GOD-BUSINESS

"You taught me to control wind. Why can't you teach me rain?"

"I can't, honey."

Faan fumed a minute, then calmed, shaking her head so the bright red and green patches of waxed and painted hair swayed like grass in a strong wind. "Why can't you?"

"Listen to me, Fa. Chumavayal controls the rain." The Sibyl lifted a hand, let it drop back. "You don't interfere with god-business, little Sorcerie. Even Tak WakKerrcarr and Settsimaksimin wouldn't take that on and they're Primes, the best there is."

The name Settsimaksimin twitched in Faan's mind. She blinked, but the faint fragrance that might have been a memory was gone. "Gods!" She chewed on her lip, sighed. "Vema. So what do we do?"

"Search."

"But. . . ."

"Through the demon worlds, not this."

"What do I do?"

The Sibyl lifted her hands, held them curved a foot apart. She spoke a WORD and a Mirror spread between her palms. "Look and tell me what you see."

Wild Magic
Jo Clayton

DAW BOOKS, INC.
DONALD A. WOLLHEIM, FOUNDER
375 Hudson Street, New York, NY 10014

ELIZABETH R. WOLLHEIM
SHEILA E. GILBERT
PUBLISHERS

First Printing, December 1991

1 2 3 4 5 6 7 8 9

DAW TRADEMARK REGISTERED
U.S. PAT OFF AND FOREIGN COUNTRIES
—MARCA REGISTRADA,
HECHO EN U.S.A.

PRINTED IN THE U.S.A.

To Penny for her help and the arguments
that opened out our minds a crack
a time or two or maybe not
and what's it matter?
A sister's a sister.

GODDANCE
The Opening Steps

The islands of the Tukery glitter with dew; the sky is dark blue burning at the edges, clear of clouds; a wandering breeze twitches at green leaves still on the trees, whirls up and drops again khaki and mustard leaves drying on the ground. The selats—the narrow winding stretches of sea between the islands—are filled with chop and shadow and drifting veils of mist.

A small boat slides gracefully along the selat that goes past Jal Virri. The hull is amber and mother-of-pearl, the single mast is yellow sandalwood, the lateen sail silk the color of beeswax; the bow curls up and over like the scroll on a violin; the stern rises in a duck-tail; delicate feathering is carved into the sides. A woman clad in veils of honey-colored mist stands in the stern, honey arms folded across her breasts, gossamer bee wings shimmering from her shoulders, antennas like curved black threads rising above huge black bee eyes.

The boat stops improbably in midstream when it reaches the part of the island where a house is visible among the trees and a broad lawn slopes to white sand and the sea water. The Bee-eyed Woman begins to hum.

> > < <

Inside the house, in a small nursery, the newly risen sun is shining through the window, turning the leaves of the vines that grow across the glass into slices of jade; leaf shadows dance on the white wall across from the crib and the child in it; the leaves scrape across the glass in soft arrhythmic sshp-sshps.

Faan rolls onto her back, kicks off the sheet, and sits up. She pulls herself onto her feet and pushes at the latch holding the side of the crib in place. She unbalances as it goes crashing down, gurgles with pleasure as the crib mattress gives under her and bounces her a few times.

She flips over, wriggles backward till her legs are hanging over the edge, lands on her feet, wobbles in a crouch till she gets her balance, then trots into her mother's bedroom.

Her mother is deep asleep, lying on her stomach with her light brown hair in a tangle over her face and shoulders. Faan holds her breath and scurries across the room. She raises on her toes, stretches up, gets her fingers on the latch handle, pulls it down, and leans into the door. It opens and she slides through the gap after a quick guilty look at her mother.

She manages to get all the way outside before the guardian sprites of Jal Virri catch her, strip off her nightgown and her damp diaper, and dress her in a dainty, lacy shift. They play with her a moment, then go back to the never-ending work of keeping the house and garden in order.

> > < <

She is watching a frog hop beside a pond when she hears the humming. For several minutes she sits on her grubby heels and listens, then she shakes her head impatiently, gets clumsily to her feet. Wiping her muddy hands on the shift she starts toward the sound. "Maksi," she says. As she trots around the house, she makes a song of the name. "Maksi, Maksi, Mak la la si la la Mak la la si la la Mak la la seeee. . . ."

When she sees the boat and the Bee-eyed Woman standing in it, she stops and stares. "Not Maksi."

The humming grows louder and more compelling.

Faan slows. She doesn't like that woman's eyes. They frighten her.

Step by step the Bee-eyed Woman hums her closer. Closer.

She is walking on sand now. She doesn't like walking on sand. It gets between her toes and makes them sore. Closer.

Mamay said never go in the water.

The sprites said never go in the water.

They aren't here now.

She whimpers, but the sprites don't come.

The water is cold. It pushes at her. She stumbles and goes floundering under the surface.

The Bee-eyed Woman reaches out, her arm stretching and stretching, plucks her from the selat.

Faan wails as she swoops across the water.

"Be quiet." The Bee-eyed Woman sits her on the deck. "You aren't hurt."

Faan ignores her and wails some more. "My Liki. I want you-ooo. Leee leeee . . . Leee keee. . . ."

The mahsar pops out of the air beside her, hisses at the Bee-eyed Woman.

"Good," she says. "I was waiting for you."

She hums and the mahsar curls up with her back against Faan, deep asleep.

Faan yawns; her eyes droop shut and she sleeps.

The Bee-eyed Woman hums another note.

A honey shimmer trembles about the child.

"Be lovéd," the Bee-eyed Woman croons over her. "Let he who finds you cherish you to death and beyond. Let them who dwell with you cherish you. Be lovéd, Honeychild, by everyone you need."

The Bee-eyed Woman hums.

A block of crystal hardens around Faan and Ailiki the mahsar.

The Bee-eyed Woman hums a double note, spreads

her arms. A dome of crystal forms about the island, stopping everything inside.

> Kori Piyolss, mother and apprentice sorceror, sleeps.
>
> Settsimaksimin, Sorceror Prime, and his lover Simms the Witch sleep side by side.
>
> The sprites melt into the soil and sleep.
>
> The trees and everything on the island freeze in place and wait.

The Bee-eyed Woman turns her head.

The honey-amber boat glides off the way it had come.

SIBYL

A mist flows from the stone, eddies and blows about in the strong wind coming up the cave from the lava lake at the heart of the mountain, a hot wind like the breath of the sun.

Near the mouth of the cave, on the dark side of the line where sunlight meets shadow, there is a chair carved from stone, broad and worn, old as the mountain.

The mist blows toward the sunlight, coalesces into a big woman with an ancient wrinkled face, iron black and collapsed on the bone; the smell of age hangs about her, musty and intimidating.

She settles in the big chair, sits there wrapped in layers of wool and silk, leaning back, relaxed, amused, her face obscured, her once-beautiful hands curled over the worn finials, a jewel on her thumb shimmering blue and green and crimson, a black opal that echoes the bright lights in her black eyes.

She opens her mouth and declaims:

> *The wheel is turning, the change is near*
> *One by one the signs come clear:*
> *Salagaum flower*
> *Through the nights and the days*
> *High Kasso seeks power*
> *In odd little ways*
> *In the Beehouse's Bower*
> *The Honeychild plays.*

>><<

She laughs, a soft growly sound like the earth shifting.

To be a sibyl, she says, it is necessary to cultivate a talent for bad verse. The seekers demand it. They will not believe you if you speak them plain.

If you want me, she says, come. I am waiting for you.

You will find this cave on the slopes of Mount Fogomalin not far below the high terrace where the Temple is, the Camuctarr of Bairroa Pili. To reach it, climb the steps and steeps of the Jiko Sagrado until you reach an ancient olive tree. It is no bigger than a bent old woman, but it has been making olives since the world began. The path begins there. Go along it, holding your clothes tight against you so the firethorn won't catch you and the boutra birds won't eat your livers. If it's Spring when you're coming, bring silk to breathe through when you pass the grove of Enyamata trees lest the pollen beguile you and keep you till you starve. Follow the cairns of black lava around the bulge of the mountain until you reach a cave mouth. Enter and I will be there.

Come with your puzzlements, come with your needs, come in the daylight or hidden by night.

You summon me into being.

Come.

>><<

I am Sibyl
I am born of earth and dream
I alone in this land exist outside the Wheel
The Wheel turns and all things change
I do not change
The Wheel turns and what was
Is now forgotten
I do not forget.

> > < <

These are things you might like to know, she says. Names, geography and rule. If such things bore you, ignore them.

This is the LAND, this is Zam Fadogurum.

The titular ruler, the Amrapake, is Famtoche Banddah, the real power mostly lies in the hands of the Maulapam—this never changes.

The First City, the Seat of Rule, is Gom Corasso; little that is important happens there.

The city below us, Bairroa Pili, is called the second city though the part that is occupied is twice the size of Corasso; it is the Mill of Plenty, grinding out the wealth of the Land.

Kasso is priest.

Kassian is priestess.

The Temples are called Camuctarrs.

> > < <

She sighs and changes the position of her hands.

I remember everything.

I remember Chumavayal dancing down Abeyhamal.

I remember language changing, law and custom, myth and history, all changing.

I remember Bairroa Pili moving from the Low City to the High, the Low City sealed and sleeping.

I remember Chumavayal as a screaming babe, a raging youth, a splendid man. As the years turned on the spindle of time, his beauty grew stolid, his alertness faded, until he became what he is today, iron grown brittle with time, jealous of the youth he once had, hoarding his strength like a miser hoards gold.

I remember Abeyhamal as a screaming babe, an impatient child, a sullen girl; she is a woman now, arrogant in her young splendor, beating her wings against the power that imprisons her.

> > < <

On the Instant that Chumavayal is danced down, he that was ancient will be newborn, knowing nothing.

On that Instant the Years of Iron will be forgotten, as if the five hundred years just completed did not exist at all, as if those five hundred years were simply erased from time.

> Abeyhamal and Chumavayal forget them.
>
> The Fadogurs of Zam Fadogurum forget them.
>
> Forget the Amrapake.
>
> Forget the Language.
>
> Forget the caste names and make them new— Maulapam the landlords and rulers, Cheoshim the warriors, Biasharim the merchants, Fundarim the artisans, Naostam the laborers, and Wascram the children born to slaves.
>
> Forget the protocols and prohibitions of Chumavayal.
>
> Forget the orders of priesthood—the Kassoate of Chumavayal:
>
> > ABOSOA who do the Family Rites of Life— birth, confirmation and marriage.
> >
> > ADJOA who tend the public worship—namings and festas and openings of every kind.
> >
> > ANACHOA who keep the Cult of the Dead
> >
> > ANAXOA who perform all sacrifices and tend the Forge Fires.
> >
> > MANASSOA who administer the Temples, Schools and, most of all, the Funds of the Orders.
> >
> > QUIAMBOA who teach and study.
>
> Forget the tables of Descent and Privilege.
>
> Forget marriage laws and marriage customs.
>
> The Fadogurs of Zam Fadogurum churn a

while in the Turn's End Chaos then settle into
a new Pattern, a new peace.

> > < <

I watch.
It is my amusement to watch the permutations and
combinations of the Change, the infinitely varied kalei-
doscopic corruscations of the Dance.
The end is always the same
The details never.

> > < <

She leans forward, bringing her aged face into the
light; the ghost of beauty clings to her bones.
I am Sibyl that reads the soul and answers as
she chooses—most of the time—whenever I'm
not sealed by those interfering ignorant gods.
*
Ah well, silence is also an answer.
*

Chapter 1
The Coming of the HONEYCHILD

Reyna Hayaka leaned against a Sequba tree at the edge of the Abey-zaza Grove, dug out his strikebox and his ti-pipe. He packed a pinch of bhaggan into the smoke-hole, fired it up, and sucked in a mouthful of the smoke. He was pleased with himself. He'd found all the herbs and roots Tai needed and got them in first light with the dew still on them. The best time.

The smoke trickled from his nose and faded into the warm green shadow.

A breeze whispered through the leaves of the canopy and in that gentle rustle he started hearing murmurs from the Sequba moththeries, translucent elusive creatures that even the Kassian Tai saw only from the corner of her eye.

Tai. Corner of her eye. Corner of her eye. Tai. Wild-magic. Never-never fly-you-by.

He smiled dreamily as a wispy something soared past on gossamer wings and swooped in and out of the feathery smoke.

In a burrow beneath the knotted roots of a nearby Sequba, a famma bird sang and his mate answered with a demure twitter. Deeper in the Grove a pan-tya chittered, broke off abruptly. All around, there were furtive rustles, small squeaks and chirrups, the thousand sounds of life beneath the trees.

Sing a song of slippery slides, atip atoop atwitter, hot hot hotter, damned dirt gets dirtier. Tiké tiki tirriah. And a twee twi twee-ee.

A bee hummed past, then another. Reyna tapped the pipe against a root, ground his heel over the ash. He stretched and yawned, settled the basket handle more comfortably over his arm and started for the River.

Reyna Hayaka was Salagaum, tall and limber with long, narrow hands and feet and the breasts of a woman. His blue-black hair was plaited in hundreds of thin braids that swung in a limber lion's mane down past his shoulders. He had honey colored eyes and his skin was burnt caramel, smooth as silk with amber lights where it was pulled tight across the bone. He wore a white cotton-and-silk underrobe, cinched tight about his waist with a wide black leather belt, a heavier overrobe with broad stripes of crimson and amber which fell in straight lines from his shoulders, blowing back as he moved to show the lining of amber silk.

Slow-dancing along in a happy languor, humming a bee-hymn, amber bangles clanking about his wrists, amber and gold hoops swinging from his earlobes, he rounded a tall broom bush—and stopped, startled, as he saw a very young child sitting on the landing, watching a strange little beast that looked like a cross between a cat and a monkey; it was jumping at famma birds hunting snails in the gravel at the waterline.

"Ulloa, honey," he said. "Where did you come from?"

She stared at him through a webbing of silky black hair, startled and afraid; she had big eyes, odd eyes, gem-colored, the right was blue, the left green.

"It's all right," Reyna said, his voice soft, soothing, making a song of the words. "It's all right, my honey. I won't hurt you." He took a step toward her.

The child whimpered, rolled onto her hands and knees and scooted away from him, heading for the end of the landing and the wide brown River beyond.

As Reyna swore under his breath, dropped the basket and ran desperately down the bank, a gray streak whipped past him, circled the child, and chittered in her face. As she slowed, startled, he dived and caught the hem of her lacy shift.

Shaken, but keeping a firm hold on the cloth in spite of the baby's howls and struggles, he sat up. "Hush, little honey," he murmured, "Hush, sweeting. No no, Reyna won't hurt you. Look here, your little friend isn't afraid of me." He held out his free hand and let the beast sniff at it.

The cat-monkey wriggled with pleasure, pushed its head against Reyna's palm and produced a loud soothing hum, then it sat on its haunches and stared at him with round intelligent eyes; it was a strange creature with its flattened little face like a miniature baby and small black hands folded over a silky white ruff.

The child stopped her struggles, her screaming diminished to a series of sniffles.

Reyna laughed comfortably, took the lower corner of his overrobe and used the lining to wipe her eyes, then her nose. "There. Isn't that better?"

" 'spa, 'nas," she said. "Poess'm? Oidat's tor? Tis su?"

"I don't understand a word of that, bébé." He smoothed the hair out of her mismated eyes; it was a waterfall of black silk and softer than anything he could remember touching. His heart turned over. "You are a mystery, oh diyo. Well, let us see, let us see. . . ."

He tapped his forefinger between his brows. "Reyna Hayaka. That's my name. Do you understand, bébé?" He tapped again. "Me. Reyna." Moving slowly so he wouldn't startle her, he touched her forehead, his finger trembling, then spread both hands in what he hoped was a universal query sign. "You. Name?"

She gurgled, a happy sound that tickled his insides, curled one small grubby hand into a fist, then used her other hand to straighten out her forefinger. She poked herself in the chest. "Faan Korispais Piyolss," she chanted, a lesson she'd learned so completely she didn't have to think.

Reyna nodded, his many black plaits swinging and slipping with the movements of his head. "And does your friend have a name?" He pointed to the cat-monkey. "Name?"

"Nainai," she said, nodding vigorously. "Ailiki. Eym mahsar." She shook her hair over her face again, looked slyly through the strands, her body shouting mischief. "Reyna," she said, then giggled.

"Diyo, you are quick, little honeychild." He chuckled. "You know you aren't supposed to go round calling adults by their use names. Someone taught you manners and did a good job of it." He gazed over her head at the River, so wide here near the estuary that the far bank was a faint fuzzy blue line. Wide and empty. "Speaking of which, my honey, how did you come here and where's your mother, hmm?" He tucked his hand under her chin and lifted her head so he could look into those bi-colored eyes. "Mama?"

She blinked at him; for a moment he thought she was going to cry. "Mamay?" Her eyes dulled as if a film had slid across them; she shivered and gulped, then she flung herself at him, hands clutching his robe, head butting into his breasts. "Mamay, Mamay," she wailed.

"Hush, bébé, hush, we'll find your mama, diyo, we will." He could feel the small body shuddering against him, feel the shudders fading; there was a last, small gulp and she lay heavy in his arms. "Diyo, my honey, oh diyo my sweeting, I wish. . . ."

Ailiki went trotting off, jumped into the small sailboat Reyna had moored to a post at the side of the landing. Her tail curled around her, the beast crouched on one of the thwarts, her head up, her ears pricked as if to say, what are you waiting for?

"Well, look at that, bébé."

Faan turned her head, blinked at the mahsar. She sighed, started sucking her thumb, too worn out, he thought, for anything more.

"That's a sign if I ever saw one, my honey." He

shifted his grip on her, got to his feet and started toward the boat.

"Abey's Sting," he said suddenly, "I'd forget my head. . . ." He looked down at the child, pulled a sad face for her that made her giggle round her thumb, then hauled her back along the landing to the basket he'd dropped when he dived for her, explaining as he walked that he didn't dare put her down, she moved too fast and chances were she'd be in that River before he'd taken two steps.

She was turning into a dead weight, heavier with every step. He shifted his grip again before he bent for the basket. "I know now why women have hips," he murmured. "How in this crazy world does a baby like you gain fifty pounds whenever she feels like it?" He straightened, jiggled her higher and got his arm crooked under her. "Vema vema, honeychild, it's back to the boat we go and off to find your mama. DownRiver first, I think, look round the Koo. If your people know they've lost you, they should be looking for you. Trouble is, a hundred things could happen so they don't know when you went off, or where."

He settled her in the bottom of the boat, set the basket beside her, nodded with satisfaction as Ailiki jumped from the thwart into her lap. "Good mahsar," he said, "keep her safe. A boat's no place for a baby, but we haven't much choice right now." He scratched at his nose and frowned down at her. The lacy shift was clean and dry. "You don't look like you've been in the water, but I don't see how else . . . vema vema, how doesn't matter right now."

> > < <

The rest of the morning Reyna crisscrossed the long narrow bay, stopping by every boat he saw, asking if they'd lost a child, if they knew anyone who had, if they'd seen any coasters coming or going, or any sign of trouble. Anything at all.

Nothing. Nothing. More nothing.

Faan was curled in the bottom of the boat, sleeping so heavily she worried him until he felt a warmth flowing across his feet; she was peeing on him in her sleep, marking him like a little dog marking his territory. You're mine, he whispered to her, by right of rescue. He laughed. "Salvage," he said aloud. "That's it." He almost stopped then and went back to the River, but he could see one more boat ahead, anchored near the mouth of the bay, the *Kiymey* owned and worked by Vumictin the Silent. He sighed and tacked across to her.

Vumictin had his nets out, his two nethands leaning against the rail taking a bagh-hit.

"Vum, you see a ship going in or coming out, early this morning, maybe just before sunup?"

The long thin man scratched thoughtfully at his arm, stared at the water then at the sky. "What's up, Rey?"

"Kuh! you're a worse clam than any you ever dug. I found a child, a baby, might've been lost off a ship. Light-skinned, probably slaveborn." He shrugged. "Or a foreigner."

"An't seen nothing like that." One of the netmen cleared his throat and spat. With a sweeping gesture, Vumictin waggled his thumb at his head, then at the spitter. "Dikhan, there, he swears he seen the Bee Mother sailing upriver. Quite a sight, he says, honey-gold in the moonlight. Maybe the kid's a little accident the god's dumped on you." He grinned. "It gets mam and da in one package and Honeymama can go play."

Reyna snorted. "You're about as funny as a wetpack, Vum. Seriously though, if you hear anything, let us know, hmm?"

Vumictin straightened. "We'll do that. Now you do us a favor, Rey, and shift youself. You in the middle the nets and we're gonna start pulling.

> > < <

It was late afternoon when Reyna broke off the futile search and wearily sailed the boat back up a River alive with traffic: fishermen out for bottom feeders and the spiny buagosta which brought more than all their fish; round-bodied merchant ships moving downRiver stuffed with ingots of copper and iron, bolts of pammacloth dyed into bright patterns and the wide-mouthed jars Bairroa Pili was known for; slimmer, smaller coasters carrying passengers and anything else that brought in cash; slave ships bouncing downRiver empty except for chains and stained benches.

" 'Loooaaah, Reeey!'' A pilot's apprentice swinging a leadline from a net slung under a merchanter's bowsprit waved at him, then went back to reading the knots.

" 'Loaaaa, Ghedd,'' Reyna called back, then gasped and snatched at Faan who'd waked from her long nap and was trying to stand up. "You been a good girl so far, honey, don't spoil it now. K'lann! I could do with some rope, run a line from you to the mast.''

Faan tilted her head, smiled uncertainly. "Ti kaps?''

"Nothing, honey, just stay still. . . .'' He returned the wave of a sailor sitting on a topmast spar, exchanged shouts and whistles with fishermen, with pilots, with traders hanging over shiprails, men he'd danced the double passage with a time or two or more. He said nothing more about Faan, he didn't exactly know why, except there was no point in it and the danger a stray child faced in the streets of Bairroa Pili was something he didn't like thinking about.

There were wharves and landings all along the north bank of the River, with barges and boats filling every inch of space, nudging at each other, swinging restlessly against their mooring cables; lines of Naostam laborers and foreigner slaves moved in and out of them like ants, carrying burdens ashore, coming empty back

for more. There were whistles and calls from a number
of them, waves and the lazy eight, Abeyhamal's sign.

Faan looked up from where she was crouching beside
Reyna's knee, tugged at the underrobe until she got his
attention. "Tis aym?"

"Hush, honey. Distraction's bad right now, Iron
Bridge coming up. I know, I know, I'm talking to them;
but I have to, you see. People I know, um . . . some
of them from times I went with Tai and nursed . . .
Abey damn that wind, why can't it . . . dosed with
tonic and purgatives . . . sh, sh, honeygirl, we can make
it, see, slip by, slide through, come out the other side
. . . friends and clients and oh you name it . . . k'lann!
you cretin, I've got windright . . . oh potz!" He
snatched up a boathook and pushed himself away from
the barge, found the sheet he'd dropped and brought the
sail around; it filled and the boat stopped gliding backward.

Tense with concentration, he maneuvered through the
River traffic, passed under the Iron Bridge, then the
Wood Bridge, tacked around the last bend and angled
in toward the dilapidated wharf at the edge of the Edge.

> > < <

The Ladroa-vivi was the last gatt (wharf) on the north
side of the River, standing more than half a mile past
the Wood Bridge. There were a small house for the
Shindagatt (when there was one) and a rotting warehouse which was empty except for dust, spiders in the
rafters, and the occasional drunk. Its interior smelled
of urine and death and no one went there except those
drunks or fugitives hiding with the spiders to get above
the stench and away from the light. Once or twice a
month the Shinda guards searched the place, confis-
cated any contraband they found hidden there. The
Shinda Prefect who ran the city threatened repeatedly
to burn it down, but he never did.

The sheds and groves around Ladroa-vivi were the meeting ground for idle porters and truant slaves, thieves and vagabonds, diseased habatrizes and overage Salagaum; they played dados with loaded dice, kucha with cards so old the cheatmarks were more legible than the pips, jiwa-bufa with bones the rats had eaten clean and stones from the River. Or they smoked tumba or drank raw mulimuli from clay jugs. Or sniffed fayyun, or smoked bhaggan, or dumped handfuls of the dust of dried pepepo—a caterpillar fed on crazyleaf—into the slugs of mulimuli and went so far off that half the time they never came back. Or ingested other drugs from the pharmacopoeia of self-destruction.

Those who hung about kept their eyes open and trusted to agility and luck to shelter them from danger—as did the Kassians, the bee-priestesses of Abeyhamal, who ventured here to bind up wounds, set broken legs, and dose the hallucinating with purges and settlers.

While Reyna Hayaka was busy knotting the painter, Ailiki leapt onto the gatt and sat on her haunches waiting. Reyna laughed, then lifted Faan up beside the beast. He set the basket on the planks, gathered the skirts of his robes to keep them clear of the muck, and climbed quickly up the short ladder.

"Something new, eh?" A Wascram smuggler with Connections, the self-appointed Shindagatt of Ladroa-vivi stepped from behind a tree and stood at the top of the gatt, his hands on his plump hips, his elbows out.

Reyna slid the basket handle over his arm, swung Faan up and held her against his breasts, half hidden by the folds of his outer robe. "Ulloa, Chez," he said. "Nothing to interest you."

"Playpretty?"

"No! I don't go that route, you know that."

"Some a you clients do."

"They don't tell me. I won't have it." He turned, putting his shoulder between Faan and the Shindagatt. "Two pradh and you don't say."

Chezar Joggaril rubbed at his broad broken nose; for a moment Reyna thought he was going to argue the price, then he shrugged. "Vema," he growled.

"One hour?"

"Bring it youself."

"Why?"

"I said."

"No trade, just coin; I'm not in the mood for games."

Chezar shrugged. "Leia got female troubles," he muttered. "Needs some more a that red stuff."

Reyna shifted his hold on Faan who was starting to wriggle, wanting down. He patted the child to quiet her and frowned at Chezar. "I'll bring a bottle. You sure that's it?"

"Same as last time."

"Vema."

With the mahsar Ailiki trotting behind him, Reyna strode into the trees. He stepped over a sprawled mule-head, started to circle around a game of jiwa-bufa scratched into the hard dry earth. One of the players, a Salagaum, looked up, pushed straggling gray hair out of his eyes.

" 'Loa, Rey." He wrinkled his brow, swayed on his knees, and peered hazily at Ailiki. "What's that?"

"Ulloa, Jumsi. Pet I picked up. 'Loa, Morg, Jago, Huz."

He moved quickly through the trees, emerged from them into a nameless wynd filled with refuse, cats and stray dogs, stopped for a moment to resettle the child in the curve of his arm. "Faan, sweeting, honeychild, be quiet now. Like a little mouse." He touched her mouth, shook his head. "There's danger here, danger until we reach Beehouse. I'm going to cover you with this robe and I want you to stay very very quiet, shhh. . . ." He hefted her higher and tugged his outer robe over her. "K'lann! wish I knew how you turn into solid lead."

He strode along the wynd, slowed as he turned into Verakay Lane, the longest and widest of the streets in the Edge. Ailiki followed close behind him, a small gray-brown shadow.

" 'Loa, Rey.'' An old Fundar woman leaned out a window, a soppy cloth trailing from her hand; she flapped it at him, splattering washwater over everything beneath her. "What you got there?''

" 'Loa, Thamman.'' He waved at her, went quickly on.

A line of Naostam boys went running past, stuttered to a stop, swung round, and shouted obscentities at him. He paid no attention to them; they were just echoing their fathers. He had Naostam clients, but they refused to know him when they passed him on the street.

He heard the clank-clash of a pair of Shinda guards before they turned the corner ahead of him, retreated a few steps and ran down a wynd between two tenements, then worked back to the Lane, dodging through porters and laborers, handcarts and oxcarts, scurrying cut-purses and lounging out-of-works squatting around jiwa-bufa circles drawn in the dust.

Mahak Peshalla stood in the door of his tavern waving a fan lazily back and forth. He had the high cheekbones, narrow face and beaky nose of his caste, rat-tail mustaches and a thin beard twisted into long tight ringlets; though he was poor Biashar, the son of a merchant who'd lost everything when a ship he'd invested in never came back, he had two official wives (of the three that Biasharim allowed themselves) and was more generous to beggars and streetfolk than most, sponsoring a score of Wascram boys in the Edgeschool. When he saw Reyna, he flicked the folding fan shut, slapped it against his arm. "Rey,'' he rumbled in a voice like a barrel rolling down a gatt, "What you got good?''

"This and that, Mak, this and that.''

Louok the Nimble was standing atop an overturned washtub making silver cemms dance between his dark fingers, the coins glinting in the morning light, changing to copper shabs, then back again, appearing and disappearing. "Now you see it," he chanted, "now you don't, silver into copper, yes, that's the way it goes, copper into air, my hands are empty, my pockets, too, yet see and see, silver." He paused in the middle of his handdance, waved to Reyna, whistled a snatch of a tune popular in the Joyhouses, went back to his performance, milking a rain of coins from the air and dropping them into a large boot. He upended it, shook his head when a moth flew out, tossed the boot to one of the Wascram boys crouched by his feet, and went on with his performance as the boys moved through the crowd, collecting coins from his audience.

On the other side of the Lane Zinar the Porter shifted his load. " 'Loa, Rey," he yelled, "Tell Dawa the Lewinkob silk's in." He slapped at the bale on his head. "He should get up to Horry's fast, or it'll be gone."

"Gotcha, Zin."

Quiambo Tanish went hurrying by, his arms loaded down with supplies for the school. He waggled an elbow at Reyna, slowed for a few steps. "Tell Pan to come by school tomorrow, I've got the talk cleared through the Manasso Head."

"Will do, Tan."

He fended off more men and women who had greetings for him, messages for Dawa or Jea, the other Salagaum living with him at the Beehouse, the Kassian Tai or Panote the Doorkeeper, nodded at them, waved, brushed hastily past. The mahsar stayed close to his heels, drawing a few stares but no comments.

The Verakay Beehouse was a blocky red-brick building rising three stories to a flat roof with a split-wood fence poking like spiky Cheoshim hair above a waist-high parapet. There was a bee carved within a cartouche above the heavy outer door and the bellpull was an amber bee on the end of a tough thin cord braided from the gut of a large fish caught in the Koo Bikiyar, stretched, rolled, and kiln dried. The followers of Abeyhamal Bee Mother avoided metals as much as they could.

Reyna let Faan slide down until she was standing on the stoop, hidden from the street by the flare of his overrobe, then he yanked at the bellpull.

The wicket slapped open and Panote peered out; he smiled, slid the shutter closed, and opened the door. He was an ascetic Naostam in service to a foreign god, Tannakés of Felhidd, a pacifist warrior god who decreed his servants should be so proficient in self-defense they would never have to use their arts. "Rey."

" 'Loa, Pan, Tanish says come by tomorrow, he's got the talk approved. Tai around?" Reyna bent, tapped Faan on the shoulder, and gave her a gentle push.

The child circled warily around Panote, went trotting over to the cape rack that stood at the far end of the small square entry; she smoothed her hand down the shining wood, patted the only cape hanging there.

"Ahsan, Rey. Diyo, she's come in. Washed her hair. Dryin it up on the roof." Panote rounded his eyes. "And who's that? A visitor or. . . ."

"Her name's Faan. That's all I know, she doesn't speak Fadogur." Reyna rubbed at his jaw. "If Tai agrees, she could be living here for a while. Silence is best on this, Pan."

"Vema, vema." Whistling a bouncy tune, he shut the door and dropped the bar into its hooks. He canted his head and inspected Faan with bright black eyes. "Char-mer," he said, then went back into his room. As Reyna slipped off the overrobe and hung it on its knob, he heard the rhythmic thumping of the doorkeeper's ritual exercises.

"Faan, come along." He stooped, took her hand and led her through the door beside the rack into a large square court filled with bloom, two trees, one a willow, one a flowering plum, a fountain in the middle and patches of short springy green grass. Morning shadows darkened the court, but the treetops shimmered with sunlight and the water droplets were diamond bright. Beyond the fountain an outside stairway jagged up the wall to a door in the roof-fence.

Faan looked around, started talking, words tumbling out of her, none of which Reyna understood.

He shook his head. "Come along, honey, I want you to meet someone; maybe she'll know what you're talking about."

> > < <

The Kassian Tai Wanameh was a tall woman, almost as tall as Reyna, and dark, a dusty inside-of-the-oven black with bluish highlights.

She was reading a leather-bound book as she lay stretched out on a longchair, her hair spread behind her on the slatted drying rack they used for the sacred linens on laundry days. She hadn't cut that hair for more than thirty years; it was a yellow-white mass thick and coarse as a horse's tail.

She looked up, lay the book face down on her stomach as Ailiki came lalumping through the door, circled round her, and stopped to sniff at her feet. Reyna was close behind, Faan clinging to his robe.

"I found everything you wanted, Tai." He set the basket on the roof tiles. "Even the ganda root."

"And a bit more, seems like."

"Faan. She was on the landing when I came from the Grove. No one else in sight, no boats upRiver or down. Reason I'm late, I've scoured the Koo and just about walked every inch of the Riverbank looking for her people."

"She can't talk?"

"She's being shy right now. And it's not much help when she does talk. She doesn't speak the Fadogur nor any tradetalk I've ever heard."

"And this little creature who's so interested in my feet?"

"Her name's Ailiki and she's a mahsar. More than that, who knows."

"Mm. Bring the child over here."

Reyna stroked Faan's small grubby hands, coaxed her into letting go of his robe and led her to Tai, pointing to Ailiki curled up in a lump next to Tai's ankles, purring loudly. Faan relaxed, curtseyed, and made a polite and formal little speech. "Aspa, tim' tethie, biosh primey'ksh."

Tai nodded. "Ah. I see what you mean. How old do you think she is?"

"Young is as close as I get. What I know about children you could paint with a whiting brush on a pinhead."

Tai tugged at an earlobe and considered Faan. "Do you mean to keep her?"

Reyna touched his face, felt the sweat beading there, his chest was tight, it was hard to breathe. He glanced at Faan, looked down at his feet. A small bit of his mind wondered why the feeling was so strong, the rest of him merely surrendered to it. "It's your house, zazi Tai. You say who stays." He hesitated, then added, "I will keep her. I must."

"Ah Rey, Rey, you're my daughter-in-Abeyhamal; that hasn't changed."

"I'm no one's daughter, Tai."

Tai spread her hands. "What's a little thing like a nuh'm matter? Truth lies in the spirit."

He pulled a clown face, his mobile mouth curving down, his eyes opening wide. "It's not so small a thing as all that."

"Boasting, Biba?"

Reyna flung his arms wide, winked at her. "Speaking the truth as you taught me, Zazi Kassian."

"Tch, it's a good thing this baby doesn't understand the Fadogur." She sobered, lay back, gazing into the cloudless sky. "Do you realize what this involves, Rey? A child's not a pet."

"I know."

"And you could lose her any moment."

"Diyo. I know."

"And you have to keep looking for her people, Rey. She's got a mother somewhere."

"A mother who didn't bother to look for her. One like mine, maybe, who'd deny her own flesh," he said bitterly. "Who'd turn away when she saw him on the street, his bones coming through his skin."

"You don't know what happened, Rey. Don't judge until you do."

Too twitchy to stay still, he went striding about the roof, fidgeting with this and that. He stroked the leaves of the white cadenthas growing as tall as he in their huge ceramic pots, shifting the mafui-flowers in their altar vases, nipping off crimson trumpets that were beginning to wilt as the morning faded.

Faan wriggled off the longchair and trotted after him, like a puppy who couldn't bear to leave her master. She patted the dark, heart-shaped leaves on the lower branches, squatted, collected the discarded flowers, piled them neatly beside one of altar table's legs.

He checked the water in the bee dish before the altar hive, walked away and began following the fence around the edge of the roof, peering through the peepholes carved into the poles.

"Subarin hasn't taken her sheets in yet; she's been sick, think we ought to give her a call? Or is her man still saying he won't see us or an abasoa kasso either? Potzhead." He didn't wait for an answer but shifted to the next hole. "Sailors snoring outside Emaur's Mule-house. Two, three, five of them. Somebody better go boot them up or . . . ah, there's the Shinda guard, they'll haul the mutts back where they belong, at least they're good for that."

Faan stood back, hands on hips watching the bees

fly, then scurried along a step or two behind him, shying away from the looming tank of the cistern, and stood close beside him when he made his brittle nervous comments.

When Reyna reached the door, he swung round, set his shoulders against the panels; Faan swung round and set her back against the brick of the parapet.

"Chez wants coin and a bottle of the red for his woman. To forget what he saw. You mind watching the baby, or should I take her down to Pan?"

"Leave her here. She won't be a bother." Tai's smile faded. "Rey. . . ."

Reyna drummed his fingers on the door. "It's what I told you, Kassian."

Faan tried to drum hers on the brick, but her hands weren't coordinated enough yet to manage it.

"This time."

"We've had this before. I need to relax, Kassian. I can quit any time I want, but I don't want to, not now. Sometimes it's . . . I need to forget for a while."

"Rey, you know you don't have to. . . ."

"So? Who'd hire a Salagaum? We need the bribe money to keep the House, we have to have water from the Shinda Cisterns—you want to chance the River?" He moved his shoulders impatiently.

Hearing the anger in his voice, Faan crept closer, clutched at his robe, and pressed herself against his leg.

"Or charge for your services? How much do we squeeze from a woman with a flux or a baby who can't breathe?" He dropped into street speech as he flew back to the bad days after his father drove him out; impatiently he shook off Faan, went striding back and forth, his soles slapping loudly on the tiles, his hands jerking through broad, angular gestures. "Starvin, tsah! I KNOW it. You took me off streets, bones out m' skin and so poxy I coon't potz straight. Owe y', diyo I KNOW it. Owe y', zazi Ma." He stopped his lope, swung to face her, arms flung wide. "I LIKE living good. I LIKE loving. Most the time. Bhagg-jag—I NEED it for the other times.'' He sighed, dropped his arms. ''Anyway, I'm not going to the gatt for a buy, just a bribe to keep that sleaze from selling news of Faan.''

Tai pressed her lips together, scowled unhappily at the tiles, but when she spoke, she'd set the old quarrel aside. ''Did he get a good look at her?''

Reyna's shoulders sagged, his anger burnt to ash. ''Good enough, I'm afraid.''

''Too bad she's such a pretty thing. Hmm. We've got to have papers if we're going to keep her, even if it's only for a short while. Juvalgrim could do that for you, couldn't he?''

''Diyo. But that's touchy.'' Reyna rubbed at his eyes, lifted the hair off his neck so a breath of air could reach the sweaty skin. ''If the Maulapam were forced to take notice of us. . . .'' He let the braids fall, moved back to the door and Faan. ''The laws and the times being what they are,'' he said wearily, ''it'd be difficult for him to refuse if I started asking him favors. And dangerous for me, because he's not a man to stand for blackmail.''

''Then you make sure he knows it's not.'' Tai sat up, pulled her hair over her shoulders; she closed her book, laid it aside and began rubbing strands of hair between her palms, squeezing the wet out. When she looked round again, Reyna was bending down, touching Faan's black hair with his fingertips, his face gone peaceful. Tai grimaced. ''If the Manassoa find out about her, you'll lose her fast; you know how rabid all of them are against the Salagaum and us heretics. Giza Kutakich . . .'' she wrinkled her long nose, ''he's the worst of a bad lot. Nearly had me burned for a witch.''

Reyna straightened. ''What? I didn't know that.''

''Before you were born. Just after I came here.'' She laughed, a soft burring at the back of her throat. ''He got his nose singed in that one. Forgot who my brother

is. That little slip in tact keeps him stuck in Bairroa;
he can't get to Corasso no matter how he yearns for it."
She got to her feet, crossed to the fence and dropped
on her knees beside Faan, held out her hand and smiled
when Faan reached over timidly to touch it. "Diyo,
honeylove, it's dark dark. I'm night and you're only
twilight." She looked up, clicked her tongue. "Go, go.
You know how fast rumor runs through the Edge."

> > < <

Reyna washed off eye paint and lip rouge, changed
into the clothes he wore when discretion was de-
manded, a loose shirt, tight trousers, a long sleeveless
jacket to further conceal the breasts he usually carried
with pride but bound down now. He kicked off his sandals, pulled on a pair of hightop boots, tugged the braids
harshly back from his face, locked them at the base of
his neck into a wooden clasp carved with the sigil of
the Fundarim caste. It was his by birthright, though his
family had disowned him and denied him when his
breasts started growing.

He inspected himself in the full length mirror that was
his most expensive possession, sighed, and went out.

Inconspicuous in his trousers and drab jacket, he walked
up the Sokajarua, threading through the throng of buyers
and sellers, then made his way through the maze of booths
and tables in the Sok Circle, the heaps of goods piled on
grass mats. He went past the Joyhouses he knew so well,
the shops and manufactures, until he reached the kariam
he sought, one of the spokes that radiated from the Sok
through the outer city, across the Lesser Ring Road that
marked the boundary between the Biasharam and Cheoshim districts, to the Greater Ring Road that connected
the city estates of the Maulapam.

He turned into Kariam Moranga, walked along in
the shadow of the Biashar towers, concrete monsters
ten stories high, raised from the ground on iron pillars

and iron arches, with iron lattices filling the window openings.

There were shadowy gardens under the arches, some of them with bee altars hidden away in bowers, women's gardens with fountains at their centers where the sun could touch them each nooning, slipping down through the hollow towers, fountains hidden away from those who walked the kariams by kichidawa hedges with thick clusters of dark green leaves and shining silvery thorns the length of a man's middle finger; the whisper of the unseen water was cool and sweetly seductive.

He crossed the Lesser Ring Road, continued along the Kariam Moranga. Outer Moranga now. On both sides of him rose the great red towers of the Cheoshim. Like the merchant's dwellings, these apartments built in a rising spiral rested on iron arches and iron pillars, but there were no gardens here. The red stone facades had iron lace set into them, endless repetitions of the warrior sigil wrought and riveted by Fundarim ironmasters. On the beaten earth of the Tower grounds Cheoshim youths were marching and training, riding in formation, shooting their bows on command. Cheoshim warriors protected the Armrapake, his household, the Maulapam and themselves, but mostly they raided neighboring lands for slaves. At least a third of the slaves in Bairroa Pili came from these raids and they collected a hefty suborrush (half the head-price) on all the rest. This was the chief source of their wealth.

It pleased Reyna to walk free past these bloodred, phallic towers and mock them secretly with everything he was. He strode along, arms swinging, wanting to whistle his defiance—but that wasn't prudent. Cheoshim cadets were squatting at the edge of the Grounds, playing dados and jiwa-bufa. They got slowly to their feet as he passed, stood watching him until he left the kariam and stepped onto the Greater Ring Road.

He turned north, walked along beside the thirty-foot stone wall that kept strays away from the Grand Sirmalas of the Maulapam families, the lords in Bairroa Pili who owned every grain of dust and sucked coin in the name of order from everyone, even the scruffiest of drugged-out beggars. Unlike the Biashar merchants and the Cheoshim warriors, who paraded their wealth and power, who liked to strut and intimidate, the Maulapam owned everything but concealed themselves behind walls—walls of stone, walls of secrecy. They were almost never seen. Slaves and servants and resident kassos did their shopping and if they wanted something special, merchants were invited into their gatehouses, though never beyond. The Kassian Tai Wanameh was Maulapam. She didn't talk much about her early life except once when she said it was boredom to the point of ossification that made her walk away from her House.

The Jiko Sagrada or Holy Way was paved with double-curved tiles of black iron, each of them the length of a man's palm, nesting curve into curve with plug-bits at the edge to straighten the line. The Jiko went up the mountainside in a leisurely arc, broke into stairs at several points and ended at the Blessing Gate.

Reyna stepped onto the iron tiles and started the long walk up the side of Fogomalin, joining the stream of other suppliants heading for the afternoon presentation of pleas and prayers to the High Kasso Juvalgrim and the council of administrators who served him and Chumavayal in him. There were mothers with sick children and well children, shopkeepers with petitions, dockworkers, players, strangers, all of them walking the Iron Way, the Blessed Way, to the Camuctarr, the Temple of Chumavayal, to get papers stamped, judgments made, petitions read, prayers purchased, every need conceivable and probably some beyond conception.

At the first flight of stairs, Reyna passed an old

woman who was struggling to carry a baby and use her
cane at the same time. He turned back, took the baby
from her, tucked it in the curve of his left arm, and
gave her his right to cling to. She labored up the seven
steps and stood panting and smiling at him, reaching
for the baby. "Ahsan, Senho."

"Nayo, nayo, Zazouivo. I'll carry the baby for you,
if you don't mind my nose in your business."

"Oh nayo, friend of the gods, don't trouble yourself.
Your legs are too long for me."

"I'm in no hurry, Zazou." He uncovered the baby's
face. A pale face the color of old cream. A slave child
with dark straight hair like spines. The old woman
was taking a bastard to the foundling wards, part
Cheoshim from the look of the hair. "Is it a girl or a
boy?"

"Girlchild, poor thing."

He nodded. There was nothing he could say to that,
it was the hard truth. If the baby were male, he could
study for one of the priest orders. An unclaimed girl
would be fostered with some Naostam family already
overburdened with mouths to feed, where she'd be
worked to death or sent to earn her bread on the streets
as soon as she was old enough.

He stroked the baby's soft cheek and felt like weep-
ing; that was Faan's life unless he could protect her.
"Does she have a name?"

"No. It's better not."

He asked no more questions but bore the weight of
the old woman and the baby the rest of the way up the
Jiko.

At the Blessing Gate, the old woman took the child
back. "Watch over the River's Gift, good Senho. And
receive a grandmother's blessing . . ." She took his
hand, wrote with her finger in his palm, then went off
with the baby up the Mercy Walk.

He stared after her, and wasn't all that surprised when
she melted into the air like fog on a sunny morning. It

was Tungjii's sign in the palm of his hand. Tungjii Luck. He passed through the gate, his heart and step suddenly light. Magic child and Tungjii's blessing. It was a wonder, that's what it was.

Chapter 2
Be lovéd, HONEYCHILD

Reyna bent over the cot. Faan was fiercely asleep, her soft mouth working, her hands closed into fists. With his fingertips he gently, carefully, brushed a tangle of black hair out of her eyes and away from her nose, tucked the strands behind her ear. *You're mine, my honey. By law and by love, you're mine.*

He closed his eyes. The past month he'd walked among the traders, asking them about a child with bi-colored eyes, getting headshakes and raised brows, but no word of where Faan might have come from; he'd repeated words and phrases she'd spoken, but none of them recognized the language—or admitted to having heard it before. With each negative he relaxed a little, though the fear was still there, churning in him, giving him nightmares. If he had to give her up. . . .

He watched her a moment longer, then eased from the dressing room, holding his breath as he pushed past the blanket he'd tacked up to make door for her so he wouldn't wake her when he came to bed himself and had to light the lamp.

Thank-offering and Evensong. Time to get ready. He pulled a hand across his face, grimaced at the sandpapery sound and feel, sniffed at his armpit and grimaced again. All that running around he'd done, he was ripe. He stripped and shaved, gave himself a sponge bath from the water in the ewer, chanting over and over the Dedication to the Honey Mother until he slid into the

calm and muted joy he felt appropriate for Evensong
and a Thank rite.

The sun was slipping away without much fuss and
evening was settling in, clear and brilliant. The cadenthas were waxy, luminous, white cups glowing against
dark stiff leaves. A few late workers from the altar hive
hummed about, moving from bloom to bloom; their
wings glittered like shards of mica in the light from
Areia One-eye's working candle, their small black bodies shimmered with gold guard hairs.

When Reyna came off the stairs, Areia One-eye was
spiking the altar candles onto the kinaries. One was
already in place in front of the hive; two others lay
beside the squat holders, waiting for her to get to them.

Like the others in the Verakay Beehouse, Areia Moha
was one of the Kassian Tai's rescues. She was about
thirteen—that was Tai's guess, Areia had no idea when
she was born, her ex-family didn't celebrate girl-births—
with the burnt amber skin of a Naostam and tight curling chestnut hair. Coming home late one night from
tending a new mother with milk fever, Tai blundered
into a gang of wild boys who were tormenting Areia;
she took her stick to them, chased them off and brought
the girl to the Verakay Beehouse for a few nights' sanctuary. In the end, Areia stayed as her novice and acolyte. She looked around when she heard the door open.
"Faan?"

"Sleeping." He set the cones on the altar beside the
candles. "Want me to do the poles?"

"If you will." Areia One-eye lifted another candle
and began pushing it down on a spike. "I didn't think
to look out the incense tray. Perhaps the Kassian will
have it when she brings the honey water."

Reyna twisted the candle into the cup at the top of
the pole, made sure it was steady, then set the kinari in
the stand. "Your nursing rounds this morning. Any talk
about Faan?"

Areia One-eye began trimming the wicks so she could light the candles. "Some."

"Bad?"

"Some grumbling, but you know Edgers. Most people mind their own business."

"Any threats to try taking her away?"

"Nayo. Rumors got about that she's spooky. Dikhan's told everyone what he thinks he saw, Bee Mother, you know."

"Good."

"Diyo."

> > < <

The Kassian Tai stood before the point of the altar, her kinari in one hand, the candle flame flickering precariously in the breeze, her fimbo gripped in the other, a staff of aromatic arazwood a foot taller than she was, with a dense ceramic sheath on the base and a point shaved to a cone, fire-hardened, then waxed and polished to a high gloss.

Carrying thinner, shorter fimbos and kinaries with thinner, shorter candles, Reyna and Dawa stood at Tai's right, Jea and Areia One-eye at her left.

The Kassian Tai opened her mouth wide, produced a humming, burring sound in the back of her throat; she stepped forward one pace, placed her kinari in the stand. One by one, the others followed her example, blending their voice with hers in a complex chord.

Dawa and Areia One-eye squatted beside the altar and tapped the rhythm on small drums while the other three danced the Bee Honors and sang the blessing words, Tai first, then Reyna and Jea.

Tai sang:

> *Honey Mother*
> *We come in the marks of our mortality*
> *Having chosen you*

Been chosen by You
We come with heads bowed and blessing in our hearts
Giver of gifts
We offer you ourselves.

Reyna sang:

I hear the hum of your wings
Honey Mother
Low and tender in the sound
I am filled with gladness
Mother of Bees
I am blessed by your Gift
Honey Mother

Dawa sang:

You glide through my bones
Honey Mother
I taste your sweetness on my fingers
I lick crystals of your love from my
    lips

Tai sang:

The river runs by day and night
And never stops
Honey Mother
So runs your mercy
The river floods and buries and retreats
Honey Mother
So floods your justice over us
Fierce and terrible is your justice
We tremble
Honey Mother

Your mercy heals and comforts us
You come to us with unveiled eyes
And speak without hurry
As honey flows
We raise our mouths and drink your words
Honey Mother
As honey flows we drink your words
As honey flows we cherish
Honeychild
As honey flows.

> > < <

Kosef Hayaka howled and brought the switch down on. . . . Reyna jerked awake. He sat up, dropped his head on his hands as he struggled to orient himself. His father was dead. He hadn't dreamed of him for. . . . He groped for the robe he'd thrown over the chair beside the bed, pulled it on, and stumbled toward the dressing room.

Faan was curled into a knot, whimpering and sobbing, her eyes squeezed shut, tears streaking her straining face. When he picked her up, she was hot as a small stove and trembling so violently he had trouble lifting her without hurting her.

He eased himself down on the cot, holding her on his lap as he rocked gently, carefully, so he wouldn't tip the tottery thing over. Patting her back, rubbing it, humming to her, singing snatches of sleepsongs he remembered his mother singing to him, talking to her, slowly, slowly he got her calm, until she was hiccupping and sighing and so relaxed her body oozed back and forth with his as he rocked.

He thought she was asleep again and tried to put her down on the cot, but her hands froze to his robe and she opened her mouth to howl. "Oh honey, honey. . . ." He grunted onto his feet and carried her into the bedroom. "Honey baby, go to sleep . . . sleep

. . . sleep. . . . '' He walked back and forth with her, back and forth. "What am I going to do with you . . . sleep, honey . . . sleep, lovey . . . sleep . . .'' Humming a bee-hymn, he carried her about the room as he collected cushions from the chair and the divan beneath the window, the blanket from the cot.

Still holding her, he arranged the pillows on the bed, then laid her down in the nest and pulled the blanket over her. When he moved away, she stirred. "Mamay . . . MAMAY!''

"Hush, honey, sh sh . . . just a minute, I'll be back. . . .'' Still talking, he discarded the robe and pulled an old shirt over his head. He slept nude, but he didn't feel right doing that with Faan on the bed beside him. "Sh sh, honey, nothing's going to hurt you, I'm here, I won't leave you, sleep, honey, sleep, lovey, sleep. . . .'' He crawled under the covers, settled himself on his side, his body curved about the nest, and laid his hand on a cushion where she could reach it, then dropped back to sleep himself.

> > < <

Reyna bent down, touched Faan's tear-streaked face, then pushed past the blanket and passed into his bedroom. Each time she saw him setting out his evening robes, she howled and clung to him, tried to keep him from leaving her; she wouldn't be satisfied with Tai or Jea or Dawa who played with her more than anyone else, she had to have Reyna. But she was asleep now. Finally asleep. He hated the thought of leaving her, but he had a long-standing arrangement with someone he was fond of.

He wore white on white, lace and broiderie blanc with gold chains about his neck, the links stylized bees. His earrings were large hoops of bee-form beads; he had more loops of those beads twisted about his wrists. His client liked a touch of danger as long as it wasn't threatening; the Bee heresy was very much to his taste. He paid well and had a gentleness that was rare among the Cheoshim, almost a perversion; Reyna found this entertaining and enjoyed the double-dance when Tumchinar was his partner.

He rummaged through his closet, found the black leather cloak he seldom wore; black was depressing and it made him feel hagged, but he needed something to moderate the effect of all that white. He swung it round his shoulders and went out.

Jea was waiting in the entry. He laughed. "K'lann, Rey, you look like a Cheossy bride boasting her virginity."

Reyna jigged in a circle, arms raised, elbows out so the cloak spread like a fan. "Sweet and sassy, oh diyo." He slapped his hands and pranced, warbling nonsense syllables like a Kalele singer, high falsetto, swooping and swinging.

Jea stamped his heels on the inlaid wood, clapped his hands a moment, then caught Reyna's wrist and swung into a degge dip, a dance some northern slaves had brought with them that Biasharim youths had taken for their own, a dance with much energy and little grace, but it got the blood moving.

Leaning in his doorway, Panote clapped his hands and added his hooming basso.

"Mamay?" Faan came through the door to the inside stairs, a strap of her sleeping shift tumbling off one shoulder, her hair tangled, her two-colored eyes wide and dark with fear.

Reyna dropped his arms, swung around. "Honey, what you doing down here? I thought you were asleep."

"Mamay, ou heym. Nayo nayo. Ou m' leps. Nayo nayoooooo." She plunged across the entry, wrapped her arms about Reyna's leg, sobbing with abandon, her body clenched and straining.

"Honey. Faan." Reyna bent, stroked her hair, tried to soothe her. "I'll be back, baby. I've gone out before and I've always come back. Sh sh, lovey. I'm not leaving you. Hush, honey. . . ."

Panote dropped beside the child, cupped his huge hands over hers. "Now now, bébé, hush your nonsense, you come with old Pan, he'll see you right, be a good girl now, come. . . ." His voice burred on.

Her crying slackened; she loosed her grip, blinked at him as if she'd never seen him before. "Maksi?"

"Pan, honey. Pan oh tay. Say it, sweetee, Pan oh tay."

"Pan oh tay?" She slid her eyes around for a quick peek at Reyna, then sidled closer to him.

He laughed, swept her up. "Come come, Honeychild, I'll show you how to make a muscle."

Reyna scowled after them.

Jea clicked his tongue. "Jealous? Shame shame, Rey. Come on, it's time we went."

>> > < <

Reyna stood twisting his silk face-scarf between his hands, staring at the empty chair. "Sibyl," he said, his voice a hoarse whisper. The cave caught the sibilant and hissed it back at him. "Sibyl," he said, more loudly this time, "Answer me."

Black smoke stirred in the chair, solidified into the bright eyed old woman. "Ask?"

"I found a child." He slid his tongue over dry lips. "Tell me who she is."

"I cannot."

"Why?"

"Nor that."

"Is there anything you can tell me?"

"Cherish her."

"I will."

"What comes will come. It is enough."

>> > < <

The days passed, slow and sweet, Nenna the month changed to Sabba, Sabba to Tikenda, Tikenda to Tamma, Tamma to Jamma as Spring ripened into Summer. Nothing was the same at the Beehouse.

At times Faan was quiet, sad, but her memories of her mother and Jal Virri faded. Even the home dreams came less and less often and finally not at all. She stopped clinging to Reyna, but she was quiet when he was out and crept up to him afterward, touching him over and over again as if she wanted to be sure he was really there. She followed him around whenever he'd let her, went with him when he visited sick women and children, playing quietly in one corner of the room while he talked to them, massaged them, did whatever he could to make them easier.

As soon as Faan picked enough Fadogur to answer questions, Tai talked to her about her mother, trying to get some idea where the child had lived for her first three years. Reyna didn't want to hear any of it; the longer Faan was with him, the harder it was to face giving her up. He didn't know if he could do it. Sometimes he wondered about the strength of his feeling, but he didn't want to question it. No one had ever given him such joy, such intense, uncomplicated love.

After the session was over, he put Faan down for her nap, crooned old songs to her until she was asleep, then he left and with dragging steps went down to Tai.

"So?"

Tai shook her head. "Not much. She lived on an island with her mother, a man called Maksi who I don't think was her father, she says he's same color as Panote. There was another man, a pale man with red hair, Sims. Her mother was just mother. She said the panumi took care of her, I couldn't get a clear idea what they were, invisible spirits of some kind. No other children about so they might be playmates she invented. Nothing to tell us where to find the place.'' She set her hand on Reyna's arm. ''Vema, my friend, we've done all we can.''

He set his forehead against the window, closed his eyes, and shuddered as tears slid down his face. Tai smoothed her hands over his back, kneaded his shoulders, the warmth of her strong thin hands sinking into him, comforting him, helping him regain control.

> > < <

Faan talked constantly to herself and to anyone who'd listen, mixing the Fadogur she was learning with her birthtongue in a hash of sound that gradually grew more comprehensible.

With Ailiki trotting behind her, she poked her nose everywhere, handled everything; got into every drawer and cabinet she could manage to open and there were few beyond her. She disrupted the Kassian Tai's meditations, knocked plant pots off the altar when she tried to climb up on it, nearly pulled the Hive over, got Areia One-eye stung by the angry bees. Panote began latching his door when he exercised after he pulled a muscle to keep from stepping on her. Jea put a hook on his door the second time he turned around and found Faan watching with fascination as he put on his makeup. Dawa played with her, sang with her, but even he couldn't give her all the time and attention she wanted. And every time Reyna went out at night, she howled and screamed until she wore herself out—and everyone else.

Nothing was the same at the Beehouse.

> > < <

His round of nursing visits finished for the day, Reyna came home and stood shifting from foot to foot as he waited for Panote to answer the bell. He'd made Faan stay home this time because he was going down to Ladroa-vivi gatt and into some tenements where he wouldn't take a dog, let alone a child. He yanked on the bee again, banged on the door. "Pan, it's hot out here," he yelled, "What's going on?" He kicked at the door and waited.

When Panote drew the slide back and saw Reyna, he twisted his face into a sorry grimace. "It's Faan, she's disappeared." He closed the shutter and pulled the door open. "We looked everywhere except your rooms."

"My rooms?"

"Couldn't get in. You must've jogged the latch when you went out."

"I didn't." Dropping his basket of remedies, Reyna ran across the entry and up the stairs. He tugged at his door, but the hook was down and it wouldn't open. "Kick it open."

They found the mahsar curled nose on tail in front of the lowboy where Reyna kept his clothing. A drawer was open the width of a finger. When Reyna pulled it all the way out, Faan was inside, curled up in a nest of rumpled silk, deep asleep and sucking her thumb, every underrobe Reyna owned damp with drool and smeared with dust. He swore and with exasperated gentleness shook her awake, lifted her from the drawer and stood her on her feet. "Little pest. Punishing me, weren't you," he muttered. "Go tell the others, Pan."

As the beat of Panote's feet faded, Reyna scowled down at the smudged sleepy child. "Nayo," he said. "This is a nayo-nay, Faan." He took one of the underrobes from the drawer, shook it out, draped it over his arm, and showed her the stains on the silk. "Look at that, Fa. Dirty."

Faan heaved a sigh. "Dirty."

"You don't sleep in drawers, Fa. You sleep in your crib. Say it. I sleep in my crib."

"Sleep m' crib."

"I'm angry with you, baby. I've got to wash all these again, maybe I've got nothing to wear tonight."

Faan flung herself at Reyna, wrapped her arms about his waist, crushing the silk of his underrobe. "Mamay Reyna," she wailed, "Mamay, Mamay, don' be mad. Din' mean to. Din' din'."

Reyna detached her. "Vema vema, honey. I know. You didn't think. Just don't do this again. Oh, we spoil you silly, we do, we do." He hoisted Faan onto his arm, drew a finger down a tearstreak. "Let's go wash your face, hmm? What a face."

Chapter 3
HONEYCHILD explores and finds more than she wants

On the Day of First Honey, one week before the Midsummer fest, Reyna left before Faan was awake to visit the hives in the Abey-zaza Grove; Jea went with him to collect changa, ponny and bala-ua to flavor the Honeybread.

Kassian Tai was on the roof, getting ready to brew next year's mead. Beside her Areia One-eye was bending over a heavy stoneware pot, moving the paddle through the hot bubbling liquid that would end as chunks of honey taffy they'd hand out to the children of the Edge on Midsummer's Day.

Panote was at the back door listening to Utsapisha gossip and tell stories while her daughters and granddaughters went like a storm through the House, dusting and straightening, scrubbing floors and windows, bagging everything that needed a washing—except the Salagaums' clothing, they didn't do clothing, and the sacred linens which the Kassian cared for herself. Utsapisha was a collection of wrinkles folded about thick old bones and her life had been harder than most, but she hadn't let age or aches kill her interest in everything going on around her. Panote liked her stories; they were earthy and full of zest and a sly malice that he knew he should deplore, but nevertheless thoroughly enjoyed.

Out in the courtyard, where Areia One-eye had deposited her to keep her out of the way of the cleaning, Faan crawled under a flowering bush, stretched out on her stomach with her doll under her arm, and watched the fountain frogs jump about. She liked frogs. She'd forgot her temperstorm—for a while, anyway. Put it aside until Reyna came home. Ailiki was prowling about the bushes, pouncing on grasshoppers and eating them.

Two of Utsapisha's granddaughters came hurrying across the court with bundles on their heads, chattering with animation and completely forgetting to close the doors behind them.

". . . and Dahlina just stood there lookin' like a fish with heaves."

"Yeh, y' know, the Pigg was doing it with Tohlin all the time Dah was thinking he was after her."

"Th' Pigg! chooee, chooee, who'd want that loser. . . ."

Their voices faded as they wound through the house. Faan crawled out and trotted after them.

Still chattering, they swept out the back door. Utsapisha was dozing in the armchair Panote had brought her. She twitched as her granddaughters passed, but didn't open her eyes. Panote was gone for the moment, fetching a mug of tea for her.

The door was open, the morning crisp and bright and beckoning.

Faan followed the girls out and down Vallaree Wynd, the rutted unpaved lane at the back of the House.

Ailiki lolloped along after her, running off to nose at the patches of grass and weeds growing in a dun and gray-green strip along back walls and rickety pole fences and send small lives skittering off in terror; she came trotting back, sniffed at Faan's legs, followed her a while, then veered off to run up a pole to a second floor balcony and peer in through the windows there. She danced along the balcony's rail, leapt across to the roof next door, came down to the alley by way of a dry and dying vine, ran back to follow Faan again.

There was a burnt-out building rotting back to earth around a bend in the wynd, with children playing in the weeds and mud where the house had been, girls six,

seven, eight years old. Faan stopped to watch; she'd
never met children before, all her life she'd lived with
adults. The girls stopped their screaming and chasing
about to stare at her, then went back to their game.

Faan walked toward them, talking as she plowed
through the weeds, mixing words she'd got from her
mother and words she'd picked up from the Kassian and
the others at the House. "Troks," she said. "To de'mai.
Ball. Me." She reached for the battered wooden sphere
as it hit the ground by her feet, but one of the girls
running after it pushed her roughly aside, knocking her
down. The girl scooped up the ball and threw it. An
older girl ran past Faan, came back and picked her up,
shoved her toward the wynd. "Go way, baby," she said,
"you too little, we don' want you." She ran back to
the game.

Faan stood in the weeds with her mouth open. She
started to cry, but no one came to soothe her. The children ignored her, the wynd was empty of adults, the
granddaughters with their bundles had turned off somewhere. She stopped crying after a few minutes, then
picked her way over the ruts and stood in the middle of
the wynd looking around. She couldn't see the Beehouse, but Ailiki was nearby and she had her doll. She
brushed it off. "Dirty girl. Bad. Angry with you,
baby."

Clutching the doll to her ribs, she went confidently
off down the wynd. Someone always turned up when
she needed help.

The sounds of the game died behind her. The backs
of the houses were shut tight. A ragged, stinking old
man was sprawled along a wall, his mouth open with
flies walking in and out of it. She moved as far from
him as she could. "Dirty," she said to the doll. She
was getting tired and hungry; she wanted Reyna Mamay to come get her and cuddle her and feed her honey-
sweetened milky coffee as he did sometimes. She held
her doll out in front of her and shook it. "Bad baby,"

she said. Ailiki came lalloping back to her and rubbed against her ankles, her fur soft and tickling. Faan tried to start walking again, but Ailiki was in front of her, leaning into her legs, trying to turn her so she'd go back the way she'd come.

She leaned down, tried to push Ailiki out of her way, overbalanced, fell heavily on her hands and knees, dropping the doll. "Bad Liki," she said. She groped for the doll, got laboriously onto her feet, and went trudging on down the Wynd.

Ailiki sat on her haunches and whined, but Faan ignored her. The mahsar groaned and trotted after her.

> > < <

The Pigg and his gang were scruffing down a side wynd, tempers on quick trigger. Tricky and his scourings had stomped them again last night, forced them to turn tail and get away any way they could. They were simmering with rage and humiliation. It didn't help that younger children leaned out from upper-story windows, yelling names at them, smacking their lips in the shame-shame noise, pointing their fingers, and laughing.

They turned into the wynd, wrestling and hitting at each other, flaring into brief shouting matches that the Pigg fisted into grudging silence, kicking at the dirt, whistling, cursing, a mob of knobby knees and flying elbows, violence barely contained.

Faan came round a bend of the wynd, dragging her doll by one arm.

The boys surged in a dark herd about her, mocking her, pulling at her hair. One of them snatched her doll away, laughed at her outraged yell, threw it to another boy; she ran after it; he threw it to a third. Frightened and angry and helpless, she started crying.

The Pigg laughed, snatched the doll, took hold of it by its china legs and slammed it against a wall, shattering the head and arms, tearing the body so the aro-

matic wood shavings spilled across the weeds at the
base of the wall. He swung the rag that was left about
his head and flung it away, then he grabbed at Faan,
caught hold of her hair, and jerked her off her feet.

She screamed.

Ailiki screamed, ran at the Pigg, black lips curled
back over her teeth.

The Pigg's lieutenant kicked at Ailiki, missed; Pigg
kicked and caught the little beast in mid-shift; he sent
the mahsar flying up and over the other boys.

And the road cracked open and huge gray
shapeless forms rose from the earth, writhing
serpent forms that reared up and over the gaping boys, roaring soundlessly, roars that hurt
the mind not the ears. A serpent plucked Ailiki from the air with its mouth, set her gently
down.

The Pigg yowled, swung a screaming bawling Faan
up and around and flung her at the serpents.

Another serpent caught her, set her down, then
reared back and darted its head at the Pigg.

He whimpered and went racing away, the rest of his
gang fleeing with him.

Faan fled blindly back along the wynd, running and
running, whimpering in terror. Ailiki ran after Faan,
squealing at her, trying to break through her panic.

The gray stone serpents undulated after Faan,
protecting her.

There were Edgers watching, children leaning out
windows, men and women gaping at her and at the
monsters undulating behind her. They stayed where they
were, too frightened to try to help. A few of the women
were lay Beeservants with enough education to know
what the serpents were; they stared at the baby and
made Abeyhamal's lazy eight. Any child who could call
elementals to her was rare, magical, and dangerous to
everyone around her. And possibly useful. More than

one gazed after the terrified child with a mix of wonder and speculation.

An Anacho priest coming from a laying ceremony for the souls of a newly dead boatman was plodding up the wynd, head down, fingering the skulls and hammerbeads on his prayerchain. He almost walked into the serpents, glanced up, and went pale. Edging cautiously backward he hugged a wall as the great gray snakes undulated past. When the wynd was clear, he hurried across it and plunged into the maze of ways and wynds beyond, interested only in putting distance between himself and that eerie manifestation of a magic he didn't want to know about.

Panote heard Faan's screams and hurried into the alley. He froze as he saw the serpents.

"Tannakés, Tannakés, Tannakés," he shouted, held his arms out before him, bent upward at the elbow, crossed at the wrist. "My shield and my strength." He ran out, knelt in the middle of the wynd, spreading his arms.

Blindly, Faan ran into them.

He held her, tenderly, gently; she struggled, bit, scratched, kicked, but he restrained her without hurting her. "Hush, Honeychild," he said, "Hush, lovey, it's just old Pan. You know old Pan, Pan oh tay." He sneaked a look past her, gulped as he saw the huge serpent heads weaving over him, then calmed as he understood they weren't threatening him.

Ailiki was sitting in the middle of the wynd, busily grooming her fur, licking at her small black hands and rubbing them over her body. She'd been hurt by something or someone, but she was healing herself as Panote watched.

Utsapisha struggled to her feet, but Panote waved her back. "Keep everyone inside," he said. She nodded, shut the door and rested her back against it.

Faan stopped struggling and begin to sob. Panote hummed a Tannak hymn and the sobbing diminished until the child was leaning exhausted and silent against his massive arm.

Silently, subtly, the serpents melted into earth and air and the stink of strange magic cleared from the Wynd.

"Broke," Faan said. "Bad boys. Dolly all broke."

Ailiki came over, put a small black hand on Faan's arm.

"Broke Liki?"

The mahsar wriggled and produced a spurt of chuckling laughter. Then she scrambled up into Faan's lap and nuzzled at her, tickling her with her wide-springing whiskers.

Utsapisha stumped over to Panote, stood hands on bony hips, gazing down at the drowsy child. "An't she somefin, eh?"

"So it seems."

Utsapisha inspected the wynd that stretched empty and shabby in the spring morning sunlight. "What were them things?"

"Earth elementals," he said. "My guess is Faan called them. To save her from . . . um . . . bad boys."

"Bad boys, hnk. Tricky or the Pigg or one a them." She snickered. "Musta scared the potz outta 'em which serves li'l bassards right."

Panote set Faan on her feet, stood, and dusted his knees off. "What I want to know is how she got out."

Utsapisha shook her head. "Kids. You turn your back a minute and off they go. That 'un gonna be a handful 'n a half w'en she get a bit older." She chuckled, a scratchy sound like rusty hinges. "A handful 'n a half. Oh diyo."

> > < <

"She wouldn't go upstairs; she screamed and struggled so hard we were afraid we'd hurt her. So we left her here till you could talk to her." Panote led Reyna into his bedroom, then backed out and shut the door.

Faan was curled in a tight knot in the middle of the bed, her head almost hidden in a pillow. When Reyna put his hand on her shoulder, she jerked away from him and wiggled toward the far side of the bed, head still buried in the pillow.

"Honey, Pan told me what happened. I sorry you were scared, but you're all right now." Reyna lowered himself onto the bed, but didn't try to touch her again.

Faan muttered something into the pillow; her small body was rigid with outrage—and temper.

"Hnh!" Reyna reached out, pulled a strand of the silky black hair. "So you're mad at me."

Faan rolled over, her face red and tearstreaked. "You lef' me."

"I came back."

"Dirty boys. They hurt me."

"They won't do it again." Reyna grinned at her, leaned over, tapped her on the nose. "You scared them so bad, I bet they haven't stopped running yet."

Faan blinked at him, a thoughtful look on her face.

"And if you try that on any of us, I'll dust your behind so hard you won't sit for a month. Come here, you." He held out his arms.

Faan scrambled into them and started to cry; her body was shaking again, but the hard rigidity was gone. "Wen' 'way," she sobbed.

"Diyo, diyo, honey, I know. I have to do things, bébé, and there's times I can't take you with me. But I'll always come back. I promise you, Honeychild, I'll always come back."

> > < <

The Kassian Tai blinked as a timid knock interrupted her meditations. She scrubbed her hand across her eyes. "Come."

Areia One-eye slid into the darkened room. "Kassian, Taravven's come for a Blessing on her prayer-beads."

"Again? Tchah, that woman's souls must be leprous if she's that worried. Bring the beads up. I don't want to see her, though, make my excuses, hmm? I don't know how it comes about, but I feel like I've been a week on bread and water after she leaves. Well?"

"She doesn't want your blessing, Kassian. The child, she said, give it to the child for me."

"Abey's Sting!" Tai slapped her hand on the table. "This is the third one nosing after Faan. It's got to be stopped now." She shook her head, got to her feet. "Interesting times, Ree. Interesting times."

GODDANCE
The Fifth Year

The huge old man sits in a naked heap huddling close to the Forgefire, his tools dropped carelessly about the stool that cupped his withered buttocks. He stares at the coals, the occasional flame licking feebly and briefly at the air.

Young and vigorous, the Bee-eyed Woman walks three times widdershins about the black stone Forge floor. Her wings vibrate, creating a thin high descant to the alto hum of her powersong. The ivory fimbo which she holds in her left hand glows palely gold.

Three times widdershins, two times otherway—then she steps onto the stone and stamps her foot.

> *Deep in the basements of the Camuctarr Chachan (The Lesser) in Bairroa Pili a wall crumbled, exposing a set of shelves, three leather-bound books on the second shelf from the top, books written in a script unknown to the Land.*

The Old Man glances at her from rheumy eyes, then goes back to staring at the fire—though one huge, ropy hand drops to rest on the shaft of the great Hammer tilted against the stool.

The Bee-eyed Woman sings her buzzing song and dances in figure eights on the far side of the fire, small tight figure eights, this is only the start of the dance, she is making her challenge, a series of subtle attacks coming at him on the veer.

> *The High Kasso Juvalgrim found the books when he*

went to inspect the foundations of the Camuctarr and
took them to the Sibyl to learn what they said.

The Old Man watches the Bee-eyed Woman without
seeming to, his hand tightening on the Hammer's Haft,
waiting for the time to strike. Watches and measures
the pace of her dance—and when she turns away in the
far loop of the figure, he brings the Hammer up and
over in a power-filled circle, strikes the Anvil such a
blow she misses a step and falters in her dance.

Wenyarum Taleza, High Maulapam, Hereditary Gen-
eral of the Armies of the Amprapake of Zam Fado-
gurum maneuvered to ensure his son would be
chosen as the Amrapake's heir.

The Bee-eyed Woman slams the butt of her fimbo on
the stone; her wings vibrate more rapidly, her hum
deepens and gets louder, driven by the force of her anger and desire.

The GodDance goes on.

SIBYL

The Wheel is turning, the Change is near
One by one the signs come clear.
Fear creeps into weary hearts
Pili dissolves to its separate parts
Honeychild burns
Draws out the strange
Wild magic churns
And trickles t'ward Change.

> > < <

Honeychild is celebrating her nameday with fire, poor baby. Eight and bewildered, she went from the loving cradle of the Beehouse to the battleground of the School. It's hard to be scorned and tormented for how you look, hard to be terrified of your own Talent.

Ah well, it means I'll have a pupil to pass my days. I believe I shall enjoy that—and hate it at the same time. I don't like being used to hone a weapon for the Honey Mother. Ahhh hahhhh.

Chumavayal is honing his own weapon. Poor little Prophet-to-be, he was happy where he was; that's finished.

The rot is starting, no one sees it yet; things will get much worse before the rains come again.

Chapter 4
The HONEYCHILD and the caste system

Dancing from foot to foot, the girl thrust her thumbs into her mouth and pulled it into a horrendous grimace, waggled her fingers at Izmit the Silversmith's Daughter and her coteries of toads who walked sedately away along the lane, pretending to ignore her. Another girl was patting her mouth and hooting.

A moment later they came skipping back to Faan who was huddling, stunned and miserable in an angle of the wall, trying to pull herself together after the nasty verbal attack by girls she hadn't even spoken to before; it wasn't what they said so much as the malice and hate she felt in them that had made her so sick.

" 'Loa, Wascra," the face-maker said; she was all elbows and knees with rusty black hair like a load of fleeces and reddish-bronze skin. "Don't let that potz play her tricks on you. All the brains she got she sits on, vema vema. I'm Ma'teesee and this's Dossan; she quiet, but she smart. You're new, huh?"

Faan nodded; the lump in her throat was still there and her eyes were burning with tears she was fiercely determined wouldn't fall. "Faan," she muttered.

"And your da tried to set y' in his caste, huh?"

Faan ran her tongue over her lips; she thought about trying to explain, but she didn't understand it herself so she just nodded.

"Sill-ly, huh, Dossy?"

The other girl smiled at Faan, patted her arm. "Das do it all the time," she said. "They don't know what it's like.'' Her voice was soft and musical. She was smaller than Ma'teesee, with curly light brown hair and skin only a few shades darker than Faan's. "You come to the Wascram class, Faan, you don't need to fool round with them."

Ma'teesee danced away. "Vema vema, true it be, no one else's smart as she." She giggled. "Le's buzzit. School's done, time for fun."

Faan straightened. "Do you rhyme all the time?"

"Oooooh she said it she said it. . . ." Ma'teesee and Dossan grabbed hands, prisoning her inside their arms, then danced around her, chanting, "Ooooh she said it ooooh she said it. . . ."

Faan giggled, ducked too quickly for them to catch her again, then the three of them went running down Verakay Lane.

>><<

"This is where I live," Faan said and pointed to the Beehouse. "I've got to go in."

Dossan's eyes went round. "You're her. The snake girl."

Ma'teesee darted forward, touched Faan's face, then went running off; Dossan followed more slowly, looking back several times before she vanished around a bend.

Faan gazed down the lane for several minutes longer, the back of her hand pressed against her mouth, then she turned, walked slowly up the steps and rang the bell so Panote would let her in.

>><<

Ma'teesee and Dossan were waiting for her when she came out the next morning.

Ma'teesee rushed up the steps and caught hold of

Faan's wrist. "Say you don' mind, Faan. Say you'll be friends. Fada, fada, say it, huh?"

Faan stared at her. "Why?"

" 'Cause."

Dossan giggled. "She told her mum what she did and her mum played pitta pat on her sitter."

"Huh!" Ma'teesee said indignantly. "I was sorry anyway. Acting like Izmit and her lot." She spat, grinned as a small black beetle scurried from under the sudden damp.

Faan wrinkled her nose. "Me, I got a scold." She caught one of Ma'teesee's curls and yanked. "That's for yesterday."

"Ow."

They walked down the steps together, joined Dossan, and strolled toward the school.

"How come you got it?" Dossan said. "You din' do nothing."

"Reyna said I should pay no mind to idiots like Izmit."

Ma'teesee nodded. "Diyo," she said. "Potzhead snerk."

Dossan touched Faan's arm and smiled.

"He said I'm gonna meet more'n I like of people like that and I sh'd figure out how to take 'em now." Faan sighed. "I said I wanted to go Wascram. Can't. He won't let me."

"Sa sa, parents." Ma'teesee skipped ahead of them, turned and danced backward. "Can you really call snakes?"

"I don't think so."

Dossan primmed her mouth. "You don't have to tell Teesee anything, Faan. M' mum says she so nosy, it'll get bit off one of these days."

"I don't mind. Anyway, it's all stupid stuff, something I don't even remember, it happened when I was just a baby."

Ma'teesee looked disappointed, then she grinned.

"Izmit don't know it. Got 'n idea, Fa. I'd do 't m'self but they won't let me in there. There's this l'il snake lives in our basement, eats mice I think, I'll catch it, you put it in her desk. That'd straighten her hair for her."

"Deeeyooooooh. . . ." Dossan breathed.

Faan swallowed. The idea terrified her, but she couldn't back down. "You bring it, I'll put it," she said.

> > < <

Izmit shrieked and went running from the room.

Faan contrived to look blandly innocent; she knew no one had seen her lift the lid on the desk and dump the snake inside.

That didn't matter. The Head's Monitor took her out of the class and Manasso Kunin gave her a dozen strokes of the switch.

> > < <

School Head Manasso Kunin drummed his fingers on the sheets of paper sewn together into a lesson booklet, the writing on them defaced by thick strokes of black ink, crudely written obscenities. "I'm waiting," he said. He had a scratchy voice, absurdly incongruent with his massive body.

Sweetly humble and the image of remorse, Izmit the Silversmith's Daughter bowed low. "I am sorry, heshim Kufuat. I offer no excuse."

Smarmy little. . . . Faan ground her teeth, then struggled to control her face as the Head glared at her.

He turned back to Izmit, his scowl smoothing out as he gave her fifty lines to write. *I will remember my duty is to charity for all and obedience to my elders.*

Izmit bowed again, all sugary compliance; as she

went out, she shot a swift side glance at Faan, her eyes gleaming with satisfaction and triumph.

"You," the Head snapped at Faan, "what's-your-name, get that insolent pout off your face." He knew her name well enough; she'd been here almost every day this month for one reason or another. "This turbulence . . . this hairpulling and vulgar scratching . . . it has to stop."

"Then stop them," she burst out. Tears stung her eyes. She knew it was futile to protest, but she couldn't help it. "You saw what she did. Her friends, they pinch me and mess my stuff, they call me names. And nobody does anything."

"Be still, fidhil!" He scowled at her, his dark face slick with perspiration. "They have provocation; they were born Fundarim." He rolled up the pages and dropped them in the wastebasket beside the desk, talking as his hands moved. "You were thrust on them by that. . . ." He scowled at her, his wide mouth twitching into an ugly knot as he reached for the limber switch she'd learned to know too well. He got up and came round the desk. "Hold out your hand."

Faan squeezed her eyes shut and turned her head away; trembling and miserable, she did as he commanded.

"You don't belong there, Wascra." His voice was harsh, filled with loathing. He slapped the switch across her palm. "You should stay with your own kind." Slap. "You will not shout at your elders and your betters." Slap. "You will show respect." Slap. "Respect." Slap. "Izmit only wrote the truth." Slap. "That unnatural whore who adopted you." Slap. "His own family threw him out." Slap. "Do you know what he does?" Slap. He went on, explaining in lip-licking detail precisely how Reyna serviced his clients. Slap. Slap. Slap.

The pain was small in the beginning, but it grew and grew until she was sick to her stomach.

Pain changed to heat.

Translucent fire danced along her arms.

"No," she cried, "no no NO! You're a liar." The pale flamelets yearned toward him. "Liar. Liar! LIAR!"

He shrank back, his mouth dropping open.

She gasped and went running from the room.

The fire faded as she fled through the halls and out into the yard, but she didn't notice.

She plunged into Verakay Lane and ran along it, head down, breath sobbing between her teeth, half-blinded by tears of pain and anger. And terror.

Desperately, she willed friends and strangers alike not to notice her, not to stop her or question her—and they didn't; they moved out of her way in an absent-minded shuffle and went on with what they were doing.

The River drew her, that slow deep flow of thick brown water. She wriggled unnoticed through the trotting porters, ducked under the noses of plodding saisai and ran down a levee workpath into the quiet and shadow beneath the Mas-Koa gatt, a small wharf busy with up-country shipping, near the west end of the Gatt Road.

A Spring flood some decades back had hollowed out the levee below Mas-Koa and the Shindagatt had replaced the earth with an eclectic mix of mussel shells, broken bricks, clay jars and discarded paving stones, covered this mass with dirt, then scattered grass seed thickly over it. Near the end of the next rainy season an old rowboat lodged against the patch and stayed there when the water went down.

Faan dropped onto hands and knees, scooted up the matted grass, flung herself on a broken paving stone and sobbed until her throat burned and her head ached. A small warm body pressed against hers, wriggled up under her arms until a cold nose was pressed against her face. "Ohhh, my Liki," she crooned hoarsely, "ohh, my Aili, people are so aw-ful."

Feet thudded back and forth above her as the porters

worked to empty the barge tied up at the gatt; hand-trucks rumbled by over her head; these noises mixed with the shouts and laughter of the sailors and the por-ters; it was a kind of sound quilt, vaguely comforting.

A voice like a mosquito hum cut through the quilt. "So, what's all this?"

Startled she shifted around on the stone, sat up, wip-ing her nose on the back of her hand. The mahsar flowed around her, curling up in her lap.

Perched on the bow of the stove-in boat was an ab-surd little figure, ancient and bearded and brown, no bigger than her fist, with shaggy green fur like seaweed on his back and around his loins.

"What are you?" Her voice was hoarse; she coughed, swallowed.

He scratched the weedy fur around his belly, found a water flea, popped it between his wee thumbnails and flung it onto the mud. "Riverman," he said. "What do they," he jerked a thumb at the planks over his head, "call you?"

Nervously she stroked Ailiki's fur, uncertain what she ought to do—but she'd been taught courtesy to elders even oddities like this little man; besides, friendliness and interest flowed sweetly from him like the incense the Kassian Tai burned for Abeyhamal. "Faan, heshim Riverman."

"Why you grievin', Faan?"

She chewed her lip, stared down at the dusty toes of her halfboots. "My mother does THINGS. For money," she burst out, the Head's hurting words tum-bling in her head. She couldn't bear to say them.

"So?" Riverman kicked his feet against the rotting planks of the boat, his shiny black eyes fixed on her.

"Ugly things. . . ." Her voice trailed off as she looked past him and saw a head poking out of the river, features sculpted in liquid crystal, delicate mouth open-ing and closing soundlessly, great lambent eyes staring at her. "What's that?"

Riverman twisted round, waved his tiny hand at the creature, got a silent laugh from it as it sank gradually into the thick brown water. "Water Elemental," he said. "Come to have a look at you."

"Me? Why?"

Riverman shrugged. "Your Ma, he's Salagaum, uh?"

"Diyo. The Head. . . ." She swallowed, pressed both hands hard on her middle. "He told me. . . ."

"Likes to hurt y', uh?"

She nodded, the two braids Reyna plaited for her every morning bouncing against her shoulders.

"Y' Ma hurt you? Hurt anyone?"

"Nayo!"

"Vema, tell me. Who's handsome, who's ugly?"

"But it's awful, what he does. Reyna, I mean. Makes me sick when I think about it. How can I go home and look at him? How can I look at my friends. If they know. . . ."

"Of course they know. Did it matter before?"

"Ma'teesee . . . I don't think ANYTHING would bother her . . . there's not much she doesn't know . . . Dossan, she's never said . . ." She pressed her hands to her eyes and began feeling better. A little. She was still sick and cold. She couldn't think about Reyna.

Others came. Tiny people, soap-bubble people, smaller than her thumb. They sang to her, eerie sounds like a wet finger rubbed round the rim of a glass. Bubbles with eyes she couldn't quite see but knew were looking at her foamed up out of the ground, bobbed in the air about her, shimmering with rainbow ripples over a transparent silver base. They danced along her arms where the flames had been, cool touches that comforted her, eased the terror that took hold of her each time she remembered how close she'd been to burning up herself and everything around her.

Then Riverman sang a skein of hissing popping sounds and the bubble people went sliding away to sink into the levee, taking their light with them, leaving her in sun-striped shadow.

"Wild Magic," Riverman said. "They like you."

She slid her palm down her arm, feeling small tingles as if the bubble people had left something of themselves behind. "My teachers say there's no such thing."

Riverman grinned at her. After a minute she grinned back.

He scratched and waited, his unhurry as soothing as the everyday sounds coming down through the planks as the porters finished the unloading. "So," he said after a long silence, "called fire, did y'?"

"Dee-yo!" She wrapped her arms about her knees, shivered.

"Scared y'self, uh?"

She blinked at him; what she mostly felt was numb, but a nebulous queasiness stirred in her. After a minute, she nodded.

"You need a teacher, little Faan. Someone who'll show you how to manage those things."

"I'm not going back to that school. Not ev-er. I don't care what Reyna says. Or Tai. Or any of them."

"Vema, vema, Sorcerie. Sibyl, that's who you need go see. Friend of mine. I'll send word and you go find her, uh?"

She blinked. "Sorcerie?"

"Sorceror in the egg. Hasn't hatched yet." He stood up, gave a hitch to the weed-fur about his middle. "Best get home, little one, there's trouble waiting." He screwed up his little round face into a clown-grimace, relaxed into a grin. "Come see me again, uh?"

> > < <

Faan stopped at the mouth of the wynd, smoothed her hands over her hair and took a last scrub at her face, then she stepped out onto the board walkway of Verakay Lane, Ailiki trotting beside her.

"Fa! Wait for us."

Dossan and Ma'teesee were running toward her, weaving through the crowd on the street, their school sacks bumping against their backs. She felt like vomiting and for a moment she thought of running away, but she straightened her shoulders and turned to face them.

"Oooo eeee, Fa." Ma'teesee swung into place at her right side and Dossan settled more quietly by her left elbow. "The mess you left!"

Dossan giggled. "Head looked like he going t' explode like a too-hot tatee, Fa. He was yelling at the teachers, 'specially Quiambo Tanish, something about Shinda and . . . uh . . . I think witches," she pinched Faan's arm, "he was gobbling so fast I couldn't really catch what he was saying."

Ma'teesee nodded. "Whatever it was you did, Fa, it scared the potz outta him. Was it magic, huh? huh?"

"Shush, Teesee, I'm telling this. Anyway, Fa, they got him quieted down and back in his ol' office, then they told everyone to go home and finish lessons there. So we left and here we are. Where you been?"

"Down by River," Faan said. "I din't want to talk to anyone, Dossy. It was ol' pie-face Izmit's fault, you know, she messed up my lesson book with really eee-vil stuff, worse'n you hear you go down by Jang." She shivered and lowered her voice as she said *Jang*. It was a bad place they weren't allowed to talk about, let alone visit.

Ma'teesee put her arm through Faan's, squeezed it. "I told y'," she said. "Shouldda come in with us Wascras. Ol' Doodoo's kinda fuzzy, but he's nice and he teaches us all kinds of naffy things, betchya a bag of taffees we learn more than that damakee Izmit and Vazi and Rullah Longnose and all them ta-tee ta-tee."

Dossan giggled, pulled Ma'teesee and Faan into a skipping dance. "Wascra Wascra we the Wascra girls. . . .

"One two three four," Teesee chanted, breaking free and clapping her hands as she jigged beside them.

"Who is it we jaja for," Dossan chanted.

"Wascra Wascra Wascra girls," the three of them screamed. They broke apart and went chasing each other down the Lane, ignoring the scolds that rippled after them as they ducked around porters and nearly ran down shopping wives and servants. Ailiki squealed and dashed ahead of them, yipped at Louok the Nimble as he came from Peshalla's tavern, leapt up on the stage Mama Kubaza was setting up for her band, yipped again as the big woman swatted at her, missing her intentionally, ran through the legs of Zinar the Porter.

> > < <

"Manasso Kunin was here an hour ago." The Kassian Tai sat in her massive Visitation Chair, the Takaffa cloth drapped over one heavily carved arm, her Visit Robes sliding into heavy, graceful folds about her thin body as she leaned forward. "Reyna and Areia Oneeye aren't back yet, which is just as well. I quashed him. For the moment."

Faan fidgeted and stared at her feet.

"You called fire. That was a stupid thing to do, honey."

Faan looked up, startled. The words were harsher than she expected, but the tone was mild. "I didn't mean to," she said.

"You never do." Tai sighed. "Well, I invoked my brother and put a scare in that cretin's head, but I can't stop tongues wagging." She leaned back, rubbed her finger along her beak of a nose. "Crops have been bad, there's talk of drought. Fa, I wish you were older and less . . . impulsive. When people are afraid, that's when witchtalk starts up; they need someone to blame."

Faan dragged her boot toe back and forth across the floor; she didn't understand all that, only that Tai was disturbed about something that didn't really have anything to do with her. "I'm not going back to that school," she said tentatively; she meant it, but she wasn't sure how Tai would take it.

"Certainly not. That's impossible. But what am I going to do with you?"

Faan jerked her head up. "The Sibyl can teach me."

"How . . . never mind. That's a very good idea. Why didn't I think of it?" Tai shook her head, sighed. "The years, the years. . . ." She got to her feet. "I'll fix a bath for you, Honeychild, then I'll stir my old bones and take a walk up mountain to see if the Sibyl will have you."

"Kassian. . . ."

"What is it, Faan?"

"Who's my mother?"

Tai backed up, settled herself in the chair. "You've never asked before."

"Well?" Sudden anger welled up inside her; at first it frightened her, then she grabbed hold of it and glared at the Kassian with a touch of desperation.

Tai smiled, her yellow eyes twinkling. "So fierce," she murmured. "Pull up that hassock and sit down, Faan, I'll tell you what I know."

> > < <

Reyna came into the sitting room, looking tired and mussed. He yawned, threw himself into a chair. "Ten kids and every one of them sick with something, toothache to colic."

Faan gulped, ran from the room.

"What was that about?"

Dawa shrugged. "She's been sneaking looks at us all afternoon, Rey. Probably one of those kids at the school said something."

Reyna swore and pulled himself onto his feet. "Where's Tai?"

"Left a note saying she was going to see the Sibyl and she'd be back for dinner." Jea came quickly across the room. "I've heard some talk, Rey. And Panote said Manasso Kunin came storming in, mad to his eyebrows about something that happened at school. Faan's had a bad day. Maybe you better let her work it out herself."

"I promised I'd be there anytime she needed help." Reyna slammed the door behind him, leaned against it for a moment, then went up the stairs, his feet dragging; he should have explained things the first time she had trouble, but she was so young, only eight years old, how could he make her understand? And I was afraid, he thought, if she couldn't accept it, if she pushed me away in disgust, k'laan! I don't know what I'd do. . . .

He knocked at her door. "Faan, I've got to talk to you."

"Nayo!" The word was muffled by walls, but he could hear the panic in her voice.

"I'm coming in, honey. I don't know what someone told you, but it's wrong, they've made it wrong." He worked the latch, pushed the door open.

She was lying curled up in the middle of the bed, her thumb in her mouth, her eyes squeezed shut.

He sat on the bed beside her, put his hand on her shoulder, agonizing as he felt the hardness of the muscles under his fingers. "What happened, Faan? You can tell me. You can tell me anything. I love you, bébé."

She gasped, then pulled her hand away and clamped her mouth shut; the only sound was a faint whine that escaped through her nose.

"Someone told you what I do. That's right, isn't it?"
Silence.

"Diyo. And they made it ugly because their minds are ugly."

Faan shuddered; at first she was pale, then flushed a bright red, then pale again. All the time her eyes were tightly shut, her face turned away from him.

"Honey, my bébé, I'm not going to ask you who said

it, or what he said; I'm just going to say he doesn't understand." He smoothed his hand over her hair, pulled a wandering strand off her face. "Don't you love me any more? Do you want to leave me?"

Faan gasped. She flung herself around and lunged at Reyna, butting her head against his breasts, hugging him. "Nayo, Mamay, nayo, nayo, nayooooo. . . ." She started crying, sobs tearing out of her, shaking her whole body.

Reyna held her and wept also, much more quietly. She loved him still. She called him mamay. A joy flooded through him so intense, it was hard to tell it from pain.

Chapter 5
The Shaping of the PROPHET begins

Wenyarum Taleza, High Maulapam and Hereditary General of the Armies of the Amrapake of Zam Fadogurum, looked with loathing at his wife, snorted, and strode with military vigor to one of the windows on the east side of the cluttered sitting room. He was not a young man, but a vigorous one, handsome in a bony way, his blue-black hide gleaming with the oils from his morning massage. The only wars he'd fought were on a chessboard, but he never appeared in public in anything but his leathers and half-armor; they reinforced his sense of his own importance, fed his ambition which was as limitless as his lack of imagination allowed.

Penhari Banadah continued to ignore him, concentrating on the stitches she was setting in the lushly burgeoning floral pattern painted onto the canvas stretched across the frame. Leaves writhed in flamelike double curves, vines twisted in and out of elaborate knots and around heavy, graceless flowers; she used primary colors throughout, saturated, clashing colors that gave a nightmare vitality to the piece.

The robe she wore was wrinkled and stained around the hem from the mud she plowed through in her gardening. Her hair was neatly braided and wired into elaborate interlacing loops because her chief maid had scolded her into sitting down and letting it be done. She had the traditional face paint on, but only the minimum required by etiquette and her ears were as bare as her fingers. She disliked jewelry and never wore it unless she was forced to. With the bluntness her brother and her husband found disconcerting and distasteful, she'd say: *I'm not a cow, I don't need tags in my ears.*

Over his shoulder Wenyarum said, "I should have poisoned you years ago."

"You didn't have the nerve then, you don't now."

"You shouldn't be so sure, my dear."

"Ha! Because my brother despises me? You know better. An attack on me is an attack on him. He'd have you garrotted before my ashes were cold." She set the last stitch in the color she was using, pulled the needle free and began searching through the tangled skeins in her workbox for the strand she wanted.

He was silent for several minutes, scratching his long, gold-painted nails on the windowsill. She shivered but said nothing.

"Your brother's patience has its limits. When it comes to the boy and what you've done to him."

"Ah. The boy." She laid the end of the yarn in a small fold of parchment, eased the parchment through the eye of the needle, ran the yarn through the canvas, then began setting stitches in the new color.

"He's a mess." He curled his hand into a fist, brought it down hard on the sill. "Kasso-coddled. Cries if he squashes a mosquito. Tchah! Disgrace. Why you put him in that school for milk-lappers. . . ." He scowled at her over his shoulder, "Turning him into. . . ." He pulled his heavy mouth into an exaggerated pout. "Into a prancing kuash slobbering over those gelded do-nothings. He's wasting his opportunities."

She continued to set her stitches without bothering to respond. Apart from a mild satisfaction that he was so disturbed by his son's idiocies, she was indifferent to both of them these days. Even the angry malevolence she'd felt from the moment morning sickness overtook her, through the difficult delivery that had nearly killed her, until she was able to pass the child to a wet nurse, even that scratchy free-form fury was washed away by the tides of her indifference.

"No more!" he shouted. "No katlin more! I'm getting him out of that nursery for fools. Sending him to the Cheoshim. Make a man out of him."

Even a year ago she might have listened, then maneuvered to thwart him. Now she didn't care. He could do what he wanted with the boy as long as he didn't bother her.

"It's time he was betrothed. He's old enough," Wenyarum said. "Make connections for him, allies." He waited for an answer but got none. "Tsah! Woman, you're his mother. It's your business to find him a wife."

She moved her shoulders impatiently. "From what you say, he wouldn't be interested."

"Chumvey! He will be if he knows what's good for him." He tapped his hand on the sill and glared out the window.

"You want a wife for him, ask one of those whores you've been tupping for years; she might know which girl's not yours, I'm sure I don't. Unless you find some titillation in the thought of the boy wedding a half-sister." She looked at him stonefaced as he swung round and took a step toward her. "If you beat me, I'll kill you and him, too."

"Unnatural woman, he's your child, born of your body."

"And I nearly died of him. Unnatural child, tearing his mother in his greed to be born." She smiled at him, her hands clasped loosely in her lap.

"Tchah! If I hadn't been besotted, I'd have repudiated you when I found you not virgin."

"Besotted with power. Don't you think I knew that? Don't you think I know what this rant of yours is really about? As for the virginity, ask my brother. He might even tell you the truth, if he's drunk enough. But be sure you're tired of living because drunk or not he'll slit your throat."

"The Amrapake. . . ."

"Oh, Famtoche wasn't the first either, my father had that honor. I think I was four at the time. By my eighth birthday, I was too old for him, so he passed me on to my brother. And Famtoche pushed me off on you. And you took me and kept your mouth shut about my . . . shall we say imperfections . . . because you were ambitious. You've been paid well for your silence and your complicity, my dear husband. Get out of here. I want to see you again as little as you want me."

He licked his lips, not daring to look at her. After a moment he swung around and stalked out.

Penhari let her eyelids droop shut a moment, then she shook herself and went back to her tapestry.

> > < <

The Quiambo Prime Walim Korongo stepped back and let the General precede him into the workroom.

A tall boy, all bone and skin, Faharmoy was bent over the Holy Texts, copying a page with meticulous care, adding his own embellishments to the plain text. He'd already illuminated the first letter with an elaborate interlacing of angular lines and forms, Chumavayal's Hammer and Anvil predominating, overlaying the black lines with brilliant color and a touch of gilding; now he was working on the columns of glyphs. His fingers trembled between strokes but were iron-steady when he was laying down the lines of ink. He was concentrating so furiously on making the page perfect he was unaware of the men standing beside him, looking down at his work.

Wenyarum Taleza reached toward his son, started to speak, but the Quiambo Prime caught his arm. "Wait," the old kasso murmured.

Wenyarum shrugged, let his hand drop. Because he couldn't bear to watch his son's finicking work, he moved across the room to one of the windows and stared out through the bubbled glass into the inner court with its sacred Fountain.

> > < <

He came back to the table when he heard the Quiambo Prime speak to the boy.

"That's fine work, Mal Faharmoy," the Quiambo said. "We will miss you here at the Camuctarr."

"Miss me? Heshim Korongo?"

"Your father has come for you, Mal Faharmoy. Your life will take another direction after this. I hope you will not forget the things you have learned here." The old man's hand closed hard on the boy's shoulder, a silent warning.

Faharmoy stood silent, contained, his confusion and anger constrained by years of discipline.

Wenyarum Taleza stared at his son with concentrated dislike, jerked his thumb at the door, and went out.

Faharmoy followed him.

> > < <

So long ago their names were lost to memory and myth, the builders raised Gom Corasso's Camuctarr on a black basalt cliff high above the inland sea they called the *Lake-That-Never-Fails*. They built the Great Wall about Gom Corasso with the blocks of stone they quarried from the side of the firemountain Choromalin when they leveled the space for the Temple and chiseled the road down to the water.

Gom Corasso. A gold and black city of towers and gardens, she sits inside a star-patterned wall with four gates and twenty towers. The shattered sapphire freshwater sea washes against her. Blue and lavender mountain ranges cup round her to merge just beyond Fireheart Choromalin.

>><<

Faharmoy stood blinking in the blinding sunlight of the Suppliant's Court, watching his father stamp around muttering curses as the minutes passed and the chair didn't come.

He slid his hand across his mouth to hide his smile, enjoying the sight of his father thwarted.

Everyone had to wait here, even the Amrapake. The mighty brought low, equal in Chumavayal's sight with the sorriest of beggars.

The bearers quick-trotted across the court, their tanned hides slick with sweat.

Wenyarum Taleza settled himself in the chair, closed the door with a snap. "Walk beside me."

Silently Faharmoy took his place.

His father slapped his hand on the door and the bearers started forward, walking a few steps, then breaking into a trot. Faharmoy loped along beside them, blessing Chumavayal that his road was down not up.

He brooded as he ran. Why now? Since he emerged from his mother's womb, his sire hadn't bothered with him beyond the yearly ceremonies of his birth, and he had to come to those or risk rumors about his son's legitimacy.

Rumors. . . .

Ah! It's true, then. Famtoche's making me his heir.

He sneaked a quick look at his father, but there was

nothing to read in that somber profile. What's he up to? What's he mean by this?

By the time the chair reached level ground and approached the Temple Gate, he was exhausted and panting, but he'd lost his fear; he was too angry any longer to care what happened to him.

GODDANCE
The Ninth Year

Abeyhamal buzzes in place, wings vibrating, larynx vibrating, bee eyes on the black old man. Abruptly she flips the fimbo up and over, holds it away from her body, parallel to the Forge Floor. She bends her knees, turns her feet out and hop-shuffles at a slant to the Forge Fire. When she is even with the fire, she stops, glides backward to her starting point, her feet moving, the rest of her quite still, then she hop-shuffles at an opposite slant, pas de vee.

Faan began to find her strength, studying with the Sibyl; she ran the ways and wynds of the Edge with her friends, a hard bite to their play.

Chumavayal surges up from the stool, stamps the Forge Floor with feet turned out until the stone booms with the weight of the blows. With his left hand he brings the iron Hammer curling up over his head; with his right he snatches the Tongs from the Anvil and brings that curling up over his head. He clashes them together. Sparks fly.

The spring rains were late in Zam Fadogur, hot winds blew eternally from the western deserts, dried the earth to dust and blew it away.

Faharmoy Taleza na Banadah encounters Reyna and from the shock the Prophet is born.

The GodDance goes on.

SIBYL

The Wheel is turning, the Change is near
One by one the signs come clear.
Drought spreads as days warm
There's death in the street
Honeychild storms
Rebellion is sweet
Magic goes freeform
And blooms in the heat

> > < <

Honeychild. Twelve now. Just tipped over puberty.

What a handful. She waxes her hair till it stands up in spikes. And she paints it green and orange and whatever color strikes her fancy—except for one long limber plait she wears falling across her face. Luck's forelock, she says. My tribute to old Tungjii and hisser bald head, she says.

Nine years.

The Sibyl shakes her massive head, pulls the veils tighter about her shoulders; the hot wind is blowing strongly up the caves from the lava lake at the heart of Fogomalin, whipping wispy ends of white hair about her face.

Nine years since the Honeychild came.

Nine years since the Goddance began.

She closes her eyes. Her hands tighten on the finials; the black opal gleams.

Changes, so many changes.

Faharmoy the dedicated young scholar is a dedicated warrior now. Fervor is fervor; he would be the same whatever he did.

The Amrapake is pleased with him; he openly speaks of Faharmoy as his heir. In spite of this he hasn't set his hand on Faharmoy's head and proclaimed: You Are He.

The Sibyl chuckles, shakes her massive head. Heirs have been known to hasten the Day.

As obtuse as ever, the General is busy making enemies with his arrogance.

Changes, so many changes.

The Salagaum grow more discreet; they carry their robes in a bag when they're out and bind down their breasts.

And the Honeychild, ahhh!

Poor little Reyna, poor little Salagaum.

You picked up what you thought was a kitten and it turned to a tigress in your hands.

And it will get worse.

Ah diyo.

> > < <

Faan dug in her shoulderbag, brought out a stub of candle and worked it into a crack in the cave floor. She poked at the wick with her finger, drew her hand back at a word from the Sibyl.

The Sibyl sang a note and the candle lit. "Focus on the flame," she said, "that's your lesson this week, that and nothing else."

Focus on the flame.

Be one with it.

Understand it.

Tease out the currents in it and see how they clash and meld to make the light take shape.

Faan fixed her eyes on the fire, reached within, and found the means.

Slowly, painfully, it began to come apart; thread by thread she combed the light and separated the twisted strands. . . .

Abruptly it broke away from her, expanded enormously and whooshed at her.

The Sibyl spoke—a word that shattered air, but made no sound.

The fire was gone. Banished.

Faan brushed ash from her face and scowled. "What did I do wrong this time?"

The Sibyl laughed. "Honey, honey, you've learned your lessons too well. Loosen up, be flexible—or barbecued."

Faan rubbed irritably at her nose. "But you said. . . ."

"That was then when you needed it. This is now, when you need something else."

"Vema. Let's try it again."

"Next lesson, honey. For now, we're going to do wind. Let's see you catch the wind."

Faan squeezed one hand inside the other. "Tell me about my mother first; you know who she is, where she is, I know you do."

"The answer is the same now as it was yesterday and the day and the day before that. I cannot speak to you of your mother."

"Then tell me where I get this. . . ." She snapped her fingers and tiny blue flames danced on the backs of her hands. "Tell me why!"

The Sibyl sighed. "The answer is the same now as it was yesterday and the day and the day before that. Consider, Honeychild. The wind blows and has power, but you can't see it. It has layers and eddies like the river. Consider them. Touch them. Turn them this way and that. Consider the wind."

Chapter 6
One night and the morning after

With Ailiki running in circles about them and chittering with excitement, Faan, Dossan and Ma'teesee slapped hands and hopped in a rocking, tail-switching dance, giggled, linked arms, and went strutting down the lane. "Wascra girls," they caroled. "We are the Wascra girls." They zigged and zagged and jigged along, broke apart to clap hands, linked elbows again. "Waste the wonkers, paste the ponkers," they chanted, "Wascra Wascra Wascra we."

A sailor off one of the coasters whistled at them, grabbed at Ma'teesee; he was soaked in mulimuli or high on bhagg, but he hadn't lost his sure hand and he was strong as a bull saisai. Ma'teesee clawed at him; Faan and Dossan kicked and scratched, but he wouldn't let go.

Peshalla the Taverner came roaring out, brought a heavy rungo down on the Mulehead's wrist and broke his grip, then grabbed his collar and the seat of his pants and threw him down the nearest wynd, speeding him on his way with a heavy boot. He came back, dusting his hands and looking satisfied. "Get outta here, you scraps." He chuckled, shook his head. "Wascra girls. Hunh!"

Two habatrizes leaned from an upper window, applauding loudly and Louok the Nimble tossed a copper moju to the girls as he went into Peshalla's for his evening meal.

"Ahsan ahsan ahsan," they chanted. "O Great

Pesha, mighty Hand of Mercy. Ahsan ahsan ahsan, Louok the Generous.'' They giggled and went switching on down the Trade Strip. ''Wascra, Wascra, Wascra girls.''

Ancient Thamman leaned from her window. ''Eh! Tchi'kas, get your tails home. Got no business out after sun's gone. Tsah tsah, what the Land is coming to.''

''Mama Thamma,'' they chanted, danced in a circle, whistled mockeries at her. ''So old she forgot what's fun.''

Other women and sometimes old men leaned out of upper windows, yelling at them to shut their mouths and get where they belonged, threatening them with Shinda guards. According to whim they ignored these shouts or stopped their strut, screamed taunts at the person interfering in their lives.

> > < <

Gozi the Ramp and his gang came prowling down the lane as Faan was using tongue and imagination on Mazabo the rag-and-bone man; they milled about listening for a moment, then added their own taunts and sass-dances. They were fourteen, fifteen, young apprentices out on a tear.

Gozi the Ramp cupped his hands about his mouth. ''Chooee, hoop hoop hoop, chooeeeee,'' he howled. ''Bite 'm, bébé, chew 'm hard and spit 'm out. Chooee, hoop hoop hoop, chooeeee.''

''Rag man bag man eat his own potz,'' Dossan chanted, clapping and stamping, slapping her arm, her mid-finger thrusting.

''Chooee, hoop hoop,'' Fugo and Wiswan hooted while they danced in a circle about their leader, snapping their fingers, jerking their heads, their hair spikes swaying.

Ma'teesee thrust two fingers in her mouth and started to whistle, then yelped and danced back as a cascade of dirty, soapy water flooded down from the upper window. As she looked up, she saw a pair of Shinda guards running toward them. "Tchi'ka, buzzit, fleas comin'."

The two sets scattered into the wynds and ways of the Backbehind of the Edge, lost the guards after the first few turns.

> > < <

The three girls sat on a deserted gatt, swinging their legs over the side and watching the torches of the priest-procession climbing the Sacred Way. Ma'teesee poked Faan. "What'd y' learn today? Show us, huh? huh?"

Faan wrinkled her nose. "You spooky, Teesee, I think you crazier 'bout this than me."

Ma'teesee giggled. "You learn it, me, I figure ways of using it. Like the time we had Rullah the snerk running down Verakay showing everything she got 'cause her skirt kept blowing up."

"Diyo. And who got singed for it? Me."

Ma'teesee punched her arm. " 'S the idee, diyo dee dee."

"That's old."

"So what's new?"

Dossan snorted. "You gonna fall for that, Fa?"

"Oh Dossy, don't be wet. You wanna see, too, I know you."

Faan and Dossan slapped hands. "Old stuff, sho' 'nuff, Teesee's stale, big's a whale." They collapsed into giggles as Ma'teesee rolled round behind them and began tickling first one, then the other, her strong agile fingers raking their ribs.

When they'd laughed themselves weak, they lay on the worn planks staring up at the sky, breathing in deep sighs, blinking at stars drifting in and out of thin dry clouds.

After a while, Ma'teesee said, "Fugo said there's gonna be a fire on the Jang tonight. Wanna go?"

Dossan sat up, fiddled with the leather thong she'd tied about her wrist, glanced sideways at Faan.

Faan looked down at Ailiki who was stretched across her stomach, looking back at her, nose twitching, ears laid back. She sat up, dislodging the mahsar. "Diyo," she said. "Le's do it."

> > < <

The Jang was at the end of Verakay Lane, a vaguely circular tract of wasteland beyond the last tumbledown shacks and hovels of the Edge—a few patches of tough short grass, stretches of dusty hardpan beaten into something like concrete by the feet of generations of youths, rustling clutches of stunted trees rising from the firethorn scrub growing round the rim of the open space. It was the unofficial meeting ground for those out of school but not yet nailed down to their life work, for outcasts and castoffs and for those who never had a place to be thrown out of. A dance floor, an assignation house without walls or roof, a place to get high on anything cheap. Or fight—there were screaming hairpulls, knife duels, gang bashes and, one night in ten, bloody riots. All three girls were forbidden to go anywhere near the place. They'd been talking about going there for weeks now.

An immense bonfire roared in the middle of the Jang, dark figures jagged back and forth, clots of them melding and breaking apart, flowing between the three improvised stages scattered around the periphery where street singers and their bands were working out. The bands came to the Jang to sing things they wouldn't dare in the street, to try modes besides the saccharine sentimental wails that brought the money from sailors and merchants, or the wordless Kalele jams; they came for the wildness, the sex and the drugs and always for the coin they could pick up there.

Titillated by fear and uncertainty, giggling nervously,

Faan and her friends drifted along the fringes of the groups, using the music to shield them from attention they weren't sure they wanted.

Two drummers tapped and caressed a triune beat from their skins. A double reed horn moaned and shrieked. An erhu keened over and around them, the player perched on a weathered box, fingers trembling as they slid up and down the two strings while he worked the arched bow delicately between them. The singer stamped and belted out his words, three light syllables and a long warbling one that lasted another three beats.

> *Doin me BA A AD*
> *Strippin m' PR I IDE*
> *Suckin m' LI I IFE*
> *Making me MA A AD*
> *Hey ey I SA A AY*
> *Kiss m' ba ACK SI IDE*
> *Hey ey I SA A AY*
> *Suck m' kni I I IFE*
> *Hey ey I SA A AY*
> *Doin me BA A AD*
> *Doin me BAD*

Gozi the Ramp elbowed his way close behind Faan.

She knew he was there, gave him an absent smile over her shoulder and went on swinging her body and clicking her fingers.

He rubbed his thumb along her neck.

She let him for a minute or two, then shied away; she didn't want him touching her any more.

"Wanna dance?"

She looked round, raising her brows, having heard only the rumble of his voice. "Huh?"

He leaned closer, shouted in her ear, "Dance. Y' wanna dance?"

She hesitated a minute, she didn't know what she wanted.

He got impatient and gave her buttock a squeeze.

She yelped and flew away from him, bounced off a half-drunk porter, wriggled away from him as he grabbed at her. When she had her breath again, she'd lost Ma'teesee and Dossan, though Ailiki was still trotting close to her ankle. The people around her were shadows and strangers, busy with their own affairs and not interested in her, so she relaxed and followed her ears over to Mama Kubaza's band.

They'd been stretching and drinking, exchanging friendly insults with the shadows standing round them, now they got into a new set, a fiddle, an erhu and a horn, with clog dancers for the beat. A man in black with an eyepatch sang in falsetto and Mama Kubaza, a big solid woman twice his size, belted out her responses in a voice so deep she was almost a basso.

> *Gonna gonna gonna GET YA,* he sang.
> *Gonna gonna gonna GET YA,* she sang.

Gonna gonna gonna get ya, the shadowy listeners sang, fighting with musicians to control the night.

> *That an't new. Nayo Nay O,*he sang.
> *NAYO NAY O,* she sang.

Nayo Nay O, the shadows sang.

> *Nayo Nay so I say,* they sang together.

> *Gonna gonna kick n' scratch,* she sang.
> *An't gonna catch me ee*
> *Gonna gonna kick n' scratch,* he sang.
> *An't gonna catch me ee.*

An't gonna catch me ee, the shadows sang.

> *Gonna see gonna see ee,* they sang together.

Gonna be free.

Free ee Free ee Free ee, the shadows sang.

THAT'S RIGHT!

The dancers and musicians joined the singers for that last powerful shout. . . .

The tension ran out of the group and they shifted to an aimless milling while the listeners snapped their fingers and whistled their approval. Mama Kubaza leaned over, took a bottle from someone Faan couldn't see, tilted her head back, and began draining it. Faan watched fascinated as her throat moved and she leaned back farther and farther until it seemed she'd strangle or fall flat if it went on any longer.

Mama brought the bottle down. "Aaah," she said hoarsely, "Real, real." Then she laughed, her laughter booming louder than the clogs had. "Real rot-your-gut, what'd you do, shunkh, piss in the thing?"

Someone pinched Faan's arm; she recoiled, ready to run again.

Ma'teesee giggled. "Dossan had 'n idee. Wanna hear?"

"Dossy or you?"

"Dossy this time, all by herself."

"What idee?"

"You know the potz her Mum put her with last month?"

"Nayo. How come you didn't tell me?"

"Shuh! Why talk 'bout it? Gonna happen to me soon enough, you, too, come to think. Well, he's a Woodman with a paintshop on the side. She sweeps up, that kind of thing. Boooring, but at least he don't bother her."

"So?"

"Come on." Ma'teesee linked arms with her. "Dossy is waitin for us down the lane." She tugged

Faan along through the crowd. "He painted the jail roof last month, you know, Midsummer comin' up, got a bucket of red left over. And since you showed us how you can peel anything clean. . . ."

Faan pulled loose, danced in a circle, ran toward Dossan who was standing in the middle of the lane, light from the Wounded Moon glowing on her fine pale hair. "Red, red, red," Faan sang. "Wascra. Wascra." She slapped hands with Dossan, wheeled and slapped hands with Ma'teesee.

They linked arms and went giggling off down Verakay Lane heading for the shop of Bamampah the Woodman.

> > < <

The guard compound beside the jail had its walls freshly whitewashed for the Midsummer festa, beautiful, smooth, white as the clouds that weren't coming this summer. A watchman was perched up in the front tower, but the Wascra-rumorline in the Edge said he spent the time drinking and spitting since nothing much ever happened around there. Not wholly trusting the whispers, the three hugged the heavy black shadow at the base of the wall until they reached the overhang by the ironbound front door. With quick sweeps of their brushes they wrote three glyphs: SHINDA+GUARDS EAT POTZ.

Fizzing with giggles they struggled to smother, they scooted off, half-terrified, half-elated by their own daring.

Dossan swore under her breath and held the bucket away from her; the paint splashed toward the rim and the bail clanked like a guard's clanger as they ran along the lane. "Slow up," she called, her voice held to a desperate whisper, "or we lose it."

Faan flicked her dripping brush at a wall, swung round, and danced backward. "Wascra," she whispered, "Wascra waa." She slowed. "Let's hit the school next."

"School?" Ma'teesee scratched at her nose, leaving behind a streak of red that the moonlight turned black. "S'pose we could." She inspected the bucket. "Got a lot left, 'f we don't spill it."

Dossan wrinkled her nose. "I wanna do Fedunzi the Silversmith. Gotta do him." She jerked her head up as Ailiki came galloping past them and she heard a distant metallic rattle; her friends called her catears because she heard things most of them couldn't. "Buzzit, fleas comin." She dived down a narrow wynd between two houses.

When the guard squad's Lanternman slipped the slide on his dark lantern and directed the beam along the wynd, Dossan and Ma'teesee were already around the corner and Faan had her body pressed into a shallow doorway. The yellow light beam caught Ailiki's backside as she scratched industriously at the dry cracked earth; the Lanternman said something Faan couldn't make out and the squad marched on.

Ailiki sat on her haunches, wriggled her nose; a moment later she trotted unhurriedly after Ma'teesee. Faan sighed and followed her.

"Guards're itchy tonight," she whispered when she was even with the others. "Maybe we should give it up and go home."

Ma'teesee shrugged, drew the drying, stiffening brush along the mudbrick of the backwall, leaving scuffs of red behind, then nothing as the paint wore off. "Maybe," she said.

Dossan frowned, shook her head. "No. Gonna tell everyone what that Kuur is. For the little 'un. You go home 'f you want."

Ma'teesee drew invisible lazy eights on the wall, the brush scratching at the soft brick. Her tongue moved quickly along her lower lip, flicking back and forth as it always did when she was disturbed about something. After a minute, she said, "Zizi? It was him?"

Dossan nodded. "Bara the Stick said so."

"Diyo, but. . . ."

"Vema vema, I know. Mulehead. But I heard him tell it. This is different." The paint bucket clanked again as she shivered violently.

Faan touched Dossan's arm. "Who's Zizi?"

Dossan grimaced, her thin face drawn and old-looking.

"C'mon, Dossy. Tell me."

"A street-rat, that's all. Little 'un. 'Bout five, something like that. Well, a bit more. Cousin of mine. His Mum's my Mum's baby sister, what she used to call her, anyway. One of them that hangs round down at Ladroa-vivi, slave till she got so far gone on fayyum her owner kicked her out. Zizi happened after that. He used to come by the kitchen and Mum would sneak him something to eat."

"So?"

"Mavucador, you know him, the crab man, he picked pieces of Zizi out of his traps last month."

"And Fedunzi put him in the River?"

"Diyo."

"Why?"

"I don' wanna talk about it. Why don't matter 'cause he's gonna do it again if we don't tell. And no one's gonna listen to us, we're kids and Wascra. So we gotta make 'em talk."

Ma'teesee grimaced. It wasn't fun any more and she didn't like being serious.

Faan sucked in a long breath and let it out. The night had gone flat for her, too, but she was ready to back Dossan wherever her idea led.

> > < <

The shop of Fedunzi the Silversmith was closed tight against the dark, heavy shutters over the windows and a half-starved hound chained beside the door. Dossan looked round the corner, saw the dog and drew back, chewing her lip. "Fa, can you sleep him like you did the rat?"

Faan looked, scratched at her ear. "I 'spose. He's a lot bigger."

Ma'teesee wriggled her body impatiently, scuffdanced around in circles, saying nothing.

Faan glanced at her, irritated, then went back to her problem. "I'm kinda tired, Dossy. Why don't we just leave it, paint something on the school wall?"

"No. Nobody but young 'uns pays any 'tention there. I want to start the old 'uns talkin. You know. Don't take much."

"Or last long." Faan rubbed her back along the wall's rough bricks. "You ought to come talk with Kassian Tai."

"At the Beehouse? I can't, Fa. Things at home are . . ." She shrugged. "Do it, huh?"

Faan kept her back against the wall and slid down until she was sitting on her heels, hands resting on her thighs; she grimaced at the scummy dirt between the silversmith's house and the next one over. "I've got to clean us up, too, 'member? Takes it out of you. . . ." She reached into a pocket in her belt, squeezed out an odd shaped pearl a water elemental had given her and tossed it to the ground in front of her knees. It lay there white and shining in the moonlight . . . shimmering . . . she focused on it, began whispering the powerwords the Sibyl had helped her find, embarrassing words she didn't want the others to hear.

Dossan looked repeatedly around the corner. As soon as she saw the hound lower his drooling jaws on his forelegs and shut his eyes, she caught up the paint bucket, beckoned to Ma'teesee, and went running for the front of the shop.

> > < <

Dossan tapped Faan on the shoulder.

Carefully, sliding from the trance as the Sibyl had taught her, Faan let the spell evaporate into the night. The hound surged onto his feet and started howling.

Ma'teesee darted around the corner, dropped the brush into the bucket. "Buzzit!" Her whisper was urgent.

Faan scooped up the pearl, staggered as she tried to stand. Ma'teesee and Dossan caught hold of her arms, heaved her onto her feet, then they ran into the maze of wynds between the houses, spurred on by the continued belling of the hound and the old man's hoarse yells.

With Ailiki trotting before them, they reached the River unnoticed, tossed the bucket and brushes into the water, and huddled under a gatt while Faan worked another spell and peeled the paint off skin and clothing. She was so tired by the time they were clean, Dossan and Ma'teesee had to pull her onto her feet and hold her up for a few steps until she was in the groove again.

There was a crowd milling about in the lane, muttering. Fedunzi had slammed his window down and retreated into a stubborn silence, refusing to answer the yells of the Shinda guards or the hammering on his front door.

ZIZI+MURDER was scrawled in huge glyphs across the front of the shop, a phallus and testicles painted on the door in swooping lines and **FEDUNZI RAPES BABIES.**

Dossan poked her elbow in Faan's ribs. "See?" she whispered.

"Vema, vema."

Ma'teesee grabbed a handful of shirt on both the others, tugged them back. "Le's bouzh, Tchi'ka. I wanna hit m' bed 'fore th' sun come up." She didn't wait for them, but went darting off toward Vallaree Wynd and her mother's house.

Dossan went with Faan until they could see the Bee-house ahead.

And two figures strolling toward it from the direction of the Sokajarua.

Faan's hand tightened on Dossan's arm. "That's trouble," she whispered. "You better go."

Dossan nodded. "Um . . . see y' tomorrow?"

"Vema," Faan said absently. She heard the soft scrape of Dossan's feet, then she went slipping through the shadows of the Lane, intent on reaching the Bee-house before Reyna and Jea got there.

> > < <

Faan lay in bed, listening to the quiet footsteps coming up the stairs. If Reyna had noticed her, he'd be in to talk soon as he'd washed up. She needed to tell him about Fedunzi, to get him to explain why . . . why . . . she needed to know if he'd ever . . . he hadn't, he COULDN'T have. . . .

She lay a long time shivering and miserable.

He didn't come and didn't come.

Then the door opened.

"It's way after midnight. Where were you? What were you doing out this late?" It was like he was beating her with the words.

She rolled onto her side, turning her back to him, pulled the quilts higher, and lay stiffly still.

His voice softened, but it was too late, his first words had wiped away everything but anger, fury, and hurt. "Faan, I'm not scolding you, I'm worried about you. The Edge is no place. . . . ahhh, honey, so many things could happen to you, bad things I wish you didn't understand, though I'm afraid you do. Children do. . . ."

With angry angular movements, Faan bounced up, jerked the quilt around her shoulders and sat in the middle of the knotted sheets glaring at Reyna. "Understand! I understand a lot of things."

Reyna snapped his head up and back as if she'd slapped him. "What's that supposed to mean?"

Faan set her mouth in a stubborn line. "I wasn't out whoring like you, if that's what you think."

Reyna drew his arm back; his hand closed into a fist, but he stopped himself before he touched her. He closed his eyes and stood shuddering. Faan could smell the anger on him and whipped up her own to match it. He drew in a long unsteady breath. "I don't know what to do with you. I just don't know."

He swung around, went out.

Faan stared at the door a moment, then wrapped the quilts around her and tried to sleep, sliding in and out of nightmare for the rest of the night.

> > < <

The drums beat like tinny hearts, *ta ta ta tii-yi ta ta tum*, the heavy throb at the end of each phrase dying into a wobbling *ta a a. Ta ta, ta ti-i-yi, ta ta tum-mta aa a*.

The daround hummed and buzzed, zou, zoul, za za za zing za.

A Kalele singer stood on a wooden drum behind the musicians, a slender coal-black man who looked much younger than he was, with a narrow naked torso and voluminous black wool trousers heavy with gold studs.

Ou sing zuul, n' gid a meeeyn, ba bi mun, the singer keened in an asexual minor moan, *ou zing zuul, gidda mii-yan,* a modulated monotone. Nonsense words meaning nothing, it was safer to mean nothing, a wrong word was like plague, sickening then killing, but— blending with the hot smoky air, the smell of bodies in heat, the uncertain flick-flick of candle flames in sooty chimneys—the sounds created a fog of desire overlaid by melancholy.

Dawa danced with his long arms curled above his thrown-back head, sway-stamp-wheel, his sandals pat-

tering on a sanded section of floor within a circle of
limelights in tin reflectors that threw their glow up from
beneath, waking oiled blue glimmers on his skin, watery shimmers in the blue satin lining of his robe. He
danced his ambiguity, his sexuality—and with his
height, his physical beauty, with all his shadows running the wrong way—he was strange and intimidating
though he did not mean to be.

> > < <

The Cheoshim Armsman slowdanced body to body
with Reyna Hayaka, then took him to one of the dim
booths lining the sidewalls; he pulled the curtains shut
and began kissing the Salagaum with rough impatience,
his hands busy on breasts and buttocks.

Reyna placed his palm over the Armsman's mouth,
leaned back against the man's knotted arm. "I am Salagaum," he murmured, "not habatrize."

The man rolled his head with an abrupt, almost violent gesture, wrenching Reyna's hand away. "I know,"
he growled when his mouth was free. "You been paid,
haven't you?"

"Yes."

"Well, what's the problem?"

"As long as you know what I am, none." Reyna
drew his fingertips down the Armsman's face. "Come
upstairs," he whispered, ignoring the man's roughness,
keeping his voice soft and beguiling. "There's no need
for such hurry. I'll please you better if you give me
time."

"No! Think I wanna be seen with somethin' like
you?" His fingers tightened on Reyna's flesh; his grip
was bruising, painful. "You do it here. Now." He
shifted his hold, slammed Reyna onto the leather covered bench at the back of the cubicle. "I want it hard,
shikko," he whispered as he tore at the thongs of his
trousers, "hurt me."

> > < <

Ta ta ta, taaa ti tum ta, the drum beat out, *ta ta taa, ti mta a tum mta.*

Za zi za zrum azrum um, the daround muttered in its lowest tones—a head-dipping, belly grinding music.

Ta ta ti tum mta, the drum growled.

Zrum zrumm um zum, the daround hoomed.

The new singer improvised against the beat—*Oh oh AH oh, pas si CO toe, pan ni PUS si, coo no PAN ni—* her voice high and swinging, *cos si to pahn ni.* Gold coins glittered on the translucent white silk of the veils that fluttered about her ripe body. *Oh ah oh pas si co,* she crooned.

> > < <

An hour before moonset there was a small confusion at the heavy velvet drapes concealing the door as half a dozen newcomers pushed through, five of them Cheoshim youths, their black spiky hair cut short, predatory eagerness in their faces. The sixth was a few years older, a sleekly muscled Mal.

Descending the stairs for the fifth time, Reyna stopped to watch the Mal, thinking he was very like Dawa, had the same kind of bones and blaze to him, although he had a finer polish than Dawa ever acquired. His hair was disciplined into a heavy braid that hung in a club down his back; he wore Cheoshim warrior leathers with careless ease and moved with the quiet, liquid grace Panote the Doorkeeper showed on one of his better days.

He let the others scatter without him and stood by the drapes, looking around, his face expressionless.

Reyna came down the last steps and drifted to one of the seats pushed up against the front wall. He was tired and feeling battered but he couldn't leave yet; the Beehouse Salagaum were hired till the EndDrum went, none of them would get their fee if any of them left early.

Pay was becoming a problem these days. The Salagaum of Bairroa Pili had to deal with increasing interference from the secular City Shindas, bribes going up and their fees going down. And there was nowhere they could troll for new clients. The Joyhouses that had been exclusively Salagaum had been harassed, then shut down by these officials—the Maulapam sent word it had to be done and it was done. At the Manassoa Order's urging, the Shinda Board had passed clothing laws that banned Salagaum robes on the street and solicitation laws that were supposed to drive from the city prostitutes of all ages and sexes, but were applied only to adult Salagaum; the children-for-rent and the female habatrizes were mostly ignored.

The young Mal dropped onto the bench beside Reyna Hayaka and sat with impassive face watching the guests labor to have fun: couples swaying in body to body hugs meant to be dancing, feet scraping over the floor, hands rubbing flesh and cloth; bhaggan smokers sitting and holding hands in reeling, babbling rings about a bubbling waterpipe; pepepo drinkers hopping alone to music they alone seemed to hear, habatrizes and the other Salagaum going up and down stairs with and without companions, parts of them, a section of face, a hand, an arm, a breast, a thigh, passing through spots of light, the rest lost in the shifting swaying clots of shadow. There were whispers all around, voices drifting in and out of the desultory tump-zing from the drums and daroud.

"It's all very dreary," the Mal said suddenly.

Reyna blinked. He didn't feel like talking, but he was being paid to respond. "I suppose so," he said. "It's late."

"Why do people do this?"

"Huh?"

"You don't seem to be enjoying it."

Alarmed, Reyna willed a smile to his face, touched the man's forearm with his fingertips. The muscle was tight under the skin and there was a film of sweat that his fingers slid on. The man . . . no, he was more like a young boy on his first date . . . he was nervous; that pretended disdain was his attempt at controlling a situation where he didn't know the rules or have the kind of edge he usually enjoyed. Reyna had seen it before, a hundred times and a hundred more, but never in an adult as old as this; even those boys the Mal brought with him had more ease about them.

He shook off his weariness and got back to work. "Oh diyo," he said, "but you know how it goes. An evening has its ebbs and flows and sometimes there's a need for quiet and sometimes there's a need to shout. You know." He stilled his fingers, let them build small pools of warmth on the young man's arm.

"That is true." The Mal smiled.

"The quiet times can be good times, though they're best when they're shared."

"Shared."

"Mmmh." Reyna lifted his hand, laid it on the silk that covered his thigh, bowed his head so the supple braids fell gleaming between him and the Mal. "You're a visitor to Bairroa Pili?"

"Yes. How did you know?"

"I haven't seen you before. I'd remember you. You have a presence, I don't know, I can't describe it, but it's there. Diyo, I'd remember you."

The Mal fidgeted, flattered but nervous. He didn't seem accustomed to compliments. "We've been on a Punish Raid. Into the Jinocaburs. It just happened that we returned to Fadogur this way."

"Ah. I've heard stories. What is it like? What is it really like?" Reyna straightened, thrust his hand beneath the braids, lifted them back behind his shoulder, settled them with a flirt of his head. "Hmm?"

The Mal sat stiffly, hands on knees, staring at the

dark figures out on the floor, though Reyna had the feeling he wasn't seeing them. After a few moments of silence he began talking, hesitantly at first as if he had trouble putting words together into coherent phrases.

Control, Reyna thought as he listened with the skill that courting strangers had given him. That's it. He hasn't opened himself to anyone for . . . years . . . probably. Abey's Sting, I hate this . . . blood and pain and death . . . punishment raid, diyo oh diyo, he's trying to justify the killing . . . he knows, surely he knows . . . this is a blooding raid for those Cheoshim boys . . . him, too, I think . . . virgin in several senses. . . .

As he talked, the Mal relaxed and warmed to Reyna who gentled him along, flattered him with soft exclamations and most of all listened with an intensity that shut the two of them into a small world of their own.

We were working from target to target, he said, along the border between the western flanks of the Jinocaburs and the Land. The last hit, it was on the tenth day we were over there, it was a mountain village, a cluster of stone houses built around a sheep barn. The barn was empty when we got there. It was just on sun-up, though that was hard to tell with all the mist hanging about, we'd been riding since moonset, running on rumor and the claims of our guide.

The men and older boys were gone, the women said they were out with the sheep. But they wouldn't say where. They were lying, of course. It was a bandit pesthole, what we'd come to get. We put the headman's wife in one of the houses and threw everything we could find that would burn in with her. Then we lit it. She was an old hag of a woman, had hands like nuts on strings. They still wouldn't tell us where the men had gone, how we could find them. Stubborn. And stupid. We killed the weak ones and the old and the babies. They were useless. Worthless. Except as a message to the men. Strangled the guide, gutless fool, couldn't even bring off a betrayal. The healthiest women we fetched back

with us, turned them over to the Cheoshim Commander
here in Bairroa Pili. Just got in last night.

He was detached, serene as he described it all—as if
it had happened to someone else. Reyna murmured and
urged him on, this was his profession and he was good
at it, though there were times when he let the braids
fall between them to hide his face as anger turned sour
in his mouth.

> > < <

The head drummer cupped his hands and beat a
steady, monotonous toom toom toom toom. . . .

Reyna looked up. The room was clearing rapidly.
The Srikkar's slaves were hauling the last of the drunk
and drugged up the stairs to the bedrooms. Dawa was
nowhere in sight; likely he'd picked up an all-nighter
with someone, even now he usually managed that. Jea
was sitting at a table, a melancholy curve over the remnants of a drink, paying no attention to what was happening around him. "They're closing. I have to go."

"I want to see you. You haven't told me your name."

"Better not. I'm not what you think, young friend.
I'm Salagaum not habatrize."

"What's that mean?"

"Ah." Reyna got his feet. "I see. Let me tell you
this. Find yourself a young habatrize, a pretty girl more
your age. Ask her what a Salagaum is and she'll tell
you. It will come better from her. Easier. No, let me
go. I have . . . enjoyed . . . listening to you." He bent,
touched the Mal's shoulder briefly, then straightened.
"Quiet shared is a blessing these days. Stay there.
Please." Without looking around, Reyna crossed the room
to Jea.

They went out together, moving in weary tandem.

> > < <

In the changing closet by the front door, Jea unbuckled his belt, curled it up, and dropped it in the cloth shoulderbag. "What was all that with the leatherman? Talky-talk and no action, hmm?"

"Innocent murderer," Reyna said. He unlaced his sandals, worked his toes. "What a night. Abey's Sting, I've got enough k'pa in my gullet to . . . well, never mind. He doesn't know what a Salagaum is, would you believe? Funny, you wouldn't think it would be my feet giving me miseries."

Jea pulled on his trousers, twitched the laces tight. "Trying it on?"

"I don't think so." Reyna shrugged out of his robe, rubbed his hands across his breasts. "Chumvay's Nuh'm, one of them had more teeth than a waterhog." He pulled a shirt over his head without bothering to undo the buttons.

"No breastband?"

"Too sore."

"How'd the leatherman manage to stay that ignorant?"

"In training for a Hero, I think. Vigils and fasts, you know." Reyna wiggled his toes again, sighed and pulled on his boots. "I think he started a pash on me. Wish we could afford a chair, the way home gets longer every time."

"Hmp." Jea took down his hooded cloak, swung it around his shoulders. "Well, pash or no, I have a feeling the less you see of that one, the better off we'll all be."

> > < <

The Wounded Moon was gibbous and low in the western sky and the night-torches had burned down to faint red glows when they left *Jigambi's Rendezvous*.

Staying in the heavier darkness by the buildings on the west of the Sokajarua so they wouldn't have to cross the street when they reached the Edge, eyes constantly moving, cloaks pulled tight about their bodies, Reyna and Jea strode rapidly along without speaking until they were off the pavement into the Edge, picking their way over the dirt ruts of Verakay Lane.

Reyna pushed the hood back, scratched vigorously under the pomaded braids behind his left ear. "Aaaah." He kicked at a dirt clod, lurched as his foot dropped into a rut. "Sicuzi says the chain I ordered 's ready, but he'll have to wait for his coin till next party." He stepped out onto the high crown of the Lane, his moon-shadow jerking across the hardpan. Over his shoulder he said, "How's your girlfriend?"

Jea drifted across, walked several minutes beside him before he answered. "Frightened," he murmured. "She's pregnant. Told me when I went to read the cards for her yesterday . . . no, day before, counting from now."

Reyna slapped his forehead. "Hoo-ah, my friend, you've got more nerve than me. You're dead if her husband finds out. Cheoshim potzhead."

"Well, it's not something we can help, you know."

Reyna closed his hand over Jea's shoulder, squeezed, then let go. "The baby, it's yours?"

"She won't say. Won't say anything, just cries."

"You better hope it isn't. You know what the Cheoshim think of bleach in their bloodlines. What are you going to do if it's yours and shows it?"

"I don't know. She won't leave him. I've tried. I've said we can go somewhere else. Well, we'd have to, wouldn't we. She's afraid."

"Raised that way, what can you expect?"

"I know."

They passed the scribbled walls of the school, rounded a bend, and saw a slight shadow gliding in and out of moonlight; it reached the Beehouse and went inside. No yanking on the bellpull, no waiting for Panote.

Neither of them said anything. They both knew who
it was. Locks and bars shifted for Faan, shifted so automatically she didn't even think about it.

> > < <

Reyna climbed to his room, stripped and washed
himself, everything wiped from his head but Faan and
what he was going to do about her. He shrugged into a
worn fleecy robe, pulled the belt tight, and sat in a chair
staring at his door and trying to think.

It'd all gone wrong when she quit school and went to
study with the Sibyl. If he asked Faan about those ses-
sions, she got angry and accused him of spying on her.
If he didn't ask, she accused him of being tired of her,
bored with her.

For a time she was obsessed with her mother; she
pestered him and Tai—the Sibyl, too, for all he knew—
for everything they knew about her, where she'd come
from. After a while, though, she dropped it. There just
weren't any answers available.

Abey's Curse on the Sibyl for teaching her how to
open locks. No keeping her inside after that.

Abeyhamal's Curse? Was that it? Wouldn't let the
baby alone, gave her that Talent . . . a Sorceror . . .
couldn't let her be a witch or something more natural
. . . a Sorceror . . . it was going to get her killed. . . .

Where did the baby go? Reyna pressed the heels of
his hands into his eyes as if that would push the pain
back. The baby who loved me without question, who
followed me everywhere. Where did she go?

Quarrels. Every time they talked. Anything he said.
He hadn't lost the memory of how he'd been when he
was that age, but he was terrified for her, he wanted to
protect her from all the horrors he'd had to face when
his father threw him out. He hadn't forgotten, no, but
nothing he did was right and he'd about run out of ideas.

At least she still came home.

And she still called him Mamay when she didn't stop to think.

He sat for almost an hour without moving, then he sighed, got wearily to his feet and walked down the hall to the small room Faan had taken for her own, opened the door and went inside.

> > < <

Faan dragged herself out of bed before the sun was up.

She scrubbed her face with angry violence, ignoring the stings as soap hit broken pimples and patches of rash from the face paint. When she was finished, she stared into the small cracked mirror, grimaced at the pale pinched face with angry oozing red spots scattered across it. Then she shrugged and began dealing with her hair, dragging a rake through the waxed spikes, combing out the plaited tress and rebraiding it. She fixed the bee-clasp on the end, shook her head, smiling grimly as the braid flipped about, the spikes shivered. The paint was flaking off the colored patches, but that didn't matter, not this morning.

She rooted through the shirt drawer until she located a faded black pullover that Reyna kept trying to throw away and she kept rescuing from the ragbag, dug out an ancient black skirt that used to belong to Areia One-eye. She dressed and left the room, carrying her sandals, her feet silent on the grass drugget that ran down the hall.

She stopped in the kitchen a moment for Riverman's treat, then left by the back door. He had a ferocious sweet tooth and made a sound like bubbles popping when she gave him honeycomb and pastry-lace and taffys from the Beehouse. HE'd listen to her without scolding her, the Wild Magic would go fizzing around her, playing their obscure games and making her laugh.

She loved it when water elementals came by, thrusting their heads into the streaked and dappled air beneath the gatt so they could look at her. They couldn't or wouldn't talk to her, but that didn't matter; she enjoyed watching them change shape, pulsing like the water lapping against the piles, and sometimes they brought her small gifts, shells and bits of coral, pearls and oddities off drowned ships.

And there was a bitty beast like a mix of mouse and boy who came and went as he chose and never spoke to her. Riverman told her one day that the mouseboy was a god, Sessa, Finder of Lost Trifles. That made her laugh, then cry—for wasn't she a lost trifle herself? And neither Riverman or Sessa could or would tell her anything about who she was. So it didn't matter they were gods or whatever, magic. They DID listen to her, though. At least there was that.

> > < <

She brought out the wedge of honeycomb she'd taken from the kitchen, unwrapped it, and tossed to Riverman. While he ate, she leaned back against the stones and watched the little people gather.

"I don't understand what's happening to me," she said finally. "There's . . . there's . . ." she groped at air in crippled, aborted gestures as if even her body was stumbling in its efforts to express what was in her, ". . . there's too . . . too MUCH! It's like I'm going to explode, bam bam splat, bits of me all over the place . . . and . . . oh . . . I don't know. . . ."

The Riverman drew his tiny gnarled hand across his mouth, then sat cradling the oozing comb. "Be specific," he said. "Elucidate." He brought the comb up to his mouth again and licked honey from one of the cells, but never took his black beady eyes off her.

Faan scowled past him at the head of a water elemental thrust up like a faceted lump of mountain stream in the midst of the muddy River. When it merged with the River and vanished, she said, "Last night . . . Tai and Areia One-eye were off to a clandestine rite in one of the Biashar towers as soon as they finished supper . . . they're gonna be sent to the mines if they get caught, they don't care . . . I get so worried . . . makes it so easy to . . . blow up . . . I've got a horrible temper . . . sometimes I want to kill . . . I can't let myself think like that or . . . things . . . happen . . . You remember first time I came here . . . I nearly burned down the school . . . and me . . . ah! diyo diyo, Riverman, I know. Stick to the subject. Reyna and Jea and Dawa, they did the evensong, then they left . . . I can't help it, I HATE what he does . . . how he can . . . he's not LIKE that, he's . . . Mamay . . . oh, I know he's not my mother . . . he's a man . . . sort of . . . um . . . one time when I was crying because Utsapisha's granddaughters teased me when they heard me calling him Mamay, he told me: *I can't be your Mamay in body, but I am in my heart. Never forget that.* That's what he's like, not . . . but he goes and does . . . what he does . . . when I'm around him, when he says ANYTHING, I feel like I'm going to explode . . . I'm afraid for him . . . I'm ashamed . . . he loves me, but he tries to make me into . . . I don't know . . . a perfect child . . . I'm not like that . . . I want . . . I want . . . I don't know . . . it's like there's a hole in me that says WANT WANT WANT and it nor nothing else will tell me what it is I do want." She laid her hands on her knees, palms up, grimaced at the damp green stains from the moss.

Slowly, painfully, she told Riverman about the quarrel last night.

". . . that's it," she said. "That's it. I got some sleep. Hour or so I suppose. Came here soon's it was light. I'm afraid, Riverman, I don't understand what's happening. . . ."

Riverman listened with all his tiny body—said **ah** at the proper places, **uh huh, go on.** He had no advice for her—what did he know of family and its terrors? He was sui generis, unique. But he let her talk and he listened, interested in this strange thing. Not like the Sibyl who seemed to know it all already.

A short while later she slipped from under the gatt and made her way to the Beehouse through the morning throngs of Verakay Lane, nothing resolved, but the storm in her blood blown away for a while.

Chapter 7
PROPHET from Pain

Late and nervous, two months after his encounter with the Mal warrior, Reyna slipped in the back door of the Jigambi Joyhouse, scrambled into his Salagaum robes in the grimy closet Srikkar Jigambi misnamed a changing room, and loped up the service stairs to the third floor where the private rooms were. He pushed past the thick red curtains into the hallway where the floor had a ten-year carpet and the walls were carved into the hammer and anvil of Chumavayal and the polished famwood gleamed pale yellow in the light from the bronze lamps whose scented oils perfumed the whole passage. It'd been a while since he'd reached these levels, and never with an anonymous client. The secrecy clamped over the rendezvous bothered him; more often than not it meant the client had serious problems which might bring death or maiming for the Salagaum involved.

He moved a few steps from the curtain, stopped before one of the gilded mirrors and drew a comb through his long hair, smoothing away the wind-blown straggles. He wore his hair loose because he was too antsy to sit long enough for Areia to plait it for him. He touched a frayed spot on the sleeve of his outer robe, sighed; his clothes were getting shabby. It was time he bought something new, but the prices weavers asked for cloth these days!

He slipped a handkerchief from his sleeve, cleaned exudate from the corner of an eye, wiped dead skin

from his lip; he reapplied liprouge, touched up his eye-
paint, made a face at himself for luck and turned away.

Room six. To the left, three doors down.

He went quickly along the passage and tapped at the
door.

There was no answer.

Potzhead, Reyna thought. Do I really want to do this?

But the fee was too good, he needed the money.
Twenty cemmas, broad silver coins in a leather pouch
waiting for him in the doorman's cage—if the client
released them to him. More than he'd earned the last
six months. He straightened his shoulders and tapped
again.

"Come." The sound was muffled, the word clipped
short.

Reyna tried a smile, sighed and shook himself into
his working mode. He squeezed the latch and pushed
the heavy door open.

Only one lamp was lit. The rest of the room was in
shadow, shifting flickering shadow; the window was
open, the warm night breeze bringing in smells from
outside, the sour waste of the Sok and the dry dessica-
tion of the city.

The client was standing beside the window, his back
to the room.

Reyna let the latch click shut. "I am Reyna, senho.
You asked for me." His voice was soft with his working
purr, the caressing gentleness which most of his clients
preferred. The man at the window didn't move. This
reassured him; the client was nervous, needed soothing. He knew how to do that. "Your wish is my delight;
let me serve you." He moved farther into the room,
stopped when he saw the man's shoulders stiffen. He
waited.

"Sit down. There, by the lamp."

Reyna moved to the divan, sat near the edge of the
lamp's glow where the play of light and shadow was
most active—and most flattering. He clasped his hands

in his lap, rested his eyes on the thick soft gold of his bracelets, deliberately not-looking at his hands, at the stringy tendons that grew more visible as the flesh melted off him. He desperately wanted a hit of bhaggan. Tomorrow, he told himself. I've got to get through this . . . go home . . . first . . . change clothes . . . why doesn't he DO something? Vema, vema, Rey, hard labor, but you can do it. "Come, sit beside me. We have the night, there's no need to hurry things. What do you wish me to call you?"

"Never mind that."

Ah. Reyna finally recognized the voice—the absurdly naive leatherman from that one-fee all-nighter . . . when was it? He couldn't place it exactly, but then he'd dropped into a bhagg-jag haze for days afterward. Didn't matter. He knew the man now and lost some of his fear; this wasn't a pain thing, he wouldn't have to play his tricks so the client thought he was getting more than he was. I can handle it, he told himself. I can handle him. "It doesn't have to be your truename, my dear." He added the last words deliberately, using them to prod a reaction from the leatherman.

The young Mal's body twitched violently and he moved a step to one side, his hands closed on the sill and he stared out over the rooftop of the nextdoor shop. Touched by the moonglow coming through the window, his skin glistened with sweat and a muscle twitched near his mouth.

Reyna touched his tongue to his lips. "Do you wish me to leave, senho? Your desire is my delight." He waited tensely.

"No." The answer came quickly this time. It was only a whisper, but it was filled with pain.

More gently than before he murmured. "Come, then, sit down. The chair by the window. It won't compromise you. The shadows are deep there and I can't see you. Sit down, put your feet on the hassock, lean back. If you want, we can talk. Or we can share a silence."

He hesitated, wondering if he should hint he recognized the client. No. It would be more tactful and certainly safer to forget about that first meeting. He kept talking, using his voice to weave a net about the client, to draw him down where the change of posture would do its business on him. "I saw something amusing today. A boy down by the River. Skinny little imp with arms and legs no thicker than twigs. Wascram, I think. He had hair like cornsilk." Reyna smiled as the leatherman moved away from the window and sat stiffly in the chair, his booted feet flat on the floor.

"The boy was playing a game," Reyna went on, "jumping from rail to rail, scooting across the decks, dodging sailors as they grabbed at him. He ran half a dozen ships before his foot finally slipped and he tumbled into the River."

The leatherman leaned back, laid his hands on the chair arms; a moment later his feet were crossed at the ankle, his bootheels digging into the cushion on the rest.

"The shipmasters were screaming curses at their men, trying to sort them out, the sailors were poking at the boy with their boathooks, trying to snag him and haul him in. He was agile as a fish in the water and got away from them all until one of the boats coming in from the Koo dropped a net on him and brought him to land dangling from the netpole. Even then he fooled them, he wriggled loose and lost them in the wynds."

The leatherman tapped his thumbs on the padding of the chair arms; his head was back, he seemed to be staring at the ceiling. "Do you like boys?"

"What?"

"Do you go with boys?"

"No. Do you want me to?"

"I. Don't. Want. Anything. From. You."

"Ah. I see."

"Salagaum. I don't believe in Salagaum."

"Water is wet. Do you believe that? Does it change anything if you don't?"

"Unnatural abomination."

"We are as we were born. The luck of the dip, not something we asked for."

"Like any sport you should be strangled at birth."

"Every boy born? Until the breasts start growing, a boy's a boy like every other."

"If you really are a man, why do you pretend? Are those breasts real or padding?"

"Shall I show you?"

"No!"

"Why am I here?"

"I don't believe you. I think you're a woman pretending to be a man. I don't know why. It's not natural, not . . . right. I couldn't. . . ." The leatherman came onto his feet with swift surge of strength that was like an explosion inside his skin; two steps and he was at the window again, staring into the night.

Reyna closed his eyes. "What do I do to earn my fee?"

"Nothing. Go away."

"You asked me to come. I came without question or cavil."

The leatherman crossed the room without looking at Reyna; he tugged at the bell cord beside the door, almost ran back to the window. Over his shoulder, he said, "Go. That releases the pledge." He was silent a moment. When he spoke again, there was a terrible compressed passion in his voice, as if his control over it and himself was nearly gone. "Go and respect this evil thing. You don't have to do this, woman. Marry, have children. You can be forgiven."

Reyna got to his feet, moving slowly, and chewing on his lip. He stopped beside the door, opened it a crack so he could run if he had to. The leatherman didn't realize it, but he'd keep coming back, calling Reyna to him . . . obsession . . . it was there, in the man's voice, in the lines of his body, the cracking of his voice . . . everything. If he wasn't stopped now, he'd be back and back, never believing Reyna, unable to escape his own needs, unable to accept those needs, back and back until he killed both of them . . . it had happened before. . . .

Though the leatherman was close to breaking now, forcing him to face the truth about Salagaum seemed to Reyna less dangerous than letting this thing go on. Hating what he had to do, raging at the rigidity and blindness of the man across the room, he slipped out of his outer robe, dropped it on the small table by the door, stripped down until he was wearing the chains about his neck, his bracelets and his sandals and nothing else. "Look at me, senho. Look at me."

"Nayo."

"I am Salagaum, senho, and I am not ashamed of it. Look at me."

The leatherman was shaking, every muscle twitching, his neck straining as his head started to turn and he wrenched it back.

"Look at me, leatherman. Are you afraid?"

The leatherman whirled. Mouth stretched in a silent shout, he stared at Reyna, his eyes shifting repeatedly up and down the lean length of the Salagaum's body.

Reyna smoothed his hands over his breasts, lifted them, let them fall back, soft, heavy breasts, the nipples dark and large, still firm and well shaped though he was past forty now. He slid his hands slowly down his body. He was beginning to get excited, the leatherman had a physical beauty that reached him and a suffering inside that spoke to him.

Leatherman stared a moment longer, then broke. He swung around, his shoulders bent, his hands clutching at the sill. "Go. Get out of here. You. You. Abomination! Thing! Get. Out. Of. Here."

Snatching up his clothing, Reyna went.

> > < <

Faharmoy heard the door click shut, then bent over the sill, fighting the sobs that tore through him. He was weak! Worse than a woman! Crying. Nayo. Nayo. Nayo. Chumavayal, nayo! He gasped and shuddered as he struggled to expel this weakness from himself. Control. That was the thing. It was loss of control that he raged against. It was loss of control that was the thing. Not the soft weakness he . . . felt . . . for that . . . that creature. Nayo, it was the loss of control. Control. He'd burned it into his bones the past nine years . . . or so he'd thought. There wasn't a man his age among the Cheoshim who could outfight him or outthink him . . . on the battlefield. On this other field he was . . . mired . . . lost. . . .

The shuddering and the tearing of the sobs he would not let escape him finally stopped, leaving him exhausted. He fell into the chair where he'd been sitting before, stretched out in it with his feet up and his eyes closed.

Gradually he pulled himself back from the situation, viewed it as a disembodied intelligence with no emotions to confuse his logic.

He was not at fault.

What he had felt was natural and good—or would have been if he had not been fooled and betrayed.

The traitor was not that creature. He . . . she . . . diyo, she was the tool of Abeyhamal who was always the enemy of Chumavayal, the bitter, bitter enemy, softness against strength, rottenness against purity.

Abeyhamal. Diyo. She and her accursed followers brought the drought on the Land by their sins and their rebellion against Truth.

Abeyhamal set the shape of woman on men and by doing so, betrayed all men. Mocked all that belonged to man.

> > < <

When the sun pressed over the horizon and its red light streamed into the window along with the growing noise of the city coming awake, he went downstairs and out the back door, ignoring the female slaves scrubbing the stairs and chattering in corners whenever they got out of the overseer's gaze, slaves who went silent and stared at him until he was past, whose whispers followed him out of the house.

When he stepped from the walkway between the Houses, boy shills for the chairmen swirled around him, not touching him but giving him no peace as they shouted out the fees and excellences of their chairs. Irritated, tired, impatient, he strode through them; he wanted to kick them away from him, slap them into silence. To do what he wanted would show weakness, loss of control, so he ignored them. And sighed with relief as he plunged into the Sok and left them behind.

The sun wasn't fully up yet and there were very few buyers in the Sok. Many of the merchants were still sweeping off their plots and hadn't yet set out their goods; those with shops were taking down their shutters and replacing their displays. A few of them stopped to stare at him. A walking Mal was a rare sight.

He found the kariam he wanted, moved briskly through the lingering coolness of the morning shadows, enjoying the play of his muscles as he walked, the perfume from the hidden flowers, the sweet seductive whisper of the unseen fountains; the Biasharim could still afford to be lavish with water from the aqueducts.

He crossed the Inner Ring Road and heard instead of water falling, the pounding feet of cadres of young Cheoshim as they marched and jumped to the shouted calls of their Drillmasters. He smiled, his soul expanding with the familiarity of those sounds.

He reached the Outer Ring Road feeling a growing harmony between himself and the world, but he needed more than harmony, he needed to understand the reasons for all this. He hurried along the Ring Road to the Jiko Sagrado where he joined the early trickle of worshipers and suppliants heading for the Camuctarr.

> > < <

The Forge Sanctuary was an immense chamber, bronze lamps on bronze chains filling the space with light and shadow, drifts of incense eddying around the kneeling stools.

Anaxoa novices led by the Anaxo Prime were cleaning the ashes from the Forge fire and renewing the coals and aromatic woods that fueled it. The Prime intoned the renewal prayers, swung the censer as he circled slowly about the Firewell; the novices chanted their responses as they worked. One by one they brought the bronze pails of ash and clinker to be censed and blessed by the Prime, then filed out, singing as they walked, their voices strong and deep and filled with power.

Faharmoy knelt at the back, half hidden by an iron column; his eyes shut, his head bowed, he bathed in the sounds and smells of adoration and felt his soul unclench, his mind smooth out.

Some time later Adjoa novices followed an Adjo priest up the aisle. The kneeling stools were filling up with anxious people from the City here to pray for the breaking of the drought. Faharmoy saw the numbers and remembered other morning services he'd gone to in Gom Corasso, services where there was only a small scatter of worshipers; if the drought brought death, it also brought the laggard back to worship. Perhaps that was what it was for, to remind people of their duties. Duties they forgot when times were good.

He closed his eyes again, listened to the service, the ringing of hammers against small personal anvils, a rhythmic ting-tang that was the song of Chumavayal.

Peace flowed into him and he felt strong enough to return to the aching uncertainties of the night.

He faced himself as honestly as he could, tried to comprehend what had happened to him. He could not accept that she was a man. He had seen, but he refused to believe that an abomination could attract him so powerfully. Why did she pull him to her even when he knew the evil that was in her? That first night . . . she seemed to understand everything, even what he had no words to say . . . her gentleness and her warmth . . . that was it. That warmth. It had to be more than pretense. Diyo, she was a whore. Diyo, it was her business to make him feel good. He understood that. And yet . . . there was something more . . . he felt it . . . she was part mother, part lover, part . . . he didn't know. And yet, how could he forget her naked . . . that tall lean figure . . . that MAN . . . that very male man . . . showing how . . . how excited he was . . . the breasts . . . the soft female breasts that he ached to touch even now . . . the thought of touching them brought a sweet agony to his loins . . . he wondered what love with that creature would be like . . . and tore his mind away from the images that exploded in his head. It was abomination. There was no one he could talk to about this, no one who would understand . . . who wouldn't recoil from him in horror.

Adjoa kassos and novices sang the noon praises, beating their small anvils in time with the basso chant, then filed out.

Faharmoy knelt in shadows, meditating, hearing distantly what was happening around him, immersing himself in the cycle of worship, accepting everything without question, bathed in the perfumes and colors and music of worship.

In the afternoon a Biasharim funeral was held, the Anacho Prime himself there to lay the two souls, earth and spirit.

The Manasso Prime led his novices in for the cleansing of their souls when the work day ended.

The Quiamboa priests brought their novices and students in, sang their praises in massed voices to the clang of Adjoa anvils.

Finally he understood what he was born for, his purpose—destroying these unnatural creatures and all the other mocking manifestations of that bitch devil Abeyhamal. Making the land pure again, gifting it fully to Chumavayal so that the rains would come again, the Land would heal, the earth would grow lush with His blessings.

That was it.

Diyo. That was it.

But not yet.

The day had shown him that.

He must purify himself before he was fit to purify the land.

He walked from the Camuctarr into the hot, dry sunset and went briskly down the Jiko Sagrada. He had to collect his cadre and arrange for their transport up River. He had to meet with the Cheoshim Commander and resign from the Border Guard. And after that was done, he had to confront the High Kasso and renounce all wealth and position. It wouldn't be easy, but it had to be done.

He was tired and hungry, but he floated as he walked, full of light and joy, all confusion gone.

GODDANCE
The Eleventh Year

Abeyhamal whirls the fimbo over her head; lightning jags from the point, crashes into the Forge iron, making it shudder and ring. The coals of the Forge Fire shudder with the iron and grey ash creeps across the dying red.

> *Faan danced on the Jang, studied with the Sibyl, was trapped into surrendering her will to the Honey Mother and ran a Barrier about the Low City.*
>
> *Reyna worked and played with equal desperation, labored with Juvalgrim the high Kasso to feed the growing numbers of the hungry and displaced.*

Chumavayal roars, his fiery breath rushes across the coals, waking them to fiercer life, envelops Abeyhamal whose gossamer wings vibrate more furiously, dissipating the heat, and whose face compresses to a scowl at the stench. He brings his sword up in a steel curve across his chest, stamps his feet to one side then the other, slashes at her, pulling yellow and crimson flame-tongues into high leaps from the smoldering coals.

> *The drought intensified. The River sank lower and lower, life grew hard for everyone, fervor increased in the cities and the farm families began leaving the dry and barren land.*

Abeyhamal catches the sword on her fimbo, deflects it, brings the fimbo around in a quick curl and slashes at Chumavayal's hands, drawing a trickle of blood as the point touches him.

> *Juvalgrim strangled Giza Kutakich, throwing the Manassoa Order into confusion, making life margin-*

*ally easier for the humbler castes. Refugees from the
Land began resettling the Low City.*

Chumavayal howls with rage, intensifies his dance.
The sword blade weaves in complex curves, glittering
red and white, sending beams of light flickering about
Abeyhamal, never quite touching her.

*The PROPHET came from the desert and preached
in the streets of Bairroa Pili.*

The Verakay Beehouse burned.

Abeyhamal leaps into the air, turning and turning,
the fimbo held horizontal above her head. She lands
with her back to Chumavayal, cries out in triumph and
hate, leaps again before he can touch her, jumping the
Forge Iron to land beside him, then somersaulting back,
heels over head; she slaps her feet down, drives the
fimbo's point at the center of his back.

Chumavayal wheels, strikes the fimbo away from him,
feints at Abeyhamal, then the two of them go round and
round and round, neither touching the other, neither
truly shaking the other. Not yet.

The GodDance goes on.

SIBYL

The Wheel is turning, the Change sets in
High and Low are caught therein
The Prophet appears, the Scourge without pity
The High Kasso turns apostate
And weaves him a plait
from anarchy
death
and true charity
The Honeychild's caught
In the goddess's plot
The Troglodite I
Watch Ephemerals die

> > < <

The Sibyl wrinkles her nose. As things get worse, so does my verse, she says.

She crosses bare feet at the ankles, wiggles her toes. Eleven years gone, she says.

The Land's drying up and blowing away.

The Lake-That-Never-Fails has fallen from the walls of Gom Corasso, leaving behind a stretch of dead fish and dried mud; the sewer outfalls are visible for the first time in any man's memory and the city stinks.

The River shrinks, the fishermen net nothing there; they go all the way down to the Koo Bikiyar for their catches these days. They prosper despite this, people still have to eat and fish is about all that's left that the poor can afford to buy.

Reyna will organize a cadre of Wascrams, women, and Salagaum who carry supplies throughout the Edge, visiting homes, leaving fruit and grain behind.

Juvalgrim will use the gold he wrings from his demon dips to bring in barrels of salt meat, sacks of tubers and grain. He has ordered the Holy Fountain conduits open, the water free to anyone who came to the Cisterns for it. He will work through the Abosoa Order because they live among the people and know the need. The Manassoate will be furious at what they consider a slight; with Giza Kutakich spurring them on, the Manassoa kassos will spy on Juvalgrim, complain to the Shinda Prefect, protest the waste to Gom Corasso, do everything they can to sabotage his efforts.

Ai-Ai, she says. This never changes, ephemerals are a constant mix of sweet and sour. What does it matter? What DOES it matter? The end comes and the players switch, the game's the same.

The Sibyl gazes a long time at the bright irregular round of the cave mouth.

She hears a rock go clattering down the slope, the scramble of feet.

It matters this much, she says. I've grown fond of two of these emphemerals. Juvalgrim, diyo. And Faan. This angry imp who's coming up the path to badger me again and entertain me with her nonsense.

>><<

"You taught me to control wind. Why can't you teach me rain?"

"I can't, honey."

"K'lann! I'm TIRED of that stupid sickly name! I'm Faan. Faan!" She fumed a minute, then calmed, shaking her head so the bright red and green patches of waxed and painted hair swayed like grass in a strong wind. "Why can't you?"

"Listen to me, Fa. Chumavayal controls the rain." The Sibyl lifted a hand, let it drop back. "You don't interfere with god-business, little Sorcerie. Even Tak WakKerrcarr and Settsimaksimin wouldn't take that on and they're Primes, the best there is."

The name Settsimaksimin twitched in Faan's mind. She blinked, but the faint fragrance that might have been a memory was gone. "Gods!" She chewed on her lip, sighed. "Vema. So what do we do?"

"Search."

"But. . . ."

"Through the demon worlds, not this."

"Vema. What do I do?"

The Sibyl lifted her hands, held them curved a foot apart. She spoke a WORD and a Mirror spread between her palms. "Look and tell me what you see."

Chapter 8
Juvalgrim, the Demon Worlds, and various kinds of Hunger

Reyna groaned awake as Juvalgrim shook him again. "Wha. . . ."

"Come come, wake up, luv." Juvalgrim's hair brushed over Reyna's torso, tickled his face as the High Kasso of Bairroa Pili bent and kissed him, a light brush of lip on lip, tickled him again as Juvalgrim straightened.

"What time is it?"

Juvalgrim finished lighting the lamp, set the candle aside before he answered. "Midwatch. The moon's down." His mouth twitched into a brief smile. "No, luv, it's not time to go yet. I need you, that's all."

Reyna sat up, swung his legs over the side of the bed. He rubbed at his eyes, stretched, dropped his hands on his thighs. "I take it you're not talking about sex this time."

"Hardly." Juvalgrim chuckled. "And no pun intended. Come on, Rey. Get dressed." He walked into the wardrobe that ran along one side of the room; his voice muffled, he added, "You're the only one I can trust to help me."

Reyna eased his legs into his trousers, stood and pulled them up, jerked the laces tight and tied them off. He rubbed at his face again, took his shirt off the chair back, shook it out and pulled it over his head. "So what is this about?"

"Open the chest there." Juvalgrim nodded at the long

carved box at the foot of the bed, took a black cloak from the wardrobe, threw it over a chair.

There were three ancient, crumbling leatherbound books in the chest and a newer one resting beside them. "Books?"

Juvalgrim dropped his hand on Reyna's shoulder, squeezed lightly. "Relics of a time not supposed to exist. Hmm." He stooped, lifted one of the ancients. "Take a look inside, will you?"

Reyna opened the book, frowned at the marks on the page. "What is this?"

Juvalgrim slid the smaller, newer book into a shoulderbag. "The language of Abeyhamal. I thought you might know it."

"No. It's scratchings, that's all. How. . . ."

"Sibyl taught me."

"Busy, isn't she."

"We all do what we must." He reached for a small darklantern, lit it from the candle, left the slide open. "I'm going to show you some things I learned from those books, Rey. And they aren't for chit-chat. Not even to Tai."

"Vema. Do you want me to swear it?"

"No." He smiled, that sudden glowing smile that never failed to make Reyna's heart turn over. "You're not afraid of demons, are you?"

"With Faan living in the house?"

"Ah. I wondered."

"Sibyl's teaching her, too."

"Diyo, I know. Vema, Rey. Keep close to me and don't talk, hmm? You've been through this often enough, you know the drill." He stepped into the wardrobe again, leaned out after a moment, and beckoned.

Reyna followed the flicker of the lantern, Juvalgrim's shadow jagging before him; down and down they went, through the narrow passage, a way he knew so well he didn't bother with light when he came and went—down and down, turning right, turning left, ducking through half-size openings, edging along sections barely wide enough to let him pass, down and around until the passage suddenly opened out into the volcanic blowtube where he usually left his own lantern. They'd passed from the Camuctarr into the heartstone of Fogomalin.

Juvalgrim bent with the grace that after all these years burned through Reyna each time he saw it, tapped the bronze case of Reyna's darklantern. The wick was turned so low it put out barely enough light to announce its presence. "Better bring this, luv, I want you to know the way; you probably won't have to walk it again, but who knows? Keep close to me, hmm? Don't want you getting lost."

He was in an odd mood, flippant and defensive, all flash and fragility. Reyna followed silently, growing more nervous with every step he took. He'd seen Juvalgrim like this before, when there was something coming that he found distasteful or frightening for one reason or another, like the last time they were together before the Amrapake was down for the reswearing of fealty, or when the High Kasso in Corasso came to inspect the records and listen to complaints.

They emerged from the winding blowtube into a stone bubble with one side broken open, the break looking straight west toward the Jinocabur Mountains; above those distant peaks *The Serpent* coiled beside *The Lion*, the stars brilliant in the cloudless sky. Juvalgrim set the lantern on a ledge of black stone. "Housework first," he said. He reached into a vertical crack, drew out a pair of twig brooms. "We've got to get this floor cleaned off, then set up some candles." He handed a broom to Reyna. "Push everything out the front, hmm?"

They worked busily, sweeping a film of dust off the polished black stone. "I thought you left this sort of thing to skivvies," Reyna said.

Juvalgrim pulled his mouth down, flared his nostrils. "Complaints complaints." He flourished the broom, sent a pile of dust flying, then cursed amiably as the wind caught the insubstantial particles and blew them back in his face. "I'll have you know, my skeptical friend, every page learns how to clean before he learns to read."

The bubble floor was flat, smooth and shiny black, with silver wire inlaid in the stone to form several five pointed stars, each in its own circle, three small pentagrams in a row along the north wall, a much larger penta in the center with odd convoluted designs scattered about, the silver lines shimmering like trapped starlight.

Reyna raised his brows. "You did this?"

Juvalgrim shook his head. "Not I nor she who wrote those books. I doubt even the Sibyl knows."

"She?"

"A Kassian. Long time ago. Here." He thrust his arm into another crack, pulled out an undyed wax candle. "That biggest penta there, put this on one of those points."

Reyna helped Juvalgrim set up and light the candles, then stood with his hands clasped behind him, waiting for an explanation.

Juvalgrim brushed his hands together, grimaced at the incipient blisters, then dropped abruptly to the stone in the center of the penta. "That's done, faster with four hands and easier," he said. "Sit down, Rey, rest your feet. We have to wait till *The Plow* rises."

Reyna sat. "I've been patient, Ju, you'd have to admit that." He brushed hair out of his eyes. "What is all this? What are you going to do? And why?"

Juvalgrim turned his head away, stared out of the stone bubble at the night sky. "The treasury is empty, Rey. Nearly. So nearly the difference doesn't matter. I've milked all I can out of the Maulapam and the Biasharim. Didn't bother with the Cheoshim. They don't think anything outside their caste is human, not even the Maulapam. The drought's going to get worse, luv. A year or two and the dying will really start." He moved his shoulders, his long blue-black hair slipping and sliding, dark as the cloak he no longer wore. The starlight touched his cheekbones, the straight stern line of his nose, the clean curve of his mouth. "I'm no Hero, Rey. But I'm curious, you know. That, and it's something I can do. Something I seem to . . . NEED . . . to do. I'm going fishing for gold, Rey, gold and food for the little ones, the ones you and Tai and the Verakay Beehouse dose and take care of. Fishing among the demon worlds. And you're going to help me."

"They'll burn you. Kutakich will find out and. . . ."

Juvalgrim grimaced. "No. Comes to that, I'm gone. Pfft. Nothing left but meat. I don't want to think about it. Hmm. Remember the quake we had a few years back? You ought to, Rey, it was that year you got Faan. Wall fell down, those books fell with them, nearly cracked my head for me. After the Sibyl taught me, I read them; they told me what I could do and how to do it. And why I should. If you don't mind, I'm not going to talk about that."

"Juva, could you teach Faan . . . those books. . . ."

"Nayo, luv." He frowned, moved his shoulders. "I don't dare . . . do you understand?"

"Give them to the Sibyl, let her. . . ."

"Rey, sweet Rey, Sibyl doesn't need the books. If she thought Faan should know, she'd tell her. Chumvey knows what harm I'd do if I got between them." He scowled down at his hands, his hair falling forward to cloak his face. When he spoke his voice was calm, but Reyna knew better than to interrupt again. "I don't really need you for the demon bit, Rey, I brought you here so you'd understand. Help me stiffen my backbone, love me a little, hmm? I'm no Hero. I said that. Well, it's true. Tell me that I'm doing right, that I'm helping where it hurts. Mostly, though, what I want from you and your friends is distribution. You know the Edge. You can get haulers who'll keep their mouth shut, take the food and pass it out where it's most needed.

The gold I'd better handle myself, no one's likely to tunk me on the head for it.''

Reyna sucked in a breath and let it out in a long slow exhalation. ''Vema. Whatever I can do. . . .''

''Thanks, luv. I knew you'd agree. Ah! *The Bull's* horns are showing. It's time.'' He jumped to his feet. ''Up, up, Rey. Stand in the middle of the star. That one over there. When the silver starts shining, don't touch the lines with flesh or leather. Got it? Good.''

Reyna hugged his arms across his breasts and watched as a huge insubstantial sphere formed at one of the penta's points, floated there while images drifted through it, nauseating, terrifying images. Juvalgrim labored on, growling and shrieking sounds that Reyna found obscene and embarrassing.

Juvalgrim's voice changed, grew harsher, louder.

Blue-green grain poured suddenly from the sphere, spread in a dimpled pile outside the penta, flowed around the penta without entering it.

His voice changed again. Fruit like apples rolled out on the grain.

Another change and coins fell in a golden rain atop the apples and the grain.

Another change. Reyna swallowed in sympathy, feeling in his own throat the rasping, tearing syllables.

The sphere went opaque, bulged and warped, shivered in midair, distorted, swirled, suddenly vanished with an absurdly tiny pop.

Juvalgrim opened his throat in a blast of ugly sound that hovered in the stone bubble for an instant, then was gone. He coughed, swallowed. Trembling he lowered himself to the stone and knelt with his shoulders bent, his head hanging. After another moment's silence, he said hoarsely, ''It's done.''

''Ju . . .''

''Do you think you could find your way here?''

''From outside?''

''Diyo. Diyo, Rey. You'll have to. I can't have this

connected to me. It's too dangerous. Do you understand?''

"Diyo.''

"Ah luv, I'm too tired to thank you the way I'd like.''

Reyna smiled. "Save it up for another night. It won't go bad for waiting.''

> > < <

Faan was a small dark shadow huddled on the top step. Reyna sucked in a breath when he saw her, fear turning him cold. Anything could have happened to her out here; the Edge was dangerous after dark, more so than ever these days. He opened his mouth to scold her, then swallowed the words. She knew everything he meant to say. What was the point of quarrelling one more time?

He sat on the step beside her. "Couldn't sleep?'' In the uncertain starlight, he saw the lines in her face soften, her mouth curve in a smile that vanished between one breath and the next.

"Nayo,'' she said. "Things. . . .'' She moved a hand in a shapeless gesture, let it drop.

It was only a few hours till dawn, but the night was hot, the air scarcely stirring. A cat yowled behind them somewhere. Someone screamed, the sound cut off quickly. Music, mostly the heavy throb of drums, drifted to them from the Jang.

"Not going to get better,'' Reyna said. He touched Faan's shoulder; she moved closer, leaning into him as she used to when she was a child. "Drought's worse out on the farms.''

"That's what he said?''

"Mm. He's going to open the temple cisterns for the Edgers so they don't have to pay Mal prices.''

"They'll let him do that?''

Reyna chuckled. "He's not going to ask.''

A lone dog came trotting down the Lane. His head

turned as he passed them, but he didn't stop and vanished round the bend a moment later. They heard some men start yelling and fighting down by the gatts; the guard horn sounded, the noise stopped a few moments later.

Faan stirred. "Sibyl's been teaching me mirrors," she said. She cupped her hands, muttered under her breath. "Look," she said.

In the dark shimmer between her hands he could see a dozen guards marching four men along the Gatt Road, then the scene vanished.

"I can't hold it long," she said. "Not yet."

"I suppose it takes practice like everything worth doing."

"Mm. I went up on the roof tonight, tried to find my mother."

Reyna stiffened; fear and jealousy made him sick. After all these years. . . .

Faan caught hold of his hand. "Nayo, Rey. Not that. It's just . . . I need to know who I am. I NEED to know."

He let out the breath he'd been holding, hugged her. "Don't mind me, Fa. I get stupid sometimes. It's just . . . you haven't said anything about her for a long time. I thought you'd forgot."

"Nayo." She sighed. "Unless you've bone for a brain, you can bang your head against a wall only so many times before you say forget it, it isn't worth the aggravation."

"What happened this time?"

"Nothing. There was a picture of a lock and the mirror went away. I was afraid I couldn't do it again, I didn't try till just now."

He got to his feet, reached down, and pulled her up. "It's time we were both in bed."

Faan put her hand on the door; after a few muted clicks from the lock and the bar, it swung silently open.

Reyna's lips twitched. "Let me tell you, girl, there's been a lot of times I wished you couldn't do that."

She giggled. "I know. But it is handy, isn't it?"

"Point of view, daughter, it's all in your point of view."

Chapter 9
HONEYCHILD copes

"Veils, veils. No slaves. Veils, veils. MOD DES TY.
No slaves. Veils, veils. PURE I TY. No slaves. Veils,
veils." The Cheoshim youths marching along Verakay
Lane howled the words as if they were curses, stamped
their boot heels to the beat of their chant; they called
themselves STRIKERS because they were striking
sparks for the Forge Fire and what they burned was sin.
They came surging at Faan the minute they saw her
walking alone. What they meant to do with her, she
wasn't sure, but she wasn't about to wait and find out.

She leapt into a wynd between two tenements, ran
around another corner and another (the howls followed
her, louder and louder), then chased Ailiki up the side
of a mudbrick house. When she reached the top of the
wall, she jumped, swung over the shaky splitwood fence
onto the flat roof. Ignoring the startled, indignant
woman tending a tiny patch of herbs, she ran across the
roof, went over the fence on the far side and half-fell,
half-climbed to the dry dusty ground below. She
scooted around behind the house next door, turned into
another wynd and ran along behind a warehouse front-
ing on the River. Behind her the chant of the STRIK-
ERS died away as they nosed about trying to find her
again, then moved off in the wrong direction.

She reached the end of the warehouse and walked
down the wynd, stepped over the legs of a sleeping
mulehead, grimaced at the avid circle of denge beetles
gorging at the pool of vomit beside him, trying to suck

it up before the sun drew all the moisture from it. She
pulled her hand across her sweaty brow, wiped it on
her skirt, sighed. Running in this heat was an idiotic
idea.

She stopped when she reached the Gatt Road, stood
in the wynd mouth and frowned at the trickle of traffic
moving along it toward the Sokajarua. The sun throbbed
in a heat-whitened sky, the River was down another five
spans, and the gatts were nearly deserted; she could
count three ships where five years ago there'd been
thirty. She wiped at her face again; her mouth was dry,
her throat sore.

> > < <

Faan slipped under the wharf and settled herself on
the dead grass, scowled at the River. Out in the center
the water had a fugitive blue glint; in close though, it
was thick and brown, more like a gel than a liquid. And
it smelled bad.

She wiped her sleeve across her face, rubbed her
hands on her skirt, pulled her legs up, rested her arms
on her knees. As she moved, thin lines of hot gold
shifted across her face and arms; the planks overhead
had dried out and pulled away from each other.

Riverman came plodding up from the water, shaking
himself and stepping delicately across the cracks in the
mud; he crouched, jumped, and landed with a grunt on
the bow of the boat, caught the bit of honeycomb she'd
fetched for him and licked eagerly at it.

Behind her the Wild Magic gathered, the bubble people shifting, melding, breaking apart, their voices like
the hiss of water over rocks.

"Trouble?" Riverman licked his fingers off and dug
into shaggy fur which had gone brown like the water.

"It's Reyna. It's a week since he's been home. The
way things are. . . ." She rubbed at her nose with the
back of her hand, fought the tears that prickled at her

eyes. "Tai's worried, too, she asked around, much as she could. And Panote's done what he could. I made my mirror, but there was the lock, that jeggin lock. And the Sibyl wouldn't try . . . she said she couldn't . . . is he in the River?"

"No." Beady black eyes fixed on her. "For sure, no."

"The Shindate . . . did . . . did the Shindate get him?"

"I don't know. River's my place, you have to ask the Wildings that."

"But will they tell me?"

"Vema, Fa. If they can. They so little, maybe the gods don't think to lock them."

"Ahhh." She dropped her head on her arms; crouched there, eyes closed, until the shaking was gone. There was a rush of pops and hissing behind her, a rain of dirt grains against her as the Wild Magic oscillated restlessly. She straightened, looked around.

Riverman had left the boat. He was standing in the middle of the bubble people while they clustered and flowed apart, shifting like soapfoam around him. A moment more, then he whistled a short phrase and stood with his hands on his furry loins as the Wild Magic vanished into the earth. He came bounding down the fill and leapt back on the bow. "No naysaying to stop them, Fa. They'll find him, if he's anywhere about. He could have been taken away, you know, sent to the mines."

She brushed her hands across her eyes. "The mines. I hadn't thought . . . could the Wildings go that far?"

"Perhaps. It would take longer and most likely would not be useful. What could you do, girl? Gird on your armor and go rescue him?"

"I don't know. Something."

He broke a sliver from the boat, shredded it into dust, brushed his tiny hands off, fixed his eyes on her. "You wouldn't be let leave the city."

"Why?"

"There are things I can say and things I cannot."

"You, too? That's what the Sibyl keeps saying."

"The constraints are the same." He got to his feet. "Watch out for the gods, Honeychild. It was Abeyhamal brought you here and Chumavayal waits to pound you. Come back at sundown. I'll tell you what we've found." He sprang down, darted along the mud and vanished into the murky water.

She stared after him for several minutes, then shook her head and crept from under the wharf, trusting her no-see-me to keep away the eyes of the few laborers hanging listlessly about, waiting for work that wouldn't come.

> > < <

She came back in the hot red light of a spectacular sundown, dipped into black shadow and knelt beside the crumbling old boat.

Riverman was already there, half out of the water, clutching a mud-caked piling to keep his place. His mosquito voice was sad and weary. "Nothing," he said. "We have asked the stones and the iron, but they have no answers. For sure, the Shinda Prefecture doesn't have him. Or the Camuctarr. Come back tomorrow sundown." He let go and vanished below the surface before she could speak.

> > < <

The Jang was a darker meaner place these days.

The shadow predators and long-gone druggers haunted the dance ground, killing one more day, preying on each other for the coin it took to stay alive, preying on the young folk who swarmed there after dark.

These younger folk were lean and hungry, searching for something to cut the heat and the monotony, drugs, alcohol, sex, music, pain, or pleasure. There was desperation and weariness in their play, but they came.

And Faan came to disable her imagination with noise and exhaustion so she wouldn't think about what could be happening to Reyna, so she wouldn't agonize over Tai and Areia One-eye defying the edicts from the Amrapake and the Camuctarr and going to sing Honey rites for the women of the Edge and elsewhere when the other Beehouses couldn't oblige. She came for the music and the dancing, the ear-hammering voices and the thick heavy stench of people around her who didn't care if she lived or died.

Dossan and Ma'teesee came with her. Dossan was tired from a long day in the Woodman's factory, but she would have come even if Faan hadn't called her out, she, too, needed some lift to her spirit, whether it was terror or raw mulimuli, or a tumble in the grass with a half drunk apprentice. Ma'teesee had her own reasons for wanting to forget her tomorrows.

They linked arms as they had so many times before and put a hop in their steps as they jigged down the Lane, giggling as they passed Fedunzi's End. The silversmith had hanged himself a year ago, shortly after a grim group of hooded men threw cruses of oil into his shop, followed it with torches, and burned it to the ground. "Wascra Wascra Wascra girls," they sang, a darker note in their voices this night. "Waste the wonkers, paste the ponkers, Wascra Wascra Wascra we."

They quieted as they got closer and heard the clashing music from the bands who'd staked claim to spots on the Ground. It was dangerous here; they had to be ready to skip and dodge, so they dropped arms and stopped their prancing, but they kept on going, dancing a step or two as a snatch of music blew toward them, carried on the hot hot wind, singing nonsense syllables as they dropped into the beat of the Jang.

Faan shied away from a shadowman crawling about

on hands and knees. "Which way, Dossy? Your turn to pick."

Dossan crossed her arms, hugged them tight to her chest. "Widdershins. I'm feeling contrary tonight; let's work a curse on the laffy Mals."

Ma'teesee giggled, then yelped and jerked her foot loose; the crawler had grabbed at her ankle, got a weak hold on it, fingers slipping on the worn leather of her boots. "Pichad," she yelled, "jegg yourself." She skipped back another step as the crawler wavered toward her again, brought her heel down on his hand. "Eat it." She circled around him and pranced after the other two.

Ailiki trotted along beside Faan, chittering almost-words at her; the mahsar loathed this place, always made a fuss. Faan ignored her. As they passed one of the bands, she caught hold of Ma'teesee and began dancing in fast-footed loops with her, then shifted to Dossan. Then she danced alone, utterly sunk into the music, sensual, abandoned, the twisting and turning of her body reaching deep into the ancient Soul of the Land at the heart of every Fadogur adopted or born.

Young men grabbed at her, but she burned too hot for them. Sucking their fingers as blisters erupted on them, shaking hands that tingled uncomfortably, they cursed then shouted to the rhythm of the band and danced in a mesmerized ring about her until the music stopped.

Dossan and Ma'teesee yanked Faan from her trance and ran off before the other dancers could close around them.

They passed a man with a burning splinter from the fire. He was a slave, a northerner, his fair skin covered with small sun cancers. He pressed the splinter against his arm, watched the fine curly hairs wither and turn to ash, the skin beneath start to bubble; he lifted the splinter, blew the coal on the end to a cherry red and put it on his arm again.

They hurried away from him and nearly ran into two men grunting and hammering at each other with their fists; it wasn't a fancy fight or a flashy one and no one was bothering to watch. They just hit and hit and hit as if they were clockwork figures.

A circle of men stood around a habatrize. As they passed, a man got up, wiped himself off with the towel a shadowy figure handed him, another man tossed a moju in a can and fell on the woman. Ma'teesee wanted to watch, but Faan and Dossan pushed her on toward the stage.

Hot hot hot hot hot hot
The singer screamed the words; behind him the tin drums sang in angry polyphony, the fiddle squealed in a floating line above the rest.

BURN!
**Hot day hot day, hot and hotter
Haaa ah aaa aaah ahhht!
Hot hot hot hot hot hot**

BURN!

**Dry day, fry day dry and dryer
Dry aye aye aye eeeeee!
Fry aye aye aye ayeeee!**

Over and over, the same rhythm, the same notes, over and over. . . .

Fry fry fry fry fry fry
BURN!

The beat exploded inside Faan, throbbed in her, the panting, insistent urgency of that music. She moved to it, dancing as she had before, seized by the music, making it tangible with her body.

Blind and unthinking, she danced in a growing circle

of watchers, danced in an ecstasy greater than she'd known before . . . and felt a force stirring in her, a power that grew and grew until it frightened her and she stopped moving. *A different power, like something trying to crawl inside her skin. Someone.*

She stood panting, sweating, the hairs on her arms erect and prickling. The music was still going on and Ma'teesee was bobbing and sweating, her face shining in the dark red light from the dying fire. Dossan was quiet, her arms crossed again, as if she hugged herself to keep out the terrors floating around her. The shadows beyond seemed to shake themselves and wake from a dream.

Suddenly sick of the place, oppressed by the people crowding around her, Faan yelled, "Dossy. Le's bouzh."

Dossan twitched, nodded at her; they grabbed Ma'teesee and started across the Jang to Verakay Lane.

Shadows collected around them, thickened in front of them. Faan swerved to go around and the clot flowed round to block her again. Men. Shifting gleams of eye-whites and teeth and skin sheened with sweat.

The fire was down to coals and the cheating clouds were blowing across the Wounded Moon, bringing darkness but no rain.

Faan zagged the other way, but they were there before her, turning her, turning them all toward the shabby rustling trees between the Jang and the River. Dossan and Ma'teesee kept close behind her; she could hear their fright in the rasp of their breathing.

Ailiki ran back and forth in front of the shadows, hissing at them, the hair standing up along her spine, her tail erect.

Faan stopped—so suddenly that Ma'teesee bumped into her and Dossan went a stumbling step past her, though she shrank back immediately and pressed herself against Ma'teesee.

Faan brought her arms up. "Stay behind me. However I turn, stay behind me.'' Then she *called* fire, the fire that ran beneath her skin all the time now, that whispered seductively to her, promising her anything she wanted if she set it free.

Wispy blue, gold and pale red flames danced along her arms. She thrust both arms before her, then bent her right arm and slid her hand under a flame dancing on the back of her left hand. She lifted it free. Then she flung it at the nearest of the shadow men.

Her control cracked a hair when she heard a high delighted giggling as the flamelet arced away from her. The other flames flickered erratically and their tiny hisses were demands to be loosed like the other.

The flamelet hit the man, flared into a skin around him, consumed him and went out with a satisfied !pop!.

Bile rose in her throat. She swallowed, caught up another flame, but the shadows were retreating, melting into the night with the pound of running feet.

''Whoosh! That was close.'' Ma'teesee shook her shoulders, her arms, danced a few tentative steps to convince herself she wasn't still scared. ''Didn't know you could do THAT, Fa.''

''Quiet.'' Faan sweated, her voice rose to a shriek. ''Get away from me.''

Dossan grabbed Ma'teesee by the upper arm, held her still, but neither girl backed off any farther; they waited tensely while Faan fought to dismiss the fire she'd called.

For several breaths she thought she wasn't going to manage it. She was so drained she could barely stand, but she knew if she didn't get rid of the flamelets, they'd eat her like the shadowman.

Ailiki came to her and pressed against her ankles. A thread of strength like a small cool stream flowed through her. She gathered herself and focused, the dismissal words came tearing from her throat—and fire was gone. She dropped her arms and walked blindly toward the Lane, Dossan and Ma'teesee following silent behind her. She could feel them starting to be afraid of her. They hadn't been before. Especially Ma'teesee, who looked on Faan's magic as a peculiar sort of toy that was hers to play with whenever she wanted. Now a man was dead. That he was dead didn't bother them all that much; these days nearly everytime they looked out a window, someone was being killed or hurt or something. It was how she killed him. How easy it looked. As if she were a pretty snake they'd played with until they found out it was a viper. Snake girl—Dossy called her that the first day they met.

She sobbed, ground her hands into her eyes.

"Don't, Fa, you couldn't help it." Dossan hugged her. "He was going to hurt us."

Ma'teesee grabbed a strand of her hair and yanked. "Silly!"

"Ow! Teesee." She leaned against Dossan, sniffed, wiped her nose with the back of her hand. "You are a pest."

Ma'teesee took her hand, swung it back and forth. "Wascra girls," she chanted.

Dossan giggled. "Wascra, Wascra, Wascra we," she sang. She danced out ahead of them, swung around and jigged backward, clapping her hands. "Wascra Wascra, watch us, hey, touch us, nay, all you ponkers walk away. . . ."

Faan looked from one to the other, laughed shakily. "I thought. . . ."

"Stoopid." Ma'teesee reached for her hair again, but this time Faan skipped out of reach, stuck her tongue out at her friend.

The three of them linked arms and went jigging along the street chanting Dossan's new verse to their theme. "Wascra Wascra, watch us, hey, touch us, nay, all you ponkers walk away. . . ."

>><<

Faan lay in bed, staring into the shifting darkness above her. She hadn't lost her friends after all, but she needed comforting, she wanted to sit in Reyna's lap as she had when she was little and have him hold her and soothe her as she cried and cried. She couldn't cry now. Dried out like the Land. She'd killed a man. She needed to tell Reyna about it, to get his . . . call it absolution . . . she needed him to tell her it was all right, she wasn't evil . . . she needed him, but he was somewhere else. Maybe as dead as that bhag-head she ashed. She pressed her hand over her mouth. She wasn't going to be sick, she refused to be sick.

It was a long time before she slept.

>><<

Riverman was waiting for her, perched on the bow of the old boat, combing his fingers through his ruffed brown fur. He grinned at her, then the grin was gone and he was shaking his head. "Found him. He's alive, just. Over in the Low City. House under the end of the Iron Bridge."

Faan closed her hands so tightly her nails cut into her palms. "What happened? Who's got him?"

"Dead man."

"What?"

"Ol' Giza Kutakich, Manasso Prime. Deader than a three-day fish. Wildings tell me he snatched Reyna because Reyna knew what Juvalgrim was doing and where he did it. Reyna didn't want to say. Wildings tell me the walls weep when they speak of it."

"Tell me the whole thing. Tell me."

"Diyo. Juvalgrim is using sorcery to find gold and food for the Edgers. He calls demons in this cave in Mount Fogomalin, not the Sibyl's, another one. Giza Kutakich was fool enough to let the High Kasso discover him spying. Juvalgrim strangled him, threw his body to a fire-demon. Handy for canceling your mistakes, having demons round the place. Far as he was concerned that was the end of it; he doesn't know about Reyna.''

''You said Reyna's alive?''

''Just. He is. . . .'' The little black eyes blinked at her; the round face looked drawn. ''Broken.''

''What can I do?''

''I told you beware the gods, Faan. SHE's touched you, but you fought HER. SHE wants you free-willed and fighting for HER. You can make a bargain with HER. Surrender and let her indwell and she'll heal Reyna, make him whole and clean.''

Her teeth clamped on her lower lip, Faan gazed at him. ''You HERS?''

''Not me. Not against her either. Little 'uns like me and the Wildings, we get mixed up in god business, we get stomped.'' He scratched at his weedfur. ''Appreciate this, Honeychild, I speak what SHE tells me. SHE's dancing her war with Chumavayal and by the Dance, SHE's built a cage that's caught you, and catching you SHE's caught us.'' He wrinkled his short broad nose, blinked his bright black eyes. ''I'm of the River, Honeychild, it's my blood, my life. It's poisoned now and diminished. I'm poisoned and diminished. When the rains come again, that'll be made right. But it'll only happen when the Godwar's finished. Abeyhamal needs you. So I need you. The Wildings want to break from from the Land and the bonds that hold them here. They need you. Do you understand what I'm saying?''

Faan closed her eyes, drew in a deep breath, let it out. ''This much. You are using me as much as SHE is.''

''As you use us, Honeychild. I have a hope and a belief that it is different between us. The take and take of friendship as well as need?''

Faan swallowed, rubbed at her eyes. ''Hope. Not

much of that around these days. Vema, vema, friend.'' When he grinned so broadly that his beady black eyes shut to slits, she relaxed. ''Tell me what I should do.''

''Find someone to help you. Cross by the Wood Bridge, not the Iron, don't touch the Iron. Carry Reyna back to the Beehouse, lay him before the Altar and make your bargain with HER.''

''How?''

''Tell the Kassian Tai what you need. She will do it.''

''Gods!''

''Diyo. Don't say more.'' He jumped from the boat to her shoulder, stroked her cheek, leapt into the water, and was gone.

> > < <

Faan pushed the door back, hesitated in the opening. ''Pan?''

The big man looked up from the boot he was cleaning and working back to suppleness. ''What is it, honey?''

''I know where Reyna is.''

''Where?'' He set the boot down, rested his large knotty hands on his knees. ''You want help? Is it trouble?''

''Diyo. All of that. We'll need a litter. Do you have a friend you can trust to help with this?''

''Have you told. . . .''

''No one. No. Please. After we bring him back, then's the time.''

''Why?'' He got to his feet as he spoke, turned his back to her, and pulled on a pair of trousers; he slid out of the houserobe and reached for an old tunic, dark brown, washed so many times it was softer than down.

Faan stared at his back for the few moments it was bare, shivered suddenly. ''You always ask why.''

"And haven't I taught you the same, my honey?" He turned round, sliding loops over the neck buttons. "So?"

"Because I have to . . . do . . . something then. . . ."

"What?"

She shook her head. "You can't help, Pan. Not this time. I've got to see Reyna first, see if. . . ." She shivered.

He touched her cheek. "You'll do what's right. I know that. Tell me where."

"A house in the Low City, it's under the end of the Iron Bridge."

"Low City?" He frowned. "What. . . ."

"I'll explain after we've got him back here."

"We? Nonsense. Charou and I'll go get him. You wait here, have the Kassian ready to help him."

"No. We have to do this without noise. The guide will show itself to me, not you. And we have to use the Wood Bridge and not touch Iron. That's. . . ." She fumbled for a word. "That's vital. It's god business, Pan."

He ran a hand over his bald head, smiled suddenly at her, the street urchin's grin that sat so oddly on his square solid face. "God wars, eh? Blessed be Tannakés. More gods like him and life'd be simpler and safer." He reached a long arm out, gathered in his staff. "I'll wait. You go get that cloak of yours with the hood. Shouldn't ha' gone out with your arms naked like that, your head uncovered. Just asking for trouble, eh? Scoot."

> > < <

The house under the Iron Bridge was squat and derelict, its thick mud bricks crumbling, the wooden shutters discolored with age and sealed to the frames as if both shutters and frames had turned to stone.

"Careful," Faan whispered. "Don't touch iron, not even with your sleeve." Avoiding the latticed metal support of the Bridge creaking and groaning overhead, she followed the pinpoint light of the Wild Magic willawis around the building to the back where a door sagged on one hinge.

The house smelled of dust and dead moss, most of all of age, yet the inner walls were in much better shape than the outside, almost as if the crumbling were a kind of camouflage.

Reyna lay naked in a small room near the front of the house, smeared with his own wastes, his body contorted, all the major bones broken, his long slender hands swollen and shapeless, his face sliced into a horror that wasn't remotely human. In the faint bluish light of the willawis, Faan looked down at him. "Vema," she said. "That's that." She stepped aside so Panote and Charou could get at him.

Faces impassive, the two men lifted Reyna as gently as they could and laid him on the litter without trying to straighten his limbs. Panote tossed an end of the sheet to Charou and they laid the clean linen over him. Panote straightened. "Has to be the Wood Bridge?"

"Diyo."

As soon as they were out of the house, she sent the willawis away and ran ahead of the men.

> > < <

Faan stood with her arms folded as Panote and Charou set the litter on the tiles in front of the altar. It was very late by now, long past moonset, and not a breath of air was stirring, even up here. Sound was oddly muffled, as if the heat were layers of felt. She shut her eyes a moment, closed her hands about the edge of the altar. The price was her soul, her life. She had no choice. None. Reyna . . . no . . . best not to think of him. "Pan, go wake the Kassian and tell her to bring candles. Tell her about Reyna. Tell her there's a bargain I need to make. Then if you want, you can go back to bed."

"Would it make trouble if I came?"

"Nayo, my friend." She swallowed. "It won't be pleasant, I think. Ahsan, Charou, I bless you for your help, but go now. Please."

> > < <

The Kassian Tai came with candles and strained honey from the jars in her room. Areia Moha One-eye followed with Tai's ancient drum that she'd inherited from the Kassian who was her teacher, who'd inherited it from hers and so on. Tai poured the honey into a crystal saucer and set the candles beside it, lit them with a coal from her fire. Holding the drum in both hands, Areia knelt beside the litter.

"Panote?" Faan said.

The Kassian Tai smiled. "He wanted to be here, but I forbade it. This is Abeyhamal's work and Tannakés has no part in it."

"I see."

"Diyo, Honeychild. Take your place." The Kassian Tai Wanameh settled the embroidered Takaffa cloth about her neck, lifted her hand for Areia Moha One-eye to begin the drumming.

Faceted shimmers formed over her eyes, her skin bleached to a dark amber, threadlike antennas curved from her brow, gossamer wings vibrated behind her. Tai+SHE turned to face Faan. "WHAT IS IT YOU REQUIRE, HONEYCHILD?"

"A bargain, O Mother of Bees." Faan sang the words; she didn't know if that was right, but it felt right. "Or a battle."

"YOU BARGAIN, FLEA?" The voice was honey sweet and thick with vibrato. The amber hands moved continually in odd, angular positions.

"A bargain or a battle."

"I COULD CRUSH YOU WITH A THOUGHT."

"Diyo, that is true. I would be a smear on the tiles and about as useful. This is your making, no doubt you know my terms before I state them. Well?"

"SAY WHAT YOU WANT. SPEAK CAREFULLY, FLEA. WHAT YOU ASK FOR, YOU SHALL RECEIVE."

"One. If all terms of the bargain are not fully complete, the bargain is nullified. Two. Reyna is to be healed of his body wounds and the addiction that is destroying him, and you will see that he does not remember these past three days, that he does not remember any pain or betrayal. Three. You will do your best to protect him from further harm. Four. I know this leaves large holes in the bargain, but I will trust your honor to see it is done. Five. On my side, I will surrender my will to you and do whatever you wish to the extent of my intelligence, my strength and my Talent, I will do your bidding even unto death." She thought a moment. "Unto MY death."

Abeyhamal in Tai laughed. "MY HONOR," she cried out, "YOU THINK TO TRUST MY HONOR."

"Diyo."

"LET IT BE DONE, FLEA. TAKE MY HAND."

"When I see Reyna whole and strong, then I will take your hand."

"YOUR TRUST IS ODDLY LIMITED, FLEA."

"It is my need that speaks, Bee Mother, not my distrust."

"SO BE IT. BEHOLD."

The stained sheet melted away. Reyna's limbs were straight, his body clean, his face had its usual austere beauty. He slept sweetly, deeply.

Faan sucked in a breath. It was hard, terribly hard to reach out to the god in the woman, to take the cool honey hand and surrender her will, to summon the god to enter and be one with her, but she'd made the bargain with open eyes and had the Riverman's warning in her ears. What the god had given, the god could reclaim. She let the air trickle through her lips and waited.

Abeyhamal was at once cool and hot, light and heavy, coming into her like honey mead; one moment she felt as if she'd burn to ash, another as if she'd turn to ice. Then she was washed out of herself, was prisoned in a cyst somewhere behind her eyes, while the god wore her body like a glove.

The Kassian Tai Wanameh crumpled to her knees, glazed eyes fixed on the tiles, the god-shape gone from her body. Areia Moha One-eye let the drumming fade. She went on her knees beside Tai and lifted her shoulders, murmuring soft encouragements into her ear.

Faan's body walked across to Reyna, took the Salagaum's hand and raised him from the litter. Reyna came up with healthy ease, his eyes still closed, his breathing slow and steady.

The god-in-Faan led Reyna down the stairs to his room on the sleeping floor, helped him into bed, and pulled the quilts up around him. She/SHE touched his brow gently, affectionately, then left him to sleep till he was ready to wake.

> > < <

The god-in-Faan deposited Faan's body on her bed. "BE READY," SHE said, the voice reverberating inside Faan's head. "WHEN I ASK, GIVE. WITHOUT HESITATION AND WITHOUT STINT."

The cyst about Faan dissolved and she was herself again, the god was gone.

She got to her feet, poured a cupful of water into the

basin, and washed her face over and over until most of the water was gone. "It's done," she said aloud. "For better or worse, it's done."

She stripped, climbed into bed, and slept without dreaming for the first time in days.

Chapter 10
The PROPHET comes from the Hills to Disturb the Land

Faharmoy woke with Chumavayal's Touch on his brow and knew it was time. His CALL had come.

>><<

Two years ago he walked into the stony wilderness of the Konduni piedmont, leaving everything behind, renouncing his father and his family, renouncing power and personal glory.

He went hungry, froze at night, burned with thirst and was tormented by his own filth, by the assaults of insects—and by memories he couldn't forget and couldn't bear to remember.

He walked blindly, following the wind.

Eventually he found a boulder-strewn wadi with a tiny spring that produced less than two cups of water a day. It was enough. He settled to pray, to meditate, to die—if that was what he was called on to do.

He slowed day by day to the unhurried flow of life around him, lost the urgencies of his regimented existence though he kept the rigidity of the framework—it was ground so deeply into him that he would never recognize how unchanging a pattern he laid over his hours.

He rose before dawn, drank three swallows of water, then three more; he walked to the sandy hole he used as a latrine and let his body act as it would. He scrubbed with sand, then washed with meticulous care and half a cup of water, then knelt naked in the morning light, his arms out, his eyes on the rising sun.

When it was directly overhead, he rose from his prayers and meditations, pulled on a coarse robe and sought food for his single meal of the day—a furry bukle or a fat lizard, a kizzai tuber or a tungah root, the fiddle curls from the tender tips of a jiji weed or whatever else came to him. He never knew exactly what he was going to find and that was good. Some days he found nothing and that, too, was good.

His beard grew. And his hair. He combed them with a scratchcone from a tiny, twisted wiba tree, cleaned his teeth with a twig he cut from that tree.

He grew calm at last. Out here the grains of sand blew across the cracks and undulations of the stone without reference to him, out here the web of life let him be.

He was happy.

> > < <

Chumavayal came to him, huge and powerful, strong and male, no ambiguities about him, everything clear and pure and true.

Chumavayal came and touched him, gently, lovingly, and told him: **YOU ARE MINE. YOU ARE MY HERO, MY CHAMPION.**

HEAR ME: WHAT IS, IS RIGHT. CHANGE IS BETRAYAL. THOSE THAT TRY TO CHANGE THINGS HAVE BROUGHT UPON THEMSELVES THE DESTRUCTION OF THE LAND. THEY WILL DIE OF HUNGER AND THIRST UNLESS THEY COME BACK TO ME—UNLESS THEY FOLLOW ME WITHOUT FALTERING OR QUESTIONING.

MY HERO, MY CHAMPION, MY WORD, MY PROPHET, FOLLOW ME WITHOUT FALTERING AND I WILL FILL YOU WITH THE HOT

IRON OF MY FORGE THAT YOU MAY BRAND
MY PEOPLE WITH MY WORDS.

YOUR VOICE WILL BE MY VOICE.

YOU WILL SCOURGE THE PEOPLE, TURN
THEM AWAY FROM THEIR SINS, BRING THEM
BACK TO ME.

YOU WILL ERASE FROM THE LAND ALL
THAT IS PERVERTED, ALL THAT IS BORN
MONSTROUS.

I WILL TAKE THOSE POOR CRIPPLED
SOULS TO MYSELF AND HOLD THEM UNTIL
THEY ARE HEALED THAT THEY MAY BE
BORN ANEW.

I AM NOT A CRUEL FATHER, BUT I DO
WHAT I MUST FOR THE HEALTH OF MY PEO-
PLE.

DISCIPLINE IS NECESSARY. YOU KNOW
THAT, HERO.

DISCIPLINE IS HEALTH.

PAIN IS GIVEN TO MAN TO TEACH HIM THE
RIGHT WAY—OTHERWISE, HOW IS HE MORE
THAN ANIMAL?

Chumavayal said these things to him, reached down
again and drew warm black fingers along the thorns
Faharmoy had woven into a scull cap to purge himself
of thoughts he should resist. THERE IS NO MORE
NEED OF THIS. YOU HAVE CAST OUT YOUR
DEMONS. THEY WILL ATTACK AGAIN, BUT
THEY HAVE NO MORE POWER OVER YOU.
YOU HAVE CAST THEM OUT AND YOU ARE
WHOLE.

GO NOW AND SPEAK THE TRUTH TO MY
PEOPLE, THAT I MAY BE MOVED AND TURN
AWAY THEIR SUFFERING.

DEMAND THAT THEY CAST OUT THE MIS-
SHAPEN AND MISBORN AMONG THEM.

DEMAND THAT THEY SEND THE FOREIGN-

ERS AWAY, RID THEMSELVES OF THAT POL-
LUTION.
  TELL THEM, MY PROPHET, MY CHAM-
PION.
  GO AND SPEAK MY WORDS.

> > < <

Faharmoy ate a tuber he'd buried beneath the fire to
cook during the night, then walked out of the camp
taking with him only the coarse brown robe he'd worn
there, the old leather sandals that were near to falling
apart, the crooked hardwood staff he'd found one day,
sandpolished and as tall as he was. Food he left to the
whims of his god, but he took the water skin, pushing
his arm through the fraying strap, settling the damp
weight against the small of his back.

The two years that had passed since he came here
had seen the drought harden on the land, streams dry
up, the River sink until the sandbars showed. Grass was
dry and brittle; most of the brush was dead.

He walked without hurrying, his long easy strides
taking him across the land with deceptive speed; he
could walk all day now without tiring, swinging the
staff, chanting Chumavayal's Law or meditating as
he moved.

An hour before sundown he searched for food, found
a few meaty beetles and some withered tungah roots.
He made a small fire, roasted the beetles and the roots,
ate them with a stolid indifference, washed the food
down with two swallows from the skin. He poured sand
over the fire and stamped it down to smother the tiniest
embers, then he slept.

On the third day he came to a scrub farm, deserted
and silent.

There was a dead cow in a rickety corral, all ribs and
skin, mummified by the heat and dryness.

Swaying listlessly in the desert wind, a short frayed

length of rope hung from the end of a cracking well-sweep. When he reached its mudbrick coping, he dropped a pebble into the well. After a while he heard a clatter, no splash. Dry. Deep and dry.

He sighed. Dropping to his knees and stretching his arms wide, he chanted Chumavayal's Blessing on the land and its people. He kept up the cycle of prayer until his mouth was dryer than the dust, his throat was raw and his lips cracking—until he felt Chumavayal's touch on his brow.

He took a swallow of water from the skin, held it in his mouth for several minutes, then let it trickle down his throat. Another sip, then he slapped the stopple home and started on his journey once again.

On the fifth day he came to a dry canal and followed it to a village. Three men sitting on a bench in the meager shade of a dead tree looked up as he stopped beside them.

"The fields are empty," he said. "Where are your children?"

"Crops ha' fail again, Prophet," one of them told him, an unlettered Naostam he was, his ancient hands twisted and knotted by a lifetime's hard labor. He jerked his thumb at the canal. "Y' see how that be. No crop 'thout water. Nothin to keep 'em here. Mal Rostocar, he send rations for the old 'uns, s' we starve slow 'stead o fast, but the young 'uns got to do fer theysefs."

"Do you have any kassos here? Abosoa? Adjoa? Anachoa?"

The old men snorted, slapped their knees, and hid toothless smiles behind withered hands. The one who'd spoken before said, "Last well he go dry, suckin yungis run like they's tail on fire."

Faharmoy shifted his grip on his staff, frowned. "Do you have ghosts that need laying?"

The speaker shrugged. "They's good folk, don' bother us."

Faharmoy scowled at the ancient, defiant faces. There

was nothing he could do here; these men were like stones, they wouldn't hear anything he said. He shook his head and started on. Clean the heart of the corruption and the body would have its health again, but as long as there was poison in the cities, there was nothing he could do for the land.

He walked through other villages, some with other old men sitting on benches talking about other old times, some empty except for the wind and now and then ghost fragments that he chanted to rest before passing on.

The fields were empty and slowly blowing away with the furnace wind. The canals that watered this once productive land were dry, even the dead fish stranded in them were so old there was no stink left, only tatters of gray-brown skin and arrangements of delicate white bone.

>><<

On his eleventh day of walking, he came to the River and followed it east to the city, which he reached late in the afternoon.

The Sequba Cloudbrushers in the Abey groves were green and pleasant in the burnt land; their roots were set so deep that droughts never troubled them. There were many of these groves scattered about the Low City, Abeyhamal's Chapels the Edgers called them. He saw them as centers of poison and corruption, seducers with their green and their shade. He circled wide about the first of them, careful that even the shadow of a tree didn't touch him. "You will burn," he murmured as he passed among the buildings. "You are perversion and will be destroyed."

Heat wavered up from the dead grass and the hardpan; sunlight glinted painfully off glass in windows whose shutters had been unbarred for the first time in centuries. They were here, all those farmers who'd abandoned the land and with it their proper roles, their needful communion with the Iron God, they were here in defiance of Chumavayal's Law and of the Amrapake's command. This must be made right.

Shadow from a wall touched him and he flinched away as if he'd been brushed by nettles. Evil.

He saw no one, but he could feel eyes on him— unseen folk in those newly opened houses peering at him from behind improvised curtains.

He moved through the Low City to the ancient Sok Circle at its heart and knelt in the dust there, his arms outstretched, his eyes closed.

After a while he heard whispers, coughs, the scraping of feet against the dusty paving stones, the rustle of cloth and a hundred other small sounds as the squatters came warily from the houses they'd appropriated and stood in a ring around the outside of the Circle. He heard them, but paid no attention to them. They were just there. Like the wind. Like the sun's heat. He was touching, tasting, getting to know the ills of this place. He wasn't strong enough to destroy it, not yet, but he could make a start.

He filled his lungs, expelled the air in a braying raucous cry: **CHUMAVAYAL!**

Eyes still squeezed shut, he felt heat brushing at his skin, then leaving him, rushing away. In his mind it was a hollow sphere of sunfire racing away from him, eating up everything it touched.

He heard screams, curses, a brief hiss of fire, then silence.

He was cold, weary. The God was gone from him.

He opened his eyes.

The walls that faced the Circle bloomed with black char; shutters were gone, baring unglazed windows like holes in skulls. In some of the kariams that led like spokes from the Circle, there were piles of rags, charred flesh, and bone.

He got to his feet, his movements slow, laborious.

From a throat scraped raw, his strained voice dropping flat against the pitted walls, he declaimed, "This place is anathema. I call upon it plague and pestilence. I declare that those who come here are corrupt and guilty. I declare that as long as there is a living soul within these walls, the drought and death will continue. I am the WORD of Chumavayal, HEAR ME! I say what HE has given me to say. HEAR ME! I am the SCOURGE of Chumavayal. Refuse my word and die."

He shook out his robe, tucked his hands in his sleeves and walked from the center of the Sok Circle; with an approving glance at the black burns on the wall beside him, he stepped over a pile of ash and bone in the mouth of a kariam and started for the Iron Bridge.

Chapter 11
HONEYCHILD Joins the Dance

Faan drew the back of her hand across her forehead, dropped the scrub brush on the tiles, and made a face at the two inches of filthy water in the bucket. Whatever else had to wait on water, the Kassian Tai insisted on keeping the altar clean and the tiles around it. And the cleaning had to be done properly. When it was her turn, Faan couldn't spell the dust away; she had to get on hands and knees and scrub.

Ailiki was curled up under the altar, head on her foreleg, twitching as she dreamed. "Aili my Liki, you have the right idea there, sleep the heat away. Trouble is, if I try that, I wake up with a head stuffed with rocks." She laughed as the mahsar opened one bright eye, closed it again, made a sound like a word. "Potz? T't t't, child, where you picking up that language? As if I didn't know. Hunh. I wonder if you really are learning to talk. Tai says you're magic from your nose to your tail. My familiar. Whatever that is." She reached for the brush and went back to scrubbing at the tiles.

Despite the heat and the withering of the pot plants, there were a few bees buzzing lazily about. One landed on the rim of the bucket, seemed to sniff at the gummy water and reject it. It looked up at her, faceted black eyes glittering. . . .

She gasped as she felt the weight of Abeyhamal come on her.

For a moment she sat on her heels with her eyes closed, struggling to accept what was happening, struggling to disengage the core of will that threatened to rebel and drive out the intruder. She forced her hands open, rested her trembling fingers on her thighs.

The Possession was different; it was not sudden, but gradual as if honey trickled down her spine, slowly, slowly, filling her. And she retained control of her body.

Words thrummed through her, low, slow—she didn't so much hear them as feel them.

She got to her feet. "I have to change my clothes." She listened again. "I know it's late, I know, I know. Diyo, of course most folk will be getting ready to eat. That's why. I can't get lost in the street crowd." She listened again. "Vema, vema, I'll hurry."

There were more people than she expected in the lane, workers trudging home, some beggars she hadn't seen before, a number of foreign sailors wobbling from drink shop to drink shop, scattered street musicians. Mama Kubaza was outside Peshalla's Tavern with Tick the Patch, a drummer, and an erhu player; she was trading zingers with sailors and merchants who lingered to watch the band setting up. Zinar the Porter and some of his friends were hanging about the metal shops, hoping to pick up work, even if it was just carrying packages. Old Utsapisha sat beside a brazier cart; while one of her granddaughters fried fishrolls and mooncakes and sold them to the sailors, other vendors, and homing workers with enough coin to buy a meal. Louok the Nimble was alternating between coin rolls, hunt-the-nut, and an inventory of sleight-of-hand tricks she remembered from the first time she'd seen him, tricks that still packed enough interest to attract a small crowd.

Down one of the walkways a clutch of streeter kids squatted against a wall, hugging a meager patch of shade; their faces were red with heat and drawn with hunger; they watched those who passed by with feral eyes, waiting for a chance to snatch and run.

The heat pressed down on everyone. Ailiki ran along

close to the house walls, keeping in the shade so she wouldn't burn her paws.

Faan sweltered in the ample skirt, the long-sleeved tunic, the hooded cloak she had to wear these days. *I'll be lucky if I don't have a heatstroke,* she told herself and the god she carried.

There was no answer unless it was the tickle behind her left ear.

She paced along slow and steady, her eyes on the ground. Abeyhamal kept prodding her to hurry, but she refused to listen. Moving faster than a crawl in this heat would attract more attention than she felt like dealing with. She didn't bother to explain that, but Abeyhamal seemed to understand after a while and let her alone.

> > < <

There were a pair of two-wheeled carts placed between the twin pillars that marked the Approach to the Wood Bridge. Two sour, sullen Cheoshim stood watch there with crossbows and short spears. Punishment detail? Probably. But they wouldn't be careless, wouldn't let her slip past however cleverly she went.

You want us to get across that Bridge anytime soon, you better come up with some way to get them out of there. She pulled the worn skirt closer about her, folded the excess cloth into a pad and eased onto her knees, then leaned forward so she could see the Bridge without being seen.

The drays were heavy and ancient; she recognized them immediately, having seen them often enough when she waited for Dossan outside the Woodman's compound. With pairs of plodding saisai hitched to them, they carried crated furniture to the gatts and brought back loads of fine woods.

Her nose twitched. Those saisai were hunks of meat now, barreled in brine; the Woodman slaughtered them when he couldn't buy feed or water for them. The

Cheoshim must have collected whatever Naostams were hanging about and forced them to haul the drays to the Bridge. Probably didn't pay them so much as a moju either.

Abeyhamel spoke.

If you're in such a hurry, you should've got me out earlier.

Abeyhamal spoke.

We could always cross by the Iron Bridge . . . nayo? Vema. Then a boat's best. Why don't we go for Reyna's cat? Ladroa-vivi's far enough on we won't have trouble with that pair.

Abeyhamal spoke emphatically.

What can you expect if you don't bother explaining? So have I got it right? I cross to the Low City on the Wood Bridge while someone else is coming across the Iron Bridge FROM the Low City? You going to explain why or who? Huh, I thought not. Then we've got ourselves a knot and not much time to untie it. I'd appreciate some suggestions.

Abeyhamal repeated what she'd said before, the exact words without explanation or amplification.

Faan's nostrils flared, but she fought down her disgust and told herself Dossan had to face this sort of thing every day—an employer was an employer, no matter hers was a god. Thick as a brick. Potz! Well, you'll live through it, Fa. So let's figure this out.

She scowled at the Bridge. The drays weren't that much of a barrier, not with those huge wheels; she could slip through easily enough, she'd hardly have to bend her head. But the men. . . .

Silvery-gray bubbles came blowing up through the dry hard earth; some of them drifted about her, slid through the black twill cloak and rested like cool thoughts about her shoulders and neck, others flitted restlessly about her, rising and falling, curling in a lazy vortex that stayed mostly at the edge of her sight—Wild Magic in the open for the first time, drawn by her need.

She heard the popping fizz of their talk, sighed because she hadn't a hope of understanding it.

Abeyhamal spoke.

Well, get on with it, you're the one that's in a hurry. Gods, she thought, Riverman was right, best to keep far away from them if you can. IF you can. Potz! Miseries miseries miseries. . . .

She shut her eyes and gasped as Abeyhamal seized her brain, drove ghost fingers through and through it, stirring it and kneading it like sticky bread dough. Pain jagged through her; she ground her teeth and culled synonyms from memory to reassure herself that her head still worked and to distance herself from what was happening to it. Agony. Affliction. Anguish. Torment. Tribulation. Torture.

When the pressure eased, she rubbed the gummy pain-tears from her eyes. *You finished reknitting my brain?*

There was no answer from Abeyhamal, just a vague sense of satisfaction.

Faan shivered. *Do you hear me, Wildings?*

The popping fizz grew more agitated, then the babble increased enormously and the whirl of the bubbles went faster and faster until she was the center of a silvery tornado. Strange. Uncomfortable. Sense of . . . something . . . an arbitrariness without limits . . . sliding, slippery contact . . . like touching . . . she couldn't find a word for the feel she got. Except for the good will that was like a sweet smell over them, the Wildings were scary. Well, no point in being a bigot about it.

I need to draw those Cheoshim off the Bridge. Can you help me?

She heard a rush of something like giggles, then the bubble people swirled away from her and went darting off like a swarm of . . . what? The way they moved, flitting and swooping in graceful arcs, reminded her of a field of butterflies shining in the sun—which she couldn't remember seeing, but the image was sharp in her head.

Abeyhamal spoke.

Vema, vema. Faan sighed and got to her feet, shook out her skirt. *Fire? Might burn the Bridge down!*

Abeyhamal spoke.

The appearance of fire? Don't know if I can do that.

Abeyhamal spoke.

Vema, vema. If you say so. Ow! Do you have to DO THAT? She lifted her arms, narrowed her eyes, built her focus on the drays . . . and waited.

The Wildings flittered about the Cheoshim, making the guards nervous with tiny nips from things they couldn't see. They scratched, stamped their feet, jigged around, stared at the drays, and cursed them as hosts for lice.

The nipping grew worse. Clawing at themselves, they put more distance between themselves and the carts.

Faan smiled, then loosed the thing she'd built. The drays seemed to explode in flames, pale, translucent red and orange tongues of fire whipping out and up. Prodded by Abeyhamal, she pulled over herself a harder cloak than usual of her no-see-me and ran for the Bridge, Ailiki lallopping ahead of her.

The Cheoshim guards were yelling and following instinct, getting out of there, scratching and cursing the heat licking at them, too busy to bother with a shadow like a drift of smoke that flowed past them and oozed between the burning drays.

By the time Faan reached the middle of the Bridge, the Wildings were back with her, bubbling about her, giggling and excited, loving the game. *More-ee, more-ee,* they fizzed at her, *givee moree. Tricky chicky ticklee donkee.*

Abeyhamal spoke.

Vema, vema. She fluttered her fingers at the Wildings. Later. *Another day for sure, another time. I give you my blessing for your help and my promise repeated.*

*I told Riverman and I tell you now, I will serve you as
I swore. Go. I have to be quiet like a mouse.*

She held her arms out from her body, the cloak fluttering in the furnace wind running along the River; the
bubble people fell away from the Bridge as if she'd
dumped them overside, then they flowed in a silver
streak across the water and melted into the Riverbank.

Abeyhamal spoke.

Faan glanced downRiver. The Iron Bridge wavered
in the heat haze, but she could see a dark figure intermittently visible between the girders. *I see him. Who is
it?*

Abeyhamal was pointedly silent and tangibly impatient.

> > < <

Faan stepped over a charred, contorted body and
walked with unhurried small steps into the center of the
Circle. She pushed back the hood of her cloak and
turned slowly, her eyes sweeping along the burn-
branded walls and across the dead lying in the kariams
leading away from the Sok. "What happened here?"
She winced as her voice broke harshly into the silence.

Abeyhamal spoke.

"Prophet? A Seer?"

Abeyhamal spoke.

"Oh. Scourge of Chumavayal. Why didn't you just
say that?"

Abeyhamal spoke with intense irritation.

"You know, if you told me a little about what was
happening, I'd be a lot more effective. Vema, vema, no
more questions. Well, this: what am I supposed to do
here?"

Abeyhamal spoke.

"Vema, vema, I'm all yours."

Faan danced.

Stamp. Sway. Shimmy.

Turn in double loops, the lazy figure eight, Abeyhamal's sign.

Dance to the music of the earth, the deep heart-throbbing that was insignificant at first, then began to boom louder and louder as waves of light and dark pulsed from her, rings of honey light, rings of hot dark fed by the fire that was with her always.

Out and out.

Lapping at the blackened walls, driving before it the resident anger and anathema spread across the Low City by Chumavayal through his Prophet Faharmoy.

Faan danced.

Abeyhamal hummed in her—yet was there only in part, was lying concealed within her, erasing through her Chumavayal's attempt to preempt HER space.

The Low City throbbed with the dance.

Stones glowed in the pulsing golden light.

The squatters came into the street and danced toward her.

Like water wheeling in a grand maelstrom they flowed round and round the Circle, humming at first, then singing syllables of sound without meaning, an antic sound that played a happy counterpoint to the earth-heart's throb. . . .

The sun dropped lower and lower, stained the sky with layers of vermillion and shell pink. . . .

Faan stopped turning.

The song of the earth slowed, the chant slowed with it.

The rings of light pulsed out from her, nudging the crowd away. Like water through a bursting dam, the squatters flowed along the kariams and into the wynds and ways of the city.

In moments Faan was the only person visible.

She rubbed at the nape of her neck, pulled the hood back up. "Anything else you want?"

Abeyhamal spoke.

"It's getting dark. I don't know if there's time for that."

Abeyhamal spoke.

"Vema, vema, I swore and I will do, if it takes the rest of the day and all night, too."

Faan walked across the Circle to the kariam that she'd come by, trotted along it until she came to the approach to the Wood Bridge.

Abeyhamal spoke.

"Vema, vema." Faan kicked off her boots and dropped them by the Approach Pillars. She wiggled her toes, sighed. "That does feel good. Don't get in a snit. Vema vema, I'll hurry." She dropped the heavy cloak over the boots. "If some potz steals these, you going to replace them for me?"

Abeyhamal spoke.

"I'm doing the job you want. What I think and what I say, that's my business."

She trotted along the Low City Gatt Road until she reached the approach to the Iron Bridge. She circled carefully around this, guided by prods from her divine rider, worked her way to the River through a double line of massive empty warehouses until she reached the last tumbledown building. She turned her back to the River, started loping along the wynd. In this heat, she thought, it's idiotic. But she kept on, circling the outer limits of the Low City in a claiming run that would seal the place to Abeyhamal.

Chapter 12
Juvalgrim and the SCOURGE of CHUMAVAYAL

Faharmoy glanced upRiver, frowned as he thought he saw a fire on the Wood Bridge; he set his hand on the iron rail and leaned out, eyes narrowed, struggling to see more clearly through the veils of heat haze. Nothing. Imagination and heatwaves, no doubt. He shrugged and went on.

The High City was hot red, the windows and the polished metal accents catching and reflecting the sunset; shadows shimmered with red edges. The towers of the Biasharim and the Cheoshim made funnels of the kariams, drawing furnace winds along them; the leaves on the trees and shrubs whipped about, more brown than green, their suppleness gone. The kichidawa hedges had died down to the deep roots, their foliage was gone, their crooked branches were as still and tangled as his uncombed beard, their fingerlong thorns gleamed like curved steel needles. The fountains in the women's gardens were dry, silencing the hidden whisper of falling water he'd found so enticing on his first visit here.

The Cheoshim towers were harder and blacker than he remembered, red-eyed from the sun, sullenly silent, though as the night crept down, a night hardly cooler than the day but without the hammering of the sun, the parade grounds were beginning to fill with listless, unenthusiastic cadets.

Faharmoy walked more slowly for a moment, watching the Armsmasters try to get some snap into the marching. He shook his head. Corruption in little, corruption in all. This place was a sinkhole.

The iron tiles of the Jiko Sagrada seared through the soles of his sandals. He accepted the burn as the cost of his sins and, murmuring the Laws of Chumavayal, he walked up the mountain with an unhurried step, his staff sounding a steady tonk tonk tonk on the tiles, punctuating his whispered chant.

He stopped at the ancient olive that marked the path to the Sibyl. "Diyo," he said. He touched his staff to the twisted trunk. **"CHUMAVAYAL BLESS!"**

He left the tree burning like a torch and walked on, stepping on coolness now, the sinuous black tiles frosting where his feet touched them.

> > < <

The Forge Sanctuary was an immense room with soaring pointed arches, the distant ceiling an intricate lacing of black iron and red fired-brick. Copper and silver inlays of chains, hammers, anvils and other signs of Chumavayal danced in an angular rhythm across black iron panels set into the brick, the polished metal wires shimmering into existence as they caught the flickering light from the Forge Fire, dying back as shadow closed over them.

The fire was small, a meager pile of split wood set in the center of the Altar. Faharmoy paced slowly up the wide center aisle between the angled lines of kneeling stools, his face grim as he watched the small weak flames. The donors were scanting their dues. Maulapam, Cheoshim, Baisharim, all of them were drawing in, hoarding their resources, letting their god-duties lapse. The High Kasso in Bairroa had gone soft, or he'd have kept them shivering in their sandals and contributing their proper share. Corruption in little, corruption in all.

He knelt on the floorstones before the Forge, black

basalt blocks worn by generations of knees into smooth
ripples like wind-ruffled water. Dropping his hands on
his thighs, palm up, he gazed at the fire and sank into
deep communion with Chumavayal, pierced by an ecstasy indistinguishable from pain.

Three·Anaxoa novices came down the aisle, heads
bent, two of them with hands hidden in the sleeves of
their robes, the third pushing the cleaning cart ahead of
him; it thumped and squeaked, the instruments on the
top tray rattled and scratched, the wood in the bin
rubbed and tunked dully.

Faharmoy heard none of this; his breathing was so
slow he might have been carved from stone like the
black stones he knelt on.

The novice with the cart stopped, blinked at the long
tangled hair and beard of the praying man, the torn
rough robe, the staff laid beside him. He caught the
sleeve of the novice behind him, pointed. "Prophet?"
he whispered.

"Don't know."

The third crowded up to them. "What we supposed
to do?"

"Don't know."

"We better go ask."

"Diyo. But who? Prime?"

"Nayo, nay, not the Prime. Teuzar, he'll know."

They left the cart and hurried out, heading for the
office of the House Master to the Anaxoa novices.

>><<

Acolyte Fitchon caught the tail of rumor and ran to
the Forge Sanctuary, crept round the edge of the chamber until he could see the Prophet's face. He sucked in
his breath, went running out again.

Outside the private apartment of the High Kasso, Fitchon smoothed his stiff coppery hair into a semblance
of order, pulled his robe straight, his sleeves down to

cover his knuckles. He knocked at the Chambermassal's wicket, sagged into a loose-kneed bow when the slide opened a crack. "Acolyte Fitchon, heshim Chambermassal," he said head down and humble, though Palag Rambazich had known him for over a decade, knew he was in charge of the High Kasso's rooms and wardrobe, knew he was free to come and go by the High Kasso's own orders. But Palag Rambazich could make Fitchon's life one long misery if he didn't go through the proper forms.

"Pass." The slide crashed shut.

Fitchon stuck out his tongue and shimmied his hips, then went more sedately along the corridor.

A brisk ta-tump on a panel of the deeply carved door, a squeeze on the latch and a shove and he was inside. He smoothed a hand across his chin, grimaced at the sandpapery rasp. Too bad the rules didn't allow beards, or maybe arranged it so his grew with a little less enthusiasm; this shaving business was getting booooring. Or maybe I should turn Prophet. Tchah! I'm wasting time. He scratched at his palm, shrugged, and went through into the sitting room.

Juvalgrim was sitting at a table by an open window, eating an apple and making notes in his journal. He shut the book when he heard Fitchon come in, set the apple on the plate at his elbow. "You're early, Fitch. Finally developed an eagerness for work?"

"Not dead yet, my friend." Fitchon dropped onto a bench, clasped his hands "Um . . . might be trouble."

"Mmh?"

"A prophet. Trancing in front of the Forge Fire, throwing the little Anaxoas into a tizzy when they came to trim the Fire for Evensong."

"Teuzar will deal with him."

"Not this one."

Juvalgrim reached for a napkin, began wiping his fingers. "Why?"

"I recognized him." He worked on a grin, but it

didn't come easy; he was worried. "Two years ago, remember, when what's his name, Faharmoy? did the I-renounce-everything thing? It's him."

"Faharmoy?"

"Vema. Looking like five years bad luck in one lump."

Juvalgrim stared out the window. "I see," he said finally, still turned away. "Lay out the red robes, I'll take Evensong myself."

"Vema. Anything else?"

"No. You might as well go to bed, be ready for anything tomorrow."

"You need someone at your back, High One. . . ."

Juvalgrim laughed, swung round again. "You haven't called me that in ears, Fitch."

He scratched at his nose. "Guess not."

"Ahsan, friend. There is one thing. After you get the robes ready, I want you to take a note to the Verakay Beehouse. All the usual cautions, Fitch. Hmm?"

"Gotcha, High one." He grinned again, more easily this time. As Juvalgrim drew a sheet of paper from a drawer and began writing, he jumped to his feet and hurried to finish his work.

>><<

Juvalgrim smoothed his hands down the embroidered panels on the front of his robe; it was a familiar feel, but not a comfortable one, not now. He took the iron chain from its hook, dropped it over his head, centered the hemisphere of cloudy crystal. The Eye of Chumavayal. It was heavy, but no weightier than usual; the god was dozing or had his attention elsewhere. He drew shaking fingers across the stone, across again, wondering if he'd at last run out of wiggle-room, if the sudden appearance of this high-born Prophet meant that Chumavayal was tired of his fiddlings and about to squash him.

He paced. Back and forth, back and forth across the oval rug that children from the Edgeschool had made for him, the Hammer and Anvil worked in black on a rusty orange ground. He was fond of that rug, told Reyna it kept him honest, but he wasn't seeing it now. He was terrified, his knees threatened to fold, and his sphincters needed only half an excuse to let go. Back and forth, back and forth.

He thrust his hand inside the robe, closed his fingers over the wax-sealed phial with the poison in it. Why wait for the stake and the fireman? Do it now. Get it over with.

Back and forth.

Can't keep this up, I've got to do something. If I'm going, I'd better get started.

Back and forth.

Send for him? Bring him here? Keep him quiet, keep it all quiet? But what if he won't come? "Chumvay!" He flung his arms wide. "Do it, idiot! Do something!"

He felt at his hair, walked quickly to the dressing table with its glass mirror, took a brush and began smoothing down the long black mass, settling it into ordered waves. He inspected his face, touched balm to his lips and along his cheekbones, worked it into his skin until it had a supple sheen, then slid on the heavy gold rings that marked his rank. "Good as it's going to get." He smiled at himself, amused at his own reactions, how this small bit of pampering had driven out a very large terror. "Vanity, oh vanity," he murmured. "How Reyna would laugh. . . ."

As he moved through the corridors of the Camuctarr, he was surprised by a twinge of guilt. He hadn't expected that, but the fervent boy for whom Chumavayal was father, protector, and source of all good was still there under the embroidery and the gold. There were oaths he'd sworn and later broken, promises implicit and explicit he'd made, then forgot as he maneuvered his way to power.

Forgot. Until now. Too late, of course.

He paced along, automatically smiling when he passed kassos, novices, and acolytes moving busily about their duties. Guilt? Was it really? He wasn't sorry for anything he'd done, only the things he'd left undone. Not guilt. No. Just fear congealing in his belly. He smiled broadly, amused again at his own reactions, then blinked as the leader of a line of foundling boys heading for supper responded to the smile with a giggle. "Ass'lim, High One," the boy called out, giggled again, impressed with his own daring.

"Ass'lim, imp. No, no." He shook his head at the Quiamboa novice who was herding them. "Let him be, Fulan." He thumped the boy on his head. "Mind your manners, kimkim, and do what your teachers tell you and then perhaps you'll live long enough to gain a little wisdom."

> > < <

"Teuzar."

"Ass'lim, Kasso."

"Have you done anything about our visitor?"

Anaxo Teuzar smiled tightly. "I sent a messenger to your office, Kasso. I know when I'm out of my depth."

"Ah. I must have just missed him. Your messenger. Send your novices in, tell them to wait on the kneeling stools while I ascertain the reasons for the visitation. Evensong may be late, but they are to be ready for it nonetheless. Curiosity and rumor will bring others, have ushers ready to get them in place without fuss. I think that's all. Let it be done." He waved Teuzar away and went into the Forge Sanctuary.

He smelled the Prophet before he got close enough for a good look. Hasn't changed his clothes since he left, or had a bath. Or shaved. Ah, the joys of holy dirt. Bless Chumavayal, I wasn't called to that. Dirt and celibacy, nayo nayo.

He crossed his long slender hands below the Eye, setting them on patches of old thread that showed off his blue-black skin and emphasized the elegance of line and shape. He moved with a quiet grace around the rough, dirty hermit and stood between him and the fire.

The ecstasy on the man's face faded with the blocking of the light; he glared up at Juvalgrim. He was almost unrecognizable, twisted, gaunt and hairy, his youth eaten up by the fervor that drove him.

Juvalgrim bowed slightly, the Eye catching the light from the wall lamps, pulsing with it as he moved. "It is time for Evensong, heshim Prophet. You may resume your meditations when our duty has been made."

Prophet Faharmoy reached for his staff and got to his feet with a wiry nervous surge of his body. His eyes peered out through a fringe of stiff, gray-streaked hair. "Duty," he cried, his voice hoarse and ugly. "You make a mockery of it, luxuriant whore! I am the Scourge of Chumavayal, hear his words. You who should be the heart of the people, you who should be the example, you have betrayed HIM. Where are the people, High Kasso? Where are the suppliants come to pray for release from their sins? You are the fountain from which corruption flows, High Kasso in Bairroa Pili. You have betrayed caste and upset the divine order of life. You have stepped between servant and master, you have acted for the low against the high. You have pampered the undeserving, you have coddled—no, worse—you have advocated perversion. You want CHANGE!" He spat the last word out as if it were the ultimate accusation. "Chumavayal put his hand upon me. Chumavayal said this to me," he opened his mouth wide and boomed out the words. "**HEAR ME: WHAT IS, IS RIGHT. CHANGE IS BETRAYAL. THOSE THAT TRY TO CHANGE THINGS HAVE BROUGHT UPON THEMSELVES THE DE-STRUCTION OF THE LAND. THEY WILL DIE OF HUNGER AND THIRST UNLESS THEY**

COME BACK TO ME—UNLESS THEY FOLLOW ME WITHOUT FALTERING OR QUESTIONING." He cleared his throat and went on in the rasping tones of his first words, "Chumavayal came to me in desert and solitude, saying tell my servants this. Tell my people this."

Once again he lifted his head, roared the words in his fierce ruined voice: "YOUR VOICE WILL BE MY VOICE, PROPHET. YOU WILL SCOURGE THE PEOPLE, TURN THEM AWAY FROM THEIR SINS, BRING THEM BACK TO ME.

YOU WILL ERASE FROM THE LAND ALL THAT IS PERVERTED, ALL THAT IS BORN MONSTROUS.

I WILL TAKE THOSE POOR CRIPPLED SOULS TO MYSELF AND HOLD THEM UNTIL THEY ARE HEALED THAT THEY MAY BE BORN ANEW.

I AM NOT A CRUEL FATHER, BUT I DO WHAT I MUST FOR THE HEALTH OF MY PEOPLE.

DISCIPLINE IS NECESSARY.

DISCIPLINE IS HEALTH.

PAIN IS GIVEN TO MAN TO TEACH HIM THE RIGHT WAY—OTHERWISE, HOW IS HE MORE THAN ANIMAL? Thus he spoke to me, thus I speak to you, hear and obey."

Without waiting for a response, he swung round and stumped out, his sandals squeaking, the butt of his staff thudding against the tiles of the mosaic floor.

>><<

Juvalgrim had come to the Sanctuary with a poison phial tucked into his sleeve, resigned to accepting whatever waited for him. With a god involved, there wasn't much else he could do. At the end of the Prophet's scold, resignation had turned to indignation; there was nothing new here. He'd listened to the same scold from the Maulapam landlords, from Cheoshim commanders, from Biasharim merchants: you're pampering the unfit, let them help themselves, let them leave if they can't feed themselves here. We've got our own to worry about. You're disturbing the order of things. You're putting desires in these people they aren't capable of handling. Nothing new. Nothing! And he'd been so terrified of this . . . this IDIOCY, he'd nearly soiled himself.

But indignation wouldn't do, not here.

He pulled himself together, pressed palm to palm, bowed his head and intoned: **"We are all guilty of doing less than we might in the service of the Iron Father. We are blessed by the gentle care of Chumavayal. I, your High Kasso, do give thanks for the chastisement of the Prophet, I bless HIM for this reminder that I must myself do better. Take to heart what you have heard, my children and give thanks yourself for HIS care."**

For the first time in years he led the Evensong, letting his deep, magnificent voice swell to fill the chamber—and by the time the rite was complete, he knew he'd canceled out most of the effect of the Prophet's scold.

He kept a gentle smile pasted on his face as he returned to his apartment, answering with genial dignity the greetings of the other kassos, the novices, the acolytes who found reasons to wander by the Sanctuary and exercise their curiosity. He'd won the exchange this time, but it was a temporary victory; he'd have to keep patching cracks and buffing egos. He'd been so busy that he'd forgotten to keep touch with his supporters. *You idiot, you really do owe the Prophet gratitude for stirring you out of this laziness.*

> > < <

Faharmoy felt the god leave him.

He stared at the impassive elegant face of the High

Kasso, then swung round and stumped out. He knew in his bones that Juvalgrim had rejected everything the Iron Father said through his mouth. The man WOULD not be saved.

He was tired to the bone. It was time to rest and restore his energies.

Ignoring attempts to speak to him, he strode through the halls of the Camuctarr until he reached the Water Court with the fountain that never went dry even in the worst of droughts.

He drank sparingly from the Fountain and settled for the night in a corner of the Court, ignoring the hunger that closed like a fist about his stomach. After a while, he slept.

> > < <

He woke before dawn and went to the towers of the Cheoshim. It was time to begin the cleansing of the High City.

Chapter 13
Fire

There was a faint pink glow on the eastern horizon and wisps of Riverfog hugging the ground when Faan limped wearily along Southbank Gatt Road. The circle was almost complete, but she was worn to a nub, hungry, thirsty, irritated with the god on her back who seemed to think she didn't need food or rest or anything as prosaic as that. When she reached the Approach to the Wood Bridge, she sank beside her boots and cloak onto the ancient surface with its mosaic of different colored woods and rested her back against the weathered rails, snapped her fingers, smiled drowsily as Ailiki jumped into her lap and tucked tail about legs. She scraped up enough energy to stroke the mahsar's back twice, then dropped her hand. "Guards still there?"

Abeyhamal spoke.

"You chase them. I couldn't light a match."

Abeyhamal spoke.

"This horse won't go. You want me to get back to the BeeHouse, you figure out a way."

Sense of impatience.

Faan let her head fall back against a post, closed her eyes and waited. *I can be as stubborn as you. It's easy when it's the only choice I've got.* In her lap Ailiki was a vibrating warm spot, purring like a dozen cats.

Abeyhamal spoke.

Faan groaned. "You would. Vema, vema, give me a minute. K'laan!" Her feet burned, she was blistered and scraped, stone-bruised and nettle stung—they were

dead nettles, but that only meant they broke apart and
rode away on her legs. "Off you go, Liki." Yelping
and groaning some more, she gathered in the boots,
draped the cloak over her arm, pulled herself up and
tottered up the slope until she was standing on the dusty
inlay between the first two piers that supported the
Bridge. "I'm here. Do it."

A warm sticky heat flowed through her, honey mead
fermenting in her, cadentha honey, the sweet-sweet perfume of cadenthas strong about her. It erased her fatigue, smoothed out her cuts and scrapes, healed her
bruises and rashes, filled her with energy—a temporary
energy; she had a felling it would burn away fast.

Abeyhamal spoke.

"Vema, vema, on my way." She started across the
Bridge, working up to a fast lope, her bare feet splatting
on the wood. Wild Magic came swooping up and
whirled about her, thick gray fog sweeping along with
her, a slightly darker scrap of mist among the other
wisps drifting along the River.

The guards were leaning against the Approach Pillars, caps pulled down over their eyes; they were more
than half-asleep, bored with watching a Bridge go nowhere.

Faan slid between the drays and trotted past them, a
patch of fog flowing off the Bridge. She darted into the
nearest wynd and stood shaking and panting, the Wild
Magic swirling around her giggling and niggling at her,
a thousand small voices impossible to understand because there were too many of them.

She wiped at her forehead, made a face at the grime
on her palm, though it was hard to see the hand through
the agitated mist. *Ahsan, ahsan, my friends, I'll see you
later, hmm? I have to rest. I can't go anymore.* She
made a dismissing gesture she'd learned from the Sibyl.

Moree moree, sweetee, honey, the Wildings teased at her,
tch'ikee sweetee, we-ee like thee.

Go home, friendlings, there'll be more. I said it be-

fore and wasn't it true? Go rest and be ready. She wiped the sweat from her head as the silver bubbles went swirling away, vanishing like soap bubbles into the hardpan of the wynd.

Without warning or explanation Abeyhamal, too, was gone.

> > < <

There were people in the wynds and the byways, trudging to work in the first light. She hurried across Verakay Lane and turned down Vallaree Wynd; it was dark and empty except for the occasional sleeper recovering from a spree in a Mulehouse on Verakay. She relaxed and slowed. "Almost home, Liki. Ooooh, I would love a long hot bath. Well, I'll have to be satisfied to crawl into bed and sleep a week."

Ailiki made a sound, another of her almost-words, then pricked up her ears. She scratched into an all-out run, vanished around a bend in the walkway.

"Huh? I do wish you could talk, Aili my Liki." She rubbed drowsily at her eyes. "Save a lot of trouble."

Ailiki came racing back, every hair on her body standing erect. She scrabbled to a stop in front of Faan, reared on her hind legs, pawed the air, dropped to four feet, reared again. "Ne ne ne," she squealed at Faan. "Ne ne ne."

"Not something else! Abeyhamal! Hai! God! I need information. You don't have to DO anything, just tell me what's going on?"

Nothing.

"Vema, vema, Riverman was right. You can only depend on them for muddle and messing up." She listened. "I don't hear anything. Ah well, Liki, we'll go along slow slow till you start having fits again. Hmm. I suppose I could climb up the back of Emaur's Mulehouse and see what's happening . . . you understand what I'm saying?" She chuckled as Ailiki sat up, clapped her delicate black hands together. "I suppose that means you do. Let's go, my Liki."

She left Vallaree Wynd, followed Ailiki deeper into the Edge through several shadowy silent ways, then back again until she was behind Emaur's, stepping cautiously over the sprawled drunks that were as ordinary here as the dead weeds along the back wall. She rested her head a moment against the wall. Tired. So tired. Sighing, she caught hold of a protruding brick, levered herself to a foothold on the sill of a shuttered window.

> > < <

As she picked her way across the cluttered roof—broken tables, cracked jars, all kinds of debris from the bar, Emaur was a compulsive hoarder, never threw anything away—she was starting to hear an intermittent rhythmic roar; it was far off still, but it made her nervous.

She knelt by the parapet overlooking Verakay Lane, scowling toward the Sokajarua, the rising sun in her eyes. The roar grew louder and more ominous and the morning wind brought her whiffs of burning oil.

Ailiki ran up her body, jumped onto the parapet and stood hissing, her body arched, her tail stiffly straight.

For a moment longer the Lane was full of people, beggars, street singers, Utsapisha and her grandaughters, Louok the Nimble, Mama Kubaza and her band, Mutri Maship and his dancers, porters and sweeps, traders from the ships, workers plodding along to the factories on the far side of the Iron Bridge, shopkeepers sweeping dust off their stoops and unlocking their shutters—then they were gone, as if some magus had snapped thumb against finger and banished them.

BURN BURN BURN. There was a flicker of light beyond the bend, faint, nearly lost in the brightness of the sun. BURN BURN BURN. And a thunder of boots beating the hard dry dirt of the Lane. **BURN BURN BURN.**

The front lines of a mob of young Cheoshim marched around the bend, torches held high, black boots swinging and hitting the earth in unison. A STRIKER band, much bigger than the one that had chased her.

"Beehouse. I know it." Faan groaned, pushed away from the wall. "Come on, Liki. We've got to warn them." Cursing the clutter, she stumbled across the roof and climbed down, ran along the wynd to the back door of the Beehouse.

As doors always did when she needed to go through them, the back door sprang open, slammed against the wall. Faan caught it as it bounded back, ran across the kitchen and up the stairs. She kicked at Reyna's door. "Up, up, there's a mob coming." She ran on, banged on Dawa's door, Areia's, hammered on the Kassian's door. "Tai, Tai, they're coming for us. We have to get out of here."

She stood panting in the hallway, swaying with fatigue, blinking sweat out of her eyes as the bedroom doors opened.

Tai shouted the others to silence. "What is it, Fa? Where've you been?"

"Never mind that, tell you later. There's a mob, I don't know how many, Cheoshim, coming down the lane, coming here, I'm sure of it. STRIKER band. Yelling burn, waving torches. We've got to get away."

Tai closed her eyes, grimaced. "Diyo, I can smell it. Areia, fetch Panote, will you? Reyna, you and Dawa collect bedding, clothes, any coin you've got stowed away. Fa, I know you're tired, but get what you can. And be ready, totta, we're going to need you. SHE has said. All of you, we'll meet in the kitchen, five minutes, that's all you've got."

>><<

The mass of Cheoshim filled the Lane wall to wall, boot heels hitting the dirt in unison, torches waving.

BURN BURN BURN.

A single man walked before them, a tall ebon figure in a torn and ragged robe, gray-streaked hair in a tangle, red eyes glaring over a gray-streaked beard, a staff in one hand, the other held out before him, palm out, fingers pointing to the sky, a bloody sky with a bloody sun just breaking free of the horizon.

BURN BURN BURN.

In the wynd across from the Beehouse, Reyna stirred. "Faharmoy?"

"Diyo," Tai whispered, "be quiet, Rey."

Faan leaned against the wall of the tenement on the west side of the wynd, her eyelids sagging, her mind barely turning over. She wanted to be away from here, but Tai wouldn't go.

BURN BURN BURN.

The Prophet stopped in front of the Beehouse.

"ANATHEMA!" he roared. **"BE CAST OUT. BE PURGED FROM THIS CITY, FROM THIS LAND."**

BURN BURN BURN, the mob roared behind him, male voices rumbling in their lowest notes, **BURN BURN BURN**.

The Prophet stepped to one side, folded his arms across his chest.

A huge heavy youth in the front rank ran to the door of the Beehouse, an oiljar in his left hand. He booted the door till it boomed. "Out," he bellowed. "Out, you kuashin guguns, out or eat fire!"

BURN BURN BURN.

So angry she forgot her fatigue, tiny tongues of flame dancing along her arms, Faan took a step toward the road—stopped at Tai's quiet "No."

The Cheoshim booted the door again, then crashed the jar of oil against it, dropped his torch into the puddle and ran back yelling, "Burn burn burn."

BURN, the Cheoshim chanted as they thinned into single file and trotted into the wynd on the west side of the house. **BURN.** They formed a circle about the Beehouse, stamping their feet and howling. **BURN BURN BURN.**

In Verakay Lane the Prophet lifted his staff, brought the butt down hard on the dirt. **"Chumavayal's Blessing"**, he cried out, **"LET IT BE DONE."**

Some heaved their jars high enough to get them over the roof fence so they crashed on the tiles, some aimed at windows or simply splattered the walls with the heavy oil. A howl blew like a gale around the house, the Cheoshim danced and whooped and waved their torches. **"BURN!"** they shouted, the sound ragged now, wilder and more terrible. **"BURN!"**

The Prophet tucked his staff under his arm and clapped his hands together, a single crack that broke through the other noise.

The Cheoshim swung their torches around their heads and hurled them at the Beehouse, then ran for the lane, arms crossed over their heads.

Like the jars, some of the torches flew up and up, turning in lazy circles, curving over the roof fence; others dropped into the pools of oil at the base of the walls.

The Beehouse burned. Flames leapt a hundred feet into the air, god-driven and terrible. In hardly a breath there was nothing but ashes left.

> > < <

Faan gazed at the blackened smoking wreck of the only home she could remember, her shoulders drooping, her eyes burning with tears that wouldn't fall.

Reyna dropped his arm on her shoulders, hugged her against him. "I know," he said.

For a moment she slumped against him, then she sighed and pulled away. "It's not finished. Not yet.

Don't do anything, Mamay, it'll only make things worse. Tai, tell him.''

"Diyo. Rey, we'll take what we can carry to the Wood Bridge. Faan will follow in a few minutes.''

Reyna stepped in front of Faan. "What is this?''

"God business. Got no choice, Rey.''

"Nayo.'' He caught her by the shoulder, held her at arms length and examined her head to toe. "What's going on, Fa? Where've you been? What happened to you?''

"Abeyhamal. Let me go.''

"Rey, don't interfere. You don't know what you're doing.''

Reyna dropped his hand. "So tell me, Tai, why does Faan look like she's been dragged through a thorn patch?''

"She made a bargain, Rey. You have to let her keep it.''

"What bargain? What are you talking about?''

"I'll explain later.'' The Kassian nodded at the others crowded into the wynd. "In private.'' She tapped his arm. "Nothing's going to happen to her, Rey. I promise. Now. Wood Bridge, my friend. Hurry.''

> > < <

Frightened but compelled, Faan walked into the middle of the Lane, Ailiki pacing at her side, Tai a step behind her.

The Cheoshim didn't notice her at first; when one did, pointed and yelled obscenities at her, the rest of them left their triumphant jigging and moved to stand in a muttering crowd behind the Prophet.

Faan stopped and gazed in silence at Faharmoy, a thin waif with hair waxed into spikes, splotches of purple and green hairpaint rubbed and shabby, a soft black plait falling forward across her shoulder; her face was smeared with gray dust, her feet were bare and dirty, her skirt torn and littered with the dead weeds she'd run through.

Abruptly, towering over her, Abeyhamal stood in the lane, singing with the wind, insubstantial as a dream, translucent; HER bee-wings vibrated, creating a thin high descant to the alto hum of HER powersong; the ivory fimbo which SHE held in HER left hand glowed palely gold.

Aged by fasting and fervor, Faharmoy was gaunt and gray, his hair and beard uncombed, his hands eroded to dry skin stretched over bone.

Chumavayal rose behind him, towering dark and powerful, insubstantial as a dream, translucent, HIS eyes red as forged iron.

The Bee-eyed Woman sang HER buzzing song and danced in figure eights behind the slight form of HER champion.

The Old Man glared at the Honey Mother from molten eyes, one huge ropy hand holding the great Hammer; HE brought the Hammer up and over in a power-filled circle, struck the earth in front of Faan, the wind of the miss stirring the spikes on her head—green eye and blue eye, she watched HIM, unmoved.

Abeyhamal slammed the butt of HER fimbo on the earth, HER wings vibrating more rapidly, HER hum deepening and growing louder, driven by the force of HER anger and desire. SHE buzzed in place, wings vibrating, larynx vibrating, bee eyes on the black old man. Abruptly SHE flipped the fimbo up and over, held it away from HER body, parallel to the ground. SHE bent HER knees, turned HER feet out and hop-shuffled at a slant to Faan. When SHE was even with the girl, SHE stopped, glided backward to HER starting point, HER feet moving, the rest of HER quite still, then SHE hop-shuffled at an opposite slant.

Chumavayal stamped the road till the shops and tenements shook with the force of HIS power and HIS fury, stamped with feet turned out, HIS elbows pointed. With

HIS left hand HE brought the Hammer curling up over HIS head; with HIS right HE snatched the Saber clipped at HIS side and brought it curling up over HIS head. HE clashed them together. Sparks flew like falling stars, vanishing before they touched the earth.

Abeyhamal whirled the fimbo over HER head; lightning jagged from the point, crashed into the Lane by Faharmoy's feet, but none came close to touching him.

Chumavayal roared, HIS fiery breath enveloped Abeyhamal and Faan without touching either. HER gossamer wings vibrated more furiously, sending the heat into the dry sterile clouds gathering over the city. He brought HIS sword down, held it across HIS chest, stamped HIS feet to one side then the other, then slashed at HER, pulling yellow and crimson flame-tongues into high leaps from the smoldering coals where the Beehouse had been.

Abeyhamal caught the sword on HER fimbo, deflected it, brought the fimbo around to slash at Chumavayal's hand, drawing a trickle of blood as the point touched HIM, blood that fell on Faharmoy, sank into him.

Chumavayal howled and made the Saber weave in complex curves, glittering red and white, sending beams of light flickering about Abeyhamal, never quite touching HER.

Abruptly the images vanished.

Faan stared at Faharmoy, he at her.

"We will meet again," he said in his ruined voice.

"Diyo," she said. "We will meet."

> > < <

Reyna and Dawa were waiting for her at the North-bank Approach; Tai and Areia One-eye were already across.

"You all right, Fa?" Reyna touched her cheek. When she nodded, he set his hands on her shoulders, clicked his tongue at the weariness he saw in her. "You better scoot across. The sooner you're in bed, the better, Fa."

"Vema to that, Rey. Come on."

"We can't, Fa. Dawa and I, we're sealed out."

"What? Jea's over there with his friend. If he's all right, why not you?"

"I can't set foot on the Bridge. I tried, but there's some kind of wall in the way. Looks like Jea was already across when it went up."

"The Barrier. SHE said . . . but SHE couldn't have meant you, you're HERS, you always have been."

"Not any more, apparently."

Faan exploded. "It's not FA AA AIR!" she shrieked. She yanked out handfuls of waxed hair, stamped her feet, whirled round and round—fury, fear and exhaustion—slammed her body into one of the pillars, beat at it with her fists until they bled—all of this the toll taken by the repression of her will to allow control by the god—flames spurted from her hands, her face, her clothing caught on fire—frustration, aggravation, vexation—she screamed, **"NO NO NO NO!"** It was NO to being stolen from her mother, NO to being different from everyone else, NO to daughterloving someone who'd been working hard at destroying himself, NO to everything horrible in her life, everything that piled up on her until she couldn't breathe any more. All the NOs she'd been storing up since she came here.

Ailiki ignored the smolders and the giggling flamelets; she leapt to Faan's shoulder, pressed her body against Faan's head, warm, furry, soft, draining off the fury.

With an absurd little squeak, Faan went still; she dropped her arms and stood trembling, smoke from burning cloth coiling up about her. Her eyes glazed over, rolled back. For the first time in her life, she fainted.

>><<

Reyna reached for her as she toppled, but she fell through the Barrier and his hands slammed into it. He beat his fist against the thing, cursing.

Dawa caught his arm. "Rey! Listen. Calm down, I'll go get someone, she's just fainted, she'll be all right."

Reyna swung round. "How do you know that? How the Jann do you know?"

"Well, yelling and thumping that thing isn't doing much good, is it? Listen, Rey, I'll go fetch old Utsapisha, I saw her out there watching the House burn." He went running off, his long hair flowing out behind him in a blue-black wave.

Reyna opened and closed his fists a few times, then dropped to squat as close to Faan as he could get. She was breathing through her mouth, he could see the dust on the planks shifting with each breath. "Secrets," he said. "Honey, what have you been up to? Why didn't you tell me? I thought we were friends again."

The gray dust danced with her breath.

Utsapisha lumbered up, leaning on Dawa's arm, two of her granddaughters with her.

"Ijjit gods," she said. "What Dawa here told us?"

Reyna slammed his fist against the Barrier. It hit hard and rebounded.

"Hunh!" Utsapisha poked her finger at the Barrier. Her hand went through as if it didn't exist. "Like I said." She waddled up the easy slant, grunted onto her knees beside Faan, thrust two thick fingers under the girl's jaw. "Vema. Good strong beat. No need to fuss y'se'f, Rey. She jes' fainted. Girls do that." She put out her arms and her granddaughters hauled her onto her feet. "The Kassian's across already?"

Reyna nodded.

"Vema. Then we'll get her to Low City. You better duck, Rey. The two of you. Don't let those STRIKER bassards get aholt a you, they gonna torch you like they did the Beehouse."

Reyna nodded. "We'll be down at Ladroa-vivi, send someone to tell me how she is, will you?"

"Sure. And don't you worry, girls this age faint when they feel like it, don't do 'em no more harm than a night's sleep."

>><<

When Faan woke, she was in a strange bed, rain pattering against the window across the room; Tai was bending over her.

"Rey?"

"Hush, honey. You're exhausted. Sleep and we'll talk tomorrow."

Faan moved her mouth; she meant to protest, but instead sank into a heavy sleep.

GODDANCE
the Twelfth Year

Honey Mother hums an angry scratching hum; she dances faster, flipping the fimbo about, jabbing at Chumavayal, never quite touching him again. Lightning jags from the tip, lacing a web of light about the broad black body of the Iron Father.

Penhari Banadah is moved onto the playing field, a potential queen ranging behind the Honeychild. The women of Bairroa Pili watch their altars burn, then take their children across the Wood Bridge and settle in the low stone houses built around the Abey Groves.

Iron Father's eyes burn red; his fire breath envelopes the Honey Mother, turns the Forge iron cherry red, sends the Fire tongues reaching for Abeyhamal, jabbing about her body, not quite touching her.

The Cheoshim STRIKER bands march to the Prophet's calling, flogging sinners and burning down Beehouses. Wenyarum Taleza bows to his son.

Honey Mother raises her hum to a gale roar, her wings vibrate so powerfully they lift her off her feet, she drives the fimbo high over her head as if she means to pierce the firmament.

Black clouds swirl violently above the ivory point; the air turns chill; the flames shrink back, huge chill drops rain onto the Forge Floor.

Iron Father opens his mouth wide, thrusts his red tongue out and out. He clangs Hammer Head against

Saber. Red fire leaps from the clashing steel, turns the rain to steam, burns away the clouds.

And the GodDance goes on.
Through Surrogate and Principal, the GodDance goes on.

SIBYL

The Sibyl tucks in a fluttering veil and wearily declaims:

The wheel is turning, the Change is here
The New Order burgeons, the Old's on its Bier
Amrapake's fist grows tight
And catches naught in its grip
Round and round in torches' light
The Anchorite strips kin- from -ship
Honeychild is Mystery
Feral Magic boiling free
The City burns with fire and fear
The Culmination hurries near.

> > < <

I am tired, she says. She smiles ruefully. The verse is worse. Bad is one thing, but this is really stretching.

She sighs, the flush of humor draining away.

The life is going out of the Land.

My students are too busy for me these days. I miss them.

Juvalgrim fights the Shinda Prefecture and the Temple, together and separately; I fear that the forces assembling against him are building too strongly. He can't last much longer.

Honeychild? She has a new guide. I am not allowed to interfere.

Diyo, I do miss them.

And I am afraid for them.

There's a fire in Juvalgrim's future; I can see him tied to a pole with the Prophet waving a torch in his face.

And Faan—the god will use her up and discard her like a dirty rag, even her memories gone. As she already has discarded the Salagaum.

The Sibyl brings her fist down on the chair arm.

I can do nothing. I am tied to this place. I can do nothing but watch.

Her head falls forward, her hands drop in her lap.

A moment later, though, she looks up, a gleam in her black-opal eyes.

Mmmh, maybe a little more than watch.

When the cats are fighting, the mice run loose.

We'll see, we'll see.

Chapter 14
PENHARI BANADAH is Shaped for Service

The Amrapake used his toe to stir Penhari's unconscious body, pulling a groan out of her, a twitch of her
fingers, but nothing more. He smiled sourly, dropped
the bloody flagellum on her back. "Should've done that
years ago." He looked at his hands, rubbed them together. "Wenyarum! Towel. Why do I have to ask?"

Wenyarum Taleza's oiled skin had an ashy look and
his eyes were uneasy. "Vema vema, Amrap. Forgive
me. A moment." He hastened out, wiping at the sweat
that popped on his brow as he stepped over the severed
head of his wife's personal Kassian. He'd seen too
much. He swallowed the bile that rose in his throat at
the memory of Famtoche kicking the door open and
slashing with his saber at the maids who were trying to
protect Penhari, then ordering Wenyarum to throw the
bodies in a pile. He could only hope his usefulness still
outweighed any flash of prudence that might strike his
unpredictable brother-by-law.

He seldom came into his wife's suite, so it took him
a while to find the water room, long enough to wet him
down with nervous sweat. Hastily he soaked a hand
towel, squeezed it out, and went rushing back.

When he reached the sitting room, Famtoche was
standing over his sister, pissing on her. Face twisted in
a grimace of fear, Wenyarum drew back and stood
swaying and holding his breath until the sound stopped;
then he went hurrying in, the towel folded on his hands.

"Hah!" Famtoche strolled from the room, cleaning

his hands, dabbing at the spots of blood on his tunic. He looked over his shoulder at Wenyarum following two steps behind. "Clean your own House, he says to me. Me! Jegging Kasso. True, though. Too long I let family feeling sway me. Well, it's done." He paused before the door into the public rooms. "One more thing, General. I've let the boy please himself. He's got spirit. Didn't want it broken. That's over." He tossed the towel on the floor. "You go down to Pili and bring him back. Don't care how you do it, get him here. We'll soon have that Prophet nonsense knocked out of him." He stepped aside and scowled at Wenyarum Taleza who hurried past him and opened the door for him. "Ten days," he said. "Want him at the Falmatarr no later'n that." He walked briskly into the entrance hall, his escort coming to practiced alert the instant the moment they saw him.

>><<

Flies buzzed about the room. One crawled up Penhari's arm, tickling unendurably. She twitched, came painfully awake. The fly kneaded at her arm with its thready legs, then crouched by one of the flagellum cuts, thrust its drinking tube into the crusted flesh. "Haah!" She shook her arm violently, arched her back and thrust herself up from the floor, rested on her hands and knees as pain lanced through her. Groaning and gasping, she staggered to her feet and groped blindly for the nearest wall.

She nearly fell over the bodies of her maids, grabbed hastily for the back of a chair as her brain whited out and her stomach convulsed.

Later—might have been a moment or half an hour—she stumbled on again, forcing herself to move though she wanted to lie down like the maids and die.

In the water room she pulled the bronze chain and stood with her bloody back pressed against the cool

tiles while the shell bath on the dais at the far end filled
with steaming water; it hurt, but it was a duller ache
than when she tried to move.

The bath overflowed; she didn't know it until she
came from a haze and saw water running across her
feet. She reached, cried out as cuts tore open, but completed the movement and pulled the chain again to shut
off the flow.

She went up the stairs on hands and knees and rolled
into the bath.

> > < <

The slave waiting for her in her bedroom was a stocky
fair woman with fine brown hair and small brown
splotches sprayed across her square cheekbones and
hooked nose.

Penhari eased herself down on the stool by her dressing table. "What's your name?" She inspected the
woman again, sighed. "Where do you usually work?"

"Desantro, heshal." Her shoulders were rounded,
her worn hands trembling. "In the garden, heshal."

"Diyo." Penhari closed her eyes. "Who told you to
wait here?"

"The Chambermassal, heshal. He wouldn't let Yea-
dah come . . . or . . . any of the chambermaids." Her
thin mouth compressed a moment and there was a dull
resentment in her eyes she wouldn't have dared show
before this. "He said . . . he made me come."

"I see." Penhari managed a slight smile. "No matter his reasons, I am happy to see you, Desantro." She
lifted an arm, winced as the movement pulled at cuts,
but continued the motion. "Go through the door there,
follow the corridor to the water room . . . which hand
do you use?"

Desantro lifted her right hand, held it palm out toward Penhari; it was lined and callused, with dirt
ground deep into the skin.

"Diyo. Put your other hand on the wall and go in the first open door you touch. You will see a chest just inside. Lift the lid and bring the red box you find there. Do you understand?''

Desantro bobbed her head. "Diyo, heshal." Her eyes shifted uneasily, then she turned and went out.

>><<

"Sa saaah, heshal." Desantro clucked over the ruin of Penhari's back and buttocks. "Men!" She poured distillate of kuzury in a small bowl, sopped a fiber ball in the liquid and began cleaning the wounds, her big hands surprisingly gentle.

Penhari chuckled, then gasped. She closed her hands into fists and ground them into her thighs as her back burned and throbbed.

"There there, luv, that's over," Desantro crooned at her. "Now this should feel a lot better, hmmm?"

Coolness. The creamy salve killed the fire and eased the stiffening of her skin. Penhari sighed, relaxed. "Diyo," she said. "You have good hands."

There was a short silence, then a hesitant laugh. "Was thinking of you like my plants, heshal, I mean, your plants, the ones I tend. If you don't mind."

Penhari smiled. "I am honored, Desantro. Plants have a proven worth, I have none." She grimaced. "In the eyes of my family."

Desantro worked a while in silence, then she said, "I've finished with the lotion; there're strips of bandage in the box. How you want me to do this?"

Penhari frowned, touched her breasts, smoothed her hand down her battered stomach; she was sore, bruised where Famtoche had used his fists on her, but the damage didn't seem to be that bad; he was too flabby to have much power behind his punch. "Bind the bandage round me, but not too tight. Enough layers so the salve doesn't leak through."

> > < <

Desantro helped Penhari to stand, then eased her arms into a wrap-around robe of linen so old and so often washed it was softer than fleece. Leaning heavily on the woman's arm, Penhari shuffled to the bed. With Desantro supporting her shoulders, she eased down on her side and lay in a loose curl with her knees bent to ease strain on her stomach bruises. She turned her head, wincing at the pull on the cuts. "Have cook make some broth for me and an infusion of singizzia."

Desantro shifted nervously. "I'll tell the Chambermassal."

Penhari managed a smile. "I think you'll find him . . . um . . . more cooperative than you expect. The Wheel turns, Desantro, he'll be remembering that about now." She lowered her head on the pillow, closed her eyes. "Tell him," she murmured, "to send you again. I find being tended like a plant comforting."

> > < <

Desantro brought the tray in, planting her sandal soles flat with each step. She shuffled to the bed, set the tray on the bedtable with a loud sigh of relief, then bent over Penhari. She hesitated, touched the back of Penhari's hand. "Heshal?"

Penhari blinked, tried to move, cried out as her body resisted and the pain she'd briefly forgotten came stabbing back.

Murmuring words in her own tongue, Desantro eased a strong arm under her, helped her to sit up, then shifted the bedtray over her knees. " 'S better to drink this when it's warm, heshal, orwise I'd a let you sleep."

Penhari wrapped both hands about the mug and with some difficulty lifted the fragrant steamy broth to her lips. She sipped, shivered with pleasure as heat curled through her. "Do you follow Abeyhamal, Desantro?"

"No, heshal." Desantro stood at the foot of the bed, her hands one atop the other at her waist, her feet spread apart. "I come from Whenapoyr. It's forests there. And mountains. My folk when they want a god, they mostly follow Geddrin the Mountain Groomer and Isshann Birthmistress. Rest a the time it's the tree spirits we talk to, Whauraka we call them. We don't take up much with strangers, be they gods or men."

"I see." Penhari ran the tip of her finger round the cup's rim. "The Kassian Kurai and the maids—has anything been done with the bodies?"

Desantro looked uneasy. "Nobody tells me aught . . . I hear . . . I don't know if it's a true thing. . . ."

"Tell me."

"They say General left word Chambermassal sh'd kick out the house every one he knows. . . ." Her eyelids fluttered. "That . . . that had the Honey taint on them. Clean house, he say. Sweep the . . . the bodies into street, shut door on them. Anyone wants them can come get them. Chambermassal he send word Ombbura Beehouse to clean street, din't want dogs and disease he say. While you sleeping, I did floor." She spread her hands, shook her head. "Not much good at cleaning. Did m' best."

"It doesn't matter, Desantro. May your gods bless you for what you tried. Take the tray and help me down. I'll sleep a while now."

Chapter 15
The PURGE Goes On and On

Faharmoy walked down Verakay Lane, angry eyes
sweeping from side to side.

He stopped across the Lane from Utsapisha and her
frycart, glared at her for several moments, then swung
round and strode off.

The old woman wrinkled her nose, lifted her veil,
and spat.

"Zazi!" Her granddaughter looked nervously around,
wiped her sleeve across her face.

"Twiddlepoop. Couldn't find his ass if he had the
runs."

"Za-zeeee."

Most of Utsapisha's vast family had packed up and
moved across the Bridge, but she grumbled she was too
old to shift her bones from the house her children and
grandchildren had been born in and too mean to be
driven out. Besides, who'd pick on a pore ol' woman
like her? She tied a rag across her face in a mockery of
a veil, had a granddaughter sew huge floppy sleeves on
her shirts and went marching along the lane swinging
her arms and body like some superannuated clown.
Giggling but nervous, one or another of her granddaughters followed her, pushing the frycart with the
chair tilted over the oilpot.

Utsapisha enjoyed these processions enormously,
bowed all round when she reached the deserted shop
where she had established her claim on the boardwalk,
settled herself with a whoomph and a wiggle and after

that traded insults with her customers. She was an institution on Verakay, selling pies and kebabs to anyone who had the money, mostly the sailors that ambled the lane hunting for whores, drink, and food.

> > < <

   chu ma vay yal chu ma vay yal
The noise whispered down the Lane along with the ominous rumble of a STRIKER band's tramping feet.

Utsapisha lifted her head, swore vigorously. "You better duck," she told the sailor who'd just handed her a copper shabo for a pie. She tucked the coin into a sleeve pocket, jerked a long bony thumb at the bend in the land. "Hear that? Them jeggers is trouble."

   chu ma vay yal chu ma vay yal
The short blond sailor licked juice off the side of his hand, shrugged. "None a my business."

"Up to you, bavv. They feel like trompin you, they gon' do it."

"Huh?"

"Might. Don' like fora-ners, that's you, bavv."

   CHU MA VAY YAL CHU MA VAY YAL
He blinked at her, listened to the SOUND getting louder, coming closer. "Ahsan, Ma." He flipped a finger at his brow and went trotting off, vanishing down the wynd between a tenement and the boarded-up shop behind her.

"Pemmie, scoot. Get home. Now."

"Zazi, you. . . ."

"I mean it. Move y' tail, hon. Or I'm gon' whip it off when I get ahold a you."

   CHU MA VAY YAL CHU MA VAY YAL
Pemmie scowled unhappily at her grandmother, then at the bend in the lane. "Vema, vema, but you take care, you hear?"

"Scat."

Pemmie walked away, dragging her feet and repeatedly looking over her shoulder.

Utsapisha kept an eye on her until she turned into a wynd, then settled herself more solidly in her chair, smoothed the rag of veil over her broad face.

CHU MA VAY YAL CHU MA VAY YAL

The STRIKER band came stomping and chanting around the bend, the Prophet a pace in front of them.

Faharmoy stopped when he came even with Utsapisha, stood in the center of the lane staring at her. "Woman," he called. "Come here."

Utsapisha sniffed, but she'd lived long enough to learn a little prudence. She bowed her head, tucked her hands in her sleeves, spoke as sweetly and softly as she could manage. "I am an old woman, heshim Prophet, walkin's hard, standin's worse." She didn't move.

He grunted and crossed the Lane to her. "Why do you expose yourself in a public street, woman? Why are you not in your house where you belong?"

Jeggin Mal, what the Jann you know about how folks live? Utsapisha sucked in a breath, wriggled her nose under the veil. "I'm a poor woman, heshim. I earn my living makin' food for hungry folk. It's honest work."

"It is not a woman's place to earn."

"I am a widow, heshim Prophet. What am I to do, starve?"

"A contumacious and contentious woman. I have seen you fouling your mouth and your sex by the filth that comes out of you. Obscene and froward, forcing your daughters before the eyes of drunkards and foreigners."

Utsapisha shivered, frightened; he was glaring at her, but she didn't think he really saw her. What he WAS seeing, she didn't know and didn't want to know.

The Prophet gestured and two of the Cheoshim ran forward, started rocking the frycart, splashing her with oil from the pot. She squealed with outrage as she slapped at the smoldering drops, gathered folds of cloth, crushing them between her hands to smother the small fires, yelled as the cart crashed onto its side, spewing oil over the boardwalk, dumping the coals in the firepan over the oil. The walk began to burn about her feet. She struggled to get up—yelled again as another two Cheoshim grabbed her arms, lifted her onto her feet and hurried her out into the Lane.

"The flogging posts," the Prophet said. "Let her learn the cost of her acts."

> > < <

CHU MA VAY YAL CHU MA VAY YAL

"This is how you treat you Ma, you jeggin potz-heads?" She snorted, tried to wrench her arms free. "You Granma?"

CHU MA VAY YAL CHU MA VAY YAL

"Hai! Prophet! Be damn to your god for a rat's ass! You Ma a poxy treez. You Pa got the Itch, been rid by every jeggin Hero in jeezin ro-yal guard. . . ." She went on and on, with every step digging up more invective from a life lived hard and colorfully. The Cheoshim holding her tightened their grip and began breathing heavily, but the Prophet walked in a cell of silence and nothing she said reached him.

CHU MA VAY YAL CHU MA VAY YAL

> > < <

In the center of the Sok Circle, with the few merchants left and fewer buyers watching silently, the Cheoshim tied her hands to the iron circle of the flogging post, wound another rope about her waist and a third about her ankles. They cut open the back of her blouse and flogged her with the five-tailed flagellum. The Cheoshim doing it would have cut the flesh from her bones because she yelled curses on him with every blow, her voice a hoarse whisper at the last of them, but Faharmoy stopped him at seven. "Enough," he said. "More would be the death of her. We must always give time for repentance." He walked around so Utsapisha could see him. "Old woman, contemplate your sins and repent your frowardness. Think on the loving care of the Iron Father."

He snapped thumb against finger and went pacing off, the STRIKER band following him.

CHU MA VAY YAL CHU MA VAY YAL
CHU MA VAY YAL CHU MA VAY YAL
chu ma vay yal chu ma vay yal

The minute they were out of sight Pemmie dashed from a kariam and ran to Utsapisha. Heavily cloaked, with the hood drawn up over his head, Reyna followed more sedately.

"Zazi. . . ." Pemmie dug frantically into a sac hanging at her belt. "Zazi, say something."

"Hunh!" The grunt was feeble, the voice shaky, but Utsapisha didn't let that stop her. "Tol' you t' go home."

"Went for Reyna 'stead." The girl began sawing at the rope around Utsapisha's waist. "Hold still, will you? Don't want to cut you."

"Hush your fuss, Pish." Reyna pushed a knife under the ropes tieing the old woman's wrists to the ring; he worked quickly, glancing from the shadow of the hood at the watching merchants. "We all know you're one mean old firemouth."

"Cess to you, tal." Utsapisha grunted as her arms fell. She leaned against the post, shaking with relief, pain, weariness—and a fury that churned so hard in her she had to shut her throat against vomiting.

Reyna took her hand, placed it on his arm. "Let's go, Pish. Who knows when he finds someone else to haul off. Lean on Pemmie and me, there's a shop near here I've got a key to. Just a few steps and we'll look at your back. Don't want you getting sick on us, huh?"

> > < <

"What's that . . . unh! . . . that girl a yours doin, Rey?" Tears leaked from under her wrinkled horny lids as Reyna cleaned the cuts as gently as he could.

"What she can. What she has to. Like us all. Tai keeps her busy." He dropped the washcloth on the table and began smoothing on salve from a small ceramic jar. "That should feel better. One of Tai's specials."

"Mmp. Heard she was . . . ahhh . . . jee-gah! . . . across here yesterday. Fooling . . . ahhhh . . . round that jeezing snake."

"Can't talk about that, Pish. Let's get that shirt off you a minute so I can wind you up like a top, eh Zazi? That's good. Round and round, Pemmie, not too tight, that's it. Pish, tell you what. Guomann went across the Bridge a couple weeks ago and isn't coming back any time soon, so there won't be anybody to bother you. There's a cot upstairs you can stretch out on and I've got a bottle of water in my bag here. Be safer after dark. Everywhere you go these days those potzheads are infesting the place."

The room at the head of the stairs was hot and airless, with hardly enough space for the three of them and the hard narrow cot. Reyna and Pemmie eased Utsapisha onto the cot, got her turned on her side with her feet drawn up, her sandals pulled off. She wouldn't lie on her stomach, said she had too much gut for that.

Reyna pushed sweat-damped gray hair off her face. "Rest now. You don't have to prove how tough you are, old woman. Just rest."

He started to straighten, but Utsapisha caught at his wrist. She didn't say anything, but her eyes slid toward Pemmie standing at the foot of the cot, then lifted with a silent plea to Reyna's face.

He tapped her hand, turned to the girl. "Pemmie, do a favor, hmm?"

"Vema, Rey. What?"

"There's a broom in the closet by the washstand in the kitchen. Go clean up down there so it isn't obvious there was somebody in here. You know, spread the dust around, get rid of blood drops, that sort of thing. Vema?"

"Vema." She caught hold of Utsapisha's great toe, shook her foot. "Behave y'sef, Zazi." She went out.

When the door shut, Utsapisha tugged her hand loose, sighed. "You a clever one, Rey," she said hoarsely. "Always were, 'f I remember right."

"So what's this about, Pish?"

"Look, only reason I never went across Bridge, I din't want t' live off m' kin. S'port m'sef on the lane. Over there, who knows? Trouble is, there's them that stayed with me. Can't ha' that any more. Got t' get out. You tell 'm, Rey. Tell 'm I say cross Bridge b'fore mornin. I'll be coming soon's I get m' feet under me. There's a time for pride and a time f' usin y' head and this's head time. Dunno what else I c'n say, 'cept Ahsan, Ahsan, Abey's Blessing on you, Rey."

Reyna patted her shoulder. "I'll take care of it, Pish, I'll take care of it all. Don't you worry."

Reyna stayed a while with Utsapisha, listened to the old woman's breathing grow slower and steadier as the heat and closeness of the room mixed with the herbs in the salve to send her deeply asleep.

Reyna smiled down at her, shook her head. "Zazi zazou, you are a one," he murmured. He closed his eyes. We all do what we can, he thought. Faany my Honeychild, why . . . ah gods, I loathe you all. . . .

After a last look at the old woman, he went downstairs to check on her granddaughter.

Chapter 16
Death Dance

Late in the afternoon, some three months after the Prophet returned to Bairroa Pili, Faan was kneeling on the damp dark earth under the Sequbas in a Grove on the east side of the Low City; with the Wild Magic drifting about her, bubbling, frothing, gently popping, she was using a pointed stick to dig a shallow furrow, reaching into the basket beside her for the eye sections she'd cut from ganda roots.

The claws closed on her brain again.

AGAIN. Every day, day on day on day, Abeyhamal seized her and danced her through the high city, drawing the women from the tenements and the towers, seducing more and more of them across the Wood Bridge into the city.

Faan jerked, dropped the stick in the furrow. Her eyes blurred and vanished behind a faceted darkness. She opened her mouth wide, poured out a deep pulsating hum. The Wild Magic flowed up and swirled about her head like shining silver bees.

She danced out of the Grove and along the lanes and wynds of the Low City, into the kariams and out again, and as she danced, girls came from the houses and the groves, from the rooftops and the gardens and danced after her, mouths wide, eyes dark, staring into dream, seeing with their feet and bodies.

Swaying and humming, silver-bubble bees swarming about them, the Honey Dancers followed the Honeychild across the Wood Bridge into the High City.

She saw Reyna standing by the Bridge watching her, angry and helpless. If she could have spoken, she'd have told him, *Mamay, we're all helpless, I did what I had to, don't hurt for me. It doesn't do any good, it only grieves you. I wish . . . ah, wishes don't count, do they? Go away from here, Mamay. Stay safe, don't waste what I've done. Mamay, don't hurt for me.*

>><<

Faharmoy gestured at the door. "Take it down."

A Cheoshim ran up the steps and swung an ax at the center panel.

Before he could get in a second chop, the door burst open and a wrinkled little Fundarim jigged from foot to foot in a panic, shrieking, "Nayo. Nay. What are you doing? Nayo. Nay. You want to come in, come. I'm not stopping you."

Faharmoy snapped thumb against finger and the Cheoshim went back to his place. "You have bees in your house," the Prophet shouted at the little man.

"I have chenz trees," the Fundarim said, voice shrill and quavery. "Come in, heshim Prophet, see for yourself, see that it's the truth. I make my duty to Chumavayal every week. I am loyal. But I can't get chenza fruits without bees to pollinate the blossoms. Come see my garden, Prophet. I give a full tithe of the fruit to the Camuctarr. Ask them. Ask the Manasso Receiver, he'll tell you."

"You are a silversmith, not a farmer. Why do you do what belongs to the Naostam?"

"I only have two trees and I don't sell the fruit. It is my pleasure and harms no one. Certainly not the Naostam."

"Contumacious! Take him." Faharmoy stepped aside

as two Cheoshim ran up the stairs. To the others, he said, "Cut down the trees and burn the hive."

> > < <

Faharmoy watched the band march the Fundarim toward the Sok Circle and the flogging post. "Excuses," he cried to the silent houses, the empty kariam. "It's always excuses. Why can't they just say **I have done wrong in your sight, Iron Father, I repent and throw myself upon your infinite mercy?** Is there SO LITTLE virtue left in the Land?"

He dropped onto his knees in the center of the kariam, lifted his face to the smoke smudged sky, the red flags of the setting sun, closed his ears to the sound of axes coming from the house. Tears of sorrow and adoration streaming unheeded past his ears and onto his ashy robe, he began to chant the Iron Litany, the Praises of Chumavayal.

> > < <

The Honey Dancers circled around the Honeychild in the kariams of the Biasharim; the spiraling towers caught the hum, played it back to them, immensely amplified. The Biashar women came out and danced with them, mothers with babies in their arms, children came, boys and girls alike, danced with their mothers, danced with the Honeygirls. The HUM grew louder and louder, rose in a solid column from the kariam.

They turned into the Inner Ring Road, went round the city, dancing, calling, more and more women coming, more and more children coming, dancing in the Ring Road, Abeyhamal forming out of the sunset before them, forming out of the HUM, her fimbo lifted into the sky, the ivory point glowing with yellow fire.

Silver bees swarmed about the Honeychild, zipping round and round in horizontal figure eights, trapped within the aura of the Honey Mother.

Round the city until they reached the first kariam, down the kariam to the Sok Circle. . . .

As the Cheoshim came with the Fundarim for flogging.

Abeyhamal shouted a soundless WORD that shook the air. From her translucent shape small lightnings jagged out, striking with hot zizzles and a thread of smoke.

Gasping with fear and annoyance, the merchants and their customers fled for whatever cover they could find.

The Wildings rose in a roaring spiral and fell among the Cheoshim like rain, but rain with a sting in every drop.

Batting at the air, cursing, the Cheoshim fled.

The little Fundarim crawled away; no one paid any attention to him.

Caught in the maelstrom of the ecstatic trance, the women danced round and round the Circle, trampling everything that lay before them, round and round until the sun was fully down and night was on them.

> < <

Exhausted and hoarse, Faan came to herself in the middle of a crowd of unsure, rather frightened women. "K'lann," she muttered, looked round uncertainly, pinching up a small smile when she saw a friendly face. "Ma'teesee, you here?"

"Choo-ee, Fa. That was some stomp." She giggled, wrinkled her nose. "We better get out of here."

"Where's Dossy?"

"Don't think you got her this time."

Ailiki chittered impatiently by Faan's bare feet. The

mahsar reached up, scratched at her ankle. "G-g-g-g," she chittered.

"Liki says its time to vacate." She held out her arms, cuddled the mahsar as the beast leapt into them. "Let's get out of here, Teesee. This place stinks."

Chapter 17
The General's Conversion

The Royal Barge moved ponderously along the shrunken River, the pilot peering anxiously at leadsmen in boats far ahead; they signaled with flags the water depths, he translated these and passed orders to the helmsmen at the sweeps.

Wenyarum Taleza paced back and forth on the quarterdeck, cursing the River, the stupidity of the bargemen, the heat, the dust, the stinking water, anything he could dredge up. Most of all he cursed Abeyhamal and all her works. He couldn't afford to be angry at the Amrapake or at Faharmoy his idiot son—it was dangerous even to think of blaming them for his discomfort and the precariousness of his position. He cursed his wife, but under his breath. One moment he wanted her to sicken and die, the next he was nauseated by the fear that she would—leaving him the sole credible witness to what was essentially her murder. That beating had dug a pit in his future that he saw no way of escaping.

The sky was white with dust, the sun hammered the Land; the River glittered at him, the glare knives in his eyes.

As the barge crawled down the River, he paced the deck, angrier every day, no place to dump his anger but Abeyhamal and the pernicious upstarts who were using her to seize power. Back and forth, back and forth. His armor rubbed rashes wherever it touched. Back and forth, back and forth. . . .

Three days after it moved away from the pier at Gom

Corasso, the barge tied up at the Camuctarr Gatt at Bairroa Pili and the General marched off, followed by the eleven-man hosta from the Corassana Royal Guard, knowing the Amrapake sent them to make sure he did what he was told and brought the boy home.

> > < <

Wenyarum Taleza, Hereditary General of the Armies of the Amrapake of Zam Fadogurum, brushed past the young acolyte guarding the door and strode into the receiving room of the High Kasso of Bairroa Pili.

Juvalgrim was seated in his audience chair, his embroidered robe pulled into graceful folds about his lean body, shining black hair with streaks of gray like polished pewter hanging loose and long over his shoulders. He was calm and smiling and a perfect Maulapam. The General hadn't met Pili's High Kasso before, though he'd heard things about him that displeased him; it was hard to believe them now he saw the man. This was his own kind he was facing, born if not bred into his own caste.

Juvalgrim lifted a hand. "It's all right, Fitchon. Close the door." He nodded at Wenyarum. "We are honored, heshim General."

Wenyarum Taleza swung round, glared at the youth with the yellow face and the spiky copper hair. "Close it with you on the other side, kuk."

The acolyte's eyes narrowed and a muscle ticked beside his mouth, but he bowed, backed out, and shut the door with a controlled, decisive click.

"Pollutes. Hunh!" Wenyarum snorted. "This being the Camuctarr, I suppose you have to put up with them. Had my way—well, didn't come here to waste time with compliments and chit-chat. Amrapake sent me to look into this Prophet thing. We hear rumors of rebellion and the flouting of authority. What's your opinion of the boy?"

"That he's far from a boy. Your son, isn't he? Or am I misinformed?"

"Got nothing to do with this, but diyo, my son. Well, he a Prophet for real or has he got knots in his head?"

"Oh, I think there's no doubt of his call. Chumavayal has walked with him."

"Who says so? Some potzhead with an overheated imagination?"

The High Kasso smiled, tented his hands, touched the tips of his fingers to his chin. "I have never considered my imagination overheated, heshim General, yet I have seen Chumavayal beside him more than once." He stroked his thumb across the curve of the Eye. "I have seen the god before so I know what I'm talking about. The Call is real. Your son has been Chosen."

"I need to talk to him."

"Vema. At the moment he's elsewhere. In the city, I suppose. If you wish, I will send novices out hunting him, but I have no power to say to him, come here, go there. Only the god can tell him that. Once they know where he is, the youngsters could take you to him."

The General grimaced. "With every nose in the city poking into my business."

"I see. Perhaps this will serve; he usually comes to us for Evensong and a few hours rest. Evensong must proceed as is prescribed, heshim General, and without interruption, but I can turn his followers from the Court and you can speak to him there with no one listening in."

"That will be adequate." The General bowed perfunctorily and marched out.

>><<

The General stood outside the pointed arch that gave entry to the Fountain Court until the hosta eleven had passed through it and established themselves with their backs to the wall, then he strode into the Court, his bootheels ringing on the flags. He stopped before his son, appalled at what he saw.

"Is this what you've made of yourself, Mal?"

Faharmoy's eyes were closed, his lips moving steadily as he passed his fingers along the bronze chain. He finished the prayer, draped the chain across his knees and looked up at his father. "Not I, but one far greater than I."

"So you say."

"So I say." His eyes went blank, his hands tightened on the chain, then relaxed.

The General stepped back and stared at the shadow spreading from the wall, hovering over and around Faharmoy.

The shadow boiled and solidified.

Blocking out the great spiral tower beyond the Court, kneeling behind Faharmoy, Chumavayal cupped immense, powerful black hands about his Chosen Word and glared at Wenyarum Taleza.

The General stared into those molten red eyes and felt the breath sucked from his body. Behind him, armor clattered and clanked as the hosta flung themselves facedown on the flags. His own knees gave under him, dropped him onto the stone paving.

"Chumavayal," he cried out. Then he, too, was facedown, plottings and fears forgotten, everything evaporated before the terror and majesty of the god.

Chapter 18
Flight Plans

On the fourth day after the beating, Penhari woke sweating with Desantro bending over her, wiping her face with a cool, damp towel.

"Hai-hai, heshal, so you're with us again." Desantro set the towel aside and went away. She was back a moment later with a mug of clear soup.

It was too warm and too salty, but Penhari drank it and felt better. "Ahsan," she murmured, closed her eyes and slept.

She woke in the middle of the night, her mouth dry, her throat sore; as she struggled up, her bandages shifted, cut into her breasts and her nightshift stuck to the salve mixture the shifting uncovered.

She'd been hurt before, but never like this, never beaten half to death. It changed things. Her. Changed her. I can't stay here. Her mouth worked and she reached for the water jug that had always been beside the bed, a stoneware bottle with a matching mug turned upside down over the neck.

It was empty. Desantro must have forgotten to fill it before she left.

For a breath and a half Penhari was furious. "I'll have her. . . ." She stared at the jug, dimly visible in the glimmer from the nightlight, ran her tongue over cracking lips. "Abey's Sting, what am I doing?" She lifted a shaking hand, rested the back of it against her brow. A month ago she'd have laughed, given the maid in charge a short scold and let the thing drop.

She got to her feet, took the jug down the hall to the water room and filled it at the tap, then gulped down a mugful of the lukewarm water, filled the mug again, drank half, and splashed the rest across her face.

Back in the bedroom, she sat on the bed, scowling at the doorwindows that opened into her garden. Famtoche had enjoyed the beating and he'd be back. Given half an excuse, he'd be back. And after a while, he wouldn't need an excuse. "I can't stay here," she said aloud. "I can't face this again. I can't."

She got to her feet, pulled on the old linen robe she'd been wearing for days. She could smell herself on the folds of the cloth, something that she found comforting and at the same time disgusting, slave-stink. She blinked, then smiled as she tied the belt. Sisters under the skin, slave and mistress, the smell of their sweat much the same. She moved restlessly about the room, lighting lamps, opening closets, pulling out bureau drawers, tipping back the lids to chests. She ran her hands along the hanging clothing, picked up things, set them down again. If she did leave this place, she had no idea what to take.

Carrying one of the lamps, she wandered into the other parts of the suite, the several sitting rooms, the sewing room, dressing room, water room, the small library. . . .

She lifted the lamp as high as she could and stared; half the scrolls were gone, others were on the floor, torn, dirty, mixed with shards of pottery from the holders. Books were thrown about, stamped on, soaked with urine. The stench was appalling.

"Everything," she cried. "They've stripped me of everything!"

Pain forgotten in her rage, she swung round and went storming through the rooms to the door into the Falmatarr's Common Hall.

A Cheoshim, one of the Royal Guard, stood slowly and turned to face her with barely concealed insolence, barring her way with his lance. "Go back to bed, Falmaree."

She shut the door, set the lamp with careful precision on the cardtable built into the jamb, and stood hugging her arms tight across her breast as sobs of rage and frustration shook her body. "Honey Mother defend me," she cried. "Help me, help. . . ."

Slowly the shudders subsided; she rubbed her hand across her eyes, clawed up the hem of her robe and wiped her nose, her cheeks. "Sleep? I can't sleep."

She took up the lamp again and wandered aimlessly through the suite, fetching up in the largest of the sitting rooms, the one where Famtoche had beaten her. Her blood was wiped off the floor, but drops of it were splattered about on the furniture. She scratched a fingernail across a crusted spot on the back of a chair. Desantro could tend plants, but she didn't know much about cleaning.

She put the lamp on a table and settled in the bloody chair, easing back until she was as comfortable as she was going to get, lifting her feet onto a rest. "I can't stay here," she repeated. "Not in the Falmatarr, not in Gom Corasso."

Where could she go? How could she get away?

"I'm ignorant. Worse than a slave."

Lamentably, dangerously ignorant.

If she tried to leave, she wouldn't get two steps before she was dragged back. She grimaced at the humiliation of that ignominious return, the fear of being beaten again. *I never understood why slaves seemed so stupid and spiritless.* It's pain. Crude brute pain they can't bring themselves to face again.

Ignorant!

She had no idea how the city was laid out, not a glimmer where she could hide if she did manage to get away from the Falmatarr. She touched the long gray hair, tangled and hanging loose over her shoulders. *I can't even do my own hair.*

"I have lived fifty-two years," she said to the ghostly shape mirrored in the window across the room. "I can read and write, I'm not stupid. I've survived rape and politics, sickness and childbirth, lust and indifference. I know the essays of Chaldeysir, the treatises on government by the Quiambo Kuigiza and his students, the philosophies of the Honey poet Yar-rai, I have read history and studied art. And I am more ignorant, certainly more helpless, than Desantro who probably can't read a word. She's come from the ends of the earth and I've never been outside the walls of this city, barely outside the walls of this one building."

Her feet were just at the edge of the circle of light. She wiggled her toes and sighed. "I am going," she said aloud. "Whatever happens out there, it will happen by my choice. At last by my own choice."

> < <

"Desantro," Penhari called out when she heard the sound of sweeping. "Come here, I need you."

Desantro came slowly into the room, her hair tied in a kerchief, a torn dustrobe over her dress. "Chambermassal says I hav'ta get the dust up t'day, heshal."

"You can go back to that in a moment. I want you to cut my hair."

Desantro blinked, backed up a step. "I'd make a mess, heshal."

"I don't care, as long as it's a short mess. Think of it as pruning."

That startled a bark of laughter out of Desantro. "You want me to fetch the pruning shears, heshal?"

"I don't believe we need go that far to validate a metaphor. The scissors in my sewing box should be adequate."

> < <

Penhari sat sideways on the garden longchair, scowling at the grass. Famtoche had even driven the bees from the garden; without them it'd turned sour for her, but Desantro wouldn't do the cutting inside.

Desantro drew the comb down through the thick, oily gray hair. "We really should wash it first, I think."

"Just cut. Till it's even with my earlobes."

"Haihai, and what if I cut them off?"

"You can sew them back on."

"Saa! That'd be a thing." She cut carefully and slowly, her face brooding as she worked, flicking the shears so the long, long strands of hair fell around Penhari, onto the chair or onto the grass.

When she was finished, she gathered every strand, took the mass of gray to the nearest flowerbed and used a spoon from the lunch tray to dig a hole and bury it.

Penhari shook her head, relishing how light and cool it felt, how naked. She blinked at Desantro. "Why are you doing that?"

Desantro stood, used the toe of her worn sandal to press the earth down about the bush. "Y' want to be careful with things that come off you," she said. " 'F you have enemies, they can use 'em 'gainst you. Witches," she said. "They tell me there be witches here, though I havna seen any myself."

"Witches, hunh. What they mean is Abeyhamal's followers. It's an excuse for a burning. There's no magic in the Land, except in idiots' heads."

"I dunno, heshal. No one talks to me 'bout that kind of thing." Desantro set her hands on her hips, tilted her head. "Better 'an I thought. You look younger even."

Penhari burst out laughing. "Vema vema, Desantro, one favor deserves another. Pour yourself some lemonade and sit a moment."

Desantro hesitated.

Penhari waved impatiently at the pitcher. "I'm still someone, woman."

When Desantro had settled to the grass, muttering she'd be more comfortable with ground under her, Penhari pulled her legs up and lay back in the chair. "Tell me about your home, Desa, what it was like, how you lived."

Desantro sipped at the lemonade, set the glass down beside her. "Long time gone," she said. "I don't think about those days much. Better not." She pulled a blade of grass free, nibbled at the greenish-white stem. "The mountains in Whenapoyr, they'd make those . . ." she flipped a hand at the Jinocaburs whose pale blue tips they could just see above the garden walls, "look like gnat bites. 'Twas cold in the winter, snow higher than the roofs. Always some'un died from the cold, old 'uns mostly or babes born too soon in the year. It c'd get so quiet you heard y' hair growing. The trees, ah the trees. . . ." She pulled another blade of grass, a longer one, stretched it vertically between thumbs pressed together and blew, producing a harsh, plaintive sound.

Penhari rubbed her back cautiously against the chair; the healing wounds were getting itchy. "What happened? How'd you come to be here?"

"Hmm. The usual way. Whenapoyr is next to Hraney and Hennermen were always raiding us. Still are, I s'pose. They came with the thaw, killed them they din't want, most a my folks. Had a brother 'n a younger sister, took them an' me, dumped us in a boat, sold us, I don't know where that market is, somewhere up north. Speculator bought me, sold me in Pili's Sok. An't seen m' sister an' brother since."

"Would you like to go back some day?"

Desantro's head came up and her eyes went blank. "Oh no, heshal. I am content."

Penhari sighed. "You don't think I'm going to run to the Chambermassal, do you? And tell him get out the whip, I've got an uppity slave plotting escape?''

Desantro pulled another blade of grass and began splitting it into hairfine strips. ''Never trust a Mal,'' she muttered.

''What?''

''The first Fadogur I learned.''

''I don't understand.'' Penhari pushed up and stared at Desantro. ''What are you talking about?''

''You'll be angry.'' Penhari had to strain to hear the murmured words. ''Then what's your word worth?''

''What I say it is. Have you ever heard else?''

Desantro rubbed green off her fingers. After a minute she shrugged. ''Maulapam keep promises they make to other castes if they wanna and forget 'em if they don't. Mostly they forget. Their word don't count 'less it's Mal to Mal. Slaves and Wascra know 't. Naostam.''

''I see.'' Penhari grimaced. ''No. I'm not angry. I believe you, Desantro. I have to, I don't know enough to dispute with you. Vema, then, I go first. I'm leaving this house as soon as I can manage it. Not just leaving, running away. I need you if you'll come. Is there anything . . . anyone . . . you'd miss?''

Desantro cupped one hand in the other, rubbed the sides of her thumbs together; for a long moment she stared at Penhari, then she looked past her at the blue peaks sketched against the blue-white sky, her hands falling apart to rest on her thighs. ''Nayo, nothing,'' she said slowly. ''I've forty years, heshal. I've birthed six children, all of 'em taken from me soon's they were weaned, two boys fostered at Camuctarr, four girls with Naostam families. I don't know where any of them are now, anyway they wouldna know me from the dog. Sometimes slave women are let keep their kids, but never if they belong to Maulapam like me. 'S a good thing a slave's kids aren't slaves, too. Fadogur is better nor some places I c'd 've been took to, but it's hard losing a babe from the breast.''

Frowning slightly, Penhari watched the woman's eyes go soft and wistful, suddenly alienated from her by more than caste. Her own son had been born in terrible, tearing pain, had cost her the ability to have more children—which she did not at all regret. She'd loathed Faharmoy from the first day of morning sickness almost as much as she loathed the husband her father and brother had forced on her, almost as much she loathed them both, her father and her brother.

Desantro's face went hard. ''Why?'' she said. ''Give me a reason I should risk the strangler's cord for you.''

''Consider this. What happens if I'm gone and you're here?''

''What happens if I go tell Chambermassal what you're getting up to?''

''Vema. You've matched me there. Consider this, then. Do you want to grow old here in the Falmatarr? You've seen what it's like; I tried to change things for my women, but that's finished now. I can't free you, a woman can't do that, not even me, but I can bribe a shipmaster to smuggle you out of the Land, give you money to live on until you can get back to your homeland or make other arrangements.''

''And if we get caught?''

''You'll be whipped to death or whatever strikes the fancy of my husband and my brother. I'll be beaten also, but no doubt I'll live through it.''

''Ah. Don't take this wrong, heshal, but I want to see the coin before I do the deed.''

''Vema. Agreed. You do get out of the Falmatarr, don't you?''

''You don't know?''

Penhari watched a single butterfly flit from bloom to bloom. ''For years,'' she said slowly, ''I have refrained

from . . . mmm . . . curiosity. It has been my best
defense. I . . . don't intend to explain that. Assume I
know nothing about what happens outside these rooms.
You won't miss truth by much."

Desantro scratched at her nose. "Vema. Le's see.
There's a Chumavayal festa every couple months. The
Primakass he makes the rule, slaves get out like the
rest, everybody has to follow it."

"Even the Maulapam?" Penhari smiled at her.

"Even the Maulapam." Desantro slanted a glance at
Penhari, her mouth twitched into a quick grin.

"So you get out. And?"

Desantro wriggled around until she was squatting
on her heels, hunched forward, knees out, with her
forearms resting on her thighs. "We s'posed to do
the worship thing, but all y' got to do is sho y' face
then scat for the dancing and all that." She twisted
her mouth into a half-pout, then clicked her tongue
against her teeth. "The Gates are left open till moonset, which means we can get outside the walls and
have some real fun. Most everybody go down beach,
dig clams and hunt the shallows for chitz an' buagosh
an' whatever else we c'n net, an' we dump them in
pots and boil 'em, an' there's homebrew an' you
name it for drinking an' bhagg for smoking an' what's
y' pleasure, an' there's fires an' someone's got erhu
or gitter or horns or somp'n, starts playing when they
feels like it, an' maybe one or two starts dancing and
then there's more dancing. . . ." She jumped to her
feet, started stamping and clapping her hands; after
a few breaths she began singing in her home tongue,
then dancing to her own singing. She had a strong
contralto voice, rough but not unpleasant. Sweat glistened on her face and arms, her body moved with a
powerful vigor.

Penhari watched with enjoyment and anger—anger at
the constraints of her caste and at herself for her years
of complacent acquiescence. *Weren't for Famtoche and*

*his flagellum, I'd be a mole all my life, blind and bur-
rowing.* She laughed aloud as Desantro whipped the
kerchief off her head and wiped at her face without
missing a beat of her swaying, stamping dance or a
syllable of her song.

"Corrupting the slaves, too, dear sister?" Famtoche
Banddah lounged in the doorwindow, one arm hanging,
the other curled about his belt. His black eyes were
empty as the windows, his smile a grimace.

Desantro's face went blank and she dropped to her
stomach, stretched out flat on the grass, her hands in
front of her, palms pressed together.

Penhari turned slowly, swinging her feet off the
longchair, pushing herself up so she was standing between Famtoche and the slave. "What do you want,
brother?"

"When I hear my sister is ill, how can I stay away?"

"Easily, dear brother. What do you want?"

He tapped his fingers against the leather of the belt;
his eyes softened and he smiled so sweetly she knew he
was remembering and as the silence stretched on, knew
he was making sure she understood the images he was
seeing.

She kept her face impassive. She'd had years of practice.

He straightened up. "Word came to me you tried to
leave your suite last night. Don't." He stepped back
into the room; over his shoulder, he said, "Or we'll
have another lesson."

> > < <

Penhari stood slumped, her hands clenched.

An arm came around her shoulders. With that gentleness of touch that always surprised her, Desantro
hugged her, then led her to the longchair.

"Hai-hai, don't you fuss youself, heshal. Rest y' now

while I finish the sweeping and see what notions I c'n dig up.''

In the doorwindow she turned, her face alive with laughter. ''One thing still on, heshal. I wanna see coin before I do aught.''

Chapter 19
The God on Her Shoulders

A gray-brown beast trotting beside her, the Honeychild danced with the Honey Dancers through the kariams of the High City, drawing women from the towers and the tenements, adding their voices to the rising-falling howl that vibrated from tower to tower. Wild Magic swirled among them, caught in the net of Abeyhamal's Summoning.

OW OOO OUM OWWW OOO AHHH UM

Their mouths gaped wide, snapped shut, stretched again, their eyes stared—they saw not the towers along the kariams but mica-bright wings like frozen light. Wild Magic grew wings that vibrated and sang so high a note the sound pierced the ears.

OW OOO OUM OWWW OOO AHHH UM

In convoluted double loops they danced, filling the kariams, crossing the Inner Ring Road to the towers of the Cheoshim. Wild Magic dipped and rose, undulating with the rise and fall of the humming howl.

OW OOO OUM OWWW OOO AHHH UM

They circled a Cheoshim tower, stomping and weaving in time with the SOUND—hundreds of women moving together, ecstatic and terrible, a maelstrom of magic force pressing against the tower. Wild Magic merged into a fog that flowed in silver-gray streamers along the lines of power.

Windows shattered and women came out to join the dance.

The air shivered.

Mica wings splintered the sunlight, swept away.

Honeychild, Honey Beast, Honey Dancers ran after them. The women ran after them.

The Wild Magic coursed with them.

OW OOO OUM OWWW OOO AHHH UM

Another tower.

Windows shattered.

Men swarmed out and tried to beat the women off.

The women ululated and ripped into them with teeth and claws, trampled them, tore them to bloody shreds and went on, following the light-splintering wings and the dancing Honeychild and the Honeychild's magic beast.

Wild Magic swept along with them.

OW OOO OUM OWWW OOO AHHH UM

>><<

The Prophet marched grim-faced along a kariam on the west side, the STRIKER band stomping behind him, the three pairs of Cheoshim in the front rank each holding the arms of a trembling man, three prisoners bound for the flogging posts.

CHU MA VAY YAL CHU MA VAY YAL

>><<

Ailiki weaving about her feet, Faan danced blank-eyed along a kariam on the east side, the Dancers from the Low City revolving in complex spirals about her, more than a thousand ecstatic women dancing behind her, maenads seized by their god.

Wild Magic came together and clustered about the Honeychild like a veil of silver toile fluttering in unfelt winds.

OW OOO OUM OWWW OOO AHHH UM

>><<

The Prophet heard the humming howl, but ignored it. He marched over the meager piles of merchandise without bothering where he put his feet; the Cheoshim following him elbowed merchants and buyers alike out of their way. Nothing mattered but the lessoning and the purifying of the City and with it the Land.

CHU MA VAY YAL CHU MA VAY YAL

> > < <

Ailiki echoing her steps, Faan danced into the Sok Circle, turning and swaying in lazy eights, veiled and revealed, veiled and revealed, while the Honey Dancers split and spun around the edges of the Circle, the hordes of women dividing and dancing after them, meeting behind the STRIKER band on the far side of the Circle, swirling in a double whirl around and around—an engine of power pouring into the Honey Mother's hands.

OW OOO OUM OWWW OOO AHHH UM

The Prophet spread his arms and glared at her. "Yellow 'Treez!" he cried. "Begone!"

Rivers of red fire burst from his palms and roared at the Honeychild.

Wild Magic became a thousand wings, brushed and blew the fire harmlessly into the sky.

Faan burned gold and white. Lightning leapt from her fingers, struck at the Prophet; it glanced off black hands that came down around him, struck several of the Cheoshim behind him and seared them to sudden ash.

The prisoners—suddenly loosed—ran blindly away.

The air in the Circle shook with heat and fire. Hair shriveled and spots on clothing smoldered.

The STRIKER band shouted CHUMAVAYAL! and rushed at the nearest women, clubs, knives, spears, torches striking at them, fists and feet striking at them.

Dancing women went down, were trampled.

A woman's skirt caught fire, turned her into a torch—

she burned in ecstacy, unafraid, leapt at a Cheoshim, curled arms and legs about him and took him with her into ash.

More women went down with smashed heads and other wounds, many dead before they hit the paving stones.

Women died and died, were mutilated, beaten, hurt.

Cheoshim died, throats ripped out by maenad teeth, smothered by women piling on them, died torn apart, arms wrenched from their bodies, wrists bitten open.

The STRIKER band died, twenty young man scattered in pieces across the Sok Circle.

For every man, four women died and another four were badly hurt, but there were hundreds of women there.

In the center of the charnel ground, the Prophet and Faan faced each other, one burning red, one burning gold.

Abruptly, the light vanished from both.

Wild Magic hovered in a fog about Faan, dulled and diminished.

The Prophet looked drained and old, though he'd lost none of his loathing for Faan and all she represented. ''Begone, habatrize,'' he croaked at her. ''Filth!''

Faan swept her eyes along his body, feet to head, then laughed, a harsh bitter sound. ''Talk about filth, louse breeder, when was your last bath? Good thing I'm downwind, or I'd be upchucking my lunch.'' She turned her back on him and sashayed off, wiggling her behind at him with mocking exaggeration.

The suddenly sobered women from the towers left the dead behind and crept back into their apartments; many of them took a last look around, packed up what they could carry, and went trudging across the Wood Bridge to the Low City.

The Prophet stomped angrily down a kariam, heading for the Outer Ring Road and Jiko Sagrada.

>><<

With Ailiki trotting beside her, brushing against her now and then, Faan limped away from the Sok Circle, battered and exhausted, cursing under her breath Abeyhamal and all her works. Tears slipped unheeded down her face.

All those women dead, burnt, heads crushed, bodies slashed and broken. Those Cheoshim boys clawed into bloody shreds. All because these cursed gods were playing their nauseating games and using people as game pieces, breaking them, discarding them. It was so wasteful, so useless. . . .

"Fa!" Reyna waved the other Salagaum on toward the Sok and came running across the kariam. "Honey. . . ."

Faan tried to smile, wiped at her streaky face. "Gods," she said. "Slaughter."

"Diyo. God business." His mouth twisted. "We kept a lookout, honey. In case you needed us. Some still alive?"

"I don't know. It's a mess."

Reyna put his arm around her, hugged her lightly. "There's a place we've been staying the past few days. Come along, honey, I'll make you some tea or something, at least you can wash your face."

Faan trudged in silence for several minutes, glancing now and then at Reyna. He looked a lot older, gaunt and graying, his hair cut shorter, shoulder length now instead of halfway down his back, but his eyes were clear and he moved with the easy looseness of good health. "Past few days?" she said.

The sudden smile that lit his face made her feel warm and happy, brought back days she'd thought were gone forever. "We keep a step or two ahead of the Shinda

Prefecture. It's a game of Hummer Stools, we move and they pounce two seats back." He made a face, reached over and took her hand. "Nobody wants the Salagaum these days. It's good to see you, Fa. I swear you've grown two inches on me."

She squeezed the hand. "I've missed you, Mamay."

He chuckled. "I know, hon. Even the shouting matches, hmm?"

"Diyo, Mamay, I was an idiot! I wish . . . I tried to talk HER into letting you come across the River."

"Down here." He tugged her into a wynd, began weaving between tenements at the inner edge of the Edge. "Don't mind it, Fa. There's too much that needs doing over here."

"You could get killed."

"So could you, hon."

"Gods!"

"Diyo."

"In here, honey." He opened a shaky stick gate at the back of a three-story tenement, took her across the sun-baked stretch of earth that had once been a garden, unlocked the kitchen door, and led her inside.

> > < <

A slender Salagaum with the spiky coarse hair of the Cheoshim, Twarra came with quick light steps into the kitchen, snapped fingers in a greeting to Faan who was sitting at a wobbly table sipping tea from a mug. He shook his head when Reyna raised an eyebrow. "We had to give grace to half a dozen women," he said. "Couldn't move them, they'd fall apart in our hands. Anyone could crawl was gone. Rest were dead. The STRIKER band, well, looked like animals had got at them. Nasty."

Reyna emptied the pot into a mug, handed it to Twarra, then hitched a hip on the wash ledge. "Any trouble?"

Twarra gulped at the strong tea, shook his head. When his mouth was clear, he said, "Nayo, Rey. If there's anyone watching, he didn't stick nose out. Dawa took t'others to pick up handcarts and they went on to stash. Figured it'd be safer to haul sacks now, STRIKER band and Shinda guards not so apt to be nosing about."

> < <

Reyna and Dawa, Thammir and Furrah pushed the handcarts onto the Approach. Dawa and the others settled down to guard them while Reyna took Faan aside to talk to her.

"Mamay, I. . . ." She broke off, lunged against him as she'd done so many times before, wrapping her arms around him and holding tight while she sobbed and shuddered, her anguish breaking suddenly through the weary numbness that had held until now.

He said nothing, just held her close, smoothing a shaking hand down and down her tangled hair until the sobbing faded and she lay against him limp with release, then he sighed, took the end of his sleeve and wiped her face. "How many times. . . ." he murmured.

She managed a watery smile. "Count the times I've made an idiot of myself."

"Honey, tell the Bitch God to go jump. Nothing's worth this."

She caught hold of his hands, but moved away from him, stood holding them and shaking her head.

"Stubborn as a waterpig, aren't you."

"Diyo. You should know by now, Mamay."

"I'll keep watching, honey."

"Don't."

"Where do you think you learned that stubbornness, Tchi'kee?"

"Ah, well." She pulled loose. "Tai'll have someone for the carts fast as she can manage. Be careful, Mamay."

> > < <

When she reached the middle of the Bridge, Faan waved to Reyna and the Salagaum, then started trotting for the Low City. She was exhausted, but she didn't want to keep the Salagaum in the open any longer than she had to.

Chapter 20
Fiddling the Escape

Desantro squatted beside the longchair, scratched at her nose. "First on, where we going?"

"I thought down the River to Bairroa Pili." Penhari swept a hand along her body. "You see what you've got to work with, Desa. I'm neither young enough nor insane enough to try crossing the mountains."

Desantro's mouth twisted into something half a smile and half a grimace. "Jumps to mind, that. We need time to get far 'nough so they can't just put thumb out and squash us."

"Do you know anything about boats?"

"Not many boats on skislope." Desantro pulled a blade of grass loose, looked at the withered stem and tossed it away. "So we buy us a sailor afore we start." She tilted her head, looked sideways at Penhari. "Need coin for him. Not gold, nayo, nayo, gold gets 'em greedy, just the shine a it. Silver, what I want. Maybe thirty, fifty, somp'n like that."

"Vema. I can arrange that."

"Be tricky, slaves an't s'posed to have anything to do with boat."

"But you can do it?"

Desantro lifted a sturdy, callused hand, spread fingers and thumb, rocked them back and forth as if to say, so so ask me no question I tell you no lie.

"When?"

"Thought about that. Wounded Moon's full five days on, there's a Festa day before, 's when 'prentice smiths, all kinds, they get raised to journeyman, being they ready for 't. One a them Festas we get off on, Primakass order, like I said. I tell Chambermassal I bring cold food in the morning, you c'n take care a youself, he'll like that. He'll be liking it so much he won't be smelling anything spooked. A good thing 'cause I c'n get hold a more food than other days, gonna be a help 'cause we'll need somp'n to eat going downRiver, can't be stopping, anyway, an't much out there these days, what I hear.'' She jumped to her feet, began pacing back and forth, excitement spilling over, brushing against Penhari, infecting her. ''Soon's it be dark, we get you out city, over to boat. Take off. Be morning afore anyone notice I'm not back, later an that when they find out you gone.'' She slapped her hands against her side. ''C'n do 't, vema, vema, we can do it!''

Penhari swung her feet off the longchair and watched Desantro go rushing out. *A quarter century's caution washed away. How easily she forgets. Trusts me. Or is she simply playing me as I've been trying to manipulate her?* She got to her feet and began moving about the garden, nipping away dead blooms, dying leaves, casting the detritus on the grass behind her. Time to consider her resources.

There were the jewels Wenyarum kept giving her. At the moment there was no way to turn these into coin; no jeweler would buy so much as a silver ring from a slave, so she couldn't send a piece out with Desantro. The jewelry would be useful, but only after she got away from here.

She straightened, frowned at the withered brown flowerhead she was holding. *If I can keep the things from being stolen.* Desantro's tales of the street and countryside were lesson enough about the difficulties travelers faced, men and women alike. *I'll have to sew hiding places in my skirts and tunics, put in padding to keep the shapes hidden.* She rubbed plant juices from her fingers, glanced at the sun. *Not now. Tonight. I don't want anyone walking in on me while I'm doing it. Not even Desantro. Particularly not Desantro. I may be ignorant, but I'm not foolish.* She made a face at the flowerhead, tossed it aside. *Not all the time, anyway.*

There was her name-day gold. Wenyarum made sure that custom was kept up. Each name-day, one broad millefur for every year of her life. Three months ago Famtoche had presented her with fifty-two millefurs. She had no illusions about Wenyarum Taleza. Most of the hoard had probably gone on habatrizes and uniforms—and on the jewelry he pressed on her (conscience money, no doubt, and bragging rights), but there should be something left. The private passage between their bedrooms must be thick with dust and spiders by now; he was the only one to use it, she'd never had the least desire to go to him, but he'd showed her the trick of the panels and she remembered. She wouldn't have to go into the outer halls and face that sneering guard. *Wonder if Famtoche set a guard on Wenyarum's suite? Hmm. I can send Desantro there tomorrow to fetch . . . what? Considering the condition of my library, a scroll . . . what does he have . . . never mind, I'll think of something later . . . if there's no guard, then that's how I get out.*

> > < <

Penhari held the lamp close to the panels on the right side of her bed. "Shoulder . . . diyo, shoulder high, him not me." The panels were carved with fertility signs, embarrassing even now when she was looking closely at them for the first time in years. She snorted as she remembered the disgust she felt when he showed her what to move. "One half turn so what was hanging is now standing high. Abey's Sting. The minds of these men."

Something clunked. The panel opened a crack, groaning as it moved. She pushed at it and with difficulty got it wide enough to let her move the lamp into the stifling darkness beyond. "Spiders, tchah!"

She set the lamp on the bedtable and went for the broom Desantro had taken to leaving in the water room so she wouldn't have to haul it back and forth each day.

>><<

The panel in Wenyarum's bedroom cracked open.

Penhari froze as she heard voices and other sounds.

She placed the broom carefully in the corner between wall and paneling, blew the lamp out, set it down and leaned against the crack. Listening.

The voices were muffled. A man and a woman, not in the bedroom but in one of the rooms beyond. She couldn't make out the words, but she didn't really need to.

She caught hold of the panel, tried to ease it farther open, winced as it groaned.

"Wha's zat?" A woman speaking.

The man's voice rumbled, impatience sharpening a few of the syllables so she could hear them, but she still couldn't make out what he was saying.

"Come from in here." The woman sounded closer.

Penhari held her breath and waited.

"Rats, that's all. Come on, you can't go in there. That jegger's nose could sniff a leaky keups like you five days gone and fifty miles off."

Chambermassal. Hunh. Talking about rats. Nay, mice. Overrunning the place the minute the cat's away. How he dares . . . Wenyarum would skin him screaming if he knew. . . .

"I swear I heard something."

"Can't have. No one comes here but that yatz."

"Don't . . . I don't like it here. If he found us. . . ."

"K'lann, Hlakki, he's down in Pili groveling around in dung and ashes with his ass in the air, tonguing ol' Prophet's filthy feet."

"You don't knooow."

"Sure I do. Comma hee-er, bébésha. Ahhh, soft, soft . . ."

"Don't! I don't like it here, I wanna go."

Penhari grimace at the sound of scuffling, glass breaking then a slap and the patter of feet, the slam of a door.

The Chambermassal cursed, stomped out, was back before Penhari could get to her feet. She heard the clink and clatter of the glass, then the brisk rasp of a scrub brush. A moment later the door slammed again.

She waited a long dreary time before she shoved at the panel again.

After lighting the lamp at the nightglow, she went cautiously into the next room, wrinkled her nose at the stink of brandy. *Fool. When the General got back. . . .* She frowned. *If he came back. . . .*

She set the lamp on the desk, went round it to inspect the elaborate carvings of the paneled wall. *This is harder . . . not so many cues. . . .* "Where was it? Where . . . was. . . ." He always brought her in here and had her take the gold from Famtoche's Mizam, made her stow it in the cavity.

"Diyo, got it." She pressed the bosses, smiled as a small square of iron-faced wood sprang at her. The opening was a foot square and an arm's length deep.

She began taking the canvas bags from the stash, setting them on the desk, not altogether surprised to find some of them much lighter than they should have been.

She emptied the stash, began going through the bags. At least half of them were plumped out with crumpled paper, there to make a show. She tossed these back inside the hole, put the others in the shoulderbag she'd cobbled together from a pillow sham and some strapping.

> < <

Penhari looked at the piles of coin scattered about the bed. Not much gold left in the mix, mostly silver and copper. Abey be blessed, the last sack still had its fifty-two gold pieces intact; the General hadn't had time to raid that one. "How am I going to work this? I'm going to have to trust her, that's all." She counted out the fifty silver cems for the boatman and his boat, set that aside, counted a hundred more of the broad silver coins, added two gold millefurs, tied them up in a bag, they were Desantro's fee. She took the rest back to the sham-sack and closed the panel on it. It was as safe there as in her jewelry box, safer probably.

She dropped on the bed, rubbed her hand across her face, then grimaced at the streaks of black dust and sweat. *Bath. Then work on the clothing, get the jewels tucked away. I can sleep in the daytime. Five days. It sounded like forever when Desantro said it. Abey's Sting, I'm going to have to work my fingers off.*

>><<

About an hour after sundown on the Vungian festa on the night of the Moondark, a tall, bent old woman dressed in coarse gray trudged out of the Falmatarr behind another, younger slave.

"Hsst." Desantro tugged at Penhari's sleeve. "Slow down," she whispered, " 'tisn't a race. Keep y' head down. You forgetting everything."

Penhari nodded, her enveloping cloak shifting against her shoulders as her head bobbed. She pulled the edges together again over the worn blouse and skirt Desantro had found for her. She was stifling in these layers of clothing, weighed down by everything she had stowed about her body, and she was sweating from excitement and an unfocused terror, her stomach knotting and burning.

The streets they hurried along were canyons between straight black walls of the Fundarim and Naostam towers, warrens that housed the Corasso poor, packed together in uneasy masses. The noise from the towers was partially muffled by the stone, but it fell on them like clubs as they went past.

"Is the city always this noisy?" Penhari murmured.

"Folk been moving off land, can't crop it without water. We turn here." Desantro tugged Penhari down a smaller side street. "Don't want to get mixed with crowd at Sok Circle. Only place they c'n go is with their kin, so there's two three times as many bodies shoved in there. That's a rowdy crowd. At the Circle, I mean. During festas."

Penhari tugged the frayed veil so she could see through the uneven eyeholes. Desantro sounded wistful, as if she'd like to be there, plunged into the middle of that noise and motion.

She followed Desantro through turn after turn, sweat streaming off her.

In the beginning she hadn't felt the weight of what she was carrying, gold coins packed into straps and wound around her legs, jewelry and more coins sewed into a thickly padded underskirt, the rolls of clothing and other items wrapped around her body, bulking out her lean Maulapam form, but after half an hour of walking, she was trembling and panting, hobbling along, moving by will alone, her knees creaking and her feet aching. *All those years of sitting about with my feet up, they're going to kill me yet.*

Desantro stopped in the inky shadow at the side of a shuttered shop that fronted on Gate Street. "Hang on a moment," she murmured. She gave Penhari a quick look-over, clicked her tongue. "You all right?"

"I'll last, don't worry. Why are we stopping?"

"There're guards at the Gate. They don't mess with people much, but y' never know. Nobody coming 'long Gate Street right now. We sh'd wait till there's a bunch going out, hitch onto it. That's the safest way."

"Vema." Penhari sighed, eased her shoulders against the wall. "How long?"

Desantro listened. "Hear that? That's a big mob coming. We gotta keep up with 'em. Can y' do it?"

"I'll do what I have to." *Brave words, I hope they're not whistling at the moon. Abey's Sting! If I fall on my face. . . .*

They left the side street and tagged after a laughing, dancing, teasing mob of young, newly-made Fundarim journeymen and a sprinkling of young women who were veiled after a fashion as a concession to the new rules, all of them noisily celebrating the the elevation of two of their members.

The mob reveled through the Gate, exchanging garbled shouts with guards leaning from the vigil windows of their turrets.

No one noticed the bulky gray figures hurrying along at the tail of that parade.

Desantro plunged into the Fringe, a maze of mud and stone houses plastered like mud-dauber nests on the waste land between the black basalt walls and the widening ring of mud at the edge of the Lake-That-Never-Fails; there were no straight streets, only narrow, eccentrically wandering wynds between the shapeless structures.

Penhari labored behind her as long as she could, then collapsed against a crumbling mud wall; she tugged the veil off, let it drop beside her and gulped in mouthful after mouthful of the hot stinking air, whining and rasping, spots wheeling and vibrating before her eyes.

Desantro came rushing back, stood over her, said something.

Penhari couldn't make out what she was saying, the blood was too loud in her ears. She managed to lift a hand, palm out. "It's ju . . ." Breath whistled out and her struggling lungs sucked in more. "Ju . . . huuuuu .. ju . . . st . . . haaaaa . . . nee . . . eed . . . huuu . . . catch . . . haaaaa . . breath!"

Desantro thrust a muscular shoulder under Penhari's arm, pulled her away from the wall, and eased her down so she was sitting on the sun-baked soil. "Whew, that stuff must weigh a ton. Y' shoulda said something."

Penhari rolled her head back and forth, tried to smile. She lifted an arm that seemed to have turned to lead, tried to wipe away the sweat that was dripping into her eyes.

Desantro clicked tongue against teeth, felt around for the veil Penhari had discarded. She shook the dust off it, wiped gently at the older woman's face. "Next time," she said, "don't be such an idiot. If you faint on me, what'n jannan am I s'posed to do?"

"Ve . . . ha . . . ma."

"Good. You sit there a minute, make believe you a poor ol' fat woman with no place t' go. Here," she wrung out the ragged veil, dropped it over Penhari's head, "way it goes, y' have t' have this. Think poor, if y' can, think I got nothing to lose so I don't give a jegg what anyone do. There's a jugshop a couple wynds over, I'm gonna get you some mulimuli, that'll have y' on y' feet and dancing." She tapped Penhari on the shoulder and went trotting off.

Penhari sat in the noisome dark, the noises of life loud and all around her, unseen but very much THERE. Murmurs. Laughter. Shouts. Screams. Howls and yowls. She was getting frightened, sitting there alone and out in the open. Desantro said be calm. Don't give in t' being afraid. Being afraid's dangerous. But this was so strange, so unlike anything she'd ever experienced, she twitched at every sound. And the smell was terrible. Appalling. Nauseating. How people could live in this kind of squalor was something she couldn't understand. It wouldn't take all that much effort to sweep away the garbage rotting in piles around her. Why didn't someone just do it? She cringed from the thought of what she was sitting on, what this dirt beneath her was made of, this hard crusty soil with not even a gesture at paving.

The tremors in her arms and legs were smoothing out and her breathing was steadying. She pulled her legs up and rested her head on arms she folded across her knees. Watching Desantro dance that day had wakened in her the sense that there was an immense ocean of life lapping against the walls of the Falmatarr but never coming inside. Now, suddenly, she was plunged into that life and finding it was one thing to dream of fleeing to freedom, but something else entirely to sit in the filth of this wynd with a stitch in her side and the shakes in every limb. *I could go back. I could knock on the door and show my face and this would all be over. Hot bath, iced lemonade . . . Abey's Sting, I'd grovel for a drink right now.* She closed her eyes and mentally wallowed in the comforts of her old life.

Reality catching up with me. What a choice. Famtoche's fists or this kind of thing for the rest of my life. She lifted her head. "No!" she said aloud and startled a squat old woman picking her way along the wynd, dragging a canvas sack behind her; gray hair straggling about a greasy, lined faced hardly visible in the darkness, hands in knotted-string mitts, the old woman glanced briefly at her, dismissed her, and went on down the wynd.

"No," Penhari whispered to herself. "No, I won't end like you. I refuse the possibility. There must be some way. . . ." She moved her head back, rested it against the wall, settling herself to wait.

> > < <

"Here, drink this. Anything happen while I was gone?"

"Old woman, two cats, and a drunk who spat at me. By luck he missed." Penhari took a mouthful of the mulimuli, sputtered with shock. Some of it went down her front, the rest down her gullet, burning as it dropped. "Gah, what foul koj. People actually drink this slop?"

"You s'posed to toss it down so it hits you belly before y' taste it. C'm on, Zazi, drink some more, it'll put stiffening in y' bones. We gotta get to boat, or he'll take off without us."

>> <<

Penhari tugged the veil tighter against her face so she could see through the eyeholes. A boat swinging lazily at the end of the stubby pier had a single mast with a frayed sail hanging in messy folds over the boom. Sitting on a bitt, kicking bare heels against it, a short skinny Naostam was watching them.

Desantro left her hobbling along the planks and charged down the pier to confront the man. "Where your jeggin' water skins, hanh?" She jabbed an accusing finger at the anonymous clutter in the bottom of the boat. "You been paid f'r it. We jannin an't gonna drink mud."

His eyes shifted under a Naostam's heavy brow ridge, the yellowed whites gleaming intermittently as they moved. With a silent insolence embedded in an exaggerated physical competence, he got to his feet, bent, caught hold of a rope tied to a cleat on the bitt and lifted, the muscles in his bare arm shifting like skinny snakes beneath his copper hide. Three dripping water skins rose from the lake. He held them up with one hand, yanked the knot loose, then lowered the skins into the boat. He swung over the edge, went down a few steps of the slimy ladder and jumped lightly into the boat, landing so evenly balanced that it hardly rocked.

He leaned over, hooked a hand over the lowest rung, and pulled the boat tight against the the ladder. And stood there waiting for them to climb down or go away, whichever pleased them.

Desantro snorted, but she didn't comment. "Zazi, I'm going first so I c'n give you a hand. Hang onto the ladder till him and I steady you. We'll get y' in, don't worry.

Penhari leaned on the bitt and watched her go down the ladder neatly and easily despite the gear she was carrying, the food and more clothing and her fee in coin and no doubt other things she liberated from the Falmatarr. She swung into the boat with an ease that almost matched the man's, slapped his shoulder and pointed up at Penhari.

Time to move. Honey Mother defend me. She lowered herself to hands and knees, reached backward with one foot until she could feel the rung; grunting and fumbling about, she finally got both feet on the ladder and started clumsily down it. The rungs were slimy with moss and smashed crawlers; she loathed having to touch them, but she told herself: I can do whatever has to be done. She said it under her breath several times as she lowered herself, but never fully believed it, even when she felt hands on her, steadying her, taking part of her weight and in the end lifting her bodily into the boat, getting her seated on a folded square of canvas placed a few inches before the mast.

Desantro knelt beside Penhari, wiping her hands with a damp cloth, fussing over her like a mother with a sickly child; she looked across the older woman's shoulder, popped out her breath in an impatient tssht!

The Naostam sat by the steering oar, watching stolidly; he might have been carved from red sida-wood except for the occasional glimmer from his eyes.

"What y' waiting for, Hahlaz? Get the sail up, le's get going, huh?"

"Women," he said and spat over the side; his voice

was reedy, with as much modulation as there was expression in his face. "Gi' penter a jerk, she come loose. An' siddown. Y' fall in, it y'r problem. Been paid f'r Pili, not f'r swanin' about."

The night was calm and hot. The boat zagged across the northern end of the Lake-That-Never-Fails, catching the vagrant breezes and using the fugitive currents to work toward the twin black towers that marked the beginning of the River.

Penhari leaned against the mast, feeling every shimmy and twist of the boat through her spine; she was deeply relaxed now, a heap of cous-cous without a bone in view, but she wasn't sleepy—her mind cycled around and around all the thoughts that had passed through her head from the moment she surfaced after the beating, leapt from that to what lay ahead, compulsive speculation insecurely based on stories from her scrolls and the few books she'd managed to get her hands on, leapt back to the pain and fear she was escaping from. Past and future, equally futile, over and over until she rebelled against treading the same ruts again and began noticing what was happening around her.

Her body was shifting with the boat, ballasted by the gold, tilting one way, then another, as the boom slammed side to side behind her, the sail bellying out, sinking, popping out again. At first she didn't understand this to-ing and fro-ing, but she had the habit of study, so she watched carefully what the man was doing and considered the results of those actions.

What wind there was came into her face, not from behind, wind out of the east—yet they were moving into the east. There had to be a reason. She listened to the sounds the sail made, looked over her shoulder at it, considered the way Hahlaz shifted the angle of the boom, how he turned the ship and sent the boom crashing to the other side, how they kept gliding forward, the black ward-towers getting closer and closer.

After an hour of this she had some understanding of the principles involved, along with an itch in her palms to take hold of the rudder and that rope and do it herself. It was frustrating sitting there, letting herself be carried along by someone else's skill. *But what else have I done all my life? Let my maids coddle me, the Kassians guide my thinking, Desantro carry me. Now that man. Who despises both of us. Abey's Sting, fifty-two years and I'm still in the egg.*

Desantro was sitting on the other side of the mast, watching Hahlaz, turning occasionally to see what was happening in front of them. "What about those?" She swung her arm, her finger sweeping from tower to tower. "Trouble?"

"Naah. Nobody home. Jeggin' guards like soft livin, an't gonna fry nuh'ms off way out here."

"Good." She settled back. "Zazi, how you doing?"

"Not bad. I'm starting to enjoy this."

Desantro laughed. "Choo-ee, swanning Ma."

> > < <

Penhari woke cramped and stiff with her bladder distended, an ache throbbing over her ears, her tongue a dead mouse in her mouth. *Mulimuli! Never again.* The boat was moving slowly around a long shallow curve, the land on both sides of the River flat and dull, no green, just shades of brown. Even the few trees that grew on the banks were half dead, the remaining leaves thick-skinned and gray with dust, hanging limply from dessicated petioles. The sun was molten and red, only halfway up, the peaks of the Kondunis like jagged black teeth across the disk, but the day was already so hot and dry she could feel cracks opening in her skin.

She eased out of the slump, moving carefully so she wouldn't wet herself. "Desa," she croaked.

"Water, Zazi?" Desantro cleared her throat, shifted enough to put a gulp in the smooth glide of the boat.

"Water I need to get rid of."

Desantro clicked her tongue, shifted again. "Hahlaz. Hai!"

"Gnuh."

"That bunch trees, c'd y' make it? Pull in over there?"

"Thought you in a hurry."

"Hurry's over. Hai, turn this thing."

"Old fish landing round next bend. Trees 'n a shack."

Desantro snorted. "Gotcha. Do it."

> > < <

Hahlaz squatted by a ring of smoke-blackened stones, shaving curls off a piece of the shack's door.

Penhari was so stiff she could barely walk. She'd been heaved out of the boat like a bale of cloth and now she had to lean on Desantro's arm or she couldn't have put one foot in front of the other. When they were behind the shack, she stopped. "This is enough. Help me out of these windings, will you? I'm about to add heatstroke to everything else."

Desantro took the cloak, snapped it out flat on the ground, then started unwinding the spare clothing from under the blouse.

As the wandering breeze stirred over her sweaty skin, Penhari sighed with pleasure. "Abey! It's almost worth it just for this."

Desantro chuckled, helped Penhari out of the under-skirt; she didn't comment at the weight, just dropped it on the rest of the pile. She rolled the cloak and its contents into a neat bundle, set it near the corner of the shack. "Can you wait a minute more?"

"If I have to."

"We need some dry leaves for wiping. I know you used to water and towels, Zazi, but you roughing it now." She went hurrying off into the scatter of trees.

Penhari leaned cautiously against the wall; it creaked but it held. There was a touch of satisfaction in Desantro's voice. *Talk about enjoying this. Should I worry? Nayo. She's a kind creature, she wouldn't do me harm. Discomfort doesn't count. Or humiliation. Getting her own back. Or a piece of it. Wouldn't I, too, if I were her? Oh, Jannam, do I ache. Hurry up, woman, I don't think I can hold it any longer.*

Desantro came hurrying out of the trees, her hands full of decaying leaves. "Here," she said when she reached Penhari, "you crumple them like this. Make a wad outta them." She grinned, her face flushed. "I learned that when I was hardly hatched. You do your thing and I'll go see what Hahlaz has got up to."

> > < <

Penhari squatted and let go, feeling more pleasure as the urine hissed than she'd ever got from sex.

She followed instructions as best she could, crumpled the leaves together, but either she did something wrong or Fadogur trees weren't like those in Whenapoyr; the leaves broke into fragments that clung and started scratching her and absorbed nothing. She used the ragged veil to finish the job and flung it away; she hated the thing anyway.

She stretched, groaned as her muscles protested, opened and shut her hands, shook herself. All that padding and weight off her body made her feel almost a girl again. She danced a few steps, the coarse gray skirt flaring out from her long thin legs, shifted into the moves Desantro showed her in the garden that day, stamping and kicking and swinging in circles. *Diyo, diyo, I can do it, I can do this, I can, I can, diyo dé, I can do it.*

Chuckling and breathless, she scooped up the bundle, grunting at the weight of it, and started round the shack.

> > < <

Hahlaz was adding a few twigs to the small fire hissing beneath a battered copper pot while Desantro slapped the stopple back in the spout of one of the water skins. As she bent with an easy shift of her body to set the depleted skin beside the others, she smiled at Penhari. "Feeling better?"

Hahlaz looked up, froze. A second later he was on his feet, running at Penhari with his knife out, shrieking, "MAAAAAAL!"

Desantro gasped and dropped to one knee, caught up a stone from the ring about the fire, flung it with hard accuracy at his head.

It hit him behind the ear with a dull thump.

He fell, sprawled, hands coming open, knife dropping hilt down beside him.

Penhari stood clutching the bundle to her middle, her mouth open, too startled to be afraid.

Desantro scrambled to her feet, ran the few steps to the unconscious man. She knelt beside him, felt under his chin, swore in her home tongue, looked up. "The jegger's still alive."

Penhari licked her lips. "Why?"

"Come at you?" Desantro shifted her position, pulled her skirt closer to her legs. "Face it, hesla. Mals an't the favorite people outside the Sirmalas." She grunted with satisfaction as she saw the knife. "No doubt he had his reasons." She wound a hand in Hah-

laz's hair, jerked his head up and away from her, and
cut his throat.

"Desa!"

Desantro wiped the knife on his shirt, set it down
away from the body. "I'm done with being slave,"
she said. She jumped to her feet. "Couldn't trust him
after this. He'd a killed you and sold me first chance
he got. Put that down and come over here. Help me
carry him."

"I don't. . . ." Penhari gazed in bewilderment at the
bundle she was clutching to her middle. "I. . . ."

"Move ass, woman. I owe y' something; I coon't be
getting loose without the coin. But I swear if you don't
get y' tail over here and grab those ankles, I'm outta
this, you c'n do what y' want."

They carried the body into the middle of the grove,
heaped leaves over it. Desantro left immediately, but
Penhari stood beside the mound for several moments,
trying to work out a way of living with what had happened. The last remnants of the indifference and with-
drawal she'd cultivated for decades were wiped away.
She'd faced shock after shock. The beating. The death
of her handmaids and the Kassian who was her closest
friend. The exhaustion, the alternating terror and exhilaration, of the escape. Now this slaughter—with her the
trigger that brought it on. . . .

She turned hastily away, leaned against a tree and
vomited up a few spoonfuls of yellow bile, then shuddered with dry heaves.

> > < <

Desantro was squatting beside the fire, stirring something in the pot; she looked up as Penhari came round
the shack. "You all right?"

"Not happy, but surviving. What are you doing?"

"Making tucker tea. The kind that crawls out the
pot if y' an't careful. I cut bread and cheese. 'S over

there." She nodded toward a board laid a short distance off. "You better eat something. Long day ahead of us."

"Eat." Penhari shuddered.

Desantro's face went hard, her eyes glittered. "Diyo. Eat. My mother was raped and murdered before m' face. I ate. Long as I stayed alive, I knew some day Hennermen would die. You told me I can do what I havta. Well, do 't."

Penhari pulled a hand across her face. "Tsah! I was thinking heroics, Desa. Eating didn't come to mind. Nayo nay." She fluttered a hand at Desantro. "Give me time. I've spent years being a slug. It slows you down, that kind of thing."

Desantro's mouth twitched, her expression softened. "Never met a galloping slug." She wrapped a scrap of cloth about the pot's handle, poured some of the turgid brown liquid into a cracked mug. "Here. Drink a this and you be dancing on water."

Penhari looked into the mug. "Do I kill it first?"

"Nay, jus' cut it with that bread 'n cheese. Now do it. . . ." She stopped talking as a small sailboat nosed round bend, out in the middle of the River, a leadman in the stern taking soundings. "Zaz, turn round, y' back to the River. And sit." She flung a cloth over her head and brought the end around her face, then calmly poured herself a cup of the tucker tea and set the pot on the ground beside her.

Penhari swung round and dropped into a squat beside the bread board, her shoulders hunched, her head drawn down. "What's happening?"

"Barge coming up River. Look over top a those trees, left side, you can see tip a the mainsail. That there going past us, that's a lead boat. River being low like it is, barge has to stick to the deepest part, they draw lotta water, them. Leadman reads channel." She laughed suddenly; danger and death seemed to spin her high. Penhari glanced at her, but Desantro's eyes were lost in the shadow of the cloth, so there was nothing there to read. "Father a my third kid was leadman, we got together at festa. Midsummer. Lakeshore. Anyway, 'tween this 'n that, I learned more 'an I want to know 'bout leadmen."

Penhari ventured a sip of the tea. It was thick and bitter, but her mouth felt clean once she swallowed it. She reached for a hunk of bread and some cheese and ate quietly, listening to the splashes and creaks from the River behind her. "Desa, there's one thing I don't understand, and the longer I know you, the less I understand it. Why didn't you get out a long time ago? The money can't have been that important."

Desantro snorted. "Mal."

"Vema then, it was. Still . . ."

"Why did you stay?"

Penhari blinked. "Because there was no reason to leave," she said slowly. "I'd made a comfortable and reasonably bearable life for myself."

"Same thing. I like plants. 'M good with them. Full belly and no bothering. Y' gardener, he double-dance with Salagaum so he leaves me alone. Through m' first two kids, I was hot t' get out, kill me some Hennermen. Find m' kin, get 'em loose an' go home. Got the five-tail on m' back 'bout every month. After a while, though, I jus' got tired. That's all."

Penhari nodded. "Tired, diyo. I know that feeling."

"Weerah! Temple barge. Nayo! Don't turn around. Some mippy type up on deck, sitting with nose in book an' half a dozen little 'uns waving fans at him. Chooee, they creeping, 'bout 'nough wind t' blow out match. Air gets lighter, poor jeggin sailormans, they'll be out front rowing and towing."

Penhari took another sip of the cooling tea, grimaced. Its bitter bite was getting to be too much for her. "What are the colors of the ensign?"

"Huh?"

"There should be a banner of some kind near the front end."

"Diyo. I see it. Hard to say, it's all crumpled together. Um. Some blue an' some green, there's another . . . ah, there 'tis. A dart of red."

"Quiambo, then. Must be Prime Korongo; he spends half the year in Pili, half in Corasso. So Faharmoy said. When he was still talking to me." After Desantro was pointedly silent for several breaths, Penhari added, "My so-loving son. Thinks he's a Prophet now, goes about flogging people for their sins. Down in Pili. We'll have to avoid him."

"Some family."

"Mmp."

The barge crept past keeping near the far bank of the long bend where the current had scoured a deeper channel, the sailors and the others on board ignoring the dumpy gray figures by the old landing.

> > < <

"Careful, Desa! I don't know if you can swim, but I surely cannot."

The sail lay limp and fluttering against the mast as Desantro struggled with the rope coming off the boom. It was hitched about a cleat with a knot she didn't know; it seemed to have swelled in place and might as well have been glued there.

She swore as she knocked another knuckle against the cleat and ripped off more skin. "Another minute a this and I take a knife to the jeggin' thing. Ahhhh." The knot suddenly came apart in her fingers, she turned to grin at Penhari and nearly got kicked in the head as the rope rushed through her fingers and the boom went crashing around. The sail filled as she closed her hand on the rope and they were suddenly going backward, heading for the far bank.

Penhari leaned on the tiller, yelled, "Desa! bring it

round like it was before. Sting!'' Hastily she shoved the tiller the other way as the turn to land grew sharper.

The sail began to slat and shudder as Desantro fought with the rope, then it seemed to vomit the air and go limp. The current took them again and they drifted back the way they'd come.

"Choo-ee, Zaz, maybe we'd better let River take us. We don't either a us have a clue 'bout handling this thing.''

"Nayo, we can't afford the delay. Hang onto the rope, wrap it round your hand or put the end under your knee or something. And let the boom swing out a little, other side this time, just a little, till the end's about halfway between the mast and the side. Vema, vema, good, that's it, there we go, little more. Hah! nothing like learn by doing, eh, Desa?''

They went downRiver in a series of jags and jerks and almost disasters, the bends in the River, the shifts in direction the changing winds all giving them moments of high terror and equally high exhilaration when they survived.

The land on both sides of the River was parched, dead and empty, the small landings they came across were deserted and starting to fall apart under the punishing sun. There was no shade in the boat; Desantro dug into Penhari's bundle and tore up one of her spare skirts, dipped the cloth into the River and fashioned turbans for them which she kept wet by filling Hahlaz's copper pot and splashing the water over her head and Penhari's.

>><<

Sundown.

Penhari moved her aching shoulders. "Well, Desa, what do you think? It's Moondark still and the wind's picking up. You want to stop for the night, or shall we take a chance?''

Desantro unwound her turban, dropped the damp cloth into her lap and ran her hands through her thick curly hair. "We could take turns sleeping . . . mmm .. I have a feeling . . . le's keep going, far as we can."

Curled up in the windowseat at one end of the long, narrow parlor, waiting for Dossan and Ma'teesee to finish packing their baskets in the kitchen, Faan stroked her hand along Ailiki's back and watched with satisfaction tempered by anxiety as the rain hissed down on the small garden outside. It would keep the pests in shelter, chase them away from the Beehouse. Most of them anyway. They weren't THAT eager for her company. Though sometimes she wondered how far they'd go. Women, a lot of them, waving beadstrings for her to bless, waggling their children at her. Bless them, she thought, more likely I'll get them killed.

One good thing, rain meant Abeyhamal was too busy herding clouds to start the Dance again. Anyway SHE'd been quiet for over a week now—as if she were waiting for something.

Faan scratched behind Ailiki's ears and let her irritation flow away. Rain was rest, but if the downpour didn't let up soon, she and the others would get wet and that was the same as shouting they'd come out of the Low City, which wasn't healthy in the Northbank Edge.

Such a stupid thing. Just because the Mums were slaves and their owners wouldn't bring them or give them leave to come, they couldn't cross the Wood Bridge. The Barrier stopped them. Like it stopped Reyna and Dawa. Stupid!

She sighed. Reyna was right. Nothing you could do about it. Abeyhamal was horribly powerful, but thick as a rock. Arguing with her was like butting your head against a mud wall. "You knock off a little dust," she told the mahsar curled in her lap, "but the wall just sits there and all you get for your trouble is a roaring headache."

She made a face, wiped the back of her hand along the window glass where her breath was making a patch of fog. Ailiki pushed at her arm with her cold nose, made sounds like *more more more*. Faan laughed and smoothed her hand along the mahsar's back.

Tai had prowled the Southbank Edge until she found this house and moved them in. The Low City squatters were annoyed with her for refusing a fancier place near the largest of the Sacred Groves, but Tai paid no attention to their grousing. Control, she told Faan, that's what they want. They want us surrounded, where they can get their hands on us any time they feel like it. Especially you, child. Well, let them want.

The new Beehouse was a low rambling structure with rooms like beads on a string laid out in a double spiral with pocket gardens of trees and flowers and grass, more grass with mossrose borders along the paths. Faan didn't like it much. Having to walk along arcs to go from room to room irritated her. And she missed Reyna and the others. Jea she never saw; she didn't know why, maybe because he was shamed that he was here, safe, while Rayna and Dawa were kept out. Sometimes when she lay in bed at night and the loneliness got to her, she thought about trying to find him and talk to him, but she never did.

Loneliness. Dossan and Ma'teesee were her best friends, but they weren't part of the Beehouse like the Salagaum had been; they just lived here and went out to work at the same kind of thing they'd been doing on the Northbank. And there was SO much she couldn't talk to them about. And they were changing. Ma'teesee's jokes weren't that funny any more; they were getting mean. Dossy was out a lot, running around

with farmboys; she didn't listen even when she was
here. Always thinking about something else. And Tai
was always busy. Besides, talking to her was like talking to the god; it turned Faan's stomach when she
thought about it. Why did everything have to go so rot-
ten!

The rain lost force, diminished to an intermittent
drip.

Dossan came in, followed by Ma'teesee.

"Fa, you ready?" Dossan's voice was hoarse from
the remnants of the cold she'd got from dancing in the
rain with that Miugi she was so dotty about these days;
she was tired and in a temper. She jabbed her elbow
toward Ma'teesee's ribs. "This one would dawdle on
her deathbed."

Ma'teesee winked at Faan, pulled her wide mouth
into an inverted curve. "Moon's got her, huh. Takes
her temper out to sea."

Faan slid off the seat, Ailiki flowing down beside her;
she reached back, thrust her arm through the basket of
fresh greens and herbs she was taking to Reyna. "Just
as well you took more time," she said as she crossed
the room. "The rain's stopping."

>><<

The three cloaked figures hurried along the wynds of
SouthEdge, Ailiki riding unsteadily on Faan's shoulder.
Except for several herds of young boys stamping the
puddles, throwing mud at each other, using broken cob-
bles to scratch insults and their vaunt-names onto the
walls, there were few people out. The peddlers had
rolled their carts or hauled their bags to the nearest
shelter, the old men and women had taken their gossip
inside, drunks and visiting sailors had learned to stay
at tavern tables during the hours each day when the
thunderstorms swept the Low City.

Near the Wood Bridge, Faan handed her basket to

Dossan, tapped Ailiki off her shoulder and folded her cloak back so her hands and arms were free. Thieves sometimes lay in ambush here to catch newcomers at their most confused and vulnerable; several times she'd had to singe muggers who tried to jump the three of them as they went back and forth across the Bridge.

There was no sign anyone was about. Which was a relief; she'd improved her control since she ashed the man on the Jang, but she never felt sure of her hold on those capricious and deadly flamelets.

Stepping onto the Bridge was like stepping into an oven. Panting and drenched with sweat, they hurried up and over the high arch. Beneath them the River was a grayish-brown, an unpleasant smell drifting up from the muddy water. There were a few coasters tied up at the Southbank wharves, only one on the north side, at the Temple Landing, east of the Iron Bridge. The fish-boats were gone; they were down in the Koo Bikiyar and wouldn't be back till tomorrow night. It was a two-day trip now; everything near the mouth of the River was either dead or too poisoned to eat.

The Wild Magic came swirling up as Faan passed the midpoint, went shooting by her in a silver-gray arrow; they slipped between the Approach Pillars on the Northbank and spread into a cloud that shimmered a neutral gray.

Ma'teesee shifted her basket to her other arm, made a face at the fine mist at the end of the Bridge. "I hate going through that stuff, Fa. Makes me feel itchy."

Faan slapped at her friend's arm. "Not stuff, Teesee. I told you. People. Wildings."

"I see stuff, I call it stuff. Hunh."

"Tsah, Teesee, they're just telling us there's no prob-lem that end. No STRIKER bands hanging about."

Dossan snorted. "Don't waste y' breath, Fa."

Ma'teesee pinched her arm, swung around, and danced backward. "Choo-eee choo-ee, Miugi the

Lump,'' she chanted, ''dump her, ooh hee he dump her, dump her, dump her, dump her.''

''Shut up, Teesee.'' Faan put her hand on Dossan's arm. ''You all right, Dossy?''

Dossan glowered at the worn wood mosaic of the Bridge floor, shrugged Faan's hand off, walked on a few steps. ''I don't want to talk about it,'' she said finally.

They trotted from the Approach and turned into the nearest wynd, walked quickly along it, a few of the Wildings drifting with Faan, flittering about her like flies. Ailiki swung her head from side to side as she trotted along, now and then baring her teeth and hissing at the hovering specks.

> < <

They rounded the end of a tenement, shied to the far side of the wynd as four looters came through a window.

The leader grinned and started for them.

Faan let fire flutter on the backs of her hands and the skinny, scarred boys went gliding off, vanishing into shadow before they'd gone half a dozen steps.

Ma'teesee clicked her tongue. ''Yaras,'' she whispered. ''I wonder who they got?''

Dossan glanced over her shoulder, shivered. ''Every time I see something like that, I think it could as easy be Mum's place.'' She hugged the two baskets closer against her, hurried ahead of the others.

''Buzzit, Teesee,'' Faan muttered. ''Likely one of 'em has a paymaster in a STRIKER band.''

''Choo-ee.'' Ma'teesee pulled the cloak closer around her and hurried after Dossan. ''Fa, you don't think. . . .''

''Rey said. . . .'' Faan trotted past the two girls, slowed, but kept a step ahead of them. ''. . . everything over here's chance these days. You don't know who's buying what with your life.''

Ma'teesee shifted the basket, rubbed at the red mark on her arm. "That jeggin' Barrier, what's Honey Mother thinking. . . ."

"T's! I don't know. I don't even care any more. Wait here a minute." She ran along the last bend of the wynd and stopped in the shadow of the tenement, frowning along Verakay Lane. "Good. They're setting out the barrels now and . . . ah . . . Mutri Maship and his band, they just this minute come out of Peshalla's Tavern. Soon's they get started, we can cut across the lane."

> > < <

Dossan gave Faan the basket she'd carried for her, whistled a quick trill, repeated it, waited.

The kitchen door opened a crack; it was dark inside except for the leftover sunset filtering in through the dusty, cramped windows.

A vague figure peered through the crack, whispered hoarsely. "Dossy?" Fasirill, Dossan's mother.

"Diyo, Mum."

"Shh, Dossy." The door opened a few grudging inches more. "He's drunk. Come on in, quick."

Faan pushed Ma'teesee ahead of her, turned, and waved to Dossan. "See you 'n an hour, Dossy."

> > < <

Ma'teesee banged on the back door. "Mum" she called, keeping her voice low, "come on, open up."

Faan's mouth thinned as she heard the undercurrent of pleading in her friend's voice; it was the same every time. Though she came on the same day each week, almost the same hour, half the time Ogadeyl forgot her daughter was due; she was fond enough of Ma'teesee, but the girl was simply not important to her.

"Teesee." Ogadeyl's high sweet voice floated into

the dusk as the door swung inward and the lanterns of
the kitchen painted a yellow rectangle on the rutted
wynd. She was a pretty woman, small-boned, skin like
amber velvet, more charm than Ma'teesee would ever
have.

"Loa, Mum." Ma'teesee moved quickly inside,
turned and waved to Faan before she pulled the door
shut. "See y' 'n a hour."

> > < <

Faan heard the music blare out and the singing begin
before she reached Verakay Lane; she shook her head,
irritated by the bubble people that flitted about her.
"Flies around a carcass," she said to Ailiki; the mahsar
reared on her hindlegs, snapped her teeth at a floating
mote. Faan laughed, shook her head again. To the
Wildings she said: *You'd better go back to your sisters,
little ones. I appreciate the warding, but I'll be safer
on the Lane if I'm not noticed.Nay nay,* they chorused in
tiny whining voices, *canna canna do. SHE say hanga with you.
True true.*

Faan sighed. *So tuck yourself in under the cloak and
keep out of sight. What SHE says, we do, but we don't
have to flaunt it.*There were three or four bonfires burning in the middle of the Lane, fueled by wood torn from
abandoned houses. On the boardwalk the Taverners and
Mulemen had set up planks on barrels as temporary
bars. There was a curfew of sorts in the Edge, decreed
by the Prophet and enforced by the STRIKER bands.
All businesses had to be closed at sundown or they'd be
burned out and their owners flogged. The drinksellers
and the pimps got around this by moving their stock
outside. None of them liked it, but the dark was their
time and they weren't about to let the profits go.

Mama Kubaza and Mutri Maship were out with their
musicians and dancers, slave women who doubled as

habatrizes between sets, taking their customers into one or another of the burnt-out buildings.

The customers were sailors bored by the tame night-life in the SouthEdge, slaves and tied-workers from the Maulapam Sirmalas, young Biasharim and Cheoshim—some of whom were in the STRIKER bands by day, drawn to the violence then as they were to the vice after dark. No real crowds, but enough custom to let the Edgers keep existing.

Ailiki gliding behind her, Faan slipped into the Lane, her cloak pulled close about her, the basket beneath it, out of sight. Verakay was dangerous for a girl alone, but the wynds and ways around it were worse; at least there was some light here and people about.

Dressed in gold tissue trousers and vest, Mutri Ma-ship stood on an upended barrel, swaying to make the sequins glitter on his vest and along his arms, singing Kalele style while his drummers tapped and brushed and the daround player's fingers crabbed across the strings so fast the blurred. *OU SING ZUUL,* Maship sang, almost shouting to break through the noise of voices and Mama's Band, though he kept an icing of lyric tone, *NA GID A MEE YUN. OU SING ZUUL GIDDA MEEYIN.*

Three young women in studded dresses danced in front of the musicians, two of them moving with lazy twists and turns to show off their bodies to the men gathering around. The third was different. She was lost in the music and happy inside her skin, enjoying the play of her muscles, bare feet stamping, kicking high, body wheeling through flips where no part of her touched the rutted dirt; a film of sweat spread over her face and arms and she seemed to glow with pleasure.

Faan stopped to watch her, smiling for the first time since she crossed the Bridge. Then a Cheoshim youth more than half drunk bumped into her, grabbed at her. Ailiki hissed a warning, raked her teeth along his leg, slicing through cloth into muscle. Faan hurried on, keeping close to the buildings, flitting from shadow to shadow, reminded that this was no longer her home-place.

When she reached Bamampah the Woodman's abandoned compound, she ran round the back, touched the gate and plunged in as soon as it flew open, Ailiki trotting beside her, tail high, a satisfied grin on her small flat face.

Reyna, Dawa and several other Salagaum had moved into the Woodhouse when Bamampah packed up his lathes and benches and everything else he could stuff in handcarts and trundled his household and business across the Wood Bridge into SouthEdge. Woodhouse was a big place with a tall brick wall around it and heavy gates of ironbound hapuawood, reasonably safe from the Prophet's torchmen and from Shindate persecution, though the Shinda Prefecture was too weak and disrupted these days to make a serious nuisance of itself.

During the day this back yard was a busy place. Using the Salagaum as his labor force, Reyna ran an infirmary from the larder next the kitchen, got sacks of food to Edge families and anyone else who needed it, and—through a web of abosoa kassos as poor as their neighbors—issued forged silver coins to buy the little water that came down the aqueducts into cisterns of the Shinda Prefecture.

Faan hauled the heavy gate shut again and slapped her hand against the wood, willing the bars into place. She didn't wait to see them chunk home, but moved quickly past the supply sheds to the kitchen door.

Thammir and Raxzin were sitting at the kitchen table sharing a pot of tea and waiting for the wash water to boil—wash water because Faan could see jugs standing beside the sink with stained cloths draped over the wide mouths. Like the rest of the Edge, Woodhouse Salagaum used River water for everything but drinking and like them strained and boiled it first; with all the abandoned and half-charred houses about, firewood was cheaper than good water.

Thammir looked up, grinned. He was a little Salagaum with hair like copper fuzz and the yellow eyes of a cat; here in the house he wore Salagaum dress again, a long white robe with a wide red leather belt cinched tight about a narrow waist. The apron he had ready for the washing up was bunched on the table beside his cup. "How's it goin, Fa?" His voice was a basso rumble, so deep it sounded as if he were growling.

Faan waggled her hand at him. "So so," she said. "Reyna in?" Ailiki trotted off, sniffing at sacks and cupboards, rearing up to peer into the water crock.

"Emergency came up. One of Mama Kubaza's women, a kid really, she ran into a pain freak."

"Already? They're just getting set up out there."

"Didn't take this shrat long to get going."

Raxzin snorted. He was Fundarim like Rey, with a thin bony face and eyebrows like inverted vees, his long black hair gathered in a tail tied with a leather thong. "You always leave everything out, Thamm. Fa, this kid, her name's Zembee, she went to see her Mum on the sly, Mum being a slave in one of the Sirmalas, and she was coming back to Mama's House when this shrat jumped her and hauled her off into one of the Greens, though you can't call it green, the way things are these days, I hear they cut off Fountain water even to the Biasharim. Well, this shrat wouldda killed her but this STRIKER band comes stomping by. As usual, they don't know what's happening, they so into that poop they do, but the shrat he don't know that and he takes off. Zembee's tough, she gets on her feet and buzzits back to Mama. Tore up pretty good, from what the boy said when he came for Rey, but not gonna die. Want a cup while you waiting?" He lifted his, raised a peaky brow.

"Ahsan, Rax, not now." Faan scratched at her arm,

frowned at the door into the front of the house. "About how long, do you think?"

Thammir rubbed at his nose. " 'Bout an hour ago he left. Shouldn't be long. You said Mama Kubaza was out on the lane?"

"Diyo."

"Then he's probably on his way back now." He nodded at the basket. "What you got good?"

Faan set the basket on the table. "Fresh greens and some medicums Tai sent along." She settled on a stool. "So what else has been happening?"

> > < <

Reyna dropped his cloak and his bag of medicines, hugged Faan vigorously, then pushed her back and stood with his hands on her shoulders, smiling down at her. "You look better." He drew the tip of his forefinger in a shallow curve under her eye. "No black bags."

"SHE's been leaving me alone. It's like SHE's waiting for something." She walked beside him, snuggled up against him, his arm around her shoulders as he moved from the entry toward the stairs. Ailiki came from shadows and glided at her heels.

He stopped by the newel post. "Go on to the sitting room, honey. I need to change my clothes and wash up."

> > < <

Dressed in a crisp white Salagaum robe, his hair brushed and wound into a loose knot atop his head, Reyna looked ten years younger. He smiled at Faan, nodded to Dawa and the other Salagaum sitting round the single lamp, repairing hems, darning holes, working over their old clothing. Cloth was almost as expensive as water these days. He dropped into a chair,

reached down to touch Faan's head as she settled on the
floor beside his knees.

Furrah set his work down. "How is she?"

"I've seen rough, we all have. Nothing so ugly."
Reyna shivered, rubbed his thumbs across his fingertips. "He did a job on her face, especially her mouth
and nose. I sewed the wounds up, but she'll have
scars." He shook his head. "She gets a look in a mirror, maybe she'll wish he finished it. Cut her on the
breasts and legs. She says he was going to gut her, then
rape her again. It got him excited, telling her all that,
where the cuts were going and how deep. A Biashar,
she said. Mama's putting the word out, we'll find him."

Goandee touched a scar slanting past the corner of
his mouth. "He get her eyes?"

"Left them alone so she could watch him strut. He
thought he cut her throat when the STRIKER band came
by, but he was in a hurry and she got her arm in the
way and he didn't stop to make sure."

Faan twisted around and looked up. "Rey, you remember the time I nearly sliced my thumb off?" She
held up her hand, fingers spread, turned it slowly in the
yellow lamplight to show them there was no scar anywhere. "When she's well enough to walk, take her to
the Sibyl."

"Fa, what Sibyl'd do for you. . . ."

"Make it a visiting night and I'll go with you." Faan
stroked her fingers down the side of her face, shivered
when she thought of the girl not that much older than
her. "We can't let the jeggers win all the time."

Silence stretched out for several minutes. Furrah went
back to embroidering with tiny precise stitches over a
tear in a white shirt. Dawa smiled at Faan, took up
another pair of trousers, and began darning a hole in
one of the knees. Reyna lay back in the stuffed chair,
his eyes half-closed, his face weary. Faan leaned against
his legs, quietly happy; it was almost like being in the
old Beehouse again, on one of the nights when Reyna

and the others stayed home and rested. If she had a choice, this was where she'd live. She closed her eyes, sighed. Choice? Tsah! the way she was now, she killed people she stayed around.

Goandee ran his finger around the cuff he'd been mending, snipped the thread loose and began folding the trousers. "Went by Ladroa-vivi this morning. Chez's place. He's down with fever. Saw three dead rats in the wynd."

Reyna opened his eyes a crack, made a face. "K'lann! It just needs that. There's already cholera about." He pulled his hand across his face. "We'd better organize flea baths and get ready to dunk the laggard. Druggers don't give a rat's ass what happens to them, they'll spread plague like fire."

Goandee spread his hands. "Maybe it isn't plague."

"And maybe it's going to rain tomorrow. Fa."

"Mmh?"

"Tell Tai about the rats. We're going to need balaar root, gauuva tincture, imba-frog paste, anything else she can think of. Oh. And all the soap she can provide. We'll have the coin for it, silver pradhs, she doesn't need to worry about that." He sat up, touched her cheek with the tips of his fingers. "All she can get, as soon as she can get it. You can take the first load of silver tonight. Pack it in your basket, hmm?"

"Vema, Rey." Faan yawned. "And I'll go see the Sibyl tomorrow morning, see what she advises." She grimaced. "If I'm let."

The door opened, Thammir came in with a platter of small cakes and Raxzin followed with a teapot and cups on a tray. "Time out," he said. "Move the lamp, hmm?"

> > < <

With Ailiki running ahead and back along the top rail, Faan, Dossan, and Ma'teesee walked slowly across the Wood Bridge, Faan brooding over what she'd heard. Halfway over, she shifted the heavy basket to her other arm. "Dossy, Teesee, were your Mums all right? Not sick or anything?"

"Why?" Dossan grabbed her arm. "You know something?"

"You're joupy as three-legged flea. Shwar't, Dossy."

"Shwar't yourself! Ol' Maumyo drinks and vomits and spews potz all day, he runs a fever but he won't take anything for it. Tell me."

Faan moved across to the rail, set the silver-heavy basket by her feet; she leaned on her forearms and stood gazing down at the dark slow water oiling below. Ailiki came back to balance beside her. "Rey says there's cholera in the edge. Maumyo probably got it from that straw mule he drinks. Rey said Aboso Shakiyr is getting water to them, so they won't catch it from the River. He says we'd better wash down good once we get home, dump our clothes in a tub with plenty soap. Teesee?"

"Kiffin's a pernickety jegger, wouldn't get near a jug of mule; he makes Mum boil everything and cook it till it's mush. Actually, you could eat off the floor in his house. Mum even makes me take away my garbage when I come see her." Ma'teesee leaned over the rail, dropped an apple core into the River. "That stuff is so gungy it doesn't even splash."

Dossan was frowning back along the Bridge. "Fa, can't you DO something? Make HER let the Mums cross."

Faan rubbed her hand along the ancient wood, smoother than silk from generation after generation of sliding hands. "I tried, Dossy. I yelled at HER till blood come out my nose. SHE doesn't listen to me. SHE tells me."

"Fa . . ." Ma'teesee pushed her hood back, caught her lip in her teeth, pointed. "There's a boat coming downRiver. More trouble?"

Faan looked along Ma'teesee's arm, saw the glimmer

of starlight on a sail; Ailiki jumped onto her shoulder
and hissed in her ear. "You thinking trouble, too, Liki,
my Aili?" As the boat came closer, she saw it was a
small one-master like Reyna's cat that got burned a few
months ago. Two people in it. "I doubt it. Probably
just a River smuggler. Trouble would come on a barge
like the General." She pushed away from the rail,
grunted when Ailiki's hind claws bit through her shirt
as the mahsar jumped down. "Buzzit, Tchi'ka, the
Kassian will be worrying about us."

Dossan went quickly along the Bridge, her head
down, worry worry worry, Ma'teesee went after her,
glancing uneasily at the River every few steps, talking
a steady stream. "Vema vema, look, it's turning t'ward
Southbank, you probably right, Fa, coming down to
connect with someone off a coaster. Coomma coomma,
Dossy, stop being a snerk. Think about Honker, he'll
give you a rub where it itches. Your Mum? Reyna'll
take care of your Mum.'Sides, Fa says she's going over
tomorrow, she'll see the Mums get what they need,
you'll do that, huh, Fa?"

Faan shifted the basket again, her eyes on the River.
"Vema vema, Teesee, early tomorrow. . . ."

The boat nosed toward one of the wharves, twitching
awkwardly, swinging out to go on by because it was
moving too fast; it cut across the River toward
NorthEdge, then circled back unsteadily, heading for
the wharf again.

Abeyhamal took Faan the moment she moved past
the Approach Pillars.

The Wild Magic came pouring from the River, swirling in a silver helix around her, a silently screaming
mist that she could hear but the others couldn't. She
tried to say something to them, but Abeyhamal wouldn't
let her speak. The god sent her loping down the Gatt
Road, Ailiki bounding at her heels, heading for the gatt
where the boat was trying to tie up.

She trotted out onto the planks and stood watching

in enforced silence as the two women climbed from the boat, women wrapped in clumsy gray robes with lengths of cloth bound about their heads and across their faces.

Abeyhamal spoke through her. ''Falmaree Penhari Banadah, be welcome, daughter.''

Chapter 22
ABEYHAMAL Advances her Queen

Desantro looped the mooring rope over the bitt, pulled the nose of the boat closer to the wharf, and went up the ladder. She knelt on the damp planks and reached down to help Penhari. "Weird," she said as the older woman came laboriously off the ladder and straightened. "Been raining here. Y' can smell it."

Penhari didn't answer. She was staring past Desantro.

Desantro eased Hahlaz's knife from the sheath she'd taken off him and turned slowly, keeping the knife behind her.

Mist like cold smoke twisting about her, a girl stood halfway out on the wharf, carrying a basket that dragged on her arm and wearing a heavy black cloak, a small beast beside her, sitting up with black paws folded across a white ruff. The girl was Wascram or slave, too pale for anything else, smooth black hair cut even with her shoulders and something odd about her eyes.

Those eyes changed suddenly into black faceted rounds that glittered in the starlight; mica wings vibrated behind her shoulders. When she spoke, there was an eerie buzz to the words. "Falmaree Penhari Banadah, be welcome, Daughter."

Penhari pulled the cloth from her head and stood holding it. "What are you saying?"

"Receive my Blessing, Faithful Daughter. You have come in the proper time to fill a great need. This girl

is my Voice and my Focus, follow her.'' The overlay
faded and the girl was simply a girl again.

Desantro pressed her lips together, took a step back,
grimacing as her foot hit a bit of gravel; the scrape was
loud as a mule's bray.

Penhari turned her head. ''Desantro?''

''The boat,'' Desantro said. ''I'd best see about getting rid of it.'' She took another step back as she spoke.
*Half a chance, Geddrin, I'll plant a hundred trees for
you. Let me get out of this and you can ask what you
want.*

The girl moved impatiently. ''Never mind that, it
doesn't matter. Come on, I'll take you to the Kassian.''

Desantro shifted again. ''You don't know what you're
talking about, baby.'' Her hip touched the bitt next the
ladder. ''Big Bro's gonna be sniffing after us any minute
now.''

The girl shifted the basket on her arm, rubbed absently at the discoloration of her pale flesh. ''Vema,
vema, I hear you. You don't want that boat any more,
heshal Falmaree?''

''My name is Penhari, child. It's all I claim these
days. No. We don't want it.''

Desantro stood silent, cursing under her breath; she
knew better than to speak up again, to say *let me take
it down past the bridges and turn it loose to float away.
Float away, hah!* She'd be in it out of here, if she got
the chance.

''My name is Faan. I stopped being a child a long
time ago. Step back, please.'' The girl whistled, made
a sweeping movement of her arm.

The silvery mist swirled faster round her, then
swooped at the boat. Round around it spun in a wide
flat vortex, then it melted into the water and the boat
was gone, not even dust left where it had floated.

''Vema.'' Faan drooped wearily; her voice was
hoarse. ''Will you come now? I'll take you to the Beehouse.''

Two girls about the same age as the first came from
the shadows and joined them, whispering vigorously,
breaking off as they saw Desantro watching them.

With the beast trotting before them, Faan and Penhari
walked down the Gatt Road. Desantro followed a step
behind, the other two girls beside her, nudging each
other and whispering again. One reminded her of the
Wharaka she'd seen when she was a child slipping out
to play in the moonlit forest, shy dark sprites flitting
from tree to tree or dancing in Whara circles in the
night mists. The other was an imp with a spray of sun-
spots across her upturned nose.

The imp whispered furiously with her friend, then
edged closer to Desantro. "Is that *really* the Falmaree?"

"Diyo." Desantro smiled. "Straight from the Falmatarr."

"Choo-ee."

Desantro looked around as she walked, beginning to
enjoy herself. The smells of damp earth and wet wood
weren't the same, of course, but they did remind her of
Whenapoyr. Her mind's eye saw soaring rough-barked
trees as huge and old as the mountains themselves, the
whitewater stream that danced down the slope beside
the sheep cote, the mountain peaks visible from the
porch: Kappawhay the Cloud Breaker, Rawhero the Sun
Spear, Whentiaka the Land Guard.

The imp tugged at her arm again. "She going to stay
with us?"

"I don't know." Desantro shook herself; she'd forgot
for a moment where she was.

It was long after moonset; the night was quiet except
for the sounds of their feet and occasional irregular drips
as leaves shed their burdens into the pools below. The
wynds were empty, the windows dark. She thought
about falling behind and getting lost in this maze of
twisting ways, but it would brand her a runaway and
she didn't think that was a good idea. Penhari promised

to get her passage on a ship. She was filled with good intentions, that Mal. *Good intentions. Hah! That and six mojus would buy a slug of mule.*

> > < <

Faan put her hand on the door and it opened. She led them into a roughly furnished sitting room lit by a single nightcandle. "If you'll wait here," she said, "I'll fetch the Kassian Tai Wanameh. Dossan, Ma'teesee, come on; you both have to work tomorrow."

They went out.

The beast stayed behind, leaping onto a window ledge, sitting with its tail wrapped across its tucked-in forepaws.

Penhari settled herself on a couch and contemplated her mud covered sandals. "Falmaree, tsah!" She yawned. "I look like that beggarwoman I saw in the Fringe."

"Mmh." Desantro moved to one of the windows. She couldn't see much in the starlight, a tree and some bushes, maybe some grass.

"Sorry about the boat, Desa. Should have let you take it."

Desantro caught her lip between her teeth, sighed. "Well, I suppose I'd ha drowned myself or run it into a mudbar."

"Be patient a few days, Desa, I'll. . . ." Penhari stopped talking as the door opened and a tall thin Mal walked in, followed by Faan and a young acolyte with an eye-patch.

Desantro slipped away from the window, went to squat in a corner behind the couch where the Falmaree was sitting.

The Kassian Tai Wanameh tilted her head in a sketch of a reverence as if to say *I recognize your status, but that's all I'm going to do.* She was a thin stick of a woman with deep laugh wrinkles about her eyes and a wide mouth that kept trying to smile. She was fifteen, maybe twenty years older than Penhari, though these Mals were hard to judge; they didn't age like the people she knew.

Penhari passed her hand over her rumpled gray hair. "Wanameh," she said, "Family Wannamm?"

"Diyo. Pili's Mal Prime is my brother. Was. When I acknowledged the Family."

Penhari gave a shout of laughter, cleared her throat. "Acknowledged the Family. I like that. I'll use it, if you permit."

"Words are still free. Like the air we breathe, though these seem to be the only free things left in the Land."

"All too true, Kassian Tai. You've had rain here."

"Abeyhamal claims this patch as her domain; she defies Chumavayal by breaking his drought."

"I see."

The Kassian made a brushing move. "What brings you here, Falmaree Penhari Banadah?"

Penhari was silent for several breaths, then spread her hands in a weary gesture. "I'm too exhausted for pride, Kassian. My brother acquired a taste for beating me. I thought I'd leave before it became lethal."

"I see. You know about the General?"

"Oh diyo. His head's gone soft and my son's his match, but don't underestimate them. They don't need intelligence, they've got power." She sighed again. "Power in the hands of fools. Think about that and shudder, Kassian Tai Wanameh."

"What do you expect from us, Falmaree?"

"What you'd do for the lowest. Sanctuary."

The lowest don't have your liabilities, Falmaree."

"True, but this is also true: sooner or later you'll have to face what I bring on you. Why not when you know it's coming?"

The Kassian Tai thought that over, her thin brows sliding together, her mouth knotted. She nodded finally, relaxed her face. "Faan told me Abeyhamal greeted you."

"So it seems."

"Seems? Honeychild is the god's Mouth, no seems about it." The Kassian glanced around, motioned to her apprentice to bring up an armchair.

Faan settled on a hassock behind the Kassian's chair; the beast jumped from the window and came to lie across her feet.

A corner of the Kassian's mouth lifted in a quick half-smile. "I must say I'm glad to see you, Falmaree." She tented her long bony hands. "I've neither training nor inclination for rule, but these idiots over here keep bothering me with their disputes. Sanctuary, eh? Well, fine. It's yours. But you'll need to work for your bread. And bread comes high these days. Just about everything we eat has to be brought in. Another thing." Tai waved a hand at Desantro. "No slaves. Order of Abeyhamal. Your companion there, if she stays, she's free."

"Desantro stopped being a slave the moment we left the Falmatarr; the laws of the Land say otherwise, but that's how I see it. Which reminds me. She needs passage out of here. Safe passage, as soon as possible."

"That might prove difficult. We don't get many ships here these days and those we do. . . ." The Kassian shook her head. "Safe isn't a word I'd use."

Faan touched the Kassian's shoulder. "I saw a ship at the Camuctarr gatt when we went across the Bridge."

The Kassian clicked her tongue. "Him? I wouldn't trust him with a pet rat, let alone a friend. That's Zmios the Phrasi and his *Gidyebar*. Connections with the slave trade. If . . . um . . . Desantro is willing to wait, Vroliko Ryo is due in with a load of corn. He's safe enough."

Penhari twisted around. "Desa?"

"I've had enough of slavers, heshal. I'll wait."

The Kassian shifted in the chair. "Vema. Falmaree, there's a House near the Sok Grove. The people here

wanted me to take it for a Beehouse, but my calling is
to serve the poor and outcast, not the smugly respect-
able. We'll get you settled there tomorrow, then you
can start organizing the chaos in the Low City.'' She
moved her shoulders, grimaced. ''There are too many
people here and no rule but mob rule. I'll back you
with whatever influence I have. Be glad to get this place
off my shoulders. Abeyhamal has already welcomed you
through Faan, so there's that, too.''

Penhari sat up. ''Why me?'' she said.

Diyo, there's bait, Desantro told herself. Run the
place. She looked past the Falmaree at the god's girl.
Faan was trying to keep her face blank, but she was too
young and probably too pampered to be good at it. She
was bored with all this, annoyed with something, maybe
these Mals sitting here and playing with people's lives.

''You're the Falmaree.''

''Hah! You know how much that means.''

''Penhari, it gives the faction leaders cover for compromise. They can go to their people and say we did it
because the Falmaree said to.''

''Desantro said to me once: Never trust a Mal. It's
the first thing she learned. And on the way here, a man
tried to cut my throat because I was a Mal.''

''They'll trust you before they trust each other, Falmaree. That doesn't mean they'll love you. Besides,
folk're used to having Maulapam tell them what to do.''

Penhari slapped her hand on her thigh. ''Then I'm
going to be more than a rug you put over a stain, Tai.
I've been reading for years about governance.'' She
laughed. ''Fifty years I sit around sewing, now I learn
how to sail a boat and it seems I'm to sail a state. You're
sure?''

''Sure? Nothing's sure, but something has to be
done.''

''Diyo, diyo. What we need at the start are Kumms
to judge disputes and set law. You know these people

. . . the women . . . I want women as Kumms. Not Kassians, just ordinary women. All castes. Then. . . ."

Kassian Tai laughed. "Slowly, slowly, Penhari Banadah. It's only a few hours till dawn. Time enough for planning when you've got some sleep."

Chapter 23
Juvalgrim Contemplates his Fate

Juvalgrim hitched a hip on the windowledge, looked down into the Fountain Court as he combed night-tangles out of his hair. "Father and son," he murmured. "Touching, isn't it."

On the far side of the long narrow room Fitchon snorted. He filled a cup with hot, steaming tea, straightened the forks and spoons, shifted the vase with the half opened tashba bud so a petal with nibbles off the edge wouldn't show. "Ready," he said. "If you haven't lost your appetite."

In the Court the Prophet stood against the back wall with arms outstretched, leading the Iron Litany.

Before him, on their knees, the General, the Royal hosta, Cheoshim from the STRIKER bands, and a scattering of men from the city, slaves and workers from the Maulapam Sirmalas, chanted the responses in deep burring voices that made the water shake and hammered at the glass in the tower behind them.

Juvalgrim slipped off the sill, strolled to his dressing table, dropped the brush, and slipped a clip over his hair to keep it out of his mouth while he was eating. He leaned closer to the mirror, ran a finger along the deepening line between his nostril and the corner of his mouth. "It would make life much simpler if I grew a beard."

Fitchon paused on his way into the next room, chuckled. "In competition with the Prophet?"

Juvalgrim straightened. "I'd keep it clean, at least,

and free of crawlers." He settled himself at his breakfast table which was set up near one of the outer windows. "Join me, Fitch; you can finish your work later."

At the foot of the Mountain lay the shrunken, deserted River and the smoldering High City. In the Edge a building suddenly belched streamers of black smoke into the red streaks lingering from sunrise.

Fitchon spread jam on a piece of toast with a liberal hand, took a large bite out of the triangle.

Juvalgrim frowned at the tea in his cup, the gold-brown liquid shivering with the barely perceptible shake of his hand; the long nights were getting to him. And this business. It wasn't going to be easy; the best he could think of was to approach it obliquely. "Have you ever wondered about your parents, Fitch?"

Fitchon's lips twitched and his eyes narrowed as they always did when he was thinking up some sass or other, but he drew his napkin across his mouth and with the jam wiped away his flippancy. "Diyo. We all do, you know. But no one says anything." He rubbed his thumb along the handle of the butterknife. "I always wondered . . ." His eyes lifted for an instant to meet Juvalgrim's, dropped quickly.

"If I'd got you on one of my bedwarmers?"

Fitchon set the knife down, scratched at a smear of jam on his napkin. "Diyo."

Juvalgrim shook his head. "Sorry, Fitch, no way. I'm sterile as a stone, lots of activity but no results." He ran his finger along his upper lip, amused and flattered by the disappointment Fitchon couldn't hide. "Singularity, hmp, it has its points." He cut a piece of sausage, looked at it, laid his fork down. "We've been friends a long time, Fitch."

His amber skin darkening with an uneasy flush, Fitchon fiddled with the napkin.

Juvalgrim's shout of laughter was loud enough to shake the tashba petals. "Nayo nay, my friend, I'm not hustling you to my bed. Though I've no doubt gossip has put you there often enough.''

"Diyo, and got me a lot of perks even you didn't know about, High One." Fitchon leaned back, grinning—as much with relief as enjoyment.

"I told Reyna once you were a conniver from the womb." Juvalgrim sobered, jabbed his thumb at the window. "Look at that, will you. Order of the day. What you can't control, destroy."

Fitchon scratched at his wrist, pulled his mouth into an upside-down curve. "Isn't that much left to burn."

"Maybe so, Fitch, but I've a proprietary interest in the tinder that's left. One of these days I'm going to look down and there'll be bundles of faggots under my feet and the Prophet dancing round me with a torch and a smug grin on his filthy face."

"That can't . . . nayo!" Fitchon slapped his hands on the table, hard enough to make the dishes jump. "We won't let it happen."

"Ghali-ghali, my friend, such passion. You've been thinking about it, haven't you."

"Nayo nay!"

"Diyo, mavi, or you wouldn't be so quick to deny."

"High One, you know we support you, us young ones. And a lot of the Primes. The Prophet wouldn't dare. . . ."

"The Prophet does what he wants." Juvalgrim shook his head. "Friends and allies, Fitch, they'll run for shadow when the crunch comes. That doesn't bother me, mavi, I'd do it myself. It's you I'm worried about. We're too tight. It's made enemies for you."

"Them! Jegging bigots, they're jealous, that's all." He pushed his chair back and got to his feet. "I won't listen to this, High One."

"Whistling at the moon, mavi. I appreciate the effort, but I haven't survived this long without keeping my eyes open even if I don't like what I see. I recommend the practice."

Fitchon's shoulders jerked, he turned his back on Juvalgrim and pressed his forehead against the window glass, his hands closed tightly about the edge of the sill.

"I'm sending you upRiver tomorrow. Quiambo Prime will take you in, put you to work in a corner somewhere, keep you out of sight until this is over."

"Nayo!"

"Diyo, mavi. Either you walk onto that barge or I'll have you carried on in chains."

Fitchon pivoted, caught hold of the back of the chair where he'd been sitting, leaned tensely toward Juvalgrim. "Come with me, this scum you're feeding and coddling, they're not worth your life."

"Scum, Fitch? You've a mother down there, perhaps even brothers."

"Mother! She threw me away, I should care about her?"

"There are other mothers, mavi. Mine among them. I was born with a Mal face, but she was a slave. What choice did she have?"

"Ahhh! All that's. . . ." He waved his hands as he searched for words. "Air! Dream! Nothing! I don't understand you. Druggers, thieves, cheats, lazy chuggs, can you deny that's what they are?"

"What does that matter? Do they have to earn my attention?" Juvalgrim leaned back, rested his hands on the slender arms of his chair. "Listen, mavi mavou, everyone else has someone or something to stand with them. Temple, Order, Family, Caste. Law and Obligation. My Scum have me." He sighed. "And the foundling school has me and the acolytes and novices depend on me. It's a heavy weight sometimes, but I," he paused, his mouth twitching into a deprecating half smile, "I like it." He looked at the pieces of sausage on his plate, wrinkled his nose, pushed away from the table.

"I know you do." Fitchon's grip tightened on the chairback. "Don't send me away. You need me."

"I need you alive." Juvalgrim crossed the room to the wardrobe, paused with his hand on the knob. Over his shoulder he said, "The third way's the best way, remember that, Fitch. When you see two bull saisai nose to nose, snorting and kicking dirt and blocking your path, go round them. One way or another. Slip and slide, Fitch, slip and slide and there you'll be peacefully on your way while they're locking horns and trying to trample each other."

"Sah! Homilies, I get enough homilies from my Housemaster." Fitchon blinked, his eyes swimming. "If you'll stop dawdling, High One. I've got work to do." He sniffed, scrubbed his sleeve across his nose. "If I'm gonna get packed by tomorrow."

> > < <

Four days later Juvalgrim sat sweltering in his Visitation Robes and contemplated the group gathered before him in the Council Chamber.

Tchah, I thought Manasso spite went with Kutakich. Looks like I removed a constrictor and got a viper in its place. Fuaz Yoyote, Manasso Prime. Does the office do it to them, or does it take that kind of man to make it there? Never been sure which it is. Sure? Fuaz surely knows how to chose a time for his strike.

Juvalgrim leaned forward, looked slowly from face to face. His strongest supporters were both away, Quiambo Prime in Corasso, Aboso Prime in the Infirmary recovering from a small stroke. He lingered on the Adjo Prime, saw him look away, drops of sweat oozing out of his burnt caramel face, as if he were starting to melt under the pressure. *He always was a feather in the wind.* Anacho looked troubled, but he was a man of ritual and pattern, with little imagination or empathy; he didn't like having to stand against a High Kasso, but he hadn't the strength to oppose the Prophet. Anaxo. . . . Juvalgrim slid a hand across his mouth to hide the twitch of his lips. Anaxo Prime had put off his black robes for the Prophet's coarse brown, let his beard and hair grow; his eyes were fierce and his posture so humble it shouted hubris. And there was young Fuaz, smug and serious.

The Prophet himself stood apart from the Primes with the General crouched at his feet like a dog. An adoring dog.

"And so?" Juvalgrim said. "What is this about?"

Fuaz bowed. "High Kasso, we have come to say the conduits from the Fountain to the city cisterns have been closed off."

Juvalgrim straightened. "My instructions were to leave them open."

"Chumavayal the Father of Waters requires it. The Prophet has given Chumavayal's command and we have obeyed."

Juvalgrim leaned back, pressed his palms together and set his middle fingers against his lips, his forefingers fitting into the dip above his chin. He was angry, very angry, but he didn't think it politic to show it. He brought his hands down, crossed them above the crystal of the Eye, and spoke softly, reasonably, using his deepest, most musical tones. "There are good people in that city, poor people, hardworking people, who can't afford to pay Mal prices for aqueduct water—if there is any water left after the Maulapam and Cheoshim are finished with it. They will be driven to the River and you know it is unclean; do you want disease in the city along with everything else? And what of the true and faithful Ironmen in the Edge, families that give generously from the little they have? Are they worth nothing to Chumavayal?"

The Prophet strode forward, banged the butt of his staff on the floor. "Chumavayal is just and compassionate. If those you speak of are truly good and faithful servants, let them come to the Fountain and be blessed. They will be given what they need. If they are sinners and recreant, it is better that they die." His eyes widened, went suddenly a brilliant red. "Chumavayal says: Look to your own soul, foolish man, it may be that I will require it soon." His mouth worked, half-lost in the tangle of mustache and beard. "Chumavayal says: Water is MY Gift. If it is misused, I will take it back." He shivered, the red faded. "The Fountain will go dry if the conduits are not sealed off."

"I see." *I do indeed; the lot of you are so frightened by this stinking fanatic, you'd castrate yourselves to please him.* He snorted. *And I'm no better. If I had a spine . . . ah well, the third way, Ju, remember what you told Fitchon. Find the third way. There's no point in disputing with this lot.* "Chumavayal's will be done." He paused, straightened and let his anger show. "Next time, however, be more faithful to the Rule. Inform me before you act, not after. For your lapse," he smiled sweetly at the new Manasso Prime, "I decree to each of you a penance; a Chant of ten Chains before the Forge. Blessed be Chumavayal."

> > < <

Reyna tightened the laces of his trousers, tied them off. He shook out the blousy black tunic, stood holding it and looking across the candle-lit bedroom at Juvalgrim who was sitting naked on a windowseat, his legs drawn up, his arms draped loosely over his knees, his long, long hair falling like black silk down his back and off the edge of the seat; he was gazing down the mountain to the dark mass of the city.

Juvalgrim sighed. "More of the Edge is burning."

"Come with me." Reyna pulled the tunic over his head, settled it on his shoulders. "There's not much you can do here any more. They're pulling the noose tighter and tighter about you."

"They?"

"You know what I mean."

Juvalgrim moved his hand in one of his graceful, meaningless gestures.

"Let Manasso carry the Eye, if that's what he wants. It's not worth this, this. . . ." Reyna spread his arms, wiggled his fingers, a sign for all the things that hung between them. "Come with me, Ju. Once you're out of it, nobody's going to bother you."

Juvalgrim moved his shoulders, shook his hair loose. "Dear Rey."

"That's no answer." Reyna caught up his cloak, swung it around his shoulders, clipped the neck cords to his belt. "I can't give you anything like you've got here, but you'd be safe."

"I'd be dead." The Wounded Moon was the finest of nail parings, only three days past Dark, but the sky was clear and the starlight lit the planes of Juvalgrim's face, slid along a body still firm and lean despite his age.

"What?"

"You heard me." He swung around, dropped his legs over the edge of the padded seat. "I might manage to escape the men, but the god, never. Rey, listen. The instant I cease to be of use to Chumavayal, I'll be a grease spot on some floor. I just have to keep hanging on and hope I can outlast the Change."

"You've lost me again."

"K'laan! Sibyl warned me not to talk about that. Trust me, Rey. If I can keep on long enough, everything will be all right." He slid off the seat and came quickly across the room; he took Reyna's hands, held them gently prisoned within his own. "Listen, luv. Take your own advice. Get out. I'll find the money for you. Next ship that leaves, you be on it."

"What about Faan?"

"You know the answer, Rey. She's caught. You can't help her, the god has her. Honey Mother will use her till there's nothing left."

"Then I stay, too. She comes to me for shelter, Ju.

All those people pulling at her, the gods fooling with her life . . . she has to have some place to rest.'' He freed his hands, lifted one of Juvalgrim's, and kissed the palm. ''She's my daughter. As long as she needs me, I'm going to be there.''

Juvalgrim sighed. ''Take care, luv.'' A corner of his mouth curled up. ''I should tell you not to come again, it's too dangerous, but I need you, too.'' He drew the pad of his thumb down the side of Reyna's face, eyes laughing. ''Not for rest.''

At the passage panel, he closed a hand about Reyna's arm. ''Come to the cave tomorrow, I'll have silver for you; you'll have to find a smith to turn it into coin. Ah, Rey, the times they do corrupt us.'' He squeezed the arm. ''Don't try to buy water yourself, luv; get Abosoa Kassos you can trust to do it.''

Reyna ducked through the short, narrow opening. ''Diyo, Mamay, I'll be good.''

> > < <

Reyna tugged at the knob on his side of the panel to make sure Juvalgrim had turned the latch; sometimes he was careless about that. He started off through the inky blackness, one hand drifting along the wall of the passage. Ahead of him there was a scraping sound like a heel against stone.

He froze.

A click.

He held his breath.

Silence.

He ghosted along the passage, ears straining, one hand in front of him, the other drifting along the wall.

Nothing.

There were other exits from this passage, his fingers read the wood as he went past them, read the accumulated grit and tickling cobwebs. If any of them had been opened, whoever it was left no sign of his passing, no disturbance to tell Reyna he wasn't dreaming.

He went down and down through the complex of passages, wondering if he'd begun imagining enemies, afraid he hadn't. If someone had been outside the panel listening to them. . . .

He didn't want to think about that. Warn Ju tomorrow. All I can do.

The lantern that he'd left where the passage became a volcanic blowhole cast a welcome light in the darkness. He wound the wick a little higher and went along the branch that led up to the Sibyl's cave. His feet knew the way well enough after so many years of traversing it, but there were too many offshoots for him to trust himself without light to see landmarks. Besides, there were bats in here and other things; he'd stepped on a poison lizard once when he was late and the lantern had burned dry, escaped by luck alone a bite that could have crippled him.

> > < <

There was someone sitting in the Sibyl's chair.

He blew out the lantern, tucked it into the crevice where he kept it between visits, loosened the rungo in its loops, the polished arm-length club he'd taken to carrying the past weeks.

Faan looked up as he came around the chair. "Loa, Rey."

She wasn't doing anything, just sitting, perhaps thinking. She was thin and worn-looking, dark circles under her eyes. "Loa, Fa." Then, because he couldn't help it, he added, "You could smuggle saisais in those bags under your eyes."

"I don't sleep much these days," she said. "Bad dreams. I Dance for Abeyhamal and . . . kill people. And the Low City folk, they want Blessings. All the

time. As if some potzy word from me would make anything better.''

"Well, you should really be in bed, sleep or not, at
least you could rest," he said. "Come, I'll walk back
with you to the Wood Bridge.''

"Still protecting me, Mamay?" She laughed and
stretched out her hand so he could pull her to her feet.
As they strolled from the cavern, she said, "None of
your Edgers would lay a finger on me, they'd be afraid
of getting it burnt off.''

Reyna flipped a finger against her cheek. "Then you
can protect me.''

Faan took his hand, squeezed it.

They walked together in companionable silence along
the twisty trail, turned at the black ruin of the ancient
olive and started down the Jiko Sagrada.

Near the last flight of stairs, Faan touched his arm.
"You love him, don't you. What's it like, being in love
with someone?''

Reyna was startled; he felt his face grow hot. It wasn't
something he'd ever thought to talk about with his
daughter, but. . . . He glanced down at her. She was
staring at the Jiko as her feet kicked out against her
skirt. What he could see of her face was intent and
serious. "In love," he said slowly. "Nayo, that's not
it, Fa. That's pretty pink pleasures, sweat and sweet
agony. I went through that a few times when I found
my first clients." He went down the stairs thinking
about it, his hands clasped behind him under the cloak;
without questioning it, he was suddenly very happy so
it was almost a dance he was doing. "Nayo. This is
different. Love? I don't know. There's friendship and
fondness, oh diyo, and passion. It's not bad, you know.
It's not bad, friendship and fondness and passion.''

"Does he love you?''

"It's hard to say with Juvalgrim. He's a secret man.
He needs me. That's enough, I think.''

"Need." She shivered. "I hate that word.''

They turned down a kariam, walked in wary silence between the dark towers of the Cheoshim, past the burnt and blackened gardens of the Biasharim, stepped into the silent starlit Sok Circle.

Faan glanced at the flogging posts clustered dark and ominous in the middle of the Circle. Small bluish flames licked along her hand.

"Nayo, Fa. You'll just make things worse."

She looked down at the little fires; after a moment they vanished. "I know."

> > < <

Faan leaned against the left-hand pillar on the Bridge Approach. "I want to stay here, Mamay. I'm sick of all that over there."

Reyna grimaced. "I wish you could, honey. I hate not being able to. . . ." He slammed his fist into the pillar. "Gods!"

"Diyo."

He caught her wrist, ran his thumb up her arm. "You've all that power, honey. Use it. Get out of this place. Once you're over the border, SHE can't. . . ."

"Oh diyo, she can. Riverman says it was HER brought me here. I know he's right and so do you, Mamay, you told about Dikhan's pipedream. Power, t's, I'm as helpless as I was when I was a baby."

He hunched his shoulders, scowled past her at the moongleams on the sluggish river.

"I've yelled and argued and tried everything I could think of, Rey, trying to get her to lift the Barrier for you. She won't listen to me. She won't do anything I ask. She just uses me."

"Gods!"

She reached up, caught a strand of his hair, tweaked it. "You're repeating yourself, Mamay. Getting senile, huh?"

"Kimkim! Respect your old ma, huh? Forgetting Abeyhamal, how's it going Southside?"

She rubbed her shoulders against the pillar. "It's a mess, Rey. Arguing all the time, fighting. People getting hit on the head, robbed. Farmers fighting Woodmen, cooks fighting brewers, everybody yelling. Pulling at ME." She pushed at her hair; it was cut short, just brushing her shoulders, fine and black, blowing in the warm wind. "They all want me, all those factions. As if having me support them validates them." She grimaced, brought Reyna's hand up, rubbed the back of it against her thin cheek. "I'm so tired, Mamay. So tired."

Reyna smiled, caught a strand of her hair, lifted it off her face. "I never thought I'd say it, but I miss your purple spikes."

"Wasn't much point keeping that up. No time for fun, can't play or sass. The paint made my head itch anyway." She leaned against him with a small sigh that squeezed his heart.

"You'd better get on home, honey. And be careful. I'll still be watching. You'll see me when you dance."

She sighed again, her breath making a small warm spot on his ribs. "Mamay."

> > < <

"High One, High One!"

Something banged hard against the door to the Audience Room, there were more bangs and scrabblings; the door opened a crack, slammed shut.

Juvalgrim lifted a brow, set his tea cup down, and crossed the room. He pulled the door open, stood there with his arms crossed, startled by the scene unfolding in the anteroom.

Shouting, wriggling vigorously, kicking and biting the young acolyte who'd replaced Fitchon, a Wascram page was struggling to break free and get back at the door.

"It's all right, Tettin, let him go." Juvalgrim grunted as the page cannoned into him. "Calmly calmly. Catch your breath and tell me what's wrong."

The boy lifted eyes the color of verdigris on bronze. "The Prophet, he's gonna flog Sivvy. In school. Says he's a blasphemer. Says he'll have the evil outta him if it takes all day. You gotta stop him, High One."

"I hear you . . . what is your name?"

"Houen, High one."

"And who is Sivvy?"

"My friend. We came to creche the same day and they put us in the same cot." Though his body shouted a terrible impatience, he spoke with the politeness that had been trained into him (it had taken better with him than it had with Fitchon; more than ever Juvalgrim missed his acolyte's acerbic tongue). "High One . . ."

"If I'm to interfere, Houen, I have to know everything. The Prophet will scold him for a while, there's no hurry. How did this get started? Tell me the truth and no excuses."

Houen was so frantic he was shaking; he tried to talk, but he couldn't.

Juvalgrim scooped him up, stood him on the table where Tettin sat during the day, working on files and arranging appointments. "Now," he said. "Take a deep breath, look me in the eye and start at the beginning." He held the boy's hands in his, smiled at him. He spoke softly, "Deep breath, that's right. Now let it out slowly slowly. Vema, Houen. How did it start?"

Houen dropped his eyes, chewed his lip; his fear having diminished, caution came flooding back. "Ummm. . . ."

Juvalgrim put his hand under the boy's chin, lifted his head. "The truth," he said.

"Well . . . um . . . Sivvy was put here 'cause his Mum belonged to a Mal. You know. But she looked for him and found him." His mouth curved into a quick grin. "Wasn't hard, he's the only one with blue eyes.

Anyway she came up here all the time to see him, but day before yesterday, another woman came, said his Mum was, well, the woman didn't say exactly, except she wasn't gonna come up here any more, she was afraid she'd get beat again. The woman started to say something else, then a Manasso come along and chased her and slapped Sivvy for fooling around with cits and slaves. And Sivvy don't say anything, but he's real mad. Well, out behind kitchen there's these bins where they dump guts and stuff. Sivvy finds some real ripe fish guts and he wraps 'em up in this gunky paper, you know, what they give out when you learning to write. And he sneaks into Manasso Prime's Sitting Room, it's just over where the Prophet does his morning prayers, you know, and he drops the gunk on the Prophet's head when he's right in the middle of a Chain. And ol' Prophet goes round smelling hands till he lights on Sivvy and he's gonna beat Sivvy and Sivvy's not gonna let him and . . . and he's gonna get killed, I just know it.''

"No, Houen, we won't let that happen." Juvalgrim swung the boy back to the floor. "Tettin, keep quiet about this. Do I have any appointments this next hour?"

There was a gray tinge to the young acolyte's face and his hands were shaking. He scurried around behind the table and consulted his lists. "Anaxo Pelekal with a list of complaints about supplies, a petition from the Sok merchants about moving the flogging posts."

"If any of them arrive before I'm back, have them wait."

"High One, the Prophet. . . ."

"Even a Prophet can make a mistake, young Tettin. Remember that." He smiled down at the page. "Give me your hand, Houen. Show me where your friend is."

> > < <

In the classroom Sivvy was stripped naked and stretched over a desk, held down by two of the Prophet's Cheoshim followers. A third waited for the Prophet to finish his scold before laying on with the five-thong flagellum which he was slapping idly against his leg.

The young Quiambo Kasso teacher struggled in the hands of another pair of Cheoshim. "You have no right here, Prophet or not, you have no right here. Leave the boy alone. . . ." He grunted as the Cheoshim twisted his arms higher behind his back.

Out in the hall, Juvalgrim tightened his grip on Houen's hand. "Be quiet," he said sternly. "Stay here. I mean it."

Houen caught his lower lip between his teeth. He blinked past the High Kasso at the scene in the classroom, nodded reluctantly.

Juvalgrim tapped him on the head, then swept into the room. "What's this? Let that man go."

The Cheoshim looked insolently at him. "The Prophet tells us, not you, old man."

"The Prophet has no authority here. Let him go." All the arrogance years of power had given him he focused on them, anger giving yet more force to his words.

They shifted their eyes after a moment, took their hands off the teacher, and backed away.

"Prophet, come here."

The gaunt bearded man turned slowly. "You do not command me, O Kasso."

"In these walls, I do, O Prophet."

"That . . . is . . . true," the Prophet said slowly. He came across the room, his feet moving more slowly than his words had. The humility that he felt was proper before man and God was struggling against Mal pride subtly reinforced by his status as the Chosen of God, the Scourge of Chumavayal. He stopped before Juvalgrim, stood with his body tense but his head bowed.

"O Prophet, explain why you have violated the quiet of this place."

The Prophet's head snapped up. "As the child, so the man. The fractious and froward boy is seed ground for evil. You are lax, O Kasso."

"I am not here to trade aphorisms with you, O Prophet, though I could say break the boy, break the man. If that's what you want, then you're well on your way to getting it. Silence! You can speak when I have finished. What you do in the city is your business, O Prophet, but you are a guest here and I require of you the demeanor and acts of a guest. You and your companions will leave. Now."

The Prophet's face hardened, his nostrils flared. "That boy. . . ."

"That boy will be punished. Appropriately. Not by flogging his skin off." Juvalgrim ran his eyes scornfully over the man before him. "Consider this, O Prophet, it is your pride that has suffered, your soaring self-exalting pride. It was not Chumavayal the boy played the trick on, it was you; it is not for Chumavayal you wish him punished, it is because he made you look a fool."

"You're the fool, pretty man," the Prophet roared, his eyes reddening with fury and a hint of the God-in-him. "You and your kind have brought the drought on us by your stubbornness and your corruption, O Kasso. Think well what you are doing. Sooner than you expect it, you will be required to answer for all you have not done."

"But not to you, O Prophet. I do not expect to see you and your . . ." he ran his eyes over the sullen Cheoshim bunched behind the Prophet, "your cohorts within these walls again. The Fountain Court is open to all, be free of it; as for the Forge Room, come and worship as all are free to come. At other times and other places, you are not welcome."

The Prophet thrust out his arms, lifted his face, his

eyes turned back. He waited. A moment later he shook himself straight. A last fulminating glare, then he swung round and marched out.

Juvalgrim snorted, turned to the boy hastily pulling his clothes on. "Sivvy?"

The boy went still.

The young Quiambo teacher sighed. "You know better, Siv. Answer the High Kasso, and politely, if you please."

Sivvy did a perfunctory bow, his face tight with rejection, his eyes like blue stones. "High Kasso," he said.

"Consider this a punishment for your foolishness, Sivvy. What you did has understandable reasons behind it, but passion, young Wascram, is a very bad master. You accomplished nothing but putting your teacher in danger and alarming your friends. I want you to consider this and remember how little you got from your joke as you are scrubbing out the offal bins for the next five days." He nodded as Sivvy started to protest, then clamped his mouth shut. "Diyo, you're not stupid, merely rash. Finish dressing. You'll find a friend of yours waiting outside. You can have half an hour with him, then report to the Kan Lougatar in the kitchen." He watched Sivvy's eyes shift. "You wouldn't make it down the mountain, boy." He didn't wait for a response, but turned to the Quiambo Kasso. "Have you had trouble before from outsiders?"

"Nayo, heshim Kasso." The young Quiambo glanced at the boy. "Not outsiders."

"I see. You're Darslin, aren't you? I remember you when you were giving your teachers fits. Your favorite word seemed to be why."

"True, heshim. The Housemaster would tell you I haven't changed." He signed permission for Sivvy to leave and the boy went trotting out. "That was close to being a declaration of war, High One. He won't forget it."

"I don't expect he will." Juvalgrim resettled his robes, grimaced. "I have more problems waiting, I'd better get to them." In the doorway he paused. "If you have trouble because of this—or for other reasons—let me know immediately. It's easier to fight devils when they're new-born."

> > < <

Juvalgrim sat in the window looking down on Bairroa Pili. The River was a curving thread of silver, the High City on the North Bank a black mass with a few red glows from smoldering fires and the scatter of torches being fired up along Verakay Lane where the Edgers struggled to keep going. He smiled fondly at the staccato red line. *My scum; takes more than a jegging Prophet to squash you.*

On the South Bank, the windows of the Low City showed yellow between the dark masses of the groves, the spray of lights muted by the dwindling rain.

He folded the letter the courier had given him an hour ago, tore it in half, tore it again and again. The Amrapake was coming with his army to reclaim his sister and clean out the Low City. "It won't be long now," he said aloud. "Ah Rey, I wish you'd been sensible and got out." He shook his head, slid off the windowseat, dropped the bits of paper into the fire and went to bed.

GODDANCE
The Twelfth Year

Abeyhamal towers over the forge, taller, juicier, stronger by far than she'd been as the dance began. Her fimbo is as thick as the Ancient God's arm; it shines with a darkly golden light. She dances power around the Iron Father, around and around as if she is spinning a web about him, gradually tightening the strands so his movements grow more restricted with every circle, more feeble.

> With the Kassian Tai and the Honeychild reinforcing her commands, the Falmaree Penhari Banadah pulled the Low City into order.
>
> Honeychild and Honeygirls danced the wynds and kariams of the High City, called women to them, leading them across the Wood Bridge, emptying the High City of all but slaves, habatrizes and shadowside women.

Chumavayal Iron Father swings his tools with increasing violence and decreasing effect. Sweat runs down his face, he strikes out at her again and again. His footing is less stable. He stumbles, nearly falls on the Forge. The fire flickers, many of the coals gray over and start to cool.

He strikes again at Abeyhamal and by the luck of the game he cuts a shallow groove in her arm and she drips honey ichor on the Forge Floor. It sizzles and boils on the stone; the sound it makes is like a whimper.

The Amrapake arrived with his army, the attack on the Low City begins. Juvalgrim fell, taking the Salagaum with him.

The GodDance goes on; the end draws near.

SIBYL

The Sybil stands beside her chair, one hand resting on the stone back. Her eyes have a distant look on them. She herself is insubstantial, little more than shaped and shadowed smoke.

> *I sit and see the Change is nigh*
> *One by one the signs drift by*
> *Life Force flows*
> *To Low from High*
> *The Forge Wind blows*
> *The Land's sucked dry*
> *Strangers fly*
> *And so must I*

>><<

I can do nothing for my pets. My mouth is sealed, my reach is gone. If either comes here or calls me, I'm nowhere.

Gods!

This is the point I loathe. I'm a fool for growing fond of these ephemerals.

Power. Why is it the stupid, the greedy, the mean who have it? Is that inherent in the weave? Is there something about power that repels intelligence and compassion? And yet there is Juvalgrim, a flawed man but a good one; he played with power like a pretty bauble, never took it seriously. Why is one emphemeral corrupted, another almost untouched? I am as old as the earth and I have not resolved that question yet.

Power. My limits grate on me.

Honeychild, High Kasso, Salagaum—somehow I'll manage to keep you clear.

Life is better than burning, memory or not; at least one can say that.

I'd best go now and think of ways of managing this rescue, if rescue there's going to be.

Chapter 24
Attack

Ma'teesee wriggled out on the limb high in the Sequba until she reached the bald spot she'd seen from below. She settled herself and looked south across the roofs of the Low City toward the South Eka Kummata. "Choo-ee." She whistled with surprise, then called down to the others, "I can see most the Eastend. Weird. There's a army out there." She giggled, a shrill sound that sent the moththeries wheeling in the air, flying away from her. "And one jegger's just bounced off the Barrier. He went riding at it flags flying and now he's on his back and his horse is running off. Sil-ly. What's that, Zindi? I didn't hear. . . ."

On the ground, the Honey Dancer Zinduki cupped her hands about her mouth, yelled what she'd said before, "You see Fa or the Kassian?"

"Nayo. Nobody out there but the lancers and the hostas unloading from the barges."

> > < <

Areia One-eye tilted the stone jar over a mug, passed it along to Dossan, shook her head at Zinduki. "Teesee wouldn't see them, you know. They're over on Wood Bridge waiting for the Amrapake's Herald."

Zinduki nodded, cupped her hands around her mouth. "Never mind Fa," she yelled up at Ma'teesee. "What else is happening?"

> > < <

Ma'teesee slapped at a moththerie she glimpsed from the corner of her eye, grabbed at a side branch as the limb shook under her.

The Lancers were riding at the Barrier, cutting at it with sabers, hurling their lances at it. The lances hit and came bouncing back at them, some of them slapping and pricking the horses who reared, screamed and bolted, some of them hitting heads butt first, knocking the men from their mounts. She enjoyed their misery, her laughter a faint snuffling at the back of her nose. It was chaos compounded by the ta-ras of the signal horns, the rattle of the cadence drums.

So excited that more than once she came close to falling off, Ma'teesee called down what she saw. The moththeries belonging to this Sequba flittered around her, sipping at her laughter like bees after nectar; she scratched absently where they landed. "And there're people out on the roofs all along the Barrier," she shouted, "far as I can see. High Kumm Penhari, she's really choused 'em out this time. Looks like they having fun, can't hear what they yelling, but I'm sure those potzes wouldn't like it if THEY could. Choo-ee, there's a bunch of fooffas riding up and yelling at them, must be the officers. Almost makes y' sorry for the poor jeggers on the ground. Ooh! He took a whip at the jegger, the yatz. Hope he tries the Barrier . . . nayo nay, not him, he's galloping back to the barges. . . ."

"Ma'teesee, come on down, that's enough." Areia One-eye tossed out the dregs in her mug, pushed the cork into the mouth of the bottle. "Dance could start any time now. It catches you up there, you'll fall and break your neck."

"Vema vema. Nothing much left to see anyway. You hear that last horn call? They backing off, making circles like they're gonna camp there till time ends."

There was a violent shaking and rustling as Ma'teesee

began back-crawling to the trunk. A moment later they saw her fitting her toes into the deep cracks in the bark, coming down almost as fast she'd climbed up.

She danced toward them, brushing herself off, scrubbing her hands along her body to get rid of bark fragments and sap. "Reea, Reea, pour me a drink, I'm dry from looking at all that dust."

Areia One-eye snorted. "You would do it, Tees."

Ma'teesee giggled, pranced before her, arms up, hands fluttering. "Gonna gonna gonna kick and scratch," she chanted. "Gonna gonna gonna. . . ." She danced away as Zinduki grabbed at her, circled around, and dropped to a squat beside Dossan. She took the mug her friend handed her, emptied it at a gulp. "You shouldda seen it, it was soooo funny."

Dossan rubbed at her face. "What's happening on Northbank, Tees? Could you see? Is it going to be worse for our Mums?"

"Not to worry, Dossy. Army's sitting on Southbank. Didn't see much doing otherside." She put the mug down, wiped the back of her hand across her mouth. "So? Reea, when do we start? I wanna stomp some Mal."

Areia One-eye shrugged. "When Abeyhamal commands. Same as always." She rose onto her knees, reached round behind her for the basket. "Come on, help me get this stuff packed away."

> > < <

Faan leaned on the railing, scowling at the noisy scene, wrinkling her nose as the horns blared, the drums beat. Each time one of the lancers seated his spear and rode at the Barrier, her skin twitched and her pulse jumped—and her cramps got worse. She swung round, pulled herself onto the rail and sat balanced there, her boot heels hooked over a lower rail, her back curved, her hands dangling between her knees.

A while later she wiped at the sweat beading up on her face, dropped her hand again; she could smell herself and she didn't like it and the monthlies sponge was rubbing her raw, felt like it had grit in it. Of all the times for the blood to come down! Now, when she was supposed to be ready for anything. All she felt ready for was curling up in bed with a hot bottle on her stomach. "Just what we needed," she muttered. "More potzheads on a tear."

Tai resettled the Takaffa cloth about her neck, smoothed the embroidered panels over her breasts, began folding back her sleeves to bare her forearms. "Fa, you've been a running sore for a week now." She was frowning, gray-white brows drawn together, the lines from her nose to her mouth-ends cut deeper.

Faan hunched her shoulders. "I'm tired, I'm tired of everything, tired of being jerked around every time the god gets a notion, I'm tired of having to cross the Bridge every time I want to see Rey, I'm tired of worrying about him, I'm tired of thugs looking to jump me, I'm tired of potzheads on this side trying to use me for everything they think they want. I'm tired of not having any fun any more." And I'm tired of listening to you, godwoman, she thought, but she didn't say it, there was no point in making an enemy where she didn't have one already. She brushed at her hair, pushed it behind her ears. "It just keeps going on and on and on, doesn't it."

Tai set her hands on her hips, inspected Faan. "Monthlies, Fa?"

"Huh! Don't talk to me."

"Tsah!" She crossed to the rail, took up the fimbo she'd leaned against it. "Here comes the Herald. On your feet, Fa. Dignity, child. Never let them see you squirm." She hugged Faan against her when she came down off the rail, then arranged her face in its sternest lines and started for the Northbank.

> > < <

The Amrapake's Herald was a Mal in bi-colored clothing riding a tall pinto. The left side of his face was painted green, his right glove was green, his left glove black, his right boot was green, his left black, his tunic and trousers were divided down the middle, the right side green, the left black. Two masked boys ran at his stirrups, the right was black from head to toe, the left green. They carried bi-colored pennons that flapped limply in the hot still air of the High City.

The pinto reared when the Herald tried to force him onto the Bridge; if the Mal hadn't been a superb rider, he'd have been on his back in the dust. He calmed the beast, then sat scowling as the Kassian Tai Wanameh and the Honeychild came walking slowly down the slope of the Bridge and stopped on the Riverside of the Approach Pillars.

Faan nudged the Kassian with her elbow. "Clown," she whispered.

"Shh. Dignity, that's the word." The Kassian Tai Wanameh stood tall and commanding, one hand on Faan's shoulder, the other clasped around her fimbo.

The pinto snorted, his hooves scraped on the dirt as he shifted nervously.

The heat was melting the Herald's facepaint; it was dripping onto his tunic. His scowl deepened. "Send forth the Falmaree," he brayed suddenly. "Renounce this blasphemy and come humbly before God and Amrapake. The magnanimity and compassion of Chumavayal are beyond your understanding. Trust in it and abase yourselves before Him. Refuse and be declared anathema. Nothing will come into that place, neither flesh nor fowl. Your children will starve, you will eat each other until only bones are left."

Before the Kassian Tai Wanameh could say anything, Abeyhamal enveloped Faan and nudged the Kassian aside. The translucent image of the god grew quickly immense, straddling the Bridge, feet in the River, head in the clouds, fimbo like a rod of light, bright wings buzzing; in a voice that hummed out over both lobes of the city, the god cried, ''Corrupt son of a feeble Father, behold how your threats trouble me.''

In all the Groves, the Honey Dancers rose as one.
OW OOO OUM OWWW OOO AHHH UMM
Their mouths gaped wide, their eyes glazed over.
OW OOO OUM OWWW OOO AHHH UMM
In convoluted double loops they danced, stomping and swaying in time with the **HUM,** hundreds of girls danced in the Groves, ecstatic and terrible, weaving through the great trees, sucking strength from the earth. Dancing up Earthfire for Abeyhamal.

Above the Low City black clouds swirled and boomed, more clouds came sweeping in from the sea, great spiraling curls of black.

Thunder crashed, lightning walked across and across the city.

Then it rained. Hard and copiously. And not just water.

Flapping and vigorous, thousands of great meaty fish fell into the streets and onto the roofs of the Low City and the SouthEdge.

Laughing and shouting, the people ran into the rain and scooped them up, dumped them in barrels and crocks and whatever was handy, went back for more.

Herds of boys and girls capered inside the Barrier, waggling fish at the lancers, jeering at the men, taunting them.

. . .

Then the god was gone.

. . .

The rain stopped, the fish-fall stopped. The Honey Dancers fell exhausted to the ground. Men and women of the Low City cleaned up the last of the fish and went to figure ways of curing and storing the bounty.

> > < <

The Kassian Tai Wanameh took Faan's arm and began walking back toward the Southbank.

Faan was exhausted, aching, and sad. Her family was scattered, her friends distracted and not really friends any more; she was too powerful and too strange now, it was as if another Barrier stood between her and them. Yet the power was useless, she couldn't get the things she wanted most. All she could do was ruin everything she touched. It wasn't fair, it just wasn't fair.

Then the Wild Magic came flowing up from the River in a stream of silver that coiled around her, caressing her, singing their fizzing songs to her, blessing her. They didn't mind her weirdness; they liked it. They liked her. That was comforting and it gave her the energy to move her feet and follow Tai back to the Low City.

Chapter 25
Gods and Rulers share the same tunnel vision

Ignoring the scandalized Anaxoa novices and the mutterings of the crowd of suppliants waiting on the kneeling stools, Famtoche Banddah stalked down the Aisle Major of the Public Audience Room, three hostas of Royal Guards behind him. He reached the stairs to the dais, clasped his hands behind him, and inspected the Primes seated in the middle three chairs of the seven. "Down," he said.

Manasso Prime Fuaz Yoyote leaned forward. "Your authority stops at the Blessing Gate, O Amrapake."

Famtoche nodded, a short sharp jerk of his head. "I see." He stepped to one side, waved his hand to his chief guard. "Do it," he said.

> > < <

Seated in the center chair, Famtoche Banddah clicked his painted nails on the wood and smiled down at the three groaning forms stretched out on the floor, their backs bloody from a guard's flagellum, their faces in the dust where the suppliant's mat had been. "My authority stops where I say it does. Fulaak."

The chief guard stepped over the legs of the Adjo Prime, bowed stiffly. "Amrap."

"Boot up one of those robes out there, send it for the High Kasso; tell it if I have to go looking for that dhun, they'll regret it more than this lot." He waved a hand at the Primes.

> > < <

Famtoche Banddah ran his thumb along his jaw and
scowled at the High Kasso as he came quietly into the
Chamber. Juvalgrim wore a plain black robe, his hands
were bare of rings, his hair brushed smoothly back,
hanging in a silver-streaked fall down past his waist, his
only adornment the cloudy crystal on the heavy black
iron chain—Chumavayal's Eye, the sign of his authority.
Despite his annoyance with the man, Famtoche was
tempted to applaud; the High Kasso dominated the room
without saying a word.

Juvalgrim stopped as he reached the feet of the groveling Primes, moved a hand in a graceful gesture that
took in them and the rows of terrified suppliants and
acolytes shivering on their stools. "You've made your
point, heshim." His voice was like honey butter on hot
bread, rich and satisfying. Famtoche lost his scowl and
the hostas stirred, their leather creaking, metal clanking
against metal. Juvalgrim brought his fingertips together,
bowed his head slightly, his hair whispering across the
rawsilk robe. "How may we serve you, O Amrapake?"

Famtoche Banddah brought his hand down flat against
the chair arm, a sharp splatting sound that shattered the
mood the High Kasso had created. "That Barrier or
whatever it is, it mocks us and Chumavayal. Why do
you permit it to exist, High Kasso?"

Juvalgrim tilted his hand in a gesture that conceded
the disruption of the mood he'd tried to create. "Permit, Amrap? It is god-business, not mine." His caressing voice once again drained much of the crackle
from the air.

"I thought god was your business."

"If Chumavayal wishes it gone, he'll take it down. I
can do nothing without his willing it. I am his servant,
not his master."

"Words!" Famtoche Banddah leaned forward.
"You're good at words, Kasso. Saying is you can talk

your way through a wormhole. Talk your way round
this. Fulaak.''

The chief guard stepped behind Juvalgrim, set the
point of his grace-dagger at the Kasso's throat.

Juvalgrim was silent for a breath, his face was as
calm as it had been from the beginning; there was a
look to him that Famtoche didn't like, a resignation that
took away one of his most powerful weapons, the fear
of death. ''You can kill me easily enough,'' the High
Kasso said. Honey-butter voice, beautiful and tranquil.
''But what will it gain you?''

''Will you bring the Barrier down?''

''I cannot.''

''Try.''

''Do you think Chumavayal is a dog to come when
he is called?''

''Try.''

''No.''

Fuaz Yoyote lifted his dirt-streaked face. ''The children,'' he said. ''The foundlings. If you want him to
act, bring them into it.''

''Ah. The Worm speaks. Stand, Worm. Betray your
fellow Worm, if you will.''

''Betray?'' Fuaz got stiffly to his feet, grunting with
pain. ''It's him who betrays us. Do-Nothing, that's what
we call him. His pretty little bedmates are all he listens
to.''

Famtoche Banddah pursed his lips, eyed Yoyote with
interest. ''Run away, little Prime, bring me back some
leverage.''

> > < <

Famtoche Banddah stroked his thumb along his jaw
and contemplated the two boys. ''Your names?''

The blue-eyed boy glared at him, pressed his lips into
a thin line.

The other one bobbed his head in a hasty bow. "Houen, heshim Amrap. And my friend is Sivvy."

Famtoche nodded, clicked his fingernails on the chair arm. "Well, Kasso? Do I have to explain? If your imagination fails you, Fulaak would be happy to provide details."

The High Kasso's eyes glittered so briefly Famtoche was unsure he saw anything, then they were blank and dull as smoked glass. "I will make the attempt, Amrap. But I tell you this, the Barrier is Abeyhamal's work. No man has power over a god."

"More than an attempt, Kasso, or these toys of yours will blood the dirt."

Juvalgrim's nostrils flared and his eyes flickered again. Over his shoulder, he said, "I will remember this, Manasso." He took a deep breath, turned to Famtoche Banddah. "If you trust that viper, you're a bigger fool than I think. I've said I'll try. I can't do more."

"We'll see. Fulaak, take the boys out, bring them to the Bridge when the Kasso's ready to work."

> > < <

"Wake up, Fa. Come on, you gotta see."

Faan groaned and turned over. "Teesee," she muttered.

"Tai said you slept long enough; you should get dressed and do some walking around." Ma'teesee slapped Faan's shoulder, then went running across the room to the wardrobe where she dug through the clothing on the hooks, began throwing things on a hassock. "It's sommme-thing," she said, "something and a half, Fa. Whole Camuctarr's marching down the mountain."

Faana pushed up, then hunched over with her arms pressed against her stomach, nauseated and filled with a low level ache. "What are you talking about?"

Ma'teesee tossed a towel at her. "Tai said the Amrapake must've bullied the High Kasso into coming at

the Barrier. I wish I'd seen that. He's a beautiful man,
the Kasso is. I ever tell you? I went up the Mountain a
couple times when he was singing the Praises at Midsummer. Just to look at him. Tai said you'd better get
dressed, Honey Mother could be calling you any minute. She's got a bath ready. Come on, Fa''

"Gods! Vema vema, I'm awake. Why aren't you
working?''

"Ol' Wewesh turned us loose for the day. No customers so he din't want to pay us. You hungry at all? The
Kassian says she gonna warm up some soup.''

"Gahhh. Don't talk about food. Hmm. I'll crawl
around in a little, wait for me in the parlor, huh?''

"Vema, Fa.''

> > < <

When the great iron gong above the Blessing Gate
began sounding the Announcement, the Salagaum
climbed to the roof and watched the Procession wind
down the Sacred Way.

Goandee hitched a hip on the parapet. "Putting on a
show for the Amrapake, that's what it is,'' he said.
"Trust Juvalgrim to do it a treat. An't that so, Rey?''
he called out to Reyna who was on the other side of the
roof, scowling at the mist eddying through the streets
of the Low City. He was worried about Faan; she hadn't
been across to see him since he found her in the Sibyl's
Chair, couldn't get past the hostas of the Amrapake, the
Cheoshim and the Guards.

"Hmm? What was that, Goa?''

"This business, it's High Kasso pulling his tricks for
the Amrapake, true?''

"Don't know. We'll find out what it's about when we
see where they're going.'' Reyna laced his fingers together, squeezed them hard as he thought about that
army and what it'd do to Low City once it got past the
Barrier. It'd get past all right, the Amrapake would see

to that. The Amrapake and the Prophet. Faan . . . I've got to get to her. Somehow. . . .

"Bet I'm right." Goandee dug in a pocket, found a battered copper coin, tossed it to the tiles, grinned at the others. "My moju in the pot, who's gonna take me?"

> > < <

Adjoa and Anaxoa novices from the foundling school marched down the Sokajarua toward the Iron Bridge, boys in the white and gold of Adjoa, the black and gold of Anaxoa, tapping small black drums with gilded sticks.

Clicka-clack clicka-clack, shuffle-shuffle of sandal soles, they came, fifty boys marching.

Adjoa and Anaxoa acolytes marched down the Sokajarua, bronze hammers beating on small bronze anvils.

Tinka-tank tinka-tank, slip and slide of sandals on the paving stones, they came, a double score of grave-faced young men marching.

Adjoa and Anaxoa kassos chanted as they shuffled down the Sokajarua, carrying the Anvil on a litter, leaning into the padded chains coming over their shoulders, chains linked to the poles of the litter.

Shhp-slide, creak and squeal, the Adjoa and Anaxoa bearers came. Black and white and gold, iron chains with the forge-sigil pendant swinging with the sway, CHUM MA VAY YAL, they chanted and slid their feet in step.

Adjoa Prime and Anaxoa Prime paced side by side behind the Anvil, white robe, black robe crusted with gold thread, staffs in their left hands, ebony bound in iron.

Tunk-tunk they came, flanked by a decade of torch bearers carrying fire from the Sacred Flame, followed by bearers with the Brazier heaped with coal.

Adjoa and Anaxoa kassos walked behind the Brazier, the oldest leaning on the arms of the young. Down and down they came, chanting as they walked, fifty kassos chanting CHUM MA VAY YAL CHUM MA VAY YAL in their deepest voices, a solid Wall of sound.

Juvalgrim High Kasso of the Camuctarr in Pili walked alone behind them, his hair unbound, blowing in the hot wind that coursed along the Sokajarua. He wore the Iron Chain and Crystal Eye, white trousers and tunic, a plain black robe closed to his waist and open below, hem fluttering about his sandals. Quietly, easily he came, the chant from those who marched before him flowing around him like a river.

Down the Sokajarua. Turn onto the Gatt Road. Down the Gatt Road to the Iron Bridge Approach.

Neatly as Cheoshim cadets on show parade, the pages and acolytes divided at the Approach and marched to their places, Adjoa to the left, Anaxoa to the right, anvils tank tick tink.

The bearer kassos hauled the Anvil onto the Bridge and eased it down on the hump at the center, set the Brazier beside it.

The Primes walked onto the Bridge, gold wire glittering in the punishing sunlight.

The kasso choir filed onto the Bridge, Adjoa to the left, Anaxoa to the right.

The torch bearers lit the coals in the Brazier and with their iron bound bellows blew the Fire alive.

They drew back, five Adjoa kassos to the left, five Anaxoa kassos to the right, holding their torches before them while the Adjoa Prime took up one great iron hammer and moved to the left, the Anaxoa Prime took up the second hammer and moved to the right. In unison they began the Great Beat on the Anvil DONNNG DONNNG DONNNG then DONNNG DONG DONNNG DONG repeated over and over. CHU ma VAY yal CHU ma VAY yal.

> > < <

On the roof of a warehouse beside the Iron Bridge,
seated in a massive chair that conscripted Naostam porters had hauled up three flights of stairs, protected from
the sun by a slatted awning, surrounded by his guard
hosta, with the Mannaso Prime Fuaz Yoyote sweating
anxiously beside him, Famtoche Banddah sipped at a
glass of iced vinyol and watched with annoyed impatience the slow unfolding of ceremony below him.

Sivvy and Houen stood by the low parapet, leashes
on their necks, their hands bound behind them.

"What's taking so long? You, Worm." A wave of his
hand brought Fuaz Yoyote to his side. "Diyo, Worm,
I'm talking to you. Why don't they just get on with it?"

"Heshim Amrap." The thin man with the coppery
skin of a Biashar and the spiky stubble of a Cheoshim
rounded his shoulders and bobbed his narrow head in
bows that seemed to have no end to them. "The Calling
must be done without flaw or the all-powerful all-
knowing Great One will not answer."

"And?"

"The High Kasso is doing what is required and
more," Yoyote said grudgingly; the sweat on his lined
face was not from the sun but from fear. His fate and
Juvalgrim's were knotted for the moment and he could
do nothing but support the man he loathed.

"I judge by the results, Worm, not the elegance of
the attempt. Now get away from me. You stink."

> > < <

The kassoa choir repeated the godname over and over
in their deepest voices, melding together in a solid
sound that shook the bones and made breathing harder.

Juvalgrim's rich baritone rang out, filling the space
between earth and heaven.

Come O Lord of the Morning
Giver of Plenty
Come to us O Father of Iron
Joy of the Faithful
Bliss of the Lawkeeper. . . .

> > < <

On the warehouse roof the Amrapake moved impatiently in his chair, then coughed and settled back to watch the rite progress.

Fuaz Yoyote wiped the fear sweat from his face, tucked his hands back in his velvet-lined sleeves.

> > < <

The choir chanted:
CHU MA VAY YAL CHU MA VAY YAL
Juvalgrim chanted:
Iron Father, come and bless us
Giver of Strength and Might
Come O Lawgiver, make this wrong right.
The choir chanted:
CHU MA VAY YAL CHU MA VAY YAL
The drums rattled tank tank t t t tank tank. . . .

The small bronze hammers beat against small bronze anvils, the tink-t-tinks sinking into the chant and emerging from it, sinking again.

Adjoa Prime and Anaxoa Prime were slick with sweat, their ropy arms starting to tremble as they brought the Great Hammers down on the Sacred Anvil DONNNG DONG DONNNG DONG DONNNG

A Red Mist rose from the Forge and spread along the Iron Bridge, turning the struts crimson as it flowed over them; when it reached the Southbank Approach it oozed along the River on both sides and seethed against the Barrier; like acid burning holes in leather it ate into the Invisibility that barred them from the Low City.

>><<

On the roof of the warehouse, the Amrapake sat up, stretched his mouth in a smile with satisfaction but no humor in it. "Chavash! The yatz is actually getting somewhere."

>><<

"K'lann!" Reyna leapt away from the parapet and ran for the stairs.

Thammir caught his arm, jerked him around. "Rey, don't be an idiot. You can't do anything."

Reyna swore, wrenched himself loose and slammed into Thammir who wrapped his long arms about him and yelled in his ear, "Rey! It's nonsense. Goandee, Furrah, help me hold him."

Reyna relaxed, seemed to listen as Thammir went on. "The Barrier. You can't get through that, and even if you could, there's the army. You know what they'd do to any Salagaum they got their hands on."

Their hands loosened as Reyna sighed, let his head fall forward. With a sudden burst of effort he broke free and was running down the stairs before they could regroup.

>><<

Honey Mother seized Faan.

Her eyes blurred, vanished behind a facetted darkness.

She opened her mouth wide, a deep pulsating HUM poured out of her.

She danced.

Stamp. Sway. Whirl.

She danced to the music of the earth, boom ba boom ba boom, the heart rhythm. Waves of dark and light pulsed from her, rings of honey light, rings of hot dark.

She danced along the ways and wynds of the Low City and as she danced, girls came from the houses and the groves, from the rooftops and the gardens. Mouths wide, eyes dark, staring into dream, the Honey Dancers followed her.

> > < <

Black clouds swirled above the Barrier, laced with wire lightning, crooked yellow streaks that jagged from lobe to lobe. A few drops of rain fell. Pause. A few more. Then again a few more.

A SOUND rose within the city.

People appeared on their roofs, handtalk drums beating a counter rhythm to the Anvil and the drumming pages.

Honeychild and Honey Dancers wove along the South Gatt Road, mouths stretching in the Abey HAUMMM.

Honey Light gushed over the Low City, yellow light that thickened and darkened, boiled and seethed. It drove back the Red Mist, filled in the Eaten Places. It grew higher and thicker and stronger, magic amber swallowing the houses and the people.

The Red Mist faltered.

On the Iron Bridge, the Primes beat faster and harder, grunts torn out of them with every stroke. The kassos' Chant grew louder, hoarser, then began to tear apart as the strain took its toll of individuals within the choir, old and young driven beyond their strength, collapsing to the iron tiles of the Bridge floor.

The High Kasso's voice soared strong and serene, singing on and on without a break. Somehow. As if breathing were not necessary. On and on. . . .

Until the Red Mist came rushing back and whirled in a funnel round and round the Primes and the High Kasso, then it sank into the Anvil on the Sacred Forge.

The Hammers fell to the tiles; the Primes collapsed.

Juvalgrim's voice soared a moment longer then cut off as he fell in a heap on the iron tiles.

The choir's chant shattered into discord, broke off.

The pages fell, their drumsticks clattering on the pavement of the North Gatt Road.

>><<

Reyna ran between the warehouses. If he could reach the water, there was still a chance. . . .

He heard a scrape behind him, tried to throw himself aside, but something crashed into his head, he saw blackness filled with jagged lines and dots of white light, then nothing. . . .

>><<

The Amrapake got to his feet, waved his guard back, and went to stand gazing down at the chaos below, his face impassive. "Worthless," he said. "I stand by my word." He turned his head, glanced at the boys, then at the men holding them. "Do it," he said.

The guards cut Sivvy's throat first, then Houen's and threw them from the roof.

Fuaz Yoyote swallowed nervously, stared at the roof tiles as if not-seeing could keep the same from happening to him.

Famtoche snapped his fingers and the hosta moved back; when there was a clear space around him, he beckoned to Fuaz Yoyote. "Here, Worm."

An ashy look to his skin, the tip of his tongue fluttering along dry lips, the Manasso Prime hastened to the Amrapake's side, bobbing in a series of jerky bows. "Heshim Amrap."

Famtoche pursed his lips, watching him from narrowed eyes. Then he smiled. "I don't interfere in the internal affairs of the Camuctarr," he murmured. Yoyote's eyes flicked up then he went back to staring at the roof tiles. "But if you don't mind a little practical advice, Manasso, this would be a good time to revise the . . . ah . . . authority structure. After this . . . ah . . . debacle, I expect you won't have much difficulty dealing with the . . . ah . . . present High Kasso."

Breathing raggedly, Yoyote bowed lower. "I hear, heshim Amrap. It will be done."

Chapter 26
Dungeon

Juvalgrim woke in darkness and pain.

There was an iron harness on his head that trapped his tongue and held his mouth immobile. He couldn't speak; he could barely grunt.

His hands had been forced into iron gloves, his arms strapped to his body; he couldn't move his fingers and the tiny shifts he could make with his arms were useless for anything but easing cramps. *They know. They have to know. Reyna tried to warn me. K'lann! Why didn't I listen? I thought I could ride this out till the Change. Wrong guess, Ju. Stupid, stupid, it's the fire for me . . . fire!*

Fire. It hit him suddenly and he panicked, struggling desperately against the unyielding iron and the broad leather straps that bound him immobile. He screamed. Tried to scream. All that came out were animal grunts. He rocked on the cot, banged against the wall, pulled at the gloves and surged against the straps, tearing open his arms and wrists, scraping skin and hair from his head; his sphincters let go and the stench of feces and urine filled the cell. He struggled on and on until he finally crashed off the cot and knocked himself out.

>><<

"Why us? Gahhh, that stinks. Why don't they make those milk-lapping Quiambos do it? I mean, this's slave work. Fit for those pollutes, not us."

"Shut up, Chutso. Ol' Yoyay, he don't trust 'em, thinks they'll let this potzpile loose. You want that? Let him . . ." he slapped Juvalgrim on the flank, "get to talking and we'll be doing worse. Witchman, they say. You wanna be a frog? Hunh! Yatz almost bled hisself dry."

Juvalgrim groaned as they shifted him roughly about, but they ignored that, finished scrubbing him clean, wrapped strips of bandages about the skin breaks, threw a blanket over him and went out, taking with them the rags of his tunic and trousers.

He shivered, chilled by the cold water and the damp in the cell. *Not many damp places this side of the River. I must be down by the cisterns.* He sneezed. *K'lann! Rey oh Rey, I should have listened to you. I should have gone with you, taken my chances out there. No, that's not true, I'd have sucked you in with me, that's all. Blessings be, you're out of this.*

He swallowed, sank into a drifting lethargy, enduring the pain and discomfort. His panic was over. There was nothing he could do but prepare himself to endure what was coming with as much dignity as he could dredge up.

Chapter 27
Defense

Two days after the collapse of the attack at the Iron Bridge, Penhari pushed straggles of hair back from her face and scowled unhappily at the young messenger. "Again?"

The Naostam girl nodded. "They marchin'. Be at the Bridge 'bout quarter 'n hour." She smoothed her hand down the gray-green tunic with its pale yellow piping, her glowing pride in the Kummo-Runner's semi-uniform giving her thin plain face a fugitive charm. "Kumm Puruka say I'm her best Runner." She grinned, showing small crooked teeth, her eyes shutting to furry slits. "She say you want me to Run for you, I sh'd do it."

"Good. I need you." Penhari moved to her desk, picked up one of the tokens threaded on a spike. "Tuck this in your pouch. Show it as you need to. I want two Runners from each Kummata, with an alternate to handle emergencies. Let me see . . . take note of what's happening outside whenever you're near the Barrier. I need to know what the army's doing. Questions?"

"Nayo, heshal." She jigged from foot to foot. "Go?"

"Go, Runner." Penhari smiled as the girl sketched a bow and went rushing out, all knees and elbows. The smile faded. "I don't like this. I don't trust him . . . if there's a way, he'll find it. . . ." She frowned at the notes she'd been making, struggling to put together a coherent plan for managing Low City and codify the practices that were developing out of need and those

that were already in place; sometimes she was terrified
things would get away from her. She tightened her lips.
It was like trying to close your hands on tadpoles; they
wiggled away in every direction. *No patterns, no order.
I have to do something . . . no time to think about that
now.* She moved her shoulders, shook her arms, and
went briskly out the door.

When Penhari stepped into her private garden at the
center of the rambling house, Desantro hit the grass in
front of her, came curling up, and went at Panote who
turned his shoulder into her and flipped her again.

"I told you," he said patiently. "Inside and low."
He saw Penhari, bowed. "Heshal."

"Pan, it's starting again. Tell Tai, will you? And see
if you can find Faan. I need to know what's happening
with her."

"Heshal," he said, went trotting off down one of the
gravel walks.

Desantro squatted on the lawn, pulled a blade of grass
and stretched it between her thumbs. She blew a shriek,
lowered her hands. "Trouble."

Penhari shook her head, sighed. "Never trust a Mal.
It seems I'm going to get you killed, Desa."

Desantro managed a shrug without loosing her balance on her toes. "Knew you might. From the beginning a this. Doesn't matter." She got to her feet. "Been
a long time afore now I haven't much liked being alive.
Least I'm not bored. What you want me to do?"

"You've made connections with the Wascram, get out
to them and let them know they'd better be ready to
fight." She ran her fingers through her hair. "Sting!
Every step I make I get pushed back two. The people
here keep expecting the Barrier to handle everything,
they grumble every time I say get ready. I've yelled so
much my throat's raw. If they think Mals are fickle. . . .
Gods!"

"Y' really think it's goin' to go down?"

"I think Abeyhamal has more on her mind than us

and we'd better be prepared for that. You boot the Wascram into getting busy and I'll set the Kummate on the others." She drew her hand across her face. "If I thought it'd to any good, Desa, I'd cross the Bridge this minute, but if I know my brother, he wants this place leveled even more than he wants me in his hands. Go, go, there's no time. There's just no time!"

> > < <

On the roofs of the solid flat buildings, Ma'teesee helped the wife of her employer light a fire under a cauldron filled with fish oil; on other roofs other women and girls got their own cauldrons ready, filled also with fish oil and melted lard, with water if there was nothing else available. In the kitchens the men bound knives to staves to make crude lances. Farmworkers, shepherds and ex-slaves carried stones for their slings onto the roofs and piled them beside the cauldrons. Farmholders, Edgers, and Naostam porters accustomed to acting as night watchmen strung bows and laid out the arrows they'd been making in their spare time. Dossan and Miugi (who'd dumped the other girl and come back to her) and dozens like them fastened washlines across the wynds, neck high, ankle high, then carted rubble and furniture to make barricades across the wynds. Children old enough to throw stones piled them up through their neighborhoods, small unobtrusive cairns, ready to hand when the need appeared. Throughout the city men and women, youths and girls collected everything that could possibly serve as a weapon.

Then they waited.

Chapter 28
Pyre

The Manasso acolytes came for Juvalgrim midmorning of the day after he woke in the cell. They threw an old patched cloak over him, then set him on his feet, unbuckled the straps about his legs and made him walk ahead of them.

It was time for his burning. He knew it though the only words they spoke were curt commands to get a move on, turn right, turn left.

Hurting and hungry, he didn't know if he had the strength to walk all the way down the Jiko without falling on his face, but he set himself to the task, one foot then the other and after a while, his body took over and his mind floated free. Fear was something far off, like a stain of smoke on the horizon.

Reyna.

He smiled as he thought about Reyna. The Salagaum that Yoyote despised was a better man than both of them. Twenty years of . . . something. Love? Who knows. It was good, what they had; no need to put a name to it.

One of the acolytes grabbed his arm and turned him onto the ramp that led down to the Outer Ring Road, sinking fingers into one of his larger bruises and startling a sound from him, a low gulping moan that he cut off as soon as he could.

The pain went away.

The cloak fluttering about him, he walked on.

The Cheoshim towers were silent, the Parade Grounds emptied out, the windows like holes in a skull.

The Biasharim towers were desolate, with broken windows, char marks from the fires that burned to ash the dried-out women's gardens.

The Prophet had purified the city all right. It was so pure, so sterile, nothing could live there.

Sadness drifted along beside him. He remembered what had been and mourned it. A little.

The Sok Circle was dusty and deserted. The hot wind blew scraps of paper, straw, cloth across the paving stones, plastered them against the pyres built there. One in the middle and a dozen others scattered around the rim of the Circle. Stacks of wood torn from abandoned houses and limbs from dead trees were piled neatly around the tall poles to make platforms for the prisoners to stand on.

The Salagaum were there, all of them that were left. Not many. Tied two to a pole, their feet sunk into the wood piles. Reyna was alone. In the middle. Tied to the pole that was waiting for him.

When Juvalgrim saw him, he struggled to say something, but all he could make was a breathy gurgling sound that no one could hear two steps away.

"Be quiet, you." One of the acolytes slapped him, hit the wound on his head, and he catapulted into darkness.

> > < <

He woke as cold water splashed into him, heard a splat and clatter as the bucket man jumped down.

He was strapped to the pole; his hands were pressed against Reyna's back; he could feel Reyna's hands against his.

His detachment frayed, blew away.

Fire.

He'd never been able to deal with pain.

All his life he'd slipped and slid to avoid even the hint of pain—and not just for himself. There was that. Not just for himself. A flare of pleasure at the thought. It died fast. Pain was now. He swallowed and struggled to keep his resolution. *Don't give them the satisfaction. Don't let them see you crawl!*

A drift of oily smoke blew into his face, stung his eyes.

Torches. They're really going to do it.

"Pervert! Destroyer of families. Demon lover!"

Juvalgrim blinked away the smoke tears that blurred his vision, angled his head so he could look down. *Prophet.* He gazed at the man with weary contempt. *Satisfied, Prophet? Behold your labors and rejoice. You've killed love and happiness, joy and sharing. You've killed the city as thoroughly as your . . . no . . . our god has killed the land. The Sibyl says it was unavoidable. I spit on unavoidable.* He managed a kind of chuckle, a gulping gurgle at the back of his throat. *Or I would if you gave me back my tongue. Afraid of a word, are you? My doom is yours, fool.* Another gurgling chuckle. *Too bad I won't be around to see it.* He trembled, wrenched his mind away from the torches and what they meant. Drooping against the straps that bound him to the pole he watched the Prophet stride about, mouthing curses and anathemas, overriding the Manasso Prime who wanted to get the burning started. *Good boy, keep it up. The longer you go on, the longer we keep breathing.*

Chapter 29
The Last Dance

On the Iron Bridge the Rite began.
                DONNNG DONG DONNNG DONG
Adjoa Prime and Anaxoa Prime were slick with sweat
again as they brought the Great Hammers down on the
Sacred Anvil:
    DONNNG DONG DONNNG DONG DONNNG.

   CHU MA VAY YAL CHU MA VAY YAL

   Iron Father, come and bless us
   Giver of Strength and Might
   Come O Lawgiver, make this wrong right. . . .
Anacho Drummers stroked the tall Drums of the Dead
doom da doom da doom. . . .
   The hand drums the pages held rattled tank t tank t t
t tank tank. . . .
   The small bronze hammers of the kassos beat against
their small bronze anvils, the tinka tinks sinking into
the chant and emerging from it, sinking again. . . .
   A wall of **SOUND** funneled along the Iron Bridge,
hammered at the Barrier.

   At the rim of the South Eka Kumata, the attack of
the army began.
   Swordsmen from the hostas spread along the Barrier,
poked and slashed at it; when they tired, others took
their places.
   Heavyarm Lancers rode their warhorses at the Bar-

rier. The horses reared, slammed their armored fore-
hooves into it, reared again and again. They withdrew.
Came at it again. Hammered at it. Hammered. Others
took their places when they tired. Hammered and hammered.

Lightarm Lancers slammed butt and point against the
Barrier, rode the rebounds, slammed at it again and
again; when they tired, others took their places.

The hosta Captains prowled along behind their men,
followed by drummer pages counting cadence to keep
the blows thumping together to set up a resonance in
the Barrier and crack it that way.

More impatient and hostile, the Cheoshim Commanders mixed with their men; even Champion Ommad, the Commander Prime of the Lancers, swung
down from his warhorse, tossed the reins to his page
and took his saber to go the Barrier.

On and on. Endlessly hammering. Slicing. Thumping. On and on.

On the Northbank of the River, Riverman stood under the Camuctarr Gatt and shook water from his ears.
He climbed the bank, hesitated on the edge of the weedy
wasteland that was the lower slopes of Mount Foga-
malin, then began toiling upward, a small brown
shadow in the dessicated dead landscape.

In the Great Grove at the center of the Low City,
teeth grinding in anger, fighting her NEED to wrench
free of the god's claws, Faan leapt and turned on the
damp earth, in and out of the arching, embracing Sequba roots, threads spinning out from her, calling to
her side the Honeygirls, calling among others Ma'teesee
and Dossan.

A sword hacked at the Barrier. She grunted with pain
and kept on dancing, a red line running across her
shoulder. Hooves slammed down. Red curves bloomed

on her thigh and she whined through her teeth—and
danced.

She drew strength from the Earthfire. From the
Honeygirls who came and danced with her, weaving
through the Grove. From the Wild Magic swirling in a
silver mist about her. And almost none from the god.

The moththeries that belonged to the trees came dripping like rain down the Sequba trunks and flittered
about her, drawn like mundane moths to a flame.

Blood bruises lacing every inch of her body, swaying
and groaning, goddriven through an endless wheeling
Dance, she fought to HOLD.

While the Prophet ranted and strode back and forth
across the High City Sok Circle. Juvalgrim drifted
among his memories. It was difficult to breathe; the
pressure from the straps and plates of the cage on his
head numbed his skin and made his tongue swell. And
he was thirsty. The heat from the punishing sun made
that worse with every breath he drew.

There was nothing he could do, no way he could
escape this, and he was no longer waiting for the Change
to rescue him. There was an odd comfort in this pas-
sivity. A rest from the weariness that had weighed him
down. He'd been working so hard for so long.

He blinked, watched with contempt as the Prophet
threw his arms out, flung himself to his knees.

"BURN," Faharmoy howled, head back, eyes shining red, a red glow about his wasted body, "BURN
AND RETURN TO THE FATHER." Eyes like furnace
holes fixed on the hot, dust-whitened sky, he began to
mutter the Praises.

Manasso Prime patted down his vestments and sent
acolytes scurrying to form up his kassos so he could
get the rite started. The Manassoa kassos were more
familiar with balance sheets than music scores, but they
fumbled themselves into the proper order, cleared their

throats, settled raggedly into the basic chant CHU MA
VAY YAL CHU MA VAY YAL.

Juvalgrim let his eyes drop shut and once more he
was playing games in the back courts of the Camuctarr,
swimming in the River, sweating and breathless in the
bed of the first woman he'd had.

He refused to think of Reyna; it was too painful. He
wanted nothing painful now.

Reyna's head ached. His body was one great bruise,
but no bones were broken and his skin was intact. *Lots
of crackling when I fry.* His swollen lips twitched into
a brief painful smile at the thought.

He could feel Juvalgrim's back against his hands.
*Crackling together. They say if you breathe the smoke,
you won't feel the fire . . . gods!*

*Faan, my Faany, my honeybaby, take care of your-
self. . . .*

Weary and so dry his skin was beginning to crack,
driven by a summons he couldn't break free of, Riverman reached the Jiko Sagrada and flinched from the
searing heat of the black iron tiles. "Please," he said
aloud. "You'll kill me. I can't . . . I can't. . . ."

The summons intensified.

He shuddered, then sat on a rock and began wrapping
strands of tough, sun-dried grass about his webbed feet.

> *Chumavayal swings his Hammer about his
> head, faster and faster until it whistles through
> air that glows red with the heat of its passage,
> round and round, then he looses it, sending it
> wheeling about Abeyhamal, wrapping a chain
> of fire about her.*

Cursing the South Eka boys jigging unreachably in
front of him, Champion Ommad brought his saber round
in a powerful circle and for the first time felt the Barrier

quiver, then yield beneath the edge. He shouted and struck again. Again. The fourth time the saber sank in and stuck; it felt like slicing through muscle into bone.

He wrenched it loose. "Here," he cried. "Wallal, Famkon, Uchovu, come here. Coordinate with me."

He brought the saber down through the softening Barrier.

In the Great Grove Faan screamed. A bruise on her arm broke open, blood sprayed over the clotted Wild Magic.

The Sequba moththeries screamed and fell like wetted thistledown onto the churned black earth.

A strand of the silver motes flew at the Honeychild, pasted themselves over the wound, holding it closed; when the healing was done, they peeled off, leaving behind a silver scar that wound like a snake about her forearm.

She screamed again. Bruises burst. Blood soaked her blouse and skirt, but she kept dancing. Round and round she danced, spraying blood on trees and earth and the Honeygirls dancing with her.

Her eyes rolled back; her mouth stretched wide in a soundless howl; she fainted.

The Barrier fell.

At South Eka, the attackers collapsed into confusion as the resistance they'd been fighting melted away. Warhorses stumbled, Lancers went to their knees, swordsmen staggered.

At the Iron Bridge the blowtorch which the Primes had evoked whooshed into the warehouses and the rambling low tenements of the Edge, burning to ash everything in its path until it beat against the rim of an Abey Grove and fell apart.

Stunned by a success they hadn't really expected, the

kassos let the beat fall to silence until the Anacho Prime threw up his arms. "Drummers, follow," he cried and plunged in the path of the fire.

CHU MA VAY YAL CHU MA VAY YAL

Doom doom da doom—weighted sticks wheeling, the drummers marched across the Bridge.

Tinka tink—hammer against anvil, the kassos picked up the beat again and crossed into the Low City.

Ma'teesee wrenched loose from the disintegrating Dance and ran to Faan who lay in a limp heap, Sequba roots like arms curled around her. "Dossy, c'mere, help me." She knelt beside Faan, straightening her out, then slapping lightly at her face. "Come on, Fa, wake up, everything's crashing. We NEED you." She pressed her fingers under Faan's jaw, sighed with relief as she felt the steady thump-thump of the pulse, looked up as Dossan stumbled over to her. "We gotta get her to Tai. Help me make a chair."

Dossan gazed vaguely at her, fumbled with her hands, let them fall.

"Bouzh it, Dossy. We don't move, we gonna get killed."

Panting and half dead, Riverman stumbled into the shade of the Sibyl's Cave; it wasn't much cooler there, but at least there was no sun. He moved his tongue over dry and cracking lips, limped deeper into the dark.

There was a small round hole gouged in the stone in front of the Sibyl's Chair. Cool clear water lapped at the edges. With a fizz-pop of intense pleasure, he plunged into the pool, sinking deep, deep into the coolness and wet that was life itself, healing the ravages of the long climb.

When he surfaced finally, he looked up to see the Sibyl sitting in the Chair. "Why?" he said. "What have I done to you?"

"Nothing, godlet. I need you, that's all."

"Need!" He pulled himself up and sat on the edge of the tiny pool, his aching feet dangling in the water. "Got more need put on me than I got skin." He scratched at a pointed ear, then dug for water mites in the rough brown weed growing about his loins.

The Sibyl tapped a long forefinger on the stone arm of her chair, then spoke a **WORD** that shook the air but made no sound.

A shimmer drifted to hang in front of Riverman, a streak of silver light the length of his arm. There was a loud PING; the shimmer solidified into a miniature saber, then splashed down in the pool just missing his webbed toes.

"You'll need that, Riverman. It'll cut through anything you want severed." The Sibyl laughed at the face he made. "Don't worry, godlet, it won't cut you. Now, here's what I want you to do. . . ."

> *Abeyhamal whirls, her fimbo held horizontally and waist high; gold fire flows from the tip, fighting and dissolving the red fire. She roars her rage and leaps across the Anvil, the butt of her Fimbo striking the Brazier and knocking it over, the coals skipping out across the Forge Floor, the red life in them slowly fading to gray.*

The kassos and the primes marched off the Iron Bridge chanting **CHU MA VAY YAL CHU MA VAY YAL,** ghost drums beating, hammers and anvils tinka tinking, tramping on the ash of the folk and buildings burned by the Fire.

Then the stones came.

From every side, the stones came.

An arrow pierced the throat of the Anacho Prime, a half dozen skewered the Anaxoa Prime.

The kassos scurried for the shelter of the Iron Bridge,

falling to stones, falling to arrows, dead and wounded
abandoned where they fell.

Champion Ommad yelled for his warhorse, cursing
as his twelve-year-old page fought toward him through
the stream of riders plunging into the South Eka Kummata. He swung into the saddle, roared at the mob,
"Get back, you jeggin' meat, FORM UP! I'll have your
guts for gitter strings. FORMATION, YOU SUCKING
TSOUS!"

A few heard him and slowed their charge, came back
to form up behind him, their faces carefully blank.

Only a few.

Confident in their training and their weapons, filled
with contempt for these squatters, these peasants, furious at the taunting they'd endured, Lancers and hostas
alike charged into the city. They'd been blooded in slave
raids and bandit chases, had never faced a hostile city
roused to resist them. They expected to ride over the
feebs and slaughter as they chose.

The wynds were narrow and crooked, and the squatters had built their barricades around curves; the warhorses crashed into these before their riders saw them,
or they stumbled over ropes strung low between the
houses; the higher ropes caught the riders in their
throats, knocked them onto the rutted earth where they
were trampled by the horses behind them and the hostas
running along beside them.

On the flat roofs of the one-story buildings the women
howled, an ululating eerie sound, then they tipped the
cauldrons over the low parapets and sent the boiling
fluids cascading onto the attackers.

Children ran from houses into side wynds, threw
stones at the intruders, scampered back inside, giggling
and triumphant. More stones rained from the roofs from
the slings of the shepherds and the others.

Squatters with hammers and kitchen knives darted

out of houses and side-wynds, swarmed over men thrown down, cut throats and hammered heads. Some were killed, but most got away with scratches and bruises.

The blundering attack degenerated into a rout. Leaving their wounded to the knives of the squatters, the Lancers and the hostas staggered from the city.

The Naostam Runner came panting into the Kummhouse Reception Room, so excited she could barely speak. "They're buzzitin', Zazi. We did it! We did it!"

Penhari lifted a hand. "Calmly, Runner. It'll be harder when they come again. Much harder." She smiled at the girl. "But we did beat them this time."

One by one the other Runners came in with reports from their Kummatas, reports of rout and people dancing in the wynds and on the rooftops, dancing in the Groves, of Cheoshim and hostas running with their tails between their legs, of kassos fleeing like frightened rats.

"Vema vema," Penhari said. "All this is grand, but it's not time for celebrating yet. They'll come again and this time they'll come as warriors, not as a mob. They'll come by inches and slaughter as they move." She smiled grimly into the suddenly sobered young faces. "I depend upon you, Runners. If you get yourselves killed, you blind me. After this, go in pairs; if one's cut down, the other can carry the word. Run the rooftops, not the wynds; it's slower, I know, but safer." She paused. "Until they decide to clear the roofs. Watch out for that." She scooped up a pile of sealed packets from her desk. "Don't let anyone see this but your Kumms. Get it to them safe and fast as you can. Bring me back any questions or objections. Do you understand? Good."

She handed out the packets with the plans she'd labored over for hours, consulting Panote, the Kassian

Tai and Desantro, pulling together the reports from the Kummate about the people and resources of their Kummatas, adding in all she remembered of the ramblings of the General about the Cheoshim and their training, all she'd learned from Faharmoy.

Runners stuffed the packets in their pouches and went trotting out.

Sting! To be so young and so eager. I never was. She shivered, swallowed the bile of ancient anger that rose in her throat. *I never had a chance to be.*

Faan woke in the Kummhouse Infirmary, blinked up into the Kassian Tai's worried face.

"Fa." Tai's voice cracked on the word. She cleared her throat. "How're you feeling?"

Faan pushed up without answering. She could hear sounds coming through the window—pans banging; the small drums that everyone seemed to have over here toom-tooming away; shouts and laughter. "I couldn't hold, Zazi."

"Don't worry, honey. We drove them back, tails tucked."

Faan shivered. "What . . . ?"

"Listen to me, Fa. It doesn't matter. They're gone. Even the kassos. They're back across the Iron Bridge. Chewed up enough to respect our teeth."

"Juvalgrim?"

"Not there this time. I expect our High Kasso has lost his footing at last."

"Mamay!" Faan swung her legs over the edge of the cot, looked frantically about. "If they got him, they got Reyna, I know it. Where're my clothes, Tai. I have to. . . ."

"Hush hush, honey." Tai reached out to touch Faan's cheek, but Faan jerked away. "I don't know what's going on over there, child. No one can cross the River now."

"No one? I can." Faan got to her feet, swung her

arms out for balance as her head swam. She stiffened her back, drew in a long breath, exploded it out. "I can," she repeated grimly. She looked down at the skimpy shift which was all she had on. "My clothes. Where are my clothes?"

"Abeyhamal. . . ."

"Abeyhamal can go jegg herself. The deal was SHE kept Rey out of trouble; well, that's off and so's the rest. I mean it, Tai, if I have to go like this, I will."

Tai looked suddenly older. "Vema, Fa. What you were wearing . . . well, we'll have to burn it. I had Dossan fetch some clean things." She gestured toward a small chest beside the door, then turned to leave. In the doorway, she paused, looked over her shoulder. "I do want to remind you, honey, Abeyhamal has a lot more than you to worry about." She closed the door gently behind her.

Faan grimaced. "Vema, Tai," she muttered, then began the loosening exercises Panote had taught her, working the dizziness from her head, the knots from her muscles. "You and I never did count, Zazi; you don't want to know it, but it's the truth."

When she was feeling steady again, she dressed and left the room, scowling, wondering where Ailiki had gotten to.

Riverman jogged down the path trying to get used to the soft shoes the Sibyl had spelled about his feet so he could run the black iron tiles without cooking himself. He slowed as he came to the charred stump of the old olive tree. A small limber shoot with shiny green leaves had grown up from the roots; he hadn't noticed it when he passed on the way to the Cave, but this time the wind shook it and it seemed to wave to him. He laughed his fizzy laugh, returned the wave, and started down the Jiko Sagrada.

He crept along the deserted kariam clinging to the ashy shadow of the dead kichidawa hedges, cautious despite the empty silence of the towers. He wrinkled his short broad nose, shifted his grip on the horn hilt of the saber, annoyed at the Sibyl for not providing a sheath for it.

He reached the Circle, ducked under the raised boardwalk in front of the shops and began circling behind the kassos and the STRIKERS, any sounds he made lost in the ragged chanting of the Manassos, the reedy voice of the Prime going on about something. He didn't bother puzzling out the Prime's words. It was all human nonsense anyway, this breast beating and reading profundities into the accidents of appetite. A god was a force you dealt with, like a blizzard or a tornado; when they were around, you kept your head down; when they weren't, you did your best not to arouse them.

He wouldn't be here now if the Sibyl hadn't laid this geas on him. Fond as he was of the Honeychild, it wasn't him she was going to lead to freedom, and as for the River—let Abeyhamal finish this thing, the rains would be back and the water clear again. Ah well, ah well, would-be was as useless as regret. Best to just get on with it.

Juvalgrim and Reyna were atop the pyre in the center of the Circle; he eyed them, sniffed with exasperation. *Into the mouth of the Beast.* He squatted under the boards, scratched his drooping weedfur and tried to figure out how he was supposed to cross that empty space without some fidgeting wander-eye spotting him and raising a shout. *Eyes everywhere. I can't do this. Sibyl, O Sibyl, I'm just a little Riverman. They'll throw me on the fire and burn me to ash.*

Sounds from across the River drifted to him on the freshening wind, sliding through the pauses between syllables—shouts, women's howling, screams, crashings; the second attack was beginning. That must be why the towers were so empty—most of the Cheoshim had crossed the River now that the Bridges were open. Too bad. There was going to be a lot of hurt and death this day. Humans. Ephemerals, Sibyl called them. Mmh! Pain was pain if you lived one year or a thousand.

"Let evil be driven from our midst," Fuaz Yoyote intoned. "All praise to all powerful all knowing Iron Father. . . ."

"CHU MA VAY YAL CHU MA VAY YAL," chanted the Manasso kassos.

The torch bearers ducked the oil-soaked batting corded about the ends of the long poles into the Sacred Brazier, marched with Cheoshim STRIKERS as escorts to the pyres at the edge of the Circle; four went to the center. Two torches each for Juvalgrim and Reyna. Sweet man, that Prime.

The kassos jabbed the butts of the poles against their feet, held the smoking torches at an angle and waited for the sign to fire up the wood.

The Prophet knelt, arms stretched out, mouthing the words of the Praises, the sound of his voice lost in the louder noise of the ritual.

> *Chumavayal dips into the dying coals of the Fire, scoops up huge handfuls and flings them at the Bee Mother, flings them to the right of HER, the left of HER and before HER and pulls flames from them, driving the fire tongues at HER.*

Wind howled through the empty wynds and kariams of the High City; threads of black cloud swirled overhead, black and heavy with wet; a spray of rain spattered on the dust and grit of the pavement.

". . . let the evil be routed, the souls of the sinners fly to the Father. NOW!" Fuaz Yoyote sputtered as a spate of raindrops hit him in the face. He wiped the water away, smiled as he saw the torch bearers whirl and thrust their fire into those piles of tinder wood.

Riverman crouched under the boardwalk, gnawing his

lip. The dry wood was going with a roar. "Oh my fur oh my feet," he wailed, ducked under the support timber and scuttled for Juvalgrim's pyre.

> *Abeyhamal roars, sweeps her massive fimbo in a circle that scatters the coals, jabs the point high. Wet black clouds swirl from it. Lightning jags from it. Wind howls round and round the floor. In the Land, wind snatches Faan off her feet, whirls her across the River.*

Thunder boomed, lightning danced in jags among the pyres, the wind rose abruptly to hurricane force, sweeping around and around the Sok Circle.

The wind pushed at Reyna, battered at him, but the ropes held, though they cut into his wrists and twisted his left arm until a long bone broke. The wind flopped him again and again against the pole, bone grating against bone, breaking through the skin, blood dripping down, mixing with the rain.

Juvalgrim heard him scream, felt him sag against the ropes. He wrenched at the straps, but he couldn't move.

Smoke from the pyres was curling round him.

He tried to speak, he fought to form the **WORD**s of power in his head and force them to work.

Nothing.

The kassians and the Cheoshim were blown out of the Circle, slammed into the shuttered and boarded up shops.

The wind swirled around the kneeling muttering Prophet; it didn't shift so much as a hair of his beard.

The smoke was thick and low; raindrops the size of olives drove through it and beat at Riverman, knocking him flat several times. Each time he scrambled to his feet and scurried on.

He reached the pyre, sprang and caught a protruding branch, pulled himself onto it, peered through the smoke for another hold. The saber was a nuisance, slowing him down, but he couldn't leave it behind, he had to have some way of cutting the ropes and straps. Flames tickling at his feet, he fought his way up the pile.

Faan dropped to the paving in front of the Prophet, an amber fimbo glowing in her right hand. For a long moment they stared at each other, then Faharmoy got to his feet.

Faan turned her back on him. "NO!" she cried. **"STOP THIS. STOP IT. THE FIRES! NO NO NO. I WILL NOT!"**

> *Abeyhamal drives the point of her fimbo at the Iron Father's chest. He lifts his Hammer to smash it, but she laughs, a mocking humming laugh, shifts direction and drives the point into the clouds above them. Rain falls in silver sheets. The last coals die.*

Rain fell in battering floods, drowning the fires.

Riverman wrapped his arms around Reyna's ankle, grabbed at his trousers, and hung on as the wind and water threatened to wash him off the pyre.

Faharmoy's hands closed about Faan's throat.

She shouted a **WORD.** Wind roared round them, swept them off their feet, flung them against the paving stones. Faharmoy hit first, he was stunned and his hands were jarred loose. By the time he was thinking again, Faan was a body-length away.

The Dance began.

Feet stamping to the beat of Earth Heart, they circled, danced breast to chest, broke apart, oscillated through arcs, shuffle to the right, shuffle to the left, back and forth, back and forth as if a resilient sphere rolled between them, blocking each from the other.

Lightning walked around them, the rain had diminished to a drizzle, the droplets settling on every fold of their clothing, on their hair and arms.

Riverman swore under his breath and began struggling up the pole, using the ropes and straps to help him climb.

"Hold still," he whispered in Juvalgrim's ear. "I'm going to cut you loose. Sibyl sent me and I'm a friend of your friend's daughter. You hear?"

Juvalgrim stiffened, then produced a low gurgle deep in his throat that Riverman took to mean assent. He inspected the hinges and straps, then began cutting cautiously, cheered to find the Sibyl was right, the saber cut steel like cheese and left living flesh alone.

He finished with the cage and the neck strap. Juvalgrim started to shake; he was trying to hold still, but he couldn't. The cage fell off, hit the top of the pyre, rolled off and clattered on the paving stones. Swearing under his breath, Riverman lowered himself to the chest rope that bound Reyna and Juvalgrim together, slashed through it, scrambled between them to the iron gloves that immobilized Juvalgrim's hands. The wind whipped grit past him; the drizzle made the pole desperately slippery, though the wet did increase his strength. He used the saber to hack toe holds in the wood, worked his way round until he could cut the straps that bound the right glove together.

It fell with a satisfactory thump. He glanced at the dancers, snorted, then wriggled around to deal with the other hand. *Getting nowhere, round and round, idiot gods, there's not going to be anything left if they don't....* He dealt with the left hand and scrambled back to cut through the ropes that tied Reyna's arms to the post, saw the jut of bone, the wash of blood, and hissed with annoyance. "Sibyl, you want this one alive, you better do something." He crawled along the arm until he reached the break. "Well?"

A snatch of breeze stirred his brown, sagging weed fur. Hold tight and lay the sword alongside the bone came whispering in his pointed ear. Tongue between his teeth, he wrapped his hand in the rags of Reyna's blouse, slapped the sword down flat on Reyna's arm.

The arm bucked and twitched, the sword sank into the dark copper skin, the wound closed over.

Riverman pulled himself back down the arm, clutched Reyna's trembling wrist. "Tsah tsah," he muttered, "now how am I supposed to. . . ."

No answer.

He wrinkled his nose, then started chewing at the rope.

The fimbo slipped in Faan's sweaty hand. She shifted her grip, wiped her palm on her shirt. The cloth was soaked, so that didn't help much. She switched hands again and tried to relax into the dance Abeyhamal was jerking her through. She didn't understand the point of this posturing and she was sick with anger because she couldn't escape the grip of the god. POWER POWER she danced. POWER. POWER. POWER. I WILL NOT, she screamed inside. I WILL NOT . . . I WILL NOT . . . LET IT HAPPEN AGAIN. I WILL NOT . . . I WILL NOT. . . . Get it done, she told herself, get this over with.

Faharmoy slapped his hands together. Tongues of fire licked at Faan.

She snorted with disgust, brought fire leaping along her arms, blue flamelets that wriggled and chattered their hunger at her. She loosed a pair of them and they engulfed the red fire, ate it, and plunged toward Faharmoy.

Chumavayal roared his anger, REACHED down and swatted the fire elementals into another universe, then slapped out, intending to crush Faan.

*Abeyhamal kicked the Brazier over, scattering
the coals; as a part of the same movement she
brought the point of the fimbo hard against the
Old God's chest, striking him over the heart.
The coals died.
Chumavayal shriveled until he was a tiny black
baby lying on the Forge Floor.*

As the tenuous black hand swept at her, Faan dropped
to her stomach.

It passed over her and was gone. She leapt to her
feet, ran at Faharmoy; the tip of the fimbo touched him
over the heart, went driving through empty space.

She scrambled frantically to keep from stepping on
the baby wailing in the rags of his brown robe; when
she was steady on her feet again, she looked around.
The people in the Circle were indistinct shadows fading
silently away into rapidly thickening fog, moving toward the River. Juvalgrim was helping Reyna down
from the pyre; they started off together.

"Mamay!" She ran after him, caught at his arm—
gasped as he looked down at her from eyes empty of
all mind or understanding. She dropped her hand.

He turned and walked after Juvalgrim with a grim,
mechanical deliberation.

A small hand slapped her leg. "Honey, give us a lift,
mmmh?"

She looked down. Riverman. "What. . . ."

"It's over, Fa. The Change is starting."

She pulled her hand across her face. "He didn't know
me. He looked at me and he didn't know me."

"It's the Change, honey. He's forgetting. That's the
way it works. If you keep after him any longer, you'll
forget, too. You want that?"

"No. . . ."

"Then you need to get to the Sibyl's Cave."

She bent, cupped her hand. He stepped into it and

held onto her sleeve as she lifted him waist high. "Ail-iki?"

"I don't know, Fa." He settled into the crook of her arm. "Quick, there isn't much time left."

She looked around a last time. There was no one left in the circle, even the baby Faharmoy had vanished. "This is what it's all about, all the starving, all the fighting, all the dying? A touch on the chest?"

"Timing's all, Faan. You and HER, touching together."

"Waste!" She blinked, shook her head, then started trotting for the nearest kariam. She was too tired and too numb to feel anything yet, grief or triumph.

> *The Forge Floor melted into the air leaving a circle of crisp green grass with a conical Hive in the center. A garden filled with the sound of water and with flowers whose perfumes drifted aimlessly on wandering breezes; gossamer bees like bits of sunlight hummed from bloom to bloom and back to the Hive. A grand Sequba grew beside a stream, its moththeries flittering about, changing color in a visual song of pleasure in their new freedom. Abeyhamal laid the baby on the grass, leaving him for the sun to feed him, the rain to quench his thirst; his excretions were perfumed and ephemeral, sublimating into the Garden air like dew evaporating in the morning.*
> *She settled herself on a Sequba root and contemplated with intense satisfaction the realm that was now hers alone.*

The Low City was silent, the wynds and ways filled with yellow-white mist. The dead lay where they fell, but the wounded rose and stood staring at nothing, their bones and muscle healing as the mist eddied about them.

Penhari sat in the Heart Garden of the Kummhouse, staring vacantly at the mist.

There was a weight in her lap. She looked down. A baby.

The baby wailed. Without thinking, she unbuttoned her blouse and put him to her breast which was suddenly heavy with milk.

At the first swallow, the baby stiffened. His body convulsed, began to change. In minutes what had been a boy child was a girl; a hungry vigorous little girl. Penhari laughed and shook her head.

And forgot.

Ailiki came lollopping from the Sibyl's Cave, circled round Faan, reared on her hind legs, and clapped her forepaws together.

Faan smiled; the lump in her throat eased a little. She set Riverman down, straightened her shoulders and walked into the shadow.

Her gear and Faan's were in two leather bags by her feet, Desantro was squatting beside the Sibyl's Chair, looking angry and confused. She stood when she saw Faan. "Maybe you can tell me. What'n jann's going on here? The beast of yours went crazy, it kept biting me like I was a sheep it was herding. The Kassian said to pack up and follow it."

"Sibyl?"

The old woman looked tired. "It was necessary. You'll need a Companion, Faan, someone to teach you how to survive once you leave the Land."

"Leave."

"You have no place here, Honeychild, not any longer. No home. No family. Nothing."

Faan clenched her teeth; her eyes prickled with tears she was too angry and too stubborn to shed.

Desantro slapped at her thigh. "Gaangah! Don't I get any say what I do or don't?"

The Sibyl turned her head, looked down. "No."

Desantro snorted, got to her feet. "One jeggin' thing atop 'nother. Well, least I get outta here."

Faan swung round, walked to the front of the Cave and looked out across the Land. All she could see below the black points that were the peaks of the Jinocabur Mountains was a billowing yellow-white fog. Her breathing was ragged, she scrubbed the heel of her hand across her eyes. The rage that filled her was trapped inside her; there was no one to vent it on. And it frightened her. *I can't deal with this. I can't.* . . .

Ailiki brushed against her legs, wove around her, warm and soft.

Faan gasped, shuddered; when Ailiki reared on her hind legs, she caught her up, held her against her face. The mahsar's purring vibrated through her, eased the tightness a little and reminded her that there was—maybe—something left. The thing she'd wanted to know and couldn't find out—who she was, where she came from. Maybe now. . . .

She turned and came slowly back to the Sibyl. "My mother. Can you tell me now? Give me a hint or something?"

The Sibyl tented her fingers, looked over them at Faan; her bright black eyes were twinkling. "More than a hint, Honeychild. Your mother is a sorceror called Kori Piyolss; you'll find her in the Myk'tat Tukery on an island called Jal Virri."

"I see. And how do I get there?"

"When the fog clears, you'll find a ship tied up at the Camuctarr Gatt, Vroliko Ryo's *Rostokul*. The crew's sleeping through the Change, but they'll wake for you." She smiled. "Don't forget your studies, little Sorcerie."

Faan shivered, went back to the Cave mouth, and stood watching the Fog boil.

GODDANCE
The Beginning

Riverman on her shoulder, the Sibyl stood at the mouth of the Cave and watched Faan run down the path, Desantro close behind her. The Change was complete, the Fog had cleared away. The morning was crisp and cold, the sky gray with clouds; underfoot Fogomalin was rumbling.

Riverman tugged at her ear. "What's bothering you, mmh?"

"Faan. What a mess these gods make. And they never clean up after themselves."

"Mmh?"

"Abeyhamal, godlet. She set a shell over Jal Virri I doubt even a sorceror could break through. Now that the Change is done, she has no doubt forgot all that and even if she hasn't. . . ." The Sibyl shrugged. "By tomorrow, godlet, your River will be flushing itself clean. Stay with me a while. Then we both can rest."

"Until it starts again."

"It already has."

*
*
*

JO CLAYTON

DAW

A Superstar in the DAW Firmament!

Mercedes Lackey

DAW

Attention:

DAW COLLECTORS

Many readers of DAW Books have written requesting information on early titles and book numbers to assist in the collection of DAW editions since the first of our titles appeared in April 1972.

We have prepared a several-pages-long list of all DAW titles, giving their sequence numbers, original and current order numbers, and ISBN numbers. And of course the authors and book titles, as well as reissues.

If you think that this list will be of help, you may have a copy by writing to the address below and enclosing one dollar in stamps or currency to cover the handling and postage costs.

DAW Books, Inc.
Dept. C
375 Hudson Street
New York, NY 10014-3658